Silver Lini KT-494-899

SHIRLEY DAVIES-OWENS was born in northern England, and emigrated to Canada with her husband when she was twenty. She has worked as a freelance secretary, administrative assistant, owned and operated her own stenography business and written management training programmes. She has two children and now lives in Washington State. *Silver Linings* is her first novel.

SHIRLEY DAVIES-OWENS

Silver Linings

This edition published 1994 by
Diamond Books
77–85 Fulham Palace Road
Hammersmith, London W6 8JB

First published in Fontana Paperbacks 1987

ISBN 0 261 66554 5

Made and printed in Great Britain

'His purposes will ripen fast,
    Unfolding every hour;
The bud may have a bitter taste,
    But sweet will be the flower.'

—William Cowper, 1731-1800

PART ONE

1877–1878

ONE

On that August afternoon in 1877, Emma Cadman could barely contain her impatience as she waited for her mother to leave.

The child drummed her small, square-tipped fingers on the edge of a mahogany table below the oval mirror into which her mother peered.

'If it had not been Jenkins's day off, I would've had him hitch up the brougham,' Beth Cadman said, pinching her cheeks until they flushed and tilting her head from side to side as if to study the effect. 'No matter, though. The walk will do me good. Emma dear' – she frowned – 'do stop that dreadful drumming.'

'Yes, Mama.' The serene smile that tilted the corners of Emma's wide mouth and the sweetness of her tone belied her irritation. Why, oh why, were the rules for grown-ups different from those for children? Surely what she was observing was vanity. And according to Mama, vanity was a sin.

Emma sighed inwardly. From beneath the dusky spikes of her lashes, her large gold-flecked eyes slid to the grandfather clock. Ten to two. She passed a weary hand across her high-domed forehead. The way Mama was primping, one would think she was set to dine with the Queen. And that awful hat – if she fussed with it once more, Emma would surely scream. With the toe of her black kid boot, she gave a disconsolate jab at the carpet.

'There.' A final smoothing behind the ears of a couple of flyaway strands of her cinnamon hair, and Beth swung about. 'Now, dear, if you will just pass my parasol off the hallstand – and my Bible – I'll be off.'

'Yes, Mama.' Emma leaped into action. 'Here, Mama.'

'Let me see.' Beth toyed with her lower lip. 'Is there anything I've forgotten?' Her bright brown eyes swept the

11

hall as though the answer might be found in its dark-panelled walls. 'Oh ... your spelling, dear. Do remember to study it while I'm gone. Your sampler, too. Work diligently on it, now. And no sloppy stiches, mind, or they will have to be pulled out.' Her grey-gloved finger wagged before Emma's nose. 'When I return, I expect – '

'*Results*,' interjected Emma.

'Quite so. Now give Mama a kiss.' She bent to offer her smooth, rose-scented cheek, then in a flurry of taffeta made for the door. There she delivered further admonitions, to which Emma nodded in mute agreement, at the same time suppressing a silent quiver of laughter caused by the feathers on the crown of her mother's hat bobbing about as if still part of the tail of a live pheasant.

'Be sure to – '

'Lock the door after you. I will, Mama.' Emma was already beginning to slide the bolt. 'And I shall not answer it to anyone, I promise.'

Emma leaned her back against the door, her ears cocked for the clang of the gate. When the welcome sound finally came, she laughed out loud and scampered through to the drawing room. At the window, she drew back the maroon velvet curtains and, with her nose flattened against the glass, watched until her mother was out of sight.

Thank the Lord for Mama's Christian work, she thought, sinking into the closest chair and unlacing her boots. Once they were off, she wriggled out of her heavy cotton stockings and flexed her toes in ecstasy.

Lovely, lovely Wednesday afternoons. How she adored the unaccustomed freedom they had brought her these summer holidays, with Mama rarely home before four and Jenkins, Cook, and Maggie gone until ten and not a soul but herself to answer to.

And today there was the added excitement of knowing Papa would be home. Contemplating her bare feet, she wrinkled her nose. Odd how the *feeling* always told her, as it had that morning when she'd awakened. It never lied. It was still there, now, below her rib cage, fluttering like captive moths. She hugged herself delightedly. An hour, maybe two, and he'd come striding up the path.

And in the meantime?

She scanned the drawing room. Beckoning her was the china cabinet, resplendent with her mother's treasures: Cadman heirlooms that one day would be Emma's, and in which she already felt a sense of ownership.

Retrieving the key from its hiding place beneath the skeleton clock on the mantel, she unlocked the cabinet and tremulously lifted from its top shelf a tiny demi-tasse. Of pale blue eggshell porcelain, it was so delicate that when she held it to the light, she could see through it shadows of her own fingertips. Next she explored the sandy texture of a bisque cupid, then the smoothness of a satin glass bowl in the palest of yellows. After that, she listened to the sound of her fingernail snapping against the rim of a crystal goblet.

Once she had tired of its contents, she locked the cabinet. And for a moment she stood, indecisive, before swiftly crossing to the fireplace – ornate with its white marble facade – where she clambered onto the heavy brass fender.

On her toes, she craned to scrutinize her reflection in the mirror over the mantel.

Bosh. More freckles. She only had to look at the sun and a new crop sprang up. Why couldn't she have inherited Mama's creamy skin? Stretching her long, slender neck, she lifted her pointed chin and made a moue. Such an ordinary nose … so short and straight.

Oh, to be all pink-and-white-and-blonde, like her best friend, Jane McDonough, whom everyone thought such a pretty little thing. She sighed. Except for Papa, no one had ever told Emma *she* was pretty. But everyone thought her *hair* pretty – everyone, that was, except Mama, who, though she never came right out and said it, gave the impression that hair as red as Emma's was vulgar. At church, a bonnet – and one which concealed every rebel of a curl – was a must.

Reaching to the back of her neck, Emma untied the plain brown ribbon of the same colour and fabric as her frock. With the toss of her head, the tight little waves sprang to life,

13

spilling about her slight shoulders like a waterfall of copper. She smiled, displaying perfectly even teeth, and then poked out her tongue, first at her image, and afterwards at the sternly disapproving faces of her paternal grandparents, housed in their tarnished frames flanking the mirror.

Dead, both of them, before she was born. She propped her chin on the mantel and glowered. Like Mama's mother and father. It wasn't fair. Everyone had relatives – loads of relatives. Look at Jane, with two grandmamas and two grandpapas, half a dozen aunts and uncles, and three brothers. Three brothers! She rolled her eyes and gave a decisive sigh. Jane was right. Better to be an only child than to have torment heaped on you threefold, for you could always make believe that you had a whole army of brothers and sisters, that your grandparents were alive, and they adored you and ... She straightened and squared her shoulders. 'You do adore me, don't you, Grandmama and Grandpapa?'

Some five minutes later, Emma darted across the front lawn to her 'sitting tree', a giant sycamore by the gate. About ten feet up, she perched in the crotch of two sturdy branches. How she loved the roughness of the bark against her bare legs and the smell of the leaves, and the way the sun, lacing through branches, made fugitive patterns on her white apron. Munching like some small rodent on a fistful of nuts and raisins filched from the pantry, she settled down to wait.

Below and behind her stretched the cobbled grey ribbon of Craven Road. It was a thoroughfare of restrained elegance, all the houses on its flanks appearing identical. Each was of red sandstone with four rectangular windows up and three down, overlooking manicured squares of green bordered by flower beds awash with pinks and purples and oranges. In each case, the same half-dozen whitewashed steps led to the same imposing front door with recumbent lions at its base, and at its centre a brass box buffed to daily perfection. Ornate black iron railings separated house from street. Off to one side, double iron gates wide enough for a horse and carriage gave onto a gravelled drive leading to a paved stable yard at the rear, with loose boxes and a detached carriage house.

Now and again, the eye was relieved by a high laurel hedge or an elm or oak encroaching on the street. Here and there, one could find apple and pear and damson trees, bejewelled with their harvests.

Only the colour of the curtains – some maroon, some bottle green or brown – distinguished one house from the next. One sensed that if a newcomer were to drape her windows in the yellow of buttercups or, Heaven forbid, scarlet, there would be a shocked outcry.

This uniformity was the mark of Craven Road. It spoke of substance, position, success. Here lived the bankers, the brokers, the merchants; the old-monied whose ancestors had been in Milchester since it was first conquered by Rome, and the new-monied, like the Cadmans, still considered outsiders by some despite their five years of residence.

Except for their nearest neighbours, few people were acquainted with the Cadmans. It was not that they were closemouthed or unfriendly. From all accounts, they were a charming duo. But George Cadman's business took him away so frequently that he was rarely seen.

It seemed to Emma that sometimes her father was gone for months, not three or four weeks. And though she missed him terribly, she understood his absences were necessary. *Sacrifices* had to be made in the name of business, he'd explained often enough. And, as General Manager of Stevenson's Hardware, suppliers of pots and pans to almost every household in Britain and the Colonies and countless countries whose names escaped Emma, her father had – now, what did he call them? – responsibilities.

Occasionally, Emma envied Jane because *her* father never went away. Then, of course, Mr McDonough had no need to, with the bank he managed in town just a mile or so down the road.

Every day Jane's father would leave at seven-thirty sharp and be home on the dot of six. Saturdays and Sundays would find him in the McDonoughs' drawing room, slumped in a wing-backed chair referred to by Jane as *the sacred chair*, since no one but her father was allowed to occupy it. There he'd read the *Guardian* while everyone crept about for fear of disturbing him. And it seemed to Emma the only time Mr McDonough spoke was to call out, 'Flora, have Lucy bring me a wee spot of tea, if you will.' Whereupon Mrs McDonough would fly to the bellpull as if God Himself had spoken.

Today, though, Emma did not envy Jane one jot. For like as not, Jane was confined to the house, attending to those horrid tasks eleven-year-olds were expected to attend to. Besides, Emma mulled, Mr McDonough never played with Jane or told her she was a princess. Never held her close and crooned her to sleep with lilting Irish lullabies. Never, aside from Christmas and birthdays, brought her gifts. While Emma's father, on the other hand, showered her with presents. Drawers, cupboards, and shelves were crammed with years' accumulation. There were dolls with perfect china faces, puppets and slippers, and scarves and rings.

Emma's expression became pensive as she wondered what her father would bring today.

Ever since her mother had taken away the parasol – a fragile confection of white organdy with an ivory handle – Emma had yearned for another. Three summers ago, her father had brought it. Remembering how her fun had been spoiled, she gnawed on her lower lip. She had been King Arthur; the parasol, Arthur's sword. Perhaps she *had* been a little eager with the sword, prodding Suzannah Parsons' fat bottom until the girl had fled, shrieking: 'Mrs Cadman, help, Emma's trying to kill me.'

At the recollection of her mother's vexation, Emma squirmed. Squinting against the sunlight she fixed her gaze on the street. A moment later, she cocked her head; her mouth tipped at its corners as she caught the sound of whistling and footsteps, punctuated by a rhythmic tapping.

There Papa was, striding along tall and straight, just

beyond the Fentons' high laurel hedge; a silver-topped cane in one hand, a black leather valise in the other.

As her father reached the gate and bent to unlatch it, Emma made a soft owl call. He froze for a minute and then straightened, shrugged, and – cane atwirl – marched down the path.

Emma stifled a giggle. '*Ta-wit-ta-woo-oo*,' she called, loudly this time.

Pausing on the top step, Papa did a quick about-face. 'Sure, and isn't it a strange time of day to be hearing an owl,' he shouted. He set down his valise and cane and, arms folded, lounged with his back to the door. 'Though, I suppose, 'tis quite possible,' he added, his chin supported on his hand now, 'that it may not be an owl at all ... but an Emma bird.'

Unable to restrain herself, Emma scrambled down the tree and, skirts hitched above her ankles, tore across the grass. She launched herself at her father and said, 'You really and truly thought I was an owl, didn't you, Papa?'

'That I did.' He held her at arm's length and chuckled. 'But only at first, mind you. Then I stopped to think – now, owls don't giggle, do they?'

'Oh, Papa.' Emma clicked her tongue against her teeth teasingly. 'You are such a caution. Do you know that I *knew* you would come today? Positively. This morning when I first woke up, I had butterflies right here.' She pressed her middle.

'Is that a fact? Sure and it must be the Irish blood in you that's giving you the second sight. And now is it after telling you what I brought, then?'

Emma's glance flicked to the valise by her feet, and she gave a little shiver of anticipation. 'What *did* you bring me, Papa? Is it in the valise' – she tugged on his coat sleeve – 'or in your pocket?'

'Patience, now.' He tweaked her cheek. 'First let me look at my wee colleen.'

'Papa.' Emma glowered disapprovingly down her nose. 'I am *not* your wee colleen. I am eleven, remember? Almost a lady.'

'Indeed you are.' Papa's hazel eyes swept from the crown of her head to her bare feet, which, judging from the way his fleshy face dimpled and his mouth quivered, he clearly found comical. But his tone was serious when he retrieved his valise and cane, bowed, and said, 'Would an almost-young-lady care to invite this poor tired gentleman into her drawing room?'

A while later, when they were settled beside each other on the sofa, Papa asked, 'And is today the day your Mama's at the rectory, darlin'?'

Emma nodded.

'Well, and it's a fine thing then, isn't it ' Papa loosened his stiff collar and untied his cravat. 'For I'll not be getting into trouble.'

'Trouble, Papa?'

'Aye. For isn't it your mother who's always saying I'll be the ruination of you, always bringing you some doodad or other? Though' – he leaned forward, fumbling in his jacket pocket while he studied Emma's face – 'I'm seeing no signs of ruination yet. All right, now, close your eyes. And no peeping.'

Emma obeyed, her lids trembling from the effort, as she listened to the rustle of paper and felt the slight pressure in her lap.

'You can be opening them now.'

A small, square package came into focus. And a conspiratorial smile passed between them as she began to tear at the wrapping.

'Oh, Papa … it's beautiful.'

'You like it, then?'

'Like it? I positively adore it.'

She ran tentative fingers over the smooth surface of the box. It was a rich red wood, the top inlaid with white flowers of mother-of-pearl. In the centre of each flower was a blue spark of glass. And when she opened the box she saw that the lining was dark green velvet like moss in a bird's nest. In the lid was a mirror, round and so minute that when she held it up, she could see only one eye at a time, or the tip of her nose or her mouth.

Papa guided her hand to a key at the back of the box and showed her how to wind it. The strains of a melody floated out – a waltz, he said, pulling her to her feet. 'Up with you, now. 'Tis high time you learned to dance. It's a simple thing, once you've the hang of the rhythm.' A quick demonstration and several minutes of one-two-threeing from Papa, and they were off, swirling and swooping like swallows under the eaves.

Emma's heart leaped. What bliss, to be waltzing like the ladies of the court. Spinning fast as a top and, beneath her ear, hearing laughter erupt in her father's stomach. She could go on forever. Round and round, faster and faster.

But stop they must, Papa gasped, bringing her to an abrupt halt before the sofa, where, together, they slumped, Papa taking great gulps of air and Emma squeezing her eyes shut against her dizziness.

Presently, the waxed tip of Papa's moustache pricked her ear. 'The music box isn't all I'm bringing you today,' he said. She felt him drape something across her lap. And when she opened her eyes and looked down, she saw a petticoat of exquisitely pale green silk, its half-dozen flounces edged in creamy lace and threaded with satin ribbon in a darker green, like summer leaves. She brought the garment to her hot cheeks.

'Oh, my, Papa. How … gallant. How truly gal – '

'*Elegant*,' Papa corrected, with a chuckle.

She scrambled upright. 'May I try it on? May I, Papa? Now?'

'Sure and why not. But the drawing room is certainly not the place for a young lady to be disrobing. Why don't you pick up your boots and we'll take ourselves upstairs. And while you change I shall splash my hands and face and rid myself of this grime.' He raked his reddish-blond hair back from his glistening brow. 'But first, you'll be tucking away the music box. We don't want to vex your dear Mama, remember.'

19

In her bedroom, some time later, Emma stood before the wardrobe's full-length mirror. When she turned from side to side, the petticoat made a pleasant swishing sound, and the silk against her bare legs was cool. She liked the way her hair caught splinters of sunshine fingering through the leaves of an elm outside the window. Papa is right, she told herself with a dreamy smile, I *am* pretty.

Hearing the clatter of jug and bowl from the adjacent room, she called, 'Papa, I'm ready.' In a minute, through the mirror, she saw him lolling in the doorway.

'Well,' she twirled about, arms outstretched, 'how do I look, Papa?'

There was a long silence before he responded with a husky, 'Lovely, my darling ... lovely.' As he advanced, stopping within arm's length of her, Emma saw at the back of his eyes something indefinable – that same something she'd seen once before, a month ago, when it had been so stifling she'd slept naked and awakened during the night to find Papa standing over her, the candle threatening to burn his fingers. His look sent a tiny tremor through her. She plucked at the lace on her bodice, watching nervously as he fingered his moustache and toyed with his shirt buttons.

Finally, he spoke. 'The music box ... where is it?' His glance skipped about. 'Oh, 'tis over there.' He swiftly crossed to the chest of drawers and called over his shoulder, 'Sure and we'll dance again. That's what we'll be doing.'

Emma sensed the agitation in his voice, saw it in the strangely tight smile when he swung about. But once she was clasped to him, her discomfort abated. And she lost herself in the joy of the dance until Papa steered her towards the bed and they both collapsed onto its vast softness.

She lay still, listening to the thump of her heart and the muted ticking of the china clock from the bedside table and the worried scratchings of the elm's branches at the window. And then, with a long, slow stretch, she let out her breath in small riffles and watched the delicate tracery made by the sun on the white ceiling.

Beside her, the steady movement of her father's chest

caught her attention. She frowned. Surely he couldn't be asleep. With her fingernail, she grazed the tip of his moustache and immediately his eyes flew open, his hand clenched about her wrist. 'Ah-hah,' he said, ''tis a clever devil I am and you an unsuspecting wee thing.'

Freeing herself, Emma laughed and scrambled to her knees. 'Now what shall we do, Papa?' When he lowered his lids again, she shook his shoulder and bounced like an impatient tot. 'Shall I rub your back? It's been simply ages since I did. And you always loved it so.'

He opened one lazy eye and nodded his agreement.

'Roll over, then, on your stomach.' Emma prodded him with her knee.

The petticoat hitched over her thighs, she straddled her father's buttocks and began to massage his shoulders. He groaned intermittently as she probed the tight muscles along his spine. After a time he twisted his head and murmured, 'That's enough, Emma. 'Tis your turn, darlin'. Lie on your stomach, now.'

Under her fathers strong hands, Emma felt as though she were melting away. Through a haze, she heard his husky, 'Don't ever cut you hair, Emma,' as he thrust up from the nape of her neck.

'Sure an' whoever said it was right.'

'Said what, Papa?'

'That a woman's hair is her ...'

'What, Papa?' Emma's eyelids felt weighted down. She fought back the heaviness.

'Her crowning glory.'

'Oh.' She smiled and nuzzled into the pillow. Her body quivered with a kind of strange hot tension that made her want to cry out when her father eased the petticoat straps off her shoulders and traced the ridge of her collarbone. 'So soft and white ... and smooth,' he said, his palms, warm and moist, insinuating under her arms and travelling down her sides beneath the bodice. With the meandering of his hands over her hips, the silk whispered. And over the whisper came the sound of his breathing, ragged, harsh, somehow disquieting. His touch, to this point firm but gentle, seemed all at once to have grown heavier, more insistent, as he explored the valley between her buttocks. In spite of herself, Emma felt an uneasy stirring that made her squirm and say, 'Papa, Mama will be home soon, won't she?'

His hand hesitated in its movement and then abruptly withdrew. She heard him rise and she flipped onto her back, hoisting up the petticoat straps, as she sat up.

Her father stood stiffly beside the bed, twisting his head back and forth as if in combat with the starch of his collar, and mopping the trickle of sweat from his flushed face with his shirtsleeve. He stared at the clock. 'God's truth and you're right. 'Tis ten to four.' He thrust one hand in his trousers pocket and plucked at his side whiskers with the other. 'You'd best be getting yourself dressed. And sharp-like.'

Why was Papa so angry? Her fist pressed to her mouth, Emma swallowed hard and swung her legs to the floor.

'Away with the petticoat, too. Hide it.' He stopped in front of the chest of drawers. 'And the music box.' He lifted its lid up and down, then wheeled about. ''Struth' - his eyes stabbed Emma -' will you look at your hair, now, 'tis a damned disaster! Brush it, tie it back ... do *some*thing with it.'

A prick of resistance rose in Emma and she thrust out a belligerent bottom lip. There was something different about Papa, something she disliked - something frightening. Close to tears, she ran to him and clasped him about the middle. 'Papa, it was a wonderful wonderful afternoon and I love the petticoat and I adore the music box and ... I love you, Papa.'

He stroked her hair. 'I know you do, darling girl. But 'tis getting yourself dressed you should be doing' - he pushed her away - 'while I run down and put the kettle on. For isn't your mother going to be dry as a bone and wanting her cup of tea when she gets home?'

It was one minute to four when Emma joined her father in the kitchen. Hearing the hiss of the kettle from the hob, she asked, 'Would you like me to make the tea, Papa, before Mama arrives?'

'Tis made,' he said without an upward glance, his fingers keeping up their tattoo on the table's scrubbed deal surface.

His terse response filled Emma with a vague anxiety. She sat opposite him and riffled through the pages of her spelling book. When *will* Mama get here, she thought. Please let it be soon.

Seconds later, the rap of the door knocker cleaved the quiet, bringing Emma instantly to her feet. 'I bolted the door, Papa, when we came in. Shall I …?'

'I'll get it, child. Stay put.'

From the hall, Papa's voice carried clearly. 'Beth darlin', the tea'll be drawn in just a jiffy. Emma and I were so wrapped up in what we were doing, we didn't notice the time.'

'And what mischief *have* you two been up to?' Mama asked.

'Sure and it's not mischief we've been up to, but back breaking work,' Papa said. 'Spelling. I've been quizzing Emma on her spelling.'

Emma frowned and tilted her head. She was still frowning a moment later when she glanced up to see Papa standing in the doorway with his arm about her mother's waist.

'Isn't that right, darlin'?' he said.

'Pardon?'

'Your spelling, child?' He gestured to the open book. 'I was just telling your mother how we've been working on your spelling. And deucedly hard, I might add.'

For an instant, Emma stared blankly. Then, when she glimpsed the smile behind her father's eyes – the small smile of warning – she stammered, 'Oh, yes – my spelling. Yes, Papa.'

TWO

'Mama, why do Mr and Mrs Cadman sleep in separate rooms, when you told me married people always share a bed,' Jane McDonough asked one afternoon in late October.

Flora McDonough bent swiftly over her crocheting, cheeks suddenly hot. She chained furiously. Lord save her! How to answer? Ignore the child, that was it. The hook flew in and out of the yarn as she counted under her breath: 'Twenty-one, twenty-two, twenty-three, twenty – '

'*Mama, is it because* – '

Flora continued counting, her voice moving up an octave: 'Thirty-one, thirty-two, thirty-three ... there!' As if it were the foremost thing on her mind, she scrutinized the work for a while and then ponderously laid it on a table at her elbow. Getting to her feet, she cast a quick sidelong glance outside.

Steven and Abraham and little Albert seemed quite happy playing at soldiering. They marched and wheeled, about-faced and saluted, and sporadically broke ranks to stagger, mortally wounded, before dropping like clay pigeons to the leaf-strewn lawn. But boys *were* unpredictable. Any moment a battle could erupt. So the half-lie she was about to tell was excusable.

'My, but just look at those boys. Didn't I ask you to keep an eye on them? Lord knows what mischief they'll be up to next if you don't get out there this instant. Off with you, now,' she said, waving her arm in a gesture of dismissal, 'before they begin fighting.'

Jane's pout changed to a smile as Flora added, 'Well, goodness sakes, if it isn't Emma coming through the gate. And I was under the impression she'd be gone at least another two ...'

Not waiting for her mother's words, Jane bolted for the

door. And seconds later, Flora watched her skip down the path to meet Emma.

Relieved, Flora sank back into her chair, scooting it close to the window for an unrestricted view of the front garden. The girls had clambered onto the lowest bough of a giant oak by the gate. Their legs swung in unison, while behind cupped hands, they whispered to each other.

Flora sighed. Such good friends those two. And what a picture they made, Emma's fiery red hair such a contrast to Jane's pale golden ringlets. Fancy Emma missing three days of school like that, to holiday with her father in London, of all places. Disapproval creased Flora's brow. Jane had certainly been lost without her friend, mooning about the house and making a pest of herself with her interminable questions and her never-ending chatter. And speaking of questions, what about this latest one? What *would* that child think of next? Flora snapped her tongue against her teeth and shook her head.

Separate rooms. Oh, dear. In Flora's mind, that could only mean trouble. As far as she was concerned, Beth Cadman had had enough to contend with the past year. And now this.

Strange. There had been no hint of a problem the last time she and Beth had talked. When had that been? Over a fortnight ago, the afternoon Abraham had put the worm down Jane's back. Flora shuddered at the thought. After executing a series of treble crochets, she paused.

No – not a solitary clue. But then, some subjects were a touch too delicate for discussion, even between friends as close as she and Beth. Gracious, they certainly were close. Sisters couldn't have shared more confidences than they had. Who would guess, looking at Beth Cadman, that she came from such humble beginnings, and was not a lady born and bred. My, but Beth's story was a Penny Dreadful novel come to life, what with her elopement and travels through Europe, and the way she'd steeped herself in culture and insisted her husband hire a tutor for her. Flora wagged her head disbelievingly. If Lavinia and Prudence and Gertrude knew, they would die of shock. But, of course, they never would.

25

Flora resumed her crocheting. Beth's secret was as safe as the money in Benjamin's bank vault.

A whoop from one of the boys brought her out of her disjointed musings and back to Jane's question.

Perhaps the Cadmans' arrangement was a temporary one. There could be any number of explanations. Flora shrugged. Besides, it hadn't been too many months since Beth had lost the baby. Three days' labour and then that precious wee scrap stillborn. James was to have been his name, or rather *was* his name – the baptism had been performed when he was hours old. So perfect he had looked, right down to the sweep of dark lashes on the wax-doll cheeks and a tender fluff of down capping the head. How terribly small the coffin had seemed. She sniffed, dabbing at her moist eyes with the edge of her shawl. Beth had taken it hard. What woman wouldn't? Surely there could be nothing more devastating.

The baby had died in early February. And no sooner was the funeral over, and the last guest departed, than Beth had taken to her sitting room. Dawn till dusk, day in, day out, week after week she'd stayed in that room, refusing visitors and insisting the curtains remain closed. And every day during those weeks, Flora had found herself intermittently glancing across the street, praying the curtains would be drawn back. For it had seemed to Flora that Beth's future – her very existence – was wrapped in the crimson folds of those curtains.

And all that time George Cadman was home. Until one May afternoon, obviously distraught, he'd come to see Flora, telling her he simply could not jeopardize his work a day longer. The summer months were his busiest, he said, and summer would soon be upon them. One could not run a household without money. Would Flora do what she could, he asked, for Beth, for Emma, too? The poor child had hardly set foot outside the house since her mother's confinement.

There was little Flora *could* do, she was convinced. Lord knew, she had tried, regularly sending across flowers and notes and aromatic broths whose preparation she had personally supervised. Time and again, too, she'd spoken to Beth through that closed sitting room door. But always the response was the same: 'Go away. Please go away. Just leave me alone.'

In the end, Flora had to agree with George Cadman: he *must* get on with his life. 'By the time you return,' she'd told him, with a bright smile that belied her feelings of hopelessness, 'things will be back to normal, you'll see.'

As it happened, Flora was right.

Her mind drifted back to that afternoon within a day or two of George's departure, when Emma, pink-checked and eyes shining, had come bounding into Flora's kitchen with Jane hard on her heels.

'Mrs McDonough,' she'd shouted, 'Mamma is better. She went out, dressed in her Sunday silk and her finest hat. And she even said what a disgrace my hair was. Isn't that wonderful?'

Perplexed, Flora had asked where on earth Beth had been going.

'To the Rectory, of course,' Emma had responded. 'Oh, I'm sorry, Mrs McDonough, how could you have known? You see, yesterday, Reverend Smythe came calling. And when Maggie announced him, Mama positively refused to see him.' With a dramatic roll of her eyes, Emma had continued: 'Well, the Reverend flung open the sitting room door (I was in the hall, so I saw and heard everything), and he threw back the curtains and said what a crime it was to sit in the dark on such a beautiful day. Then he turned on Mama. And in what Papa would call his *you-are-all-sinners-and-bound-straight-for-Hell* voice, he said, "Beth Cadman, you are not the first woman to lose a child, nor will you be the last. And who are you to question the Lord's will? While you sit there on your fine *posterior*"' – Flora recalled how Emma had giggled over the word *posterior* – '"there are scores of homeless children at the Orphanage needing care. So it is high time you got up off your *bustle*, Madam, and made yourself useful." And he finished,' Emma continued, 'by

27

making it plain that he expected to see Mama at the meeting of the Circle the next day.'

Never, Flora had thought. Reverend Smythe saying such things! Surely the child must've exaggerated. Yet it had been more or less confirmed some weeks later, when Beth had confided, 'I remember wondering that afternoon, Flora, as the Reverend ranted and raved (and you would be amazed what a veritable fiend that man can be), which of us was the lunatic. I'd be loath to repeat what he said. But he certainly was no gentleman, I can assure you. Come to think, though,' Beth had sniggered behind her hand, 'it was hardly ladylike of me to have the profoundest urge to smash my prize aspidistra over his bald pate.'

Only after Beth's disclosure had Flora seen the method to Reverend Smythe's madness. With the true wisdom of a fine cleric, he had recognized that without purpose and a sense of being needed, Beth would've been lost.

Flora allowed her thoughts to meander pleasantly back to the present. Numb from sitting, she shifted in her chair, her eyes sweeping the garden and coming to rest on her own flock.

The tight little circle of crouching figures against the dappled pattern of the lawn all at once unravelled and became a joyful tangle of tousled heads and flailing arms and running legs. Five pairs of feet pounded on the stone path and five figures streaked by the window, laughter bouncing off the glass as they passed.

Smiling, Flora pressed her palms to the rounded belly beneath the folds of her skirt. Indeed, how important it was to be needed. And she certainly was, with four children and another on the way. Sometimes it was overwhelming. Yet what a blessing it was. Basking in the thought, she leaned back in her seat and felt contentment wash over her.

Her euphoria was short-lived, sent to its death with a sharp slam of the door and Steven's high-pitched 'Mama, Mama!' She jolted upright as the boy burst in.

'You'd best come quick. Emma ... Jane ...' He fought for

28

breath, dancing about like a prize fighter. 'They're scratching and biting ... and kicking!'

'Very well.' With a cluck of exasperation, Flora scrambled upright. 'I am sure there is no cause for hysteria, Steven. Do calm yourself.'

'But Mama, they're pretty near killing each other – leastways Emma is killing Jane. Honest!' The glee in the boy's voice was barely disguised and he clawed at Flora's sleeve. 'Hurry, Mama. Hurry!'

'All right, all right.' Flora trailed after her son and rolled her eyes heavenward. Indeed, it *was* wonderful to be needed.

In her agitation, Flora had arranged and rearranged the china cups and saucers on the low rosewood table before the sofa at least a dozen times. She shook her head in mute disbelief. Emma was normally such a pleasant child. Mischievous, yes, as all children were. But *this!* It had required all her strength to drag Emma off Jane. And the girl's language! Vile. Flora gave an inward shiver as Emma's words ran through her head. 'Jane McDonough, you know what you are? A fornicating bitch!'

Of course, there had been nothing else for it but to send the child packing and later, once Jane was cleaned up and resting in her room, have Steven deliver a note to Beth: Could she come at three to discuss a matter of some importance? On no account, Flora had admonished Steven, was he to breathe a word of what had occurred.

The clock struck three. Flora started. The doorbell rang. And with the sound of approaching footsteps, her heart palpitated. How she hated unpleasantness. But what else could she do? Beth must be told. When the anticipated tap at the door came, she fixed a smile on her face.

'Beth, dear, how good of you to come. Do sit down.' She gestured to a chair opposite the sofa, searching Beth's pallid face as she settled herself. Poor dear, how tired she looked. It would be best not to broach the subject right off. First, they would have a nice chat to smooth the way.

Over tea, they discussed the weather and how it had

improved the past few days. Wasn't it capital to see the sun again after those dreadfully dull days? Oh, had Beth heard about the Mattsons' downstairs maid? Gracious, she hadn't? Well, that terrible girl had apparently staggered into the Mattsons' drawing room the previous Wednesday afternoon, positively reeking of gin. Imagine! Then, along with the plate of cucumber sandwiches she'd been carrying, she had promptly fallen into Mrs Fortescue's lap. Yes. *The* Mrs Fortescue – Chairwoman of the Temperance League. Needless to say, Mrs Mattson had been absolutely livid.

Once their laughter had subsided, an uneasy silence fell. And in Flora's mind, the ticking of the clock became unduly loud. She cleared her throat. 'More tea, Beth?'

'No, not just now, thank you, Flora.'

Draining her cup, Beth set it on its saucer. 'Your note, Flora. You said you had something …'

'Oh, yes.' Slowly, Flora nodded. 'My note.' Playing with the lace doily beneath the cake plate before her, she drew in a breath. 'Well, you know, of course, that I am not one to carry tales, Beth dear. But …'

'It's Emma, isn't it,' Beth broke in.

'Actually … yes.'

'I knew it.' Beth slumped back in the chair, her eyes momentarily closed, and with one weary hand massaged the nape of her neck below the heavy coil of her hair. 'What has the child done?' she asked in a flat voice.

'Dear me, dear me. How to … Er, she set upon Jane like … a wild beast.'

Beth's face contracted. Her hands fluttered to her lap, where they lay limp against the dark blue merino of her skirt.

'It took all my strength to drag her off Jane,' Flora continued. 'Lord knows what might've happened if Steven hadn't fetched me when he did. I have not been able to get to the bottom of it yet. But I *will*, mark my words. It was useless trying to talk to Jane earlier – she was close to hysteria. And if I'm to believe the boys – and I have no reason not to – Emma started the whole affair. At least, she was the one to strike the first blow. Of course, that isn't to say Jane didn't goad her into it. Her tongue can run away with her sometimes. Nevertheless ...'

'Is she still here?'

'Emma? Goodness, no. I sent her home, immediately.'

Beth frowned. 'Then she must've gone upstairs while I was resting in the sitting room. Oh, that child.' She clapped her hands to the sides of her head. 'What am I to do with her?' Pounding her fists on her knees, she went on. 'She's changed, utterly changed. Before the trip with George, it was bad enough. Now it is ten times worse. Rude. Irritable. She doesn't even want to sit down to dinner with us when her father's home. Moody. The slightest provocation and she bursts into tears.' Beth rose and began pacing. 'She was always an easy child, with such a sweet disposition. But now ...'

Taking another quick swallow of tea, Flora watched Beth over the rim of her cup. She set down the cup and picked a currant from the slice of cake on her plate, rolling it between her fingertips. 'I'm afraid there is more, Beth.'

'More?' Beth stood rigid, her thin eyebrows making oblique slashes against her broad white forehead. She pulled distractedly at the cameo in the froth of pale blue lace at her throat as she slipped back into her chair.

'Yes, more.' Flora averted her gaze. 'Emma's language was positively vile.'

'Vile? What exactly did she say?'

Flora looked up. 'It hardly bears repeating. She told Jane she was a –' Flora drew in a breath and, as she exhaled, said quickly, 'Fornicating bitch'.

Beth blanched. 'Oh, my Heavens!' She gripped the wooden arms of the chair, her knuckles turning white. 'What am I to do, Flora? Everything is falling apart.'

Instantly at Beth's side, Flora wrested Beth's hands from her face. 'Oh, come now. It's not *that* bad. A suitably severe punishment should take care of it. Obviously, Emma is out of sorts. Anyway, for goodness sake, it wouldn't be the first time a child used a vulgar word or two.' She patted Beth's shoulder. 'Now, wipe your eyes while I pour you a fresh cup of tea.'

If she were my child, Flora thought, busying herself with the teapot, she'd get the hairbrush across her bottom and her mouth well and truly scoured with carbolic soap.

'Here.' Flora slid the freshly filled cup across the table and then thrust a plate under Beth's nose. 'Do have a piece of this cake. Cook outdid herself. It's delicious.'

With a dumb shake of her head, Beth pushed the plate away.

'There, dear. I understand.' Reaching across the table, Flora patted Beth's knee. 'Try not to worry about Emma, now. We both know she's a good girl. A firm hand is all she needs.'

'Oh, it's not just Emma, Flora.' Beth's voice was gritty. 'I cannot – I mean, since James's birth, I have been unable to ...' She brought her fists to her mouth, 'I have been unable to fulfil my duty as a wife. There is a name for the condition. "Vaginismus," the doctor called it. A condition brought on by "a hysterical fear of conception," and one that makes it impossible for a husband to ... well, er –'

'I think I understand,' Flora said quietly. 'And is there anything that can be done?'

'I have medicine.' Beth ran her hands over her face and examined her fingernails. 'Medicine to calm my nerves. Though, with the turn of events lately, my nerves have been reduced to shreds. You see' – she stared down at her lap for a time, smoothing the fabric over her knees – 'it is having the most devastating effect on my relationship with George. The last time he was home, four weeks ago, he moved into the study and –'

Flora smoothed out the linen napkin on the tea tray. So that was what it was all about. 'Go on, dear.'

Before continuing, Beth blew her nose briskly. 'He said that, under the circumstances, it was the best solution. And Flora ... I was actually *relieved*. Isn't that a dreadful admission for a wife to make?'

'No, I don't think it's dreadful at all, dear.' Flora cut herself another sliver of cake and popped a piece in her mouth. 'Heavens, there's been many a time I wished Benjamin and I had separate rooms. I mean, it's not as if any of us relish that side of our marriages. And do you know what else I think? That you are making mountains out of molehills.'

'You do?'

'Yes. And I think you are putting yourself through unnecessary torment. Time, dear ... time is what you need to regain your strength. You and George will weather this setback.'

Beth smiled fleetingly. 'I suppose you are right.'

'Of course I am right. George couldn't ask for a better wife, a better mother for his child.'

'Mother!' Beth threw her hands up. 'Emma ... Lord! What am I to do about her? If George were here, and he won't be home until Friday, I'd have him give her a good dressing down. It would have far more effect coming from him. Though knowing the way he ruins her, I ...'

'Beth, dear.' Flora nodded in the direction of the mantel. 'I *do* hate to cut you off, but it *is* twenty past four.'

A glance at the clock, and Beth was on her feet, smoothing her skirts and pulling on her gloves, full of apologies for having taken up Flora's afternoon and full of thanks for Flora's help.

Brushing aside the apologies and thanks with an insouciant wave of her hand, Flora said she had merely listened as any friend would. And the solutions arrived at had been Beth's own.

As they parted, they agreed to speak with their respective daughters and arranged to meet the following day.

'You'll see,' Flora said, masking her vague sense of unease with a cheerful smile. 'Between the two of us, we will have this entire affair ironed out in no time.'

When she heard Lucy close the front door after Beth, Flora crossed to the window, where she watched until Beth was through the gate. She turned and, with a firm set to her mouth and a purposeful stride, made for the door. Now was as good a time as any to begin the ironing-out process.

'All I said was that she was making it all up, Mama. I didn't exactly call her a liar. And then she slapped me really hard, right across the face.' Jane's voice whined about the chintz-papered walls and, as she settled on her back and glowered up at the ceiling, glowing dimly from the lamp on the chest of drawers, the bed creaked.

Seated on its edge, Flora leaned over to touch the child's cheek, letting the silence hang for a minute. 'Making all what up, dear?'

Jane hoisted herself onto her elbows. 'Oh ... the things she said her father makes her do.'

Raising a quizzical eyebrow, Flora asked with a hint of amusement in her voice, 'And what things are those?'

Jane wrinkled her nose. 'I'm not really supposed to tell. I mean, I promised. But that was *before*. And Emma *was* mean and nasty to me.' Squirming to an upright position, she sat cross-legged. 'It's all a lot of silly lies, anyway.'

'What is, dear?' With a benign smile, Flora reached for Jane's hand and clasped it between her own.

'The dancing.' Jane shrugged and wriggled her hand free of her mother's. 'She says her father makes her dance' – averting her eyes, she lowered her voice to a whisper – 'without any clothes on.'

Flora felt a flush start at her neck and creep up into her cheeks. Abruptly, she turned away and made a show of coughing. Lord above, what was the child saying? Fighting for composure, she swivelled to face Jane. 'Go on, dear.'

'And he touches her, she says,' Jane snickered into her hands, 'on her private parts.'

Oh, that girl! That Emma! The child had to be demented to concoct such a tale. Flora got up very slowly and, with studied indifference, crossed to the window, where she stood rigid, her back to Jane. But how could Emma possibly know about such things? There was no way conceivable. Unless ... unless the girl spoke from experience.

Mentally, Flora shook her head against the thought. But the awful realization flashed upon her: it *had* to be the truth. God in Heaven, it was disgusting. She clamped a horrified hand to her mouth, tasting the revulsion at the back of her throat. Then she made her lips move. 'My, that is *quite* a tale.' With a hollow laugh, she went on, 'What an imagination Emma has.' Her hands moved involuntarily to the folds of the curtains, pleating and repleating them. That child. That poor defenceless child. No wonder she had been behaving so strangely.

Fragmented thoughts scrambled at the rim of Flora's mind. Benjamin gone. Why tonight, of all nights? Bankers' conference. Not back until Friday. Must tell somebody. Must decide what to do.

Nine o'clock, Flora saw as she lowered the wick on the sperm lamp beside her bed. The house was blissfully silent. How she had managed to get through the dinner hour, with all its bickering and tittering and kicking under the table, the Lord only knew. Thank God she had herded the children into bed by eight, all the time remaining outwardly calm.

But still no solution. Nothing to be done tonight. Tomorrow, she'd tackle it again tomorrow. She would think of some way to tell Beth. At least the child was safe tonight, with her father gone the rest of the week. That final thought was of small comfort, but it was enough to send Flora over the edge of wakefulness into a fitful sleep.

Some half an hour later, George Cadman came sauntering along Craven Road, whistling softly. What a stroke of luck, he thought, that the meeting had been cancelled at the last minute and in plenty of time for him to catch the train.

By the gate, he paused under the gas lamp and pulled his watch from inside his jacket. Nine-thirty. Glancing up to the second floor, he narrowed his eyes speculatively. If Beth wasn't asleep already, she soon would be.

THREE

Emma must have slept, for she experienced a plunging sensation when she became conscious of a noise from beyond the bedroom door. It took only an instant for her to recognize it as the creaking of loose boards on the landing. Night after night, she had listened for it these past weeks. It was a sound that made her blood pound in her ears and her mouth become dry.

Please God, not tonight. She tossed her head to and fro. It wasn't supposed to happen tonight. Friday, Mama had said. 'Your father will deal with you when he gets home on Friday.'

The footsteps drew nearer. They had a strange, uneven rhythm, as if they were those of a lame man. Emma hitched herself onto her side, facing the door, which was illumined by a swatch of curdled-milk light sent through a gap in the curtains by the moon. Taut with apprehension, she drew her knees to her chest and pulled the quilt over her ears. From under her lashes, she watched as the door swung open.

Framed in the grey rectangle was the swaying black silhouette of her father. As his shadowed bulk approached the bed, she snapped her eyes shut.

Seconds of elastic silence punctuated the rasp of his breathing. 'Emma ... my wee darlin', Papa's home.' His voice, barely above a whisper, seemed to fill the room.

Feigning sleep, Emma forced tiny, even puffs of air between her slightly parted lips. There was a rustle of movement, then she felt the mattress beside her give. A hot, dry fingertip grazed the tip of her nose and traced her cheekbones. Moist lips moved along her jawline. And the sweet, sickly odour of port crept into her nostrils. Her stomach made a fist as his hand, beneath the covers, clamped on her shoulder. He shook her. 'Wake up, my sweet. Papa made a special trip to see you.'

The pressure in her head built to a steady throb. Leave me alone, she wanted to scream.

As though responding to her mute plea, he loosened his grip. She felt him rise. Was he leaving? Sucking in air through her lower teeth, she held her breath at the shuffle of his feet across the floorboards. Squinting in the dimness, she could see his dark outline bent over the chest of drawers. What was he doing? And that noise? That scratching. What was it? There it went again. The answer came to her in the smell of sulphur and the thrust of amber light beneath her lids the instant before she lowered them.

From the bedside table came the metallic scrape of the lamp being set down, followed by the sputtering of the flame.

He chuckled close to her ear. 'Sure and you *are* awake. I guessed as much. Can't fool Papa.' He hiccoughed. 'No one can fool Papa, least of all you, darlin' girl.' He gave a loud belch and mumbled under his breath, 'Damnably hot. Damnably thirsty. Must have a drink.' His lips, moist as a worm, suddenly moved against her earlobe. 'Papa's going now. But it'll not be for long. Just a few minutes. Five or ten at the most. And then there'll be no more teasing, no more pretending when Papa returns. Little Emma'll be wide awake and ready to be nice to her poor, tired Papa.'

Motionless, Emma waited. As soon as the door closed after him, she threw back the quilt and swung out of bed. Irresolute, she stood clutching the bedpost for support and shivering against the chill air. Looking desperately about, she brought her hand to her mouth.

Tonight she was afraid. Tonight he would be mean. The signs were there in his slurred words and the way he moved and the stink of his breath. He would pinch and poke and pry.

There had to be some way to stop him. But how?

Run to Mama? No! She blinked back her tears as his warning rolled through her mind. 'If you ever tell a living soul, and especially your Mama, there could be the most fearful consequences.'

37

Consequences. Things that could happen – sometimes good, often bad – if you acted a certain way.

Emma trudged to the window and stood with her forehead against the frame. He was right. Already there had been dreadful consequences because she'd broken her word and let the secret slip. But this secret was different. Painful. Terrifying. And she hadn't meant to tell. Jane hadn't believed her anyway. Now, Jane hated her. And Mama? Did Mama hate her? Surely, she must.

'Oh, Emma, what could've possessed you to use such abominable language, and Jane your dearest friend,' she'd said. 'And *where* in the name of all that's holy did you learn such filth?'

Emma's silence had turned her mother's eyes to flat, muddy pebbles. 'So you refuse to say. In that case, I have no alternative but to speak to your father on his return and discuss with him what's to be done about your shameful behaviour.'

Whimpering, Emma pressed her forehead even harder against the window frame. Had she been free to answer, what could she have said?

'But, Mama, I didn't know it was wicked. I didn't *know* those words were filthy. Because last week at the hotel, Papa called me that name after he held my nose and tried to force his awful brandy down my throat, and I was sick all over the front of his shirt.'

Mama would never have believed it.

Emma turned from the window, shuddering against the memory of her father's rage. In weary disgust, she sat on the edge of the bed. With her fists, she pummelled her thighs. Her heart pulsed at her temples. Any minute now, and he'd be back.

Think. She squeezed her eyes in concentration, slowly opening them seconds later, as the idea began to take shape. Angling her head, she raked a hand through her hair. It *might* work. Absently, she wound a curl around her forefinger. A sidelong glance at the wicker sewing basket on the desktop, and she nodded. It *would* work. It had to.

Swathed in a sheet, its edges twisted in a knot held firm by her chin, Emma sat with her back pressed against the bedhead. As the door opened, her jaw tightened.

He advanced, smiling, hands thrust in the pockets of his green velvet smoking jacket. 'Well, well. Wide awake, I see. And what have we here?' He fingered the sheet. 'A fashionable new frock?'

'I was cold, Papa.'

'Cold, you say? Well, and isn't that an easy thing to be taking care of,' he chuckled, leaning over to kiss the tip of her nose, enveloping her in that sickly stench and making her flinch inwardly. 'You just snuggle down, now, poppet' – he straightened and loomed over her for a moment, his eyes narrowed to hot, glowing slits – 'and Papa will soon warm you.'

The instant he turned away, Emma loosened the sheet and shrugged it off. And as he began to untie the cord at his waist, she posed straight-backed, chest out, her chin thrust forward at a defiant angle.

She swallowed hard. 'What do you think, Papa?'

Whistling softly, he swung about. At the sight of her, the whistle froze on his lips. His mouth went slack. 'Holy Mother of God ...' He grabbed the lamp and held it over her. 'What is it you've done to yourself?'

The pain and horror Emma saw in her father's face sent a surge of power through her. She ran a casual hand across her scalp, exploring the bristly tufts. 'I cut my hair, Papa. Don't you like it?'

Unafraid yet confused, Emma watched him. How much longer would he sit like that, not moving, not speaking? She had expected anger, disgust. But not this.

He was on the floor beside her, one foot tucked under him, the other stretched out. Head hanging down. Chin on his chest. To one side of him, on the polished wooden boards, was the lamp. Centered on the oval rug in front of him were the scissors, blades open. Flanking them, like twin sleeping snakes, the glistening copper coils of her hair. And strewn about – flotsam on a patterned turquoise sea – were fragments of red wood, icicles of glass, velvet scraps, tiny cogs and wheels, and the spiral of the music box's spring.

Slowly, he raised his head, levelling his gaze at her. Tears bled down his cheeks. Emma squirmed. A needle of fear pricked her consciousness. Papa crying?

'Why, oh why, Emma? Your beautiful, beautiful hair.' He shook his head heavily and reached for one of the coils, unwinding it and draping it across his palm. The minutes dragged by while he contemplated it. Finally, he let it slip to the rug. And his head snapped up. 'Is it deaf y'are, child. I asked you *why!*' he said in a chilling voice, lunging for the lamp and scrambling upright.

In an attempt to conceal her alarm, Emma looked away. 'I didn't like it,' she mumbled.

'You didn't *like* it?' His words came out in a shower of spittle as he leaned over her, breathing hard. 'And do you realize what it is that you've done?'

Emma stared up at him in mute horror.

'You've ruined yourself … made yourself ugly, you have. *Ugly*, do you hear? Without your hair, you're nothing. *Nothing!*' He brought his face close to hers. She could see the purple veins at his temples, the foamy flecks at the corners of his mouth, the web of red lines in his bulging eyes. 'Oh, but you'll not be getting away with it. Oh, no!' Reaching across her, he slammed the lamp down on the table and then abruptly turned away.

His back was towards Emma. It was the moment to move. Blindly, she felt for the tiny metal knob. Her fingers trembled as she rotated it clockwise. The flame flickered once, twice, then died.

There was silence. A harsh intake of breath. A muttered curse.

'Emma.'

'Yes, Papa.' Swinging her feet to the floor, she dropped to her knees and began to crawl across the room.

'Get the matches, girl. They're on the chest of drawers. And hurry – I cannot see a blasted thing.'

Her hand crept higher until it closed around the door-knob. Slowly, carefully, she pulled herself up.

'Well, child, did you find them?'

'Yes, Papa. I have them.' She inched open the door.

'Bring them here, then. The lamp, too.'

She slipped out onto the landing, easing the door closed after her. Now what? She stood rigid. Run? Hide? Wake Mama? Scream? Oh, please Lord, help me.

'Emma.' The whisper came from behind her.

Panic spun her around.

In the ghost light, his face gleamed faintly. 'Emma, darlin',' he whispered, 'sure, and Papa didn't mean to be frightening you. Come here.'

The glitter of the scissors as he beckoned.

Terror wringing the air from her lungs, filling her mouth with a coppery taste, she backed against the bannister. It quivered slightly.

A hand clutched at her. As she sidestepped, from some place far away came the sounds of her nightgown ripping, the clatter of metal, wood splintering – and the muted explosion of breath that was her own silent scream.

And with the final, terrible thud from below, Emma seemed to float away horizontally.

.

FOUR

From that first late October day, the wreath hung on the front door of the Cadman residence was like a blister on the heel of Craven Road.

Bad enough that the accident had happened. But to be haunted by it daily, to have one's eyes inexorably drawn to the twining black-silk opulence of that circle of doom, was to be reminded of the tenuousness of life itself. Death was disconcerting; violent death, horrifying.

Worse yet was the scandal of it: a neighbourhood's reputation sullied in an instant; respectability snuffed with the snap of George Cadman's neck.

Of course, it was a tragedy. There was no denying that. But from all accounts, the man *had* been drunk – or so went the story, one that began (as all such stories did) below stairs.

'It was the child who found him, you know.'

'Really? I heard it was the wife ... that she was there when he fell. And her screams woke the child.'

'Oh, no! You are both wrong. I heard from Lavinia Parsons that the child was *with* him when it happened.'

'You mean, she actually witnessed the whole thing?'

'I most certainly do.'

'I suppose you could be right. We all know the girl has been ill since the accident. And no wonder, seeing her father plummet to his death like that – and a father they say she idolized.'

'Frankly, I'm bored, completely and utterly bored with the entire subject. For a fortnight now, all I have listened to is this nonsense. And as far as we can determine, only one person knows what *really* happened. George Cadman. Now he's dead and buried. And the truth – whatever it is – is buried with him.'

Through it all, Emma Cadman was lost in a different world, where voices that were sometimes sad and soft and pleading, often sharp and intrusive, but always without meaning, penetrated layers of half-dream, half-reality.

There were moments when, motionless, mute, and seemingly suspended by an invisible cord, she observed below her the lifeless form of a girl, white as the sheets of the bed on which she lay; and beside the bed, a figure dressed in black, kneeling, praying. Or was it a doll with a porcelain face and painted lips and red, red tufts of hair? And not a bed at all, but a shoe box lined with tissue?

Then came the day when Emma swam up through a warm,

grey void towards a spark of light and, surfacing, found that *she* was in a bed – a lavender-scented bed in a room vaguely familiar, with its pale flowered wallpaper and tall rectangular window draped in crimson velvet, beyond which she could see scurrying cloud wisps above the skeleton of a tree etched in charcoal on the sky.

Whose room? Not hers. That much she knew instantly. Raising herself up on her elbows, she looked around, searching for clues.

Beneath the window was a chintz-covered chaise, with embroidered pillows; and next to the chaise, a square white wicker table bearing a lamp of rose-pink glass, with a round base, a slender hollow stem, and a cuplike top from which hung ruby-coloured prisms.

At the foot of the bed was a kidney-shaped dressing table skirted in the same chintz as the chaise and holding an assortment of pill and pin boxes, hair tidies and ring holders. Centred beneath an oblong mirror was a grouping of crystal perfume bottles, most half full, all silver-stoppered. On the same wall, between a wardrobe and a tallboy, was a washstand, with a jug and bowl in crackled duck-egg blue and cream.

Her neck and shoulders grown stiff, Emma sank back onto her pillow. Glancing sidelong, she saw a fireplace, small and neat, with a mantel whose only ornament was a clock. Mama's clock ... she was in Mama's room. She scratched her head. But where was Mama? Her fingers moved frantically over her scalp. Horrors, her hair! Someone had cut it as short as a boy's. Hot tears sprang to her eyes and spilled down her cheeks. Why? Why, too, when she tried to move, were her legs so disobedient?

Sick, that was it. She must have been ill, to be in Mama's bed. Her heart stopped in midbeat and she clamped her teeth. The pox! Or worse! Gingerly, she lifted back the sheets and fumbled with her nightgown until she had it up around her chest. Holding her breath, she flashed a look at her torso. No telltale sores, not so much as a freckle. 'Thank you, Lord,' she whispered, 'thank you.' Then, exhausted, she drifted off into sleep.

When next she opened her eyes, warm air flowed soft about her head. A fire burned in the grate, logs bursting into bright flames, coal hissing angrily. Suddenly, the door creaked wide. And a woman paused on the threshold, muttering to herself between great rasping breaths, 'Them stairs'll be the death of me.' Hands clapped to the majestic prow of her bosom, she closed the door with a jerk of her huge bottom and trudged to the fireplace, where she stood with her back to Emma.

After several minutes of studying the strange figure, Emma said quietly, 'Excuse me, ma'am, but who are you?'

The woman spun about. In the half-light, her eyes, magnified by the spectacles perched on the ridge of her nose, were like two ebony buttons. She clutched her throat. 'Lord o' mercy, child, I thought it was the Holy Virgin 'erself speakin' to me. Frightened me clear out of my stays, you did!' She and the bed wheezed in unison as she sat down. 'I'm Mrs Flaherty, darlin', brought in to nurse you back to health.'

'Have I been very ill?' Emma struggled to sit. But when her head began to spin, she thought better of it.

'That you have. It's the reason you're feeling so weak, child.'

'How long have I been ill?'

'How long?' Mrs Flaherty toyed with a hairy mole on her chin and stared ceilingward. 'October the twenty-seventh it was … and today is November the twelfth. If I'm not mistaken, that's over two weeks.'

November? Emma frowned. Odd. Somehow she'd imagined it to be summer.

'Thought you was lost, we did,' the woman's voice intruded. 'Lyin' here day after day, with your poor mother an' me havin' to force the broth down you. And you spittin' it up an' hardly takin' enough to keep a flea alive.'

'My mother! Where is Mama?'

Mrs Flaherty threw up her hands and got to her feet. 'Your

44

Ma is downstairs, she is, havin' her dinner. An' me sittin' here blatherin' while the poor dear soul is worryin' herself sick, thinkin' the worst. Now don't you move.' Waddling across the room, she called over her shoulder, 'Stay right where y'are, you hear me?'

Grinning to herself, for she could not have moved if she'd wanted to, Emma listened to Mrs Flaherty's slow, receding footfalls on the stairs.

Presently, a door slammed somewhere below. A voice shouted, 'Maggie, run and fetch Dr Bicknall. Quickly, now.' A flurry of swift, light steps, and the voice came again, this time calling, 'Emma darling, mama's coming.'

Seconds later, the door flew open. Mama! For an instant, she paused motionless, light and shadow playing on the pale oval of her face. With a strange little whimpering sound, she stumbled to the bedside and stood looking down. Through the spill of tears, she smiled, her gaze sweeping with love and wonder over Emma's face. 'Darling, darling child,' she said, her voice catching, 'you are back.'

It was late – nine o'clock, Emma saw – and still Dr Bicknall was not done with her.

All the time he had been checking her pulse, listening to her heart, instructing her to wiggle her toes and stare at a lighted match he waved before her nose, Emma had been casting puzzled looks at her mother, who sat knitting on the chaise, in the halo of pink light from the lamp.

Had it really been Mama who earlier had clasped Emma to her bosom, kissed her and crooned in her ear the tender phrases she had never thought to hear because – for some untold reason – she had imagined Mama angry with her? Or had it been the sickness playing tricks with her brain?

No. It *had* been real. As real as Mama's smile now, as she paused to set aside her work and glanced up, pulling from her sleeve a black handkerchief and dabbing it at her nose and eyes. A black handkerchief? Odd. A black dress, too. Black beads at her throat. It was the *same* black gown. The *same* black beads Mama had worn after baby James had gone to

45

Heaven. Mourning, that was it. But who was Mama mourning now?

'I'm not dead!' Emma heard her own voice shrill in the silence.

'You are certainly not, young lady.' Dr Bicknall chuckled and toyed with his cropped white beard. 'Far from it, if what Cook tells me is true: that you ate everything on your tray and even asked for more. I would say you're very much alive. Now ...' His hand cupped her chin. 'Turn your head this way. Good. Now the other. Excellent!'

With a slight jerk of his head, he signalled Mama to join them. Setting her knitting aside, she quickly rose and came to stand beside him.

Dr Bicknall took Emma's hand. 'Now, child, do you remember anything about the accident?'

The accident. What accident? She had been sick was all. Shrugging uncertainly, she nodded no.

'You don't remember any fall?' He released her hand.

Her thumb found its way to her mouth and she gnawed on it, conscious of their eyes upon her, watchful, as if her answers were important. She fidgeted. 'No.'

'And your father, Emma, do you recall the last time you saw him?'

Her father? Strange, she hadn't even thought of Papa until now. But then it was so long since she had seen him. Months and months. So how could she be expected to remember? Anyway, it made her head hurt to try. She pouted. 'No ... my Papa goes away. He is hardly ever home.'

She caught the look of dismay that passed between the doctor and Mama. It brought a vague feeling of uneasiness. Her discomfort grew when they both crossed to the window, where, with heads together, they began to converse in low voices. Once in a while, snatches of the conversation, which made no sense at all, came to her.

'It is as I suspected. No memory of it whatsoever. Too painful ...'

'... Ever come back to her, Doctor? I mean, will we ever know what happened?'

46

'Just don't know enough about these cases ... knowledge very limited. 'Days ... months ... years, even. Maybe never.'

'... Must tell her, mustn't I, Doctor?'

'Absolutely. And the sooner, the better.'

In what appeared to be a comforting gesture, Dr Bicknall squeezed Mama's shoulder. And then they both turned and approached the bed. 'I'll be on my way now, Beth,' the doctor said. 'And as for you, young lady' – he brushed Emma's cheek with the back of his hand – 'you do as your Mama tells you – lots of rest and plenty to eat. And I shall be back to see you in a day or two.'

Once the door closed behind Dr Bicknall, Mama sat beside Emma on the bed. Stroking Emma's hair back from her forehead, she said, 'I have something to tell you, dear. Come here.' Encircling Emma with her arm, she pulled her close. 'It is something very difficult, and you must be very brave. It's Papa,' she whispered. 'There was a terrible accident, you see.' She shuddered. 'And the Lord took Papa to be with Him.' She eased Emma away from her and grasped her by the shoulders, turning her so that their eyes met. 'You understand, child, what I am saying? Your poor dear father is dead.'

Emma eased herself from the warm curve of the body next to hers; the measured breathing signalled that Mama was finally asleep. Tentatively, she swung out of bed. For a time, she stood flexing her uncertain legs and adjusting her eyes to the dimness. Unsteady, she crept towards the window and slowly, carefully, parted the curtains. Grasping the sill for support, she lifted her eyes to the midnight sky. At that instant, the moon slid from behind a cloud and hung like a great silver locket.

So that was where he was, her father. Gone forever. Dead.

Odd, but still she felt no grief. If grief was that terrible sad ache she'd had last year, when her kitten died under the wheels of a brougham.

She felt something – that same something she'd felt earlier, when Mama told her – and she had tried so hard to cry because, with news of a death, one always cried. And yet, then as now, the tears refused to come.

Whatever it was – this hot, bittersweet flow that seemed to bubble from her centre, filling her bones, her veins, her heart – it was nice. And she was home, back, as Mama had put it, from wherever it was she had been. And that was even nicer.

FIVE

Had it not been for the huge coal fire blazing in the grate, the clutter of papers and ledgers and journals and periodicals on every available surface, and the redolence of beeswax, pipe tobacco, and mildew, Benjamin McDonough's office might have seemed forbidding to Beth, for it was a vast, lofty-ceilinged room, dominated by a massive oak desk and broad bay window. This latter was draped in velvet the same weary green as the carpet, and it afforded the visitor – seated as Beth was in one of the two hard and wholesome wooden chairs – merely a view of rooftops and a drab sky pierced by a distant steeple.

Hanging on the inlaid panelling above the fireplace were the likenesses of a bastion of banking hierarchy, long-departed. Opposite, centered on the longest wall, was a bureau bookcase, solid, utilitarian, and filled with leather-bound volumes, much like the one lying open at Benjamin's elbow, whose pages he scanned from time to time as he spoke.

He would be with Beth shortly, Benjamin had said a quarter of an hour earlier, when an eager young clerk had ushered her in and Benjamin, with an obsequious smile, had motioned her to sit.

The wait was somehow nerve-racking – the minutes marked by the sombre ticking of a brass-faced mantel clock, the scratch of Benjamin's pen, the shuffling of papers, and his chair springs' intermittent groan when he shifted position.

Finally, he spoke. 'There.' Blotting the paper before him and propping his pen in a square-cut crystal inkwell, he peered at Beth over a pair of pince-nez perched on the carmine-veined bulb of his nose. 'I'm afraid the news isn't good, my dear. Not good at all.' He shook his head heavily, and the ruddy jowls spilling over his starched shirt collar quivered.

Apprehension crawled up Beth's spine and settled at the back of her neck.

'In fact ...' Letting the sentence trail off, he threw up his hands in a gesture of helplessness. He sat back, thumbs hooked under a gold watch chain hooked across the immense expanse of his belly. His eyes swept the ceiling and he muttered under his breath, 'A dreadful situation.'

Gripping the arms of her chair, Beth sat frozen and, in a voice sharpened by fear, replied, 'You'll forgive my impatience, Benjamin, but if you have something to say, I would be obliged if you would just say it. Jenkins is waiting with the hack, and the poor fellow will –'

'Yes, of course, my dear.' Benjamin exhaled audibly and then swivelled towards the window behind him, his head angled.

'By Jove ... beastly-looking day. Shouldn't be a bit surprised if it snows. Then it's all one can expect ...' He swung back. 'Snow in November. Oh, but the children do love it so, especially young Albert.' Smiling, he, stared beyond Beth, seemingly oblivious of her anxious knuckles drumming on the edge of the desk.

'The situation, Benjamin? Speak plainly, *please*.' Beth felt the last thread of her patience ready to snap. 'I assure you there is no danger of my swooning. More than anything, I'm anxious to hear exactly where I stand.'

He smiled a touch sadly. 'Of course you are, Beth.' Removing the pince-nez, he polished them against his sleeve and set them aside. With thumb and forefinger, he massaged the angry little indentations each side of his nose. 'I really am frightfully sorry to have kept you this long. But going over the figures with Bromley, your bank manager, took rather more time than anticipated.' His mouth made a reflective curve. 'Good fellow, Bromley. A bit stand-offish at first, mind you … until I gave your letter authorizing release of all the pertinent information.' He riffled through the ledger pages. 'But I couldn't have asked for a more thorough accounting. Chap has a superb eye for detail. Deucedly fine job.' He touched his fat fingers together in emphasis and then, with a slight movement of his head toward the sheaf of papers, added, 'It's all here, the whole lamentable mess.'

Half-rising, Beth braced herself on the arms of the chair. 'What, Benjamin? *What* lamentable mess? What exactly are you trying to tell me?'

Benjamin flushed slightly, cleared his throat, and said softly, apologetically, 'I am trying to tell you, dear lady, that your husband left you penniless.'

For a long time after Beth's departure, Benjamin stood at the window, his eyes fixed in space, contempt for George Cadman an unyielding lump in his throat. Lord forgive him for thinking ill of the dead, but on top of everything else (and Flora had told him all she knew), the man had been an irresponsible wretch.

Frowning, he chewed on the stem of his pipe. Had he been right, he wondered, in glossing over the whole distasteful affair and sparing Beth the lurid details, trusting that rumours would never reach her of the gambling and the drinking? But the facts. Inescapable facts. The creditors. The horrendous overdraft and the promises to cover it – promises never fulfilled.

Bromley had been damn near apoplectic when it had come to light. 'Three thousand pounds, you say? Three thousand *pounds?*' Benjamin had heard him shriek from the next room when he'd interrupted his meeting with Benjamin to hold a hurried conference with two clerks, clerks whose heads would undoubtedly roll before the day was out. And rightly so. It was inexcusable. Though, *had* Bromley been alerted earlier, it could hardly have made a difference, since from all accounts (and good, reliable sources) Cadman's insolvency was inevitable.

Yes, telling Beth that the situation had come about through her husband's mismanagement of his financial affairs was a small deceit, an oversimplification perhaps. But kinder, much kinder, than the truth. An ugly truth that would serve no purpose other than to take away what respect she had for the man. Benjamin clamped his teeth on his pipe stem as if to affirm his rationale. Let her at least keep that respect. Lord knew, she would be left with little else.

Once the machinery of reprisal was set in motion, it would move swiftly, relentlessly. A bank had no heartstrings to be tugged at, only stockholders to answer to. And the plight of one unfortunate widow? Inconsequential. At least in the eyes of a succinct Bromley. 'Wherever our sympathies may lie,' he'd said, 'we must *always* put the interests of the bank first.'

Benjamin nodded. Bromley was right, of course. Emotional detachment was the quintessence of banking; subjectivity, an anathema. But when the bank involved was not one's own? And the person involved was one's wife's closest friend? Surely there was no harm in being a trifle subjective. No ... not subjective. Concerned.

Turning from the window, he trudged the few paces to the desk, where, realizing numbly how weary he was, he sank into his chair.

Yes. Debits and credits, checks and balances were one thing. But Beth Cadman was another.

Worrying at the tobacco in the bowl of his pipe with a pearl-handled knife, he hunched over the desk top. In his experience, adversity had a way of bringing out the best or the worst in people; in Beth's case, the former was true. By Jove, one had to admire her spunk. None of the hysteria he'd anticipated – dreaded even. And, Heaven knew, he had dealt with enough distraught widows in his time to be able to predict their reactions. Not a one, though, had been like Beth.

His pipe lit, he puffed thoughtfully, recalling how

throughout his narrative she'd remained outwardly calm. Only her eyes had given her away, as the implications of his various statements, with all their ramifications, were mentally noted.

In the upward spiral of grey smoke, he caught an image of Beth's face: pale, almost translucent against the black bonnet. Lips tight, nostrils flared, and a brave thrust to the chin, as she'd said with an ironic twist to her mouth, 'So, I'm to join the ranks of the destitute, am I, Benjamin? Do you think we will make good pickpockets, Emma and me?' She had punctuated the question with a hollow little laugh and then, obviously sensing his discomfort, apologized.

'Will they allow me to keep anything, Benjamin? Or will they demand the clothes off my back?' she had asked. 'And how much time do I have? As you know, Emma was quite ill after the accident. She is on the mend, now, of course. But any more upheaval could be quite detrimental.'

About the clothes, he'd been able to reassure her. As for the time? He understood the bank would require her to vacate within thirty days. And the rest? What she'd be allowed to keep? Policies differed from bank to bank, he'd said. And though he could not speak for Bromley, he *could* speak for himself. Pack away any jewelry and personal effects, he had told her, small items that wouldn't be missed. He and Flora would be glad to store a trunk or two for Beth, for as long as necessary. And if she had any funds of her own – a nest egg perhaps – she should hide it and not divulge its existence to a soul. When it came to questions from Bromley or his staff, she should play the innocent, for if Benjamin's advice ever came to light, it could prove most embarrassing for him.

Recollection, now, of Beth's gratitude filled Benjamin with the same sense of impotence he had felt earlier. For really what *had* he done? Nothing of consequence. A few calculations. An inquiry here and there. A smattering of advice. And to what avail?

What would she do? From what Flora had told him, Beth had a sister, but one she hadn't seen in years, and there seemed to be a hint of some rift or other. What *did* someone in her position do? Go into service? Become a governess? God forbid that a woman of Beth's sensitivities should have to resort to such things.

The chime of the clock – dismally echoing his mood – intruded on his thoughts. And he watched the pendulum swing, musing that life went on in spite of everything. As it would, he felt sure, for Beth and her child.

He scooped up the Cadman papers, regarded them sorrowfully, and then with a sigh dropped them into the top drawer.

There was not a thing more to be done. The rest was up to Beth.

SIX

So this was it. January sixth, 1878. Emma's throat tightened. The dreaded, irrevocable day had come.

Standing at Jane's bedroom window, Emma watched through the spot where her warm breath had melted the frost-etched ferns and flowers from the glass, as Roscoe hefted her mother's three trunks onto the McDonoughs' brougham, while the pair of dappled greys, tossing their manes and pawing at the gravelled drive, snorted steamy plumes into the raw morning air.

The poignant finality of the scene suddenly sent Emma sobbing from the room and down the stairs. Outside the drawing room door, she paused for an instant, chagrined to hear the happy babble from within. It wasn't fair, that they – the McDonoughs and Mama, whose sporadic laughter rang over the buzz of conversation – should be so cheerful. How could Mama laugh on such a day as this, Emma asked herself, choking back her sobs and stumbling through the hall, out the front door, and across the glistening white crispness of the lawn, to the oak by the gate.

Panting, she embraced the tree and pressed her face hard against the knurled bark. A moment later, the crunch of footsteps came from behind, and a voice she recognized as Jane's said, 'Are you terribly sad to be leaving, Emma?'

'Of course I am.' She let her arms go limp at her sides and turned. 'I shall hate them, my aunt and my uncle and my cousin. I know I shall. And the school – a *factory* school, Mama says – and different altogether from Miss Faverley's.' Hands thrust inside her muff, she brought the soft fur to her face and rubbed her cheek over it. 'And the town.' She stood on tiptoe and reached for an overhead branch, snapping off a dry, dead twig and drawing it through the air in aimless patterns. 'So far away it might as well be across the ocean.'

'That far?' Jane's eyes widened and her mouth went slack.

'Yes. Glinton, Mama says, is in the Midlands. That's somewhere between London and the Scottish border.'

'But it might be nice, Emma. I mean, I am sure there are places just as nice as Milchester.'

Emma scowled. 'Not Glinton, though. Sounds perfectly horrid. According to Mama, it's a factory town and' – she curled her mouth in disgust – 'noted for its soap. Nearly every last person in the town, including Uncle Eustace, works at the soap factory. He's a caustic soda-maker.' She shrugged. 'Whatever that means.'

'Oh my, Emma.' Jane clapped her gloved hands. 'You mean your uncle actually *works* in a factory?'

'Yes.' Emma nodded dolefully. 'And that's not the worst of it.' Her gaze averted, she twisted the cord of the muff around the twig. 'Aunt Kate –' Pausing, she disentangled the twig from the cord and wagged it before Jane's nose. 'Now you must swear you won't tell a soul. I should positively die if anyone else knew about it –'

Jane crossed herself. 'I swear, I swear.'

'Aunt Kate' – Emma swallowed hard – 'takes in washing.'

'Washing … other people's dirty clothes. Oh, how frightful!'

'Isn't it though?' Emma winced. 'There's more. I and Mama will be expected to help her. Now you see why I would just as soon die as go to that awful place. It's been bad enough, lately, having to help Mama with the cooking and the cleaning and emptying the slop pails and – other things.'

Jane linked her arm in Emma's. 'Oh, you poor, poor thing,' she said, shivering and drawing her heavy coat about herself. 'I really am freezing, Emma. Do you think we could walk while we talk?'

'All right.' Emma dropped the twig and ground it under her heel as, paces matching, they began to slowly circle the garden.

Grateful for Jane's silence, Emma began to think of the past weeks.

It was at the beginning of December that Mama had taken Emma aside and told her of the changes that would come during the following month – changes neither of them would welcome, but that had to be bravely accepted.

Mama had made a long speech containing phrases such as *untimely demise* and *dire financial straits*, which Emma had translated to mean that Papa should not have died when he did, but because he had, they were dreadfully poor.

The house, Mama had said, with an expression that appeared to Emma as a mixture of sadness and anger, had to be sold. The furniture, too. But for reasons Emma could not be expected to understand, since after all she *was* just a child, the money from the sale would go to the bank and not to Mama.

This, of course, meant they would have to move, and by December seventeenth. Thank Heavens, Mama had said, the McDonoughs had been kind enough to invite them to stay through Christmas. New Year, too, if necessary.

And after that? Then where would they go? Emma had asked.

'At this moment, dear,' Mama had said with a worried look, 'our only hope is my sister, Kate. Though I must admit, it will be a miracle if she responds, and an even bigger miracle if she agrees to take us in. You see, although she brought me up and was like mother and father to me, when I left home and married your Papa she was very angry … for reasons that are too complicated to explain. She never wanted to see or hear from me again, she said. And if it wasn't for the fact that your Uncle Eustace dropped me the occasional secret note over the years, I might have lost touch altogether.'

'But what if they say no, Mama?' Emma asked.

'Then Lord help us, child, I just don't know *what* we'll do.'

Seeing the tears gather in her mother's eyes, Emma had right then begun to pray as she had never prayed before. And when the letter had finally arrived on the eleventh, and Mama had torn at the envelope as fiercely as an owl tearing at a mouse – her anxious eyes scanning the two sheets of paper that would not stay still because her hand was shaking so badly – and laughingly said, 'Praise the Lord, child, Eustace says they will take us,' Emma had been caught up in the excitement of the moment. After all, it wasn't often one was party to a miracle.

Only later, when the contents of the letter had revealed to Emma a hint of what lay ahead of them, had the misgivings begun.

Misgivings about Aunt Kate. Would she be nice? Or just the opposite? Not merely easily vexed, as Mama sometimes was, but downright *mean*? When Emma had asked if Aunt Kate was nice, Mama had mulled over the question for a long time, before describing her sister as *God-fearing … hard working … thrifty*.

Misgivings about school. One room and everyone mixed in like vegetables in a stew. Little children, big children – and boys! Perhaps rough and rude and smelly boys, like the ones Emma had observed on Market Day, tearing in and out of the stalls and yelling nasty things and spitting at every turn.

Misgivings about her cousin. Surely, no one could be that good, that perfect. Mama had quoted Uncle Eustace: 'Leticia is a joy to us both. Sings in the choir, and sweet as a lark. Set to become a milliner. Already turning the lads' heads, and she barely fourteen.'

Those same misgivings crowded in on Emma now,

though she tried to press them back. With her breath catching in her throat, she voiced her fears out loud. 'Oh, why, *why* does it all have to change?' she said.

Jane responded with a squeeze of Emma's arm that was clearly meant to be reassuring. 'I heard Mama saying to Papa just last night that change is good sometimes. And for you and your mother, she said, it surely was the best thing in the world. A fresh start, she called it.'

Jerking her arm free of Jane's, Emma thrust her hands in her coat pockets. 'Huh. Fresh! There is nothing fresh about it. It's stale and beastly, if you ask me.'

At the iron gates, Emma stopped and clambered onto the bottom strut. Grasping two of the vertical bars, she rested her chin against the cold metal and stared glumly across the street.

Jane tapped her arm. 'I think they are ready,' she said, gesturing towards the house.

'Girls,' Mrs McDonough shouted, 'come along, now. And open the gates if you will, dears.'

Silently, they climbed down, simultaneously glancing over their shoulders at the front steps, where everyone was assembled and Roscoe was standing beside the brougham, steadying the horses' heads.

Once they had opened the gates and slipped the bolts into their sockets, the girls faced each other in awkward silence. Emma's breath came shudderingly as she struggled to hold back the tears. And Jane began to cry in quiet little hiccoughs. She stumbled towards Emma. They clutched at each other.

'Promise me you'll write, Emma,' Jane sobbed.

Not trusting herself to speak and easing herself out of Jane's embrace, Emma bobbed her head.

One final, swift hug and they trudged, hand in hand, across the lawn.

For Emma, the following minutes were lost in a confusion of hugging and crying and kissing and jostling and joking, and Albert's squeals and the whinnying of the horses.

All too soon, Mrs McDonough was handing Emma into

the brougham and, brushing Emma's cheek with her plump hand, saying, 'We shall miss you child, and your dear, dear Mama. May the Lord watch over you both.'

Roscoe, seated up front, yelled, 'Giddyup, now!' The brougham lurched forward, sending Emma slithering across the leather seat and hard against her mother. As they headed down the drive and through the gates, the McDonoughs ran alongside. Emma shouted, 'Goodbye, Jane. I'll write ... I promise.' But her words were drowned in the cacophony of churning wheels and creaking springs and pounding hooves and the snap of Roscoe's whip.

Now they were speeding along Craven Road. When Emma glanced back, she could see them all standing by the gates waving, their small forms becoming smaller and smaller, their hands at last dropping to their sides.

And she knew, with a terrible pain, it was the last time she would see them.

On the way to the station, she watched the town rush by. Her town. Her school. Her park, now so still and empty and bereft. Her dressmaker's. Her boot shop. Her lending library, tucked in the mildewy depths of the tobacconist's. And the milliner's where Mama bought her hats.

As her eyes dwelled on the familiar streets and structures stretched out behind her, her anguish grew. She wanted to say, 'Mama, please ... can't we stay?' But she sat, mute, until the brougham pulled up in front of the station and Roscoe helped them down, telling Mama he would make sure their trunks were safely stowed for the journey.

Standing on the platform beside Mama, Emma could see the train, with its long load of roaring coaches, careening in upon the track; then drawing to a creaking, lumbering stop, its funnel belching great clouds of steam.

And in what seemed like no time at all, Mama was ushering Emma ahead of her up the steep flight of steps into the compartment.

Inside, Emma stared dumbstruck at the two hard wooden benches facing each other and the grimy, bare floorboards. Where were the upholstered seats and the thick carpet and the dark-panelled walls, so shiny you could almost see your face in them, that somewhere at the back of her mind she had expected? 'Mama,' she said over her shoulder, 'there are no cushions – nothing soft to sit on.' She turned to see her mother bent over, shoving suitcases under the bench.

'That's right,' Mama said, straightening and passing a weary hand across her flushed face. 'I do not know how many times I have to tell you this, dear: we are poor.' She drew out the word *poor*, letting it hang for a moment. 'And we have to live within our means, meagre as they may be. We do not have the money for such luxuries as soft seats.'

Well, piffle and bosh, thought Emma; she had not asked for a speech. It had been a simple question. And Mama was not done, even now.

'Just be thankful,' Mama continued, 'that we are travelling second-class and that at least we have windows and will not freeze to death.' She felt for Emma's hand. 'I know this is all very confusing for you, child. But everything will work out, you'll see. At least we know we'll have a roof over our heads when we get to Glinton. And' – she tweaked Emma's cheek – 'we do have each other. That's certainly worth a great deal. And look!' She swung her arm in a wide arc. 'We have the entire compartment to ourselves. Now isn't that a pleasant way to start the journey? I suppose that's the advantage to travelling this time of the year. I must admit, the one thing that worried me most about the journey was the riffraff we might encounter.'

Frowning in puzzlement, Emma leaned forward and looked up into Mama's face.

'Riffraff, dear. Unsuitable sorts of people. But it seems we'll have no need to worry on that score. We will have all the peace we need.'

Peace. Would there ever be peace again? Emma wondered, turning to the window and, eyes closed, pressing her face into the smooth coldness of the glass. Her heart seemed to pound in the same even, mechanical rhythm as the speeding train. And her thoughts began to bob about on the tide of her changing emotions – misery, fear, and anger lapping the shores of her mind until she drifted off into an uneasy sleep.

The next thing Emma knew, someone or something was rocking her. Nuzzling into her pillow, she felt it move under her ear. And when she turned her head, the fabric beneath her cheek was strangely rough. An odd kind of rumbling sound came from somewhere below her, and every so often she felt herself jolted.

Slowly, she opened her eyes and let her gaze move upward. She puzzled over the row of shiny, gold coins she saw, one above the other, on a background of dark green. She blinked a couple of times. Of course. They were buttons, not coins, brass buttons on a coat. Mama's coat.

Now Emma remembered: she was on the train. Oh, and how dreadfully stiff and sore she was – numb from waist to feet. And her stomach was hollow. How she wished she'd eaten the eggs and bacon, the sausages and kidneys Mrs McDonough had heaped on her plate at breakfast. Mama had told her it would be hours and hours until their next meal. But Emma had hardly been able to swallow a bite.

She turned and stared beyond the window at the rushing treetops and the pewter sky. But watching it made her eyes blurry. She closed them again. It was then that she heard the voices from behind. She listened indifferently, too lethargic to move.

There were two voices – men's voices. One was high and thin and quavery; the other, gruff and wheezy.

'By Gawd, Albert,' the wheezy man said,' nothin' like a tot o' gin to warm the awd bones.'

There was a good deal of what sounded like lip-smacking before the other man responded.

'Aye, Barnaby,' he said, ''tis powerful good, alright.'

'Eeee, Albert, will yer look at them fields out there, whooshin' by. A bloody marvel.'

'Aye, no denyin' it. Remember, in the awd days when we was young 'uns, 'ow you an' me an' Jake – bless 'is dear departed soul – used to take the coach down to London?'

'That I do. Must o' took us nigh on thirteen hours. An' all that joggin'. Always said that's wot loosed me teeth.'

There was a pause here, and a chuckle. And then the quavery-voiced man said, 'Loosed a lot more'n teeth if you asks me. An' cold! Ridin' atop like we did. 'Twere enough to freeze yer arse off ...'

'Yer balls, too, when yer went to take a piss ...'

'Gentlemen!' Mama's sudden shriek from overhead startled Emma out of her lethargy. Snapping open her eyes, she looked up. Mama's fury was evident in the set of her jaw and her pursed lips; from neck to hairline, she was bright pink. Her hand slapped against her knee, barely missing Emma's cheek, as she said between her teeth, 'I will thank you both to keep your vulgarities to yourself,' and added under her breath, 'Disgusting riffraff.'

Whatever response her mother's outburst brought was lost in the piteous wailing that all at once started. Over the wails, a woman shouted, ''Ush, child, it's alright. 'Ush now.' Whereupon the cries dissolved into soft sobs, punctuated by sniffs and loud sucking sounds.

Inquisitive now, Emma scrambled upright. Flexing her tired muscles and yawning, she surveyed the bench opposite.

Obviously, the cries had come from the toddler slumped against the chest of the weary-looking, pale-faced woman who was seated by the window directly across from Emma. Pulling fretfully at its drab wool bonnet, the child was chewing on the edge of its mother's shawl.

In Emma's experience, babies were clean and pink, angelic and sweet-smelling. But this was a nasty creature with a runny nose. Emma turned away in disgust and focused on the two old men at the other end of the bench.

Clearly, these men were the source of the conversation that, for some untold reason, had enraged her mother. Mama's words must have had the desired effect, Emma concluded, for both were sound asleep and snoring softly.

So this was 'riffraff.' They certainly were horrid. She regarded them with a mixture of revulsion and fascination.

One was huge. He wore a grimy black frock coat, whose

buttons strained with the steady movements of his vast belly. His baggy trousers were of a brash red-and-white houndstooth check. Below their frayed bottoms was a pair of feet clad in down-at-heel brown boots with thick mud-encrusted soles. Emma couldn't see his face, for it was hidden beneath a battered top hat. But somewhere in the tangle of a grubby beard below the torn rim of the hat was a pair of lips, parted over three or four yellow teeth.

The other man was similarly attired but was bone thin. His eyes bulged in their sockets, under closed lids. The greyish skin of his face hung in crusty folds. Even in sleep, his mouth continually ticked, as did his purple-veined hands.

A sudden tap on Emma's arm intruded on her observations. 'It's rude to stare, child. You know that.'

Surprised, Emma whispered, 'But Mama, they *are* riffraff, aren't they?'

The corners of Mama's mouth made a slight upward curve and she coughed behind her hand before responding. 'Whatever they are, Emma, it is still impolite. Now why don't you read your *Hymns in Prose* for a while. I have it here in my handbag. If you put your mind to work, time will go so much faster.'

While Mama resettled herself and went back to her reading, Emma opened the hymnal. Dull, dull. She focused on the words, but could hardly make them out with the jostling of the train. Thinking that maybe she could sleep away the rest of the journey, she closed her eyes. No sooner were they closed, it seemed, than the baby opposite began to whimper. So she opened them again.

Just now the train was churning through a gorge where sandstone outcrops mingled with terraces of drab houses. Narrow, twisting streets crowded up a steep hill topped by a church whose steeple was all but obscured by the layer of black smoke snaking from the tall chimneys of a many-storied building on the church's flank.

How grim, how horrid it looked. And how awful to have to live like that. Nudging her mother, she said, 'Mama, look

… we're coming into a town. What place do you suppose this is?'

Mama performed a series of stretches and yawns, before finally leaning into the window. She craned her neck. 'I'm loath to say it, dear, but there's really only one place it can be.' She bit her lower lip and slanted a sad look at Emma. 'This is Glinton … our new home.'

PART TWO

1878–1882

SEVEN

Alone by the kitchen fire at midnight on that last Sunday in January, Kate Sheene set down her darning and leaned back in her chair. 'You can't go on punishing her forever.' Eustace's words echoed in her head and, fists clenching and unclenching in her lap, she gave a furious little shudder.

To think you could live a lifetime with someone – figure you knew them inside and out – and then ... She pressed her knuckles to her mouth. Meek Eustace, who bowed to her every whim; never so much as raising his voice in seventeen years of marriage. And then to find out that all this time he'd been sneaking behind her back, writing to Beth. And as if that weren't enough, laying the law down as he had. 'She's your sister, Kate. And she's in trouble. I've stood by all these years and said nothing. But enough's enough. It's time to let bygones be bygones. I'm posting the letter tomorrow. So you'd best set to and get things ready for the pair of them.'

Bygones be bygones, indeed. Kate gritted her teeth. He wasn't the one who'd sacrificed everything from the time she was ten years old to raise a sister. He wasn't the one who'd been made a laughingstock when that sister had thrown over the richest man in the county to run off with a no-account Irishman – and a Catholic to boot.

Damn fool Eustace! Not sense enough to realize where they could have been today if Beth had married Jethro Bates. God Almighty, the man would have set them up on their own farm – given them the Chiswick place; he as much as said so the night he'd come to ask her for Beth's hand. And they wouldn't have had to pack up and move to Glinton because there was more money to be made in the factories than there was as a farm labourer.

Damn fool Beth, as well. Old man Bates wouldn't have lasted more than ten years anyway. She could have been a rich widow – instead of a penniless one. Business troubles, indeed! Like as not, it was the card tables and drink and Lord knew what else. Like as not, too, it was the drinking that did him in. A person couldn't be sober and end up the way George Cadman had.

Kate retrieved her darning and attacked the hole in Eustace's sock with renewed vigour. Imagine him going through all his money like that. He must have had his share for them to have gone gallivanting all over creation before they finally settled in Milchester. Three trunks to her name after sixteen years. And a few fancy frocks. Fancy ways, too. Oh, she was a lady alright and no denying it. With her la-di-da talk. And those soft hands, white as starch and fingernails like pearl buttons. Not for long, though; give Beth a week at Brummerley's and those fine hands of hers would be as rough as Kate's own.

As she rose and straightened, intending to give the ashes a jab, Kate caught a glimpse of herself in the pitted little mirror that hung alongside the fireplace. She ran her fingertip over the bluish pouches beneath her eyes and laughed a low, derisive laugh. She'd surely lost *her* bloom. To think she'd once been called a handsome woman. That was before life furrowed her brow and robbed what had once been plump, rosy cheeks of their flesh.

The sourness of her mood was reflected in her image. She turned away abruptly, anxious to be done with a self-appraisal that only served to reinforce her bitterness.

'You can't go on punishing her for ever.' The phrase continued to play annoyingly across her mind as she sat. 'Maybe, maybe not,' she said out loud, stretching Eustace's sock over the wooden mushroom and giving it a fierce poke with her needle.

They were here anyway. Nothing to be done about that. And since they'd been thrust upon her, wasn't it only right that she should get what she could out of the arrangement? Of course it was. Two pairs of extra hands could go a long way towards helping her achieve *her* dream. Her gaze moved to the top shelf of the pine dresser. Fifty guineas in the tobacco jar now. Half as much again, and she'd be able to pull it off.

Detached; it would have to be a detached house. Nothing worse than having your neighbours living in your pocket, only a wall separating you, not being able to so much as pass wind without them knowing. Perhaps an iron verandah, painted green, and a garden with hollyhocks planted by the front door. In the country, but still within walking distance of Brummerley's – of course. For there was Eustace's job to consider. It'd be a good fifteen years before *he'd* be ready to hang up his cap.

A plodder, was Eustace. Not an ounce of ambition in the man. Aye, she nodded, it was the women of this family who had the ambition: Look at Leticia. Barely fourteen – less than a year into her apprenticeship – and her sights already set on a shop of her own. If determination had anything to do with it, she'd have it, too. Unless some young man came along and her plans went by the board. More than likely they would, though. Lordsakes, hardly a day went by that there wasn't some lad or other mooning after her. Had her Ma's drive, alright. But her Pa's looks, with that buxom figure of hers: hourglass, they called it, didn't they? And that black hair.

Who'd ever guess she and that scrawny Emma were cousins. Kate plucked at the sagging flesh below her jaw. Proper strange, that niece of hers; holding herself stiff as a washboard when Eustace had gone to give her a goodnight peck on the cheek. Nothing to say for herself except, 'Yes, Aunt Kate … no, Aunt Kate.' Saved all her talking for during the night, from all accounts. Wasn't natural. Wasn't right, either, that Leticia should have to put up with it. Needed her sleep, she did. If it went on much longer, something'd have to be done. Maybe school would put paid to it. Idle hands made for addled heads, didn't they? And the child's head must surely be addled. What else could account for such carryings-on?

Kate rose woodenly and, yawning, scrubbed at her gritty eyes. This week would tell, wouldn't it? At least it would make her six shillings better off, when Saturday came and, with it, half of Beth's wages.

Massaging her lower back, she trudged to the kitchen table and turned down the lamp's wick. One last lingering look through the darkness, in the direction of the tobacco jar, and she plodded for the door.

Hearing the creak of the staircase, Beth swiftly extinguished the tallow candle on the nightstand at her elbow and then wafted her arms about to dispel the telltale odour that pervaded the room – an odour which smacked of rancid mutton. On the edge of the bed, she sat stock still. Great God, Kate would have a fit, after that long lecture she'd delivered about the cost of everything – candles included – if she were to discover Beth's ration (two a week) was already half-gone.

The footsteps halted before Beth's door. And she held her breath until they resumed, cocking her head for the muted thud of Kate's door. When it came, she relit the candle and smoothed out the sheet of paper centred on her satinwood lap desk. Lord save her, where had the time gone? Quarter to one, her watch told her. Almost two hours to write one letter.

Then it had been no easy task: keeping the tone cheerful, throwing a pleasant mantle over grim reality. And it certainly was grim. This miserable little monk's cell, with barely enough room for her to lace her stays. And its pockmarked iron bedstead, iron washstand, night table, and one rickety chair, plus, of course, her three trunks, set one on top of the other.

Had she succeeded, *that* was the thing. She perused the letter afresh. 'Dear Flora …' she mumbled through the salutation and the opening lines, stopping when she came to 'We have been terribly busy settling in.'

Settling in! Slaving was more like it, slaving from dawn till dusk. Every waking hour devoured by the interminable tasks. The kitchen grate to be cleaned out, the fire laid and the ashes riddled so that the larger pieces of clinker could be used over. The entire fireplace (ovens and surround) black-leaded.

70

Meals prepared. Water drawn and heated for th
Dusting, sweeping, scrubbing. The endless
Kate's brasses – fenders, trivets, kettles, pans, s
And Kate acting the brigadier general, lacking
bugle for the sounding of reveille.

Lacking much more, too. Forgiveness; since, appare
marrying the man you loved instead of the one your siste.
had selected for you was reason for needing forgiveness.
Sisterly affection. Beth blinked back the tears of disillusion-
ment that came with the recollection of Kate's contemptuous
'I might have known it would come to this.' She had been
foolish to expect anything but harsh judgement.

She shrugged her shawl about her shoulders against the
damp chill and tucked her chin into her chest. Well, at least
tomorrow she would be free of Kate's continuous diatribe.
And there would be a weekly wage to look forward to,
meagre as it might be.

But, Father in Heaven, at what cost? To have to earn one's
money in such a place. She shivered uncontrollably at the
memory of the great blackened hulk of the Brummerley
Soapworks, with its spewing stacks.

The letter – back to the letter: 'Glinton is quite different
from Milchester. But I'll warrant, in time, we shall grow used
to it.'

Never! She shook her head morosely as a vision of the
town played across her mind. Row upon row of horrid,
pokey houses, each joined to the next and, from a distance,
looking like dominoes with their soot-encrusted brickwork
and dots of windows. Every corner boasting a public house,
with the stench enough to bowl one over.

Cesspits – evil-smelling, inviting disease. Narrow twisting
streets, resounding with the cries of the rag-and-bone
merchants. And one such merchant, owner of that decrepit,
smelly cart that had transported them from the station,
Eustace's friend.

Not a single garden. Only cobbled rectangles of back-
yards, each with a washhouse, coal shed, and closet. Oh, how
she longed already for the sight of something green. For the

g of the perpetual shroud that hung over the rooftops, a glimpse of the sun. For the scent of a Milchester orning. For ...

She shook herself, suddenly, out of her self-pity, refocusing on the letter. 'Of course,' she read, 'we have many challenges to meet. I have not a doubt, though, that we shall bravely make the necessary adjustments.'

Not a doubt. She laughed a soft, bitter laugh. Overnight, she had become as adept a fiction-writer as the Brontë sisters. And what was the truth, now that the illusions were gone? What Kate had implied – that she had come from nothing, only to return to it?

She had, hadn't she? She'd come full circle. Her tearful gaze moved to the clogs on the floor.

Lord ... that she should have come to this.

In the room across the hall, Emma lay staring into the darkness, wrestling with doubts that loomed larger by the minute.

She had slept intermittently during the evening hours. But with Leticia's noisy entrance at a little after ten, Emma had jerked awake. Squirming against the discomfort of her lumpy straw mattress, she listened to her cousin's measured breathing from beyond the curtain – hung by Uncle Eustace at Leticia' direction – over the exact spot where the chalked line on the floorboards intersected the room – two-thirds Leticia's, one-third Emma's.

'Since I'm forced to share with you, let's make one thing clear, right off. Set foot on my side, and it'll be woe betide you.' Recollection of Leticia's warning returned to Emma; and with it came anger so strong she could taste it. Propping herself on her elbows, she stuck out her tongue in the direction of Leticia's vast featherbed. She smiled. If Leticia only knew. Since that order had been issued, Emma had done much more than *set foot* in the forbidden territory: she had, at every opportunity, explored each surface, examined each trinket, poked into drawers, sniffed the contents of the various pots and bottles on the dressing table, and once – *la pièce de résistance*, as Miss Faverley would have said – coaxed Rex, Uncle Eustace's beagle, up onto Leticia's bed, where he had abandoned himself to a frenzy of rolling and grunting and scratching, and (judging from Leticia's attack of St Vitus' dance the next day) lived up to Aunt Kate's opinion that he was a 'flea-ridden cur'.

Giggling softly, Emma sank back onto her pillow. It served her right. Who did she think she was anyway? Just because she was fourteen and an apprentice milliner. Oh, and the way she had sniggered behind her hand the day of their arrival, her fat cheeks puffing out like twin cricket balls, when Emma had removed her bonnet and Aunt Kate said, 'Lord o' mercy, the child looks like a Charity Girl. Whatever possessed you to crop 'er hair that way?' It had had to be done when Emma was ill, was all Mama had said.

'Course you know, don't you, why they shear the hair of Charity Girls? To rid 'em of lice,' Leticia had said with obvious delight, later, when she and Emma were alone. Lice. Emma felt her scalp creep.

What if everyone at the new school were to laugh at her, ridicule her, as Leticia had – call her that horrid name reserved for the workhouse girls? She ran her hand distractedly through her hair.

She would keep her bonnet on, that's what she'd do. Why did she have to go to school, anyway? And what if she lost her way and forgot all those left turns and right turns Aunt Kate had drilled into her head at teatime?

'I cannot possibly go with you, dear,' Mama had said. 'I'm to be at the factory at six. And six is far too early for you. I cannot just deposit you on the doorstep and leave you there to freeze.'

Alone. She must face the ordeal alone. Tears scalded her eyes. And she turned her face into the pillow, sobbing quietly, for fear of waking Leticia.

Finally, in damp, cold misery, she fell asleep.

EIGHT

The next morning, Emma's worst fears were confirmed when she stood on the threshold of Glinton Factory School. Like most of the amenities in the town – the shops, public houses, public baths, and the two scrubby acres next to the Canal, with the unlikely name *Waterview Park* – it owed its existence to Ralph Brummerley.

Poulton had its Church of England school, as did Brewster, but though Glinton boasted a fine Anglican church with a Norman tower, an imposing spire, and a reasonably healthy congregation, it had no C. of E. school.

As long as Ralph Brummerley, out of the goodness of his benevolent heart (though the parents of each girl child were required to pay sixpence a week), was willing to support the Factory School and thus provide an education for his workers' offspring, far be it from the Bishop to complain; for the monies saved could be put to use in the saving of souls, the conversion of heathens, and the modernization of a rectory that had fought the good fight for more than a century.

Glinton Factory School had fought that same fight, but had long since surrendered to the ravages of time and the neglect of a benefactor who had not set foot on the premises for two decades past.

If Mama had warned Emma – and aside from one or two vague references to the building's state of dilapidation and Emma's need to wear her flannel drawers, flannel chemise, and flannel petticoat, in addition to her usual starched under-petticoat and muslin top-petticoat, she had not – it could not have prevented Emma's being struck dumb by mildewed walls that bled moisture and floors strewn with tattered exercise books and broken slates, and the deafening yells and

74

shrieks of occupants every bit as unruly as the mob that stormed the Bastille.

A jab in Emma's ribs, accompanied by 'New, ain't you?' returned Emma to earth. And she found herself staring up into the thin, olive-skinned face of a girl she guessed to be about her own age. 'Name's Jessie,' she shouted over the din, her dark, slanting eyes moving over Emma in frank appraisal, 'Jessie Dobbins. What's yours?'

'Emma Cadman.' She had to repeat it to make herself heard.

'We'd best find you a seat. Come on.' With a jerk of her head towards the back of the room, the girl signalled Emma to follow. 'This one ain't taken.' The girl halted, motioning Emma to sit at a narrow desk whose sloping surface bore twin indentations where, over the decades, countless elbows had rested. 'It's a good place,' she said, 'away from the window. Been broke for two years, it has. And not likely to get mended, neither.' She unwound the faded blue muffler from around her head. And her hair sprang eagerly from its centre parting in a wild, sooty frizz.

Watching her own breath plume in the chalk-heavy air, Emma shivered and tucked her mittened hands into her armpits. 'It's freezing,' she said, her teeth chipping at the words.

The sonorous booming of the clock, close by on the wall, sent the girl and her fellow students into a desperate scramble for their seats. As the last gong faded away with the whispers, the door to Emma's right slowly opened.

The black-clad twig of a man, whose bald head wobbled like a too-heavy bloom on the stalk of a neck, would have been tall, Emma supposed, were it not for the hump on his back that caused him to bend almost double.

With the aid of a walking stick, as gnarled and misshapen as he was, he shuffled towards the table centred on a raised platform at the front of the room. In profile, with his hooked nose and slack mouth, he had the appearance of a gaunt bird of prey.

My, but he was old, Emma thought. So old, in fact, that

75

when he finally reached the table and lowered himself painfully into his chair, she imagined she could hear the creaking of his joints.

Hunched over the tabletop, he perused the uppermost of a sheaf of papers at his elbow. 'Good morning, children,' he wheezed without looking up, his head moving in the same palsied motion Emma had observed earlier.

'Good morning, Mr Opey,' came the answering chorus.

'Today' – he fumbled in his top pocket, brought out a pair of spectacles, and polished them against his lapel. Settling them halfway down his nose, he peered over their rims, his straggly white eyebrows knitted together so that they formed one continuous line. 'Today,' he repeated, 'we have in our midst a new pupil.'

Emma clenched her fists inside her mittens.

'…Cadman, Emma Cadman. Where, may I ask,' he craned his neck, 'is this Miss Cadman?'

Every head swivelled in Emma's direction.

'Back there, are you? Well, stand up, girl, so we can get a good look at you.'

Emma rose, her neck and face grown suddenly hot.

'Into the aisle, girl, where I see you proper.'

She shuffled sidelong and stood inanely, staring at her boot toes.

'As you've doubtless gathered, I am Mr Opey. Look at me when I'm talking, child.'

She brought her head up.

'That's more like it. Come forward.' He gestured impatiently, tottering to his feet and supporting himself on the edge of the table as she advanced.

'Here, beside me,' he said, as she reached the platform.

Her knees threatened to buckle as she clambered up and fought off the sudden impulse to flee.

Oh, but he was ugly, with his stubbled chin and glinting little eyes and a neck like a turkey's, all flaps and folds. And there was a sour odour about him. She swallowed hard and tried to hold her breath. But his 'That's an uncommonly fine bonnet you have' demanded a response.

'Thank you,' she said.

'Not at all.' His lips parted over toothless gums in something resembling a smile. 'Turn and show your classmates your finery, girl.'

Feeling all at once like a freak at a country fair, and wishing the floorboards would open, Emma obeyed. Among the myriad curious eyes focused upon her, she caught those of Jessie Dobbins. The girl winced in apparent sympathy, as Mr Opey said, 'We've a rule about bonnets, haven't we, children?'

'Yes, Mr Opey,' the pupils chanted.

'And what is that rule?'

'All bonnets must be removed,' the children answered in one resounding voice.

'All headgear must be removed,' Mr Opey said in a dangerously quiet tone. 'We give no preferences, boys and girls alike. So ...' Emma felt a tap on her shoulder, and she wheeled about.

'Off with it. And sharp-like.'

Averting her gaze, Emma mumbled, 'I'd rather not.'

'What was that?'

She lifted her chin and regarded him squarely. 'I said I would rather not.'

He recoiled as if from a physical blow, his parchment cheeks flooding crimson. His Adam's apple worked furiously and he made as if to speak, though all that came out of his mouth was a dribble of saliva.

After a moment that seemed to Emma as long as eternity, he croaked, his head now shaking uncontrollably, 'Do you hear that, my dears? Little Miss Cadman would *rather* not.'

The ruffle of titters instantly subsided when he seized Emma's arm in a painful grip and shouted, 'Only one thing for it, then. I shall have to do it for 'er, shan't I?' Like a talon, his free hand clawed at the ribbon beneath her chin. And with a maniacal light in his eyes, he yanked off her bonnet, holding it aloft, as wave upon wave of laughter crashed in on Emma.

NINE

The bonnet episode was only one of many humiliations Emma was to suffer at the hands of Mr Opey.

From the first, his greatest delight seemed to come from taunting her. If she raised her hand to answer a question, he rarely acknowledged her. And when he did, he had a habit of twisting her words and tying her into such knots that she was reduced (in her own eyes) to near-idiocy. When she sought escape in daydreams, he caught her out and dispatched her, with a kind of infantile relish, to the dunce's corner, where she would stand in mute contemplation of the peeling plaster, consoling herself with the knowledge that, at least while she wore the dunce's cap, her shorn hair was safe from the ridicule of her classmates.

If Jessie Dobbins had had her way – 'Leave the poor girl be,' she said, 'an' don't be such a rotten lot, all of you' – it might have ended there. But as soon as Jessie's thirteenth birthday came on the first of February, she was off to work at Brummerley's. And for those left behind at Glinton School, the newcomer still provided plenty of sport.

Everything about Emma Cadman struck them as different, not just her hair, but her manner, her speech, and her fancy clothes. Above all, though, her stubborn refusal to break before their collective will goaded her fellow students on.

Lard smeared on 'er chair. And there she'd sat on 'er greasy bottom like a bleedin' duchess, as if it was the natural thing to be slitherin' around. Her cheese sandwich switched for a *meat* sandwich, and the meat a dead mouse. Oh, 'er eyes had got big as a pair of pan lids, alright, at the sight of the beast. But that was all. The spiders in 'er desk. Whoppin' big 'uns. An' not a peep out of 'er. The chanting, every mornin' as she rounded the schoolhouse corner, 'Here comes Lady Muck...

here comes Lady Muck.' And what does she do, but sail forth with 'er nose in the air.

'I think when they cut 'er hair, they cut out 'er brains, too,' one frustrated prankster was heard to say.

'Or stuck a pin in 'er head an' sucked 'em out, like you an' me did with them sparrow eggs,' another offered.

'Naw,' May Stokes said. 'Prob'ly does 'er blubberin' – an' I'll wager she does plenty – when she goes home an' sits in Mama's lap.'

'Well wouldn't you?' It was John this time, wiry little John O'Malley, late of County Cork. Hadn't he had to put up with their shenanigans himself, not more than a year ago, with them callin' him all the names under the sun an' not givin' him a minute's peace until he bust the teeth of one lad and bloodied the nose of another? 'Sure an' I think she's a plucky one is Emma Cadman. Me Da says it's the quiet ones as has the strength.'

Of the two, John and May, it was May who possessed the insight. For Emma's outward show of stoicism was a facade behind which she cowered in utter hopelessness.

She would have given anything to crawl into her mother's lap and unburden herself, to feel the comfort of Mama's soft bosom and soothing words. But Mama had enough to cope with, didn't she? And there were certain things you had to try and solve yourself, especially when you were going on twelve. Even if you had not a notion which way to turn.

And it wasn't that Mama was unfeeling, either. It was just that she was too exhausted by her own daily grind. It was obvious from her pallor and her struggle to stay awake beyond the seven o'clock evening meal. And she *had* asked, once or twice during the first week or so, how Emma was faring in school. But Emma's 'Not very well' had fallen on deaf ears. In fact, the only receptive ears in the entire Sheene household were those of Rex.

'You are my only friend,' Emma bent to whisper against the dog's sleek neck, as he sat at her feet by the kitchen fire one Friday evening in early March – one of those rare evenings when she was alone, with Aunt Kate, Uncle

79

Eustace, and Mama off to St Peter's for a choir concert, where Leticia would be giving two solos. Surprisingly, Mama had seemed actually to be looking forward to it. Friday nights she always had more energy, probably because Saturdays meant only six hours' work instead of the usual twelve, but how anyone could relish the idea of listening to Leticia was beyond Emma. She had had the dubious pleasure of hearing her cousin's rendition of 'The Last Rose of Summer' the Sunday before, when the Beatons (old friends of the Sheenes) had stopped in for tea. That afternoon there'd been no necessity for Emma to feign a headache, as she had tonight. Five minutes of Leticia's high soprano, and every nerve in Emma's body (some she had not known she possessed) was on edge. And poor Rex, howling like a demon, had shot for the front door.

'Dear Rex' – Emma chucked him under the chin – 'to think what you've suffered all these years.' Your entire life spent listening to that ungodly caterwauling.' Her sorrowful *tut* brought a responsive thump of the dog's tail against the chair leg. 'And no escape.' She stroked his velvety head and then leaned back, hands clasped behind her neck. 'We should run away, you and me. You'd adore Milchester. Lots of meadows on the outskirts of town ... and woods, with rabbit burrows galore. Oh, and Craven Road, the road our house is on – rather *was* on – has at least two dozen lamp posts.' She sat forward, nodding ruefully at the sight of the dog's inert form. Why, the scoundrel had fallen asleep. She nudged him with her boot toe. 'Lamp posts, Rex ... do you hear me?' His tail gave a lacklustre wag. He opened one bloodshot eye and promptly closed it.

Emma sighed and slumped down in her seat. So much for her only friend. Well, perhaps, not her *only* friend. There was still Jane. The letter was in her apron pocket. Unopened as yet, because there hadn't been time earlier.

A regular epistle, too, judging from the bulky envelope under her fingertips. Oh, dear, had she done the right thing – after her firm resolve to find her own solutions – in spilling all to Jane? Would Jane think her a namby-pamby? Nervously, she fingered the envelope.

What was it Mama had called it the other Sunday when, astonished by the tone of Mama's letter to Mrs McDonough, Emma had asked why everything had been made to sound absolutely wonderful?

Putting up a cheerful front, that was it – when you covered, or bent, the truth. When you said things like, 'Kate is quite the organizer,' when what you meant was, 'Kate is a mean old witch.' Or in her own case, 'There are several pleasant girls in my class, though I have not yet had a chance to get to know them,' when the truth was there *had* been one half-pleasant girl – at least she'd been helpful that first day – but that had been as far as it went, since the girl had left school to work at Brummerley's after little more than a fortnight.

Not that Emma had said that, of course, about the pleasant girls. She had been perfectly honest, describing her daily torment in minute detail.

She drew Jane's letter out of her pocket and ran her fingernail under the envelope's flap, recalling Mama's explanation of that glowing report to Mrs McDonough. 'It's a matter of pride, dear. I should hate the McDonoughs to think that we Cadmans fall apart at the slightest hardship. Besides, it just isn't done to bare one's soul; to burden friends with one's trials and tribulations. And you be sure and remember that when you write to Jane.'

But remembering and doing were not the same thing. Emma squeezed her eyes tight for an instant. 'Please, Jane,' she whispered, 'be my dear, dear friend. Make me glad I did not put up a cheerful front.'

Jane did much more than that. Her letter fairly sang Emma's praises. 'How terribly brave you are,' she wrote. 'And what a good Christian, turning the other cheek like that. If it were me, I could not have endured it. I would most certainly have lost my temper, forgotten everything I ever learned about being a lady, and promptly put an end to the whole affair.'

It was this latter sentence – and especially the phrase 'promptly put an end to the whole affair' – that weighed on Emma's mind in the week following, and finally led her to the conclusion that by ignoring the slights of her classmates she was, in all likelihood, spurring them on to even greater mischief.

There was only one thing for it then, wasn't there? To change her tune from one of silent suffering and gird herself for battle.

In this frame of mind, Emma set off for school on that decisive morning.

Emma was not the only one to have a change of heart. About the time she was impatiently waiting at the intersection of Marley and Castle Streets for a break in the endless stream of horse-drawn wagonettes, a group of her classmates were assembled beneath the clock in the schoolroom.

There was not one dissenter among their ranks. ''Tis agreed, then,' John O'Malley said, 'no more baitin' of the girl. For she's proved 'erself to have more pluck than all of us put together. And for that, she deserves our friendship. Right?'

'Aye,' came the unanimous response.

'Then I say all of us give 'er the good news soon as she gets here.'

Was it an omen? Emma laboured up the final steep stretch, her head bent against the biting wind, her heart racing. First the delay caused by the traffic. Then the splattering of mud from the cart wheels. And now the stitch in her side, slowing her down when it surely must be close to nine. And she'd seen what happened to latecomers. Kept after school, alone with Mr Opey, and made to write two hundred times, 'I must learn to be punctual.'

Cresting the hill now and ignoring her pain, she broke into a run.

When she reached the schoolroom door, she stopped to collect herself. None of the usual din. It could mean only one thing – that it was after nine. She drew in a shuddering breath and pushed open the door.

Hallelujah. Five minutes to spare. Oblivious of everything but the hands of the clock, she headed for her seat. With a caution learned from experience, she lifted the lid of her desk. Nothing untoward: her slate, her exercise book. No doubt they had other mischief planned for her today. But they had best mind their P's and Q's, hadn't they? Or …

'Emma.'

She looked up in surprise. Someone actually calling her by her first name, her real name. It was that Irish boy, standing so close she could feel his breath. Oh, and now the others – a dozen at least, advancing on her, surrounding her. The slate in one hand, she let the desk lid slam shut, her resolve at once wavering and firming as she slowly came to her feet.

'We, er … that is, I …'

'Shut up,' Emma shrieked. 'And get away from me.' She shoved the boy and he keeled over and went down. 'And you' – her eyes swept the circle of slack-jawed bystanders – 'don't dare come near me. Because if you do …' She gestured wildly with the slate. 'I'll crown the first one.' She was shaking and panting at the same time. And when the Irish boy scrambled up and said, 'Now hold on, Emma, she closed her eyes and screamed at the top of her lungs, 'Shut up! Shut up!'

And then the words dissolved into one long infuriated cry – a disembodied cry that echoed hollowly in her head.

Thwack! In the same moment the slap on her cheek registered and her throat clamped over the scream, she struck out blindly with the slate.

And as her eyes flew open, she saw Mr Opey staggering back, his hand clutched to his bloody forehead.

TEN

This time, the dream was more horrifying than usual. For instead of the lone pursuer – that dreaded pursuer relentlessly dogging her but never revealing himself – an army of ghostly, dark-blue uniformed figures, truncheons raised and buttons glinting like a thousand watchful eyes, loomed out of the cloying mists, chanting, 'Murderess – murderess – murderess.' Now they fanned out. To the left, the right, gaining on her. Their litany filling her with paralytic terror.

A hand fell on her shoulder and she screamed, 'No, no, no,' clawing at the air and pitching forward, down into a bottomless black void.

'Emma, for pity's sake, wake up!'

The enraged whisper slammed Emma back. Heart thudding in her neck, she lay motionless.

'I said wake up, do you hear me?' The voice had risen to a whine now.

Leticia. The realization cut through Emma's sense of disorientation, and she felt a great sweep of gratitude. 'I hear you,' she murmured into her pillow, struggling to dislodge the ball of bedclothes under her stomach and then turning over onto her back. 'Oh, and thank you, Leticia, thank you for ...'

'You've no call to be thankin' me.' There was the sound of the dividing curtain being drawn and, seconds after, the creaking of Leticia's bed. 'Twasn't for your benefit I did it, but my own. You'd have to be daft not to know that. I mean, how many times 'as it been, now? I said, how ...'

'Quite a few. I'm sor ...'

'Quite a few.' Leticia gave a brittle laugh. 'I don't call every other night quite a few. Well, tonight's the end of it. Enough's enough.' A flurry of what must have been pillow-

84

thumping drowned out her voice. A minute of silence, and she resumed, droning on like an angry gnat. 'All very well for you, isn't it. No school tomorrow, 'cause it's Saturday. But ...'

The word 'school' triggered the memory, diverting Emma's thoughts from the familiar dirge, spinning them back to the terrifying events of the day before.

The slate. Mr Opey. Her flight to Brummerley's and Mama's stunned reaction to the news that the Peelers must surely be hot on Emma's trail, for she had killed Mr Opey. The agonizing wait - 'Go straight home,' Mama had said. 'Aunt Kate will be at the market all morning and you know where the key is.' The longest two hours of Emma's life, and finally the news from Mama that, thank the Merciful Lord, Emma had not killed the man. Though the wound was serious enough to require a doctor's attention and to cause Mr Opey to cancel school for the day. 'I caught him just as he was leaving,' Mama said. 'I tried talking to him, but he would have none of it. The most he would do was agree to meet me tomorrow afternoon to discuss - as he put it - your "vicious and unprovoked attack".'

'Vicious' Emma understood. 'Unprovoked' had no meaning for her. But it had been obvious from Mama's stern expression that this was not the time for the solving of puzzles.

Throughout Emma's account of her weeks of torment, Mama had sat quietly, occasionally prompting with the lift of an eyebrow or a nod, and not interrupting until Emma said, 'I thought it was one of those beastly children hitting me and I didn't ...'

'Someone actually struck you?' Mama leaped to her feet, her eyes blazing.

'Mr Opey, Mama. I remember seeing his arm raised when I opened my eyes and ...'

'Why didn't you tell me this before?'

'I ... I thought ...' Emma massaged her temples in confusion.

'Unprovoked, indeed.' Mama gritted her teeth and

clenched her fists, her expression one of such fury that Emma could no longer hold back her pent-up tears. 'I'm sorry, Mama,' she wailed.

'Oh my dear, dear child.' Mama was all at once kneeling before Emma's chair, her hands gripping Emma's. 'I am sorry, too. That you didn't confide in me. For all you've had to endure. Sorry for my failure as a mother, sorry for our lives.' She wiped away Emma's tears with the edge of her shawl. 'But I fear all the sorrow in the world cannot undo what has already been done. There is no going back.'

Mama was right. There *was* no going back. Emma's day of disgrace had ended three hours before, the clock dial told her. Cautiously, she lifted her head from the pillow, suspicious of the blissful silence she had returned to – a silence that might, at any instant, be broken. But no, the faint rasping sounds of Leticia's breathing told her she was safe.

Sitting up, Emma contemplated the cold pool of moon-light in her lap. What would her punishment be? She shivered as her imagination went to work. The pillory? There was one in the square. A public whipping? The birch-rod? Or worse?

'There was no reasoning with the man,' Beth wrote, her pen skimming over the paper as if of its own violition.

I did everything short of grovelling at his feet, but he was adamant. The only punishment for a misdeed as dire as Emma's was expulsion. In his estimation, as well as being violent, lazy, defiant, and uncooperative, Emma is incorrigible. If only she had confided in me, Flora. Then, the whole dreadful affair might have been avoided. Why was I blessed with such a closemouthed child? Your Jane always seemed so open a girl. I realize, of course, that we mothers cannot protect our children from everything, least of all the cruelty of their peers, for Lord knows, we have all, at one time or another, had to contend with such cruelty. I realize, too, that had I been more observant, less involved in my own thoughts, I might have seen the signs that led to this lamentable event and interceded before it went too far. But the milk is already spilled, isn't it? We can only press on. The irony is that Emma is actually happy with the outcome. Not that she said so – but it was apparent, this afternoon, when I gave her the news. In some ways she is utterly transparent, in others deep as a ditch. I told her that, first thing Monday, her Uncle Eustace would be making arrangements for her to start at Brummerley's next month. I told her, too, what backbreaking work it will be. But all she could do was smile and nod.

I suppose there's a bright side to it all (at least from Kate's viewpoint) in that Emma will shortly be a wage-earner. And Kate may well be right when she says a good day's work should put an end to Emma's other problem. The nightmares: at least once, sometimes twice a week, since we arrived. Needless to say, they disrupt the entire household, making Leticia complain bitterly to her mother, who in turn complains to me and expects me to be able to order them stopped! Chances are, with the torment of school behind her, Emma will settle down and we shall, at last, have some peace.

Of course, the thought of Emma earning a wage is of no consolation to me, for I'd far rather see the child complete her education in school. As it is, I feel duty-bound from now on to assign her (and oversee) two hours' homework a day.

Lord … she had been gripping the pen so tightly, her fingers had grown numb. She set aside her lap desk and flexed her hands. The wind keened against the house, and beyond the window the Sunday afternoon sky was as sullen a grey as Beth's mood.

Reverend Witherspoon's sermon that morning had done nothing to lift her spirits. Nor was there comfort in the rare silence of the house, with the Sheenes off visiting and Emma downstairs seeing to her studies. Poor child. She'd had to take a drubbing from Leticia last night. From the room across the hall, Beth had heard her niece carrying on until well past ten.

No more of a drubbing, though, than Beth herself would take when tomorrow morning came. How the tongues would wag. She rose and stretched. But she'd lived through it before, hadn't she? And still held her head high. She laughed disenchantedly. And discovered who her friends were, a bare handful when it came right down to it. And of those, only the McDonoughs truly steadfast.

But, really, how far could that steadfastness go? It was all well and good to purge oneself. She sat on the bed again, her gaze resting uneasily on the letter. And she'd certainly done that. Unintentionally, granted. It was to have been one of her usual rose-coloured accounts, but her pen had galloped away from her. Best now to tear up the dreary epistle and start over. On the other hand, Flora had often said if there was ever anything she could do … and perhaps there was. Even if it only amounted to a different perspective, a more objective view of the situation. After all, when it came to motherhood, Flora was a woman of vast experience.

It took several minutes of soul-searching before Beth made her decision. Pride was fine, but there came a time to set it aside in favour of a friend's insight.

Flora's response came in record speed. Less than one week later, as Beth walked in the door, Kate handed her the envelope. 'Lord knows what you find to write about,' she said with a disapproving set to her mouth.

Whatever it is, it's no business of yours, thought Beth, popping the letter in her pocket and tossing over her shoulder as she headed for the stairs, 'I'll be down directly, as soon as I've washed my face.'

'The table needs setting. And there's spuds to be peeled. Tell Emma she'd best finish up with the dusting now.'

'I heard,' Emma's voice came from the landing. 'I'm coming.'

Beth started upstairs and met Emma halfway. The child's face was a study in dejection until Beth gave her a quick hug and whispered, 'We'll have a nice little visit later.'

'In your room, Mama?'

'Yes. Now off you go, your aunt's waiting. And remember not to cut away half the potatoes when you peel them.'

'I will,' Emma sighed, dragging her duster over the bannister as she descended.

In her room, Beth sank onto the chair with the sagging cane seat. Easing her feet from her clogs, she wiggled her toes. Bliss. Odd what constituted bliss these days. Just to be able to sit was Heaven. As she slipped off her shawl and reached to toss it across the bed, the letter in her pocket rustled. Should she read it now, or at bedtime when she could savour its contents? A quick scan, first, just to reassure herself that she hadn't overstepped the bounds of friendship by baring her soul to Flora.

Obviously, she had not, she saw, when she read the opening paragraph.

How my heart went out to you, dear, when I received your letter. And how glad I was that you put enough store in our friendship to feel you could unburden yourself.

Beth exhaled in relief and read eagerly on.

I, too, recognizing the strength of our friendship, as well as the possibility that what I have to say may put it in jeopardy, feel the need (perhaps compulsion would be the better word) to unburden myself. I would have done so sooner. In fact, it has been weighing mightily on my conscience that I did not. But with the tragedy of your husband's death, your concern over Emma those weeks she was so ill, and, of course, the aftermath, I just could not bring myself to do so until now.

Beth tore her gaze away from the sheet of paper and drew several steadying breaths to quell the tightening in her stomach before refocusing on the bold handwriting.

You remember, I'm certain, the dreadful fight the girls had and my subsequent promise to get to the bottom of it. Well, I did, that very night – the night of George's accident. And I learned from Jane the whole sordid truth.

It seems that for some time (exactly how long I have no way

89

*of ascertaining), your late husband had been interfering
with Emma. Lord knows how far this interference went. Let
us hope and pray not too far. I do know, however, that it
involved Emma being made to dance naked for her father
and his touching her on her private parts.*

God in Heaven! Beth slapped her palms over the letter and
took a great gasping breath. What was Flora saying? George?
Emma? Was she saying that … No, no, it couldn't be true. She
wouldn't read another word of such … But Flora was her
friend. Flora wouldn't – Her heart beat wildly and she
pressed her hands to her breast, forcing her eyes back to the
letter.

*Please understand how difficult it is for me to be the bearer of
such tidings, and be assured, also, that this secret is entirely
safe with me (Jane was instructed never to mention it and
has, I am certain, long-since forgotten the whole affair). Like
me, you may at first discount the story, but conclude as I did:
that the minds of innocent children can conjure only so much.*

*I am sure you realize, too, that my purpose in finally
divulging all this is not to upset you, but to help you and dear
Emma. Imagine what the poor child has had to endure. It is
no wonder she suffers from nightmares and that she is not, as
you put it, an 'open child'. It is also understandable that she
should have responded to a threatening situation with a
violent outburst as you described.*

*I am well aware of Emma's memory loss as regards her
Papa's death and the prior months. But I feel certain that if
you were to gently probe into the past with the utmost care –
to help Emma bring out what has been buried – you would see
an end to her problems. This is not idle advice, Beth dear, but
comes from experience in dealing with my own brood. Often,
children want to tell us what is on their minds, but fear of
retribution or shame prevents it. It is, I believe, a proclivity all
children share. And it is up to us parents to help them
overcome it. If we have a splinter in our finger, then better to
suffer the pain of the needle than ignore the splinter.*

90

So, I beg you, dear friend, to set aside your own feelings and talk to Emma. Nothing but good ...

The letter fluttered from Beth's hands to the floor. And she stared numbly at the scattered sheets, her fingers creeping through the folds of her skirt. The knot in her stomach worked its way, like some living thing, up her gullet, exploding hot and acrid in her mouth and sending her stumbling for the washstand, where she vomited until her throat was on fire. Then, in a quaking cold sweat, she collapsed on the bed.

No ... *no!* She gripped the iron bars of the bedhead and whipped her head from side to side. Not George and Emma. Please God. Tell me it isn't true.

Come now, her conscience derided. *Would Flora lie?* Beth's head halted in its frenzied movements. She brought her hands to her sides and lay inert.

And remember, when he moved into the study ... how you found his bed empty? And what about the whisperings from Emma's room? His death, too? What was Emma doing on the landing that night? Didn't you ever stop to wonder about that? And the scissors? Her hair? And remember the way he used to look at her? You surely recognized that hot gleam for what it was ...

On and on the voice went, relentlessly hammering in her head until she finally held up her arms as if to ward off a blow and whispered, 'Oh please ... please. Yes, I was blind. Blind and foolish. But nothing else, I swear.'

Nothing else but a failure as a wife. She covered her mouth with her fist and gave in to the first of a series of dry, wracking sobs. For why else would her husband have become a monster? She had had to turn away his advances. And she had been relieved to be done with that side of their union, a side which brought her only distaste and fear: raw, paralysing fear that another child would result, a child that might kill her – a child that might die as James had.

Yes, in the end, it had been a question of survival, hadn't it? She sat up slowly. And it was done with, wasn't it? Buried with George. Hadn't the doctors said the chances of Emma's

91

ever remembering were infinitesimal? Dredging it up now would be like exhuming a rotting corpse, laying herself and Emma open to its putrefaction.

No! Beth clasped her hands together in an unconscious gesture of prayer. Flora was wrong, no matter what her experiences had taught her. Whatever Emma had suffered could, *would*, be undone with a mother's support and comfort. And with the salve of time.

There would be no probing into the past. Emma must never be allowed to remember the monstrous truth.

It was two weeks before Beth could bring herself to answer Flora.

My dear friend

I could not have been more shattered, more horrified by your news, than if you had told me that you had seen Emma push her father over the bannister that night. That is all I can say about my feelings. For the wound is too raw, the pain of admitting that my husband was a monster, a betrayer of the innocent, too excruciating. You were right to tell me. Never doubt that for a moment. You were right, also, to advise me as you did. Emma's welfare is the crucial issue. And with that thought in mind, I took your advice and talked to Emma, gently, carefully wormed the truth out of her. Thankfully, she did unburden herself. So, it is over and we need never discuss it again. And it was exactly as you said it would be. Now that everything between us is out in the open, Emma is a changed child.

ELEVEN

Indeed, Emma *was* a changed child, and happier than she had been in months.

In retrospect, she could point to the day, to the very hour, that her happiness began. It was the dinner hour on that Monday three days after her expulsion.

Anticipating another meal of long tense silences and accusing looks, she had already developed the familiar knot in her stomach as they gathered around the table. And the sight of Mama's red-rimmed eyes and her odd transparent pallor only added to the child's misgivings.

As soon as grace was over, Mama turned to Aunt Kate and said with a calmness belying the agitated motion of her hands within the folds of her napkin, 'It is high time we dealt with the problems of Leticia's disturbed nights. I think the only solution is for Emma to move in with me.'

Emma's knot instantly dissolved. Suddenly, the unappetizing mound of turnips on her plate no longer fazed her. At that moment, she could have cheerfully eaten a platterful of fatty mutton.

Uncle Eustace frowned, his silver-white brows coming together over brown eyes that had the same mournful quality as Rex's. 'Sounds a mite daft to me,' he said, leaning back in the chair, his thumbs hooked under his jacket lapels.

'What's daft about it?' Aunt Kate's nostrils flared slightly. She set down her knife and fork and propped herself on one challenging elbow.

'Yes, Pa.' Leticia wiped a smear of gravy from the corner of her mouth and glared at her father. 'What's daft about it?'

Scratching his bald spot, Uncle Eustace sat forward. Then he pinched the hawklike bridge of his nose, as was his habit when deep in thought. 'Well,' he said, taking the cut-glass stopper from the vinegar bottle by his plate and twirling it between his fingers, 'it seems as if it'd make a lot more sense if Beth moved in with Emma and Leticia moved into the little ...'

'I will *not*,' Leticia screeched, with an affronted toss of

93

her black curls, her pudgy cheeks colouring fiercely. 'Why should I ...'

'Leticia, love, don't take on so.' A flush crept up Aunt Kate's neck and into her sallow face as she leaned sideways and stroked her daughter's arm. 'Of course, you shan't, my pet,' she said, her voice at odds with the look of silent fury she flashed at her husband.

Leticia's chin came up triumphantly and she cast a side-long 'I-told-you-so' glance in her father's direction.

He shrugged, replaced the stopper, and returned his attention to the food on his plate. 'I just thought it'd be easier on everyone if ...'

Aunt Kate's 'Eustace!' and Mama's 'Gracious!' simultaneously drowned him out.

Mama, who all this time had been intent on cutting her potato into minute cubes, dropped her cutlery. 'I assure you all, I had no intention of starting another Waterloo. I *said* ...' She paused, passing her hand over her brow in a gesture of vague weariness, while everyone stared at her. 'Emma could move in with me. And as far as I'm concerned, that is that.'

Leticia patted her hair into place and smiled a smile of obvious victory. 'Thank you, Auntie,' she said.

And thus it was settled.

Accomplishing the move the following weekend was a simple task, for it was merely a matter of finding space for the tin trunk that contained Emma's clothes and a few personal treasures. Luckily, there was room for it beneath Mama's double bed.

Of course, sharing those cramped quarters was a challenge. But as Mama laughingly put it one day when they were squeezing by each other, 'At least our waistlines should benefit from this constant sucking-in of our breaths.'

And what a joy it was for Emma to fall asleep each night with the reassuring contact of Mama's body next to hers. Sometimes they would whisper back and forth through the darkness about their dreams of a future beyond Glinton, dreams that, according to Mama, would be that much closer to reality once Emma became a wage-earner, as she was slated to do the third Monday in April.

As the days passed, the thought of the important new role she was to play, coupled with the knowledge that now she had an ally in Mama, was enough to dilute Emma's occasional trepidation.

At first, it was odd thinking of Mama as a friend and confidante – hearing her say such things as, 'I want us to be close as sisters' – when Emma had always sensed a hidden reserve in Mama. What was odder still was the realization that this shift in their relationship had happened somewhere around the time of Emma's expulsion from school.

Despite all the horrendous punishments she'd visualized for herself, not a single one had come about. If anything, she had been rewarded: school behind her forever, salvation from her cousin's nightly wrath, and the discovery of a new and wonderful side to Mama. And as if that wasn't enough, she was no longer – miracle of miracles – plagued by the dreams. After almost three weeks of undisturbed nights, she was happily convinced that the dreams, too, were a thing of the past.

But on the eve of her debut at Brummerley's, the terror returned. This time, though, Mama was there to save her from the dreaded pursuer, to cradle and soothe her with assurances that nothing could hurt her.

The next morning, as they passed through the gates of Brummerley's Soapworks, Mama repeated those assurances, shouting through the dank yellow air over the clatter of hundreds of clogs across a central quadrangle, and the neighing of a team of steaming horses turning in ahead of them and pulling a cart whose wheels churned up a muddy wake.

When they reached the centre of the vast cobbled square, the river of workers that bore them along split into four distinct streams. Mama veered to the left and Emma stumbled after her, her feet sliding about in her new clogs.

'That is where you will be working,' Mama yelled, pointing to one of four two-storied brick buildings with twin stacks, from which columns of black smoke rose. 'I work in the one to your left.'

Anxiety thrummed in Emma's chest. Clutching at her mother's sleeve, she drew in a deep breath. The acrid air invaded her throat, caught at her lungs, so that it was a minute before she could stammer, 'You mean, you are not coming with me?'

'I told you, dear, that is just not possible.' Mama took Emma's elbow, coaxing her along. 'Remember, we discussed it. You'll be just fine. You have absolutely nothing to fear as long as you work hard and do exactly as you are told. It'll be strange at first. It was for me; it is for everyone.'

Now they were in the shadow of the building. A few more yards and they came to the foot of a flight of worn steps leading up to the entrance. Mama halted. 'This is where we part company,' she said, rummaging in her basket and then pressing into Emma's hands a linen-wrapped package, which Emma regarded dully.

'Your sandwich, dear. We mustn't forget that. Oh ... and I slipped in a slice of Dundee cake when your aunt's back was turned.'

Emma wanted to return Mama's smile. But her mouth refused to respond. The frightened child in her struggled against the urge to cling to her mother. And in the end, the only thing that prevented it was Mama's confident 'Well, young woman, I know you'll make me proud of you.'

'Oh, I'll try ... I honestly will,' Emma said, giving Mama a swift kiss and then running up the steps before her courage deserted her.

TWELVE

'Sunday, May 12th, 1878.' Emma added curlicues to the *y*'s in 'Sunday' and 'May,' then she twirled a strand of hair around her forefinger while she mulled over which of the items scribbled on the paper at her elbow should be imparted to Jane. There were about ten pencilled notations, none of which would have made sense to anyone but Emma, since they consisted of sentence fragments and single words, such as 'pay,' 'Theodore,' 'Frampton – fat,' 'my mighty deed,' all designed to jog Emma's memory and provide the fuel for her pen, for she was determined to impress Jane with the fullness of her life in Glinton.

Granted, it was not a social fullness; there were no soirées or dances or problems with her dressmaker, no dreary lessons in deportment with the works of Mr Thackeray or Mr Dickens balanced on one's head.

Nor, of course, was it an educational fullness. And thank goodness for that. Only a little reading, writing, and arithmetic – an hour a day since she'd begun working at Brummerley's. No Latin verbs to conjugate, no struggles over French pronunciation.

Yet it *was* a fullness, and of a sort that defied description. Emma picked at a groove in the bleached top of the kitchen table. Her world was now a grown-up world. Not that she was grown-up, at least not in the physical sense. She made a moue and looked down her cheeks at her chest. It was still a chest and no sign of its becoming anything more. And her bottom – she shifted uncomfortably in the hard wooden seat – was as bony as ever. Someday she would have 'natural' padding – the kind that came with maturity. Like Leticia's. Only less, of course. Lord, a great deal less! Like Mama's. She propped her elbows on the table and cupped her chin in her hands. Yes, it would be nice to have Mama's slender waist, gently curving hips, and rounded bosom.

Imagine, in the space of a few months she had seen two naked bosoms. The first, when she had peeped through a tiny hole in the divider curtain and watched Leticia at the washstand. Oh, and what a horrifyingly ugly sight it'd been. Those great white swinging things, surely abnormal for a girl her age and bearing no resemblance to Mama's, which she'd glimpsed silhouetted in the moonlight just last evening.

'Breasts,' Emma doodled on the paper and then glanced guiltily over her shoulder, grabbing her India rubber and quickly erasing the word, though there was no one to see it. This afternoon was a 'tea-at-the Beatons' Sunday. And to the obvious chagrin of his wife and daughter, Uncle Eustace had invited Mama along.

Emma dipped her pen in the ink and wiped off the excess on the edge of the pot. 'My dearest Jane,' she wrote, experimenting with the slope of her letters – there was something decidedly grown-up to a slanted hand – 'I was thrilled to hear from you.' Thrilled? She'd been ecstatic. But annoyed, too, that it had taken Jane so terribly long to answer. Of course, she dare not say anything, for there was always the chance her friend would take offence and cease writing altogether.

Puckering her mouth, she studied the opening line. It would be impolite to launch into her own news without first commenting on Jane's. She reached across the table for Jane's letter, glowering as she read the constant references to Phoebe Benridge. New friend, indeed. She sounded like a positive bore. A brief paragraph was all it took to deal with Phoebe Benridge. And then Emma consulted her notes.

'Pay.' Mama would say it was in bad taste to discuss wages. And perhaps she was right. Besides, a crown a week would surely seem a pittance to Jane. And though they *were* (Phoebe or no Phoebe) the best of friends, how could she convey to Jane (on paper, anyway) the sense of pride and satisfaction she felt each Saturday when she handed two-and-six to Aunt

Kate, one-and-nine to Mama, and kept ninepence (the agreed-upon amount) for herself, to do with exactly as she wished. With a wry shrug, Emma drew her pencil through the word.

'Theodore.' Oh, but she absolutely must tell about Theodore Brummerley, Mr Theo, as the women called him. Such a pleasant young man, she thought. Dark good looks. Ready laugh. So kind and courteous, too, the way he had singled her out that first morning and taken her, as though she were some visiting dignitary, on a tour of the factory.

They had begun with the building that housed the monstrous vats of bubbling fat, where the heat was so fierce that within minutes she'd been drenched in sweat. And obviously, judging from his comment that he'd seen right off what a smart girl she was, he'd taken her stunned silence and constant nods (she'd been afraid to breathe the malodorous air) as a sign she understood his explanation of the process he called 'saponification.'

Approaching the second building, she'd heard a sound similar to that of the roll of thunder. 'The machine room,' he had said. 'It's here that the slabs are made into flakes and bars before they go on to the packing house. You might find it a trifle noisy.'

A trifle noisy! The din had been hideous, the floor trembling beneath her with the vibrations of gigantic machines which squeaked and whirred and clacked and banged with such a force that even covering her ears made no difference.

After that, he had shown her the printing department, which occupied the upper floor of the building Mama had pointed out earlier as being hers. Here enormous presses, under the watchful eyes of their operators, spat out wrappers and labels and wafer-thin sheets of cardboard that would be made into boxes. And though there seemed to be scores of people scurrying about, Emma saw no sign of her mother.

Next was the laboratory, where two chemists experimented with scents and dyes. Fascinated with the peaceful room that smelled of lily of the valley and honeysuckle, roses and lavender, and contained an awesome maze of glass tubing and bottles and phials filled with liquids in every hue imaginable, Emma had been reluctant to leave. But Mr Theo threw a panicky look at the wall clock, mumbled something about 'Pater,' and ushered her posthaste back to the packing room.

Yes. She dipped her pen again. Mr Theo was certainly worthy of a mention.

Lips firm with concentration, Emma wrote a vivid description of the tour, adding with a feeling of importance, 'He said if I ever needed help, I was to come and see him in his office. Oh, you should have seen the women after he left, positively green with envy and gathering around me as if I were a Queen bee.'

No need for Jane to know their reason for gathering round her had been to warn her, though she still had not been able to make any sense out of those warnings, except to conclude that perhaps the man had a violent side to him.

Moll Bowers, the overseer, a big slovenly woman with a careworn face, but a kindly manner, had been the first. 'If you know what's good for you, you'll stay away from that one,' she said.

Emma stared blankly, her head still in a whirl.

'The gaffer's son … Mr Theo. Dangerous, 'e is. No girl's safe with 'im on the prowl.'

'Reckon Emma can take care of 'erself,' one consumptive-looking girl who punctuated her words with a hollow cough piped up. 'Took care of old Opey, didn't she?'

'That's right. Gave it to 'im proper, you did' – this from a fat girl with rank breath, who identified herself as Prue. 'Wished I'd done it meself, 'fore I left school last year. Still got 'is mark on me knuckles.' She brandished a fist before Emma's nose: 'See?'

Someone else slapped Emma on the shoulder and said, 'What you done was a real favour to us all. There's not a one of us wouldn't've done the same if we'd had your gumption.'

Gracious, thought Emma, they obviously viewed her attack on Mr Opey as a heroic deed. 'Thank you,' she murmured, feeling herself blush under their approving attention.

'Alright now, back to work the lot o' you.' Moll thrust her way into the midst of the melee and shooed Emma's admirers off.

'Like I said' – she took Emma's elbow and steered her toward a long table where about two dozen girls sat, wrapping cakes of soap with a speed that boggled the mind – 'stay away from Mr Theo. You may well 'ave spunk, girl, but spunk won't do you no good with the likes of 'im. An' don't let that tour business go to your head.' She motioned Emma to sit beside a pretty blonde-haired girl of enormous girth, who kept to her task, apparently oblivious of everything but the soap and wrappers and glue pot before her. 'Ruth, here,' Moll whispered next to Emma's ear, 'was the last one to get the royal treatment, an' you can see where it got 'er.'

But Emma had not, for the life of her, been able to see the connection between Mr Theo's kindness and Ruth Frampton. Nor had the mystery come any closer to solution during the past fortnight. Doubtless it would, though, in the weeks ahead. She teased her lower lip with the tip of her pen. Once she'd overcome her shyness enough to join in the lunchtime conversation – the gossip and the jokes, the fast and clever talk that had so far overwhelmed her.

And even though the girls had not yet taken her into their confidence, they did admire her for her 'mighty deed.' Jane must hear about that. And about Prue and Moll, and Harriet and Liza and Charlotte. Ruth too, poor girl, who seemed to be growing larger by the day and finding it increasingly difficult to squeeze into her seat.

Resuming the letter, Emma smiled to herself. It was like composing a story, breathing life into the characters, as Miss Faverley used to say. Just wait till Jane read it. She would be bursting to hear more. The thought sent Emma's pen scudding across the paper. Yes, this time Jane would not lose a minute in responding.

Emma was wrong. June was half over before Jane's answer arrived.

With her pay jangling in her pocket on that Saturday afternoon, and the unaccustomed warmth of the sun (anaemic though it was) on her face, Emma was in a cheerful frame of mind as she and Mama rounded the bend onto Milton Street.

'There's the postman,' Mama said. 'Maybe he'll have a letter for you today.'

Emma quickened her pace. 'Maybe he will at that, Mama.'

They caught up with him as he came level with the Sheenes'.

'Afternoon, ladies.' He doffed his cap.

'Good afternoon. Anything for number seventeen?' Mama said.

'Reckon there was something.' He riffled through a pile of envelopes. 'Yes, here we are. One for the little miss.'

'Oh, thank you.' Emma grabbed the letter and skipped on ahead of Mama to the front door. Sinking to the step, she tore open the envelope.

It was a disappointingly short note, with only a cursory acknowledgement of Emma's news and the rest of it divided between an excited account of the arrival of baby Seraphine on the tenth (which Emma already knew about from Mama) and Jane's proposed visit to Paris in August, with Phoebe and her parents.

In a fit of pique, Emma crumpled the letter in her fist and glowered down at her dusty boot toes.

'Gracious, whatever is the matter?' Mama sat beside her. 'It was a letter from Jane, wasn't it?'

Emma nodded.

'And you're not happy to get it?' Mama's arm encircled Emma's shoulders as they lifted in a dispirited shrug.

'But all these weeks you've been waiting for the postman to come. Did Jane say something hurtful?'

'No.' Emma watched the progress of a shiny greenish-black beetle just beyond her feet.

'Well, what on earth *did* she say?'

'Nothing.'

'Oh, come now, she must have said something.'

The hint of amusement she heard in Mama's voice only added to Emma's ill-humour and she blurted, 'Nothing worthy of mention, except for the baby. Silly old trip to Paris. Who gives a fig for Paris? She's not interested in me, Mama. She has Phoebe now. I told her all sorts of exciting things and she didn't even have the good manners to ...'

'Of course, Jane is interested in you.' Mama gave her a squeeze. 'It's just that, well ... sometimes people grow apart. It's nobody's fault. Their lives take a different course, that's all.'

'But what about you and Mrs McDonough? She writes almost every fortnight and ...'

'I know, dear. Our friendship is a unique one, and –' 'A what one?' Emma cut in.

'A special one. And I pray to God it endures. But, like you' – Mama removed her arm from Emma's shoulders, stretched her legs before her, and smoothed her skirts over her knees – 'I must face the possibility that someday Flora may ...' She caught herself and glanced sidelong. 'You trust me, don't you, dear?'

'Yes, Mama.' Emma positioned her legs alongside her mother's, noting how much more she would have to grow before she was as tall.

'Then trust me when I tell you that you *will* make new friends. It may be one of the girls you work with or someone you don't yet know. I'm so convinced, in fact' – Mama had a mischievous look about her now – 'that although you know I abhor gambling, I am willing to wager a shilling on it.'

Emma tugged at her earlobe in puzzlement. 'What does that mean, Mama?'

'It means,' Mama said, wagging a teasing finger, 'that if you make a friend – a true friend, not just an acquaintance – by, let me see now ... we will have to set a date ... December first, you will owe me a shilling. And if you do not, then I will owe you a shilling. So what do you think?'

'Alright,' Emma said without an instant's hesitation.

'Very well.' Mama rose and extended her hand to Emma. 'I do believe, then, that custom dictates we shake on it.'

THIRTEEN

If there was one thing Emma wanted more than anything, it was to lose the wager. As the months passed, however, her hopes dwindled.

The girls at Brummerley's, long established in their own cliques, made no overtures to her. That was understandable, she supposed, considering she was so much younger than any of them and different in background, manners, and speech. (In their estimation, she talked like a 'toff,' which according to Mama was a good thing, because it meant she had the diction of a lady.)

Not that her co-workers were unpleasant. They were really quite nice. But their niceness wavered between a kind of affectionate teasing and a tiresome protectiveness that had them constantly warning her about (though never stopping to explain) the mysterious dangers associated with Mr Brummerley's son.

She must on no account linger after hours. As if she would. The second the six o'clock whistle went, she was right there, with the rest of them, scrambling for the door. She must not so much as smile at the man. For she might be considered easy. It was easiness that had been Ruth Frampton's ruination, got her into such a terrible fix. Did they mean her size? They must. For to look as enormous as Mrs McDonough had looked the summer she had been in 'that certain condition' was surely a terrible fix for any girl to be in. But what on earth was the connection between Ruth's odd shape and smiling at Mr Theo? And what did they mean when they said he was a 'rake' and a 'lecture'?

It was all dreadfully confusing. In the context in which they were used, the girls' words were foreign to Emma. 'Easy' was the opposite of 'difficult.' A 'rake' was for raking. And a 'lecture' was what resulted when she expressed her confusion to her mother.

'It's obvious,' Mama said with a flustered little shudder, 'that you have been listening to gossip. Ladies, Emma – and despite our current circumstances we *are* ladies – do not waste their time on, nor lend their ears to, gossip.'

She was not wasting her time on that October morning. The six dozen bars of soap she'd already wrapped and glued after less than an hour's work were proof enough of that. But she *was* lending her ears to gossip. For how else would she learn? Oh, and what fascinating gossip it was. About Harriet's beau, and whether or not he was good enough for Harriet. About Mr Theo's long trip to Germany, which would take him away for months. It was worth not being a lady to hear *that* welcome titbit. The conversation, accompanied by a good deal of sniggering, moved on to the subject of Mr Theo's business, and how it was unlikely he'd get much accomplished by the time he was done chasing after something that sounded like 'frawleens.' Now Prue and Liza were whispering together. Straining forward, Emma paused in mid-dab.

'Alright, you lot,' Moll's voice boomed from behind her, giving her such a start that she dropped the glue brush. 'Get your 'eads down.'

Emma quickly retrieved her brush and was about to resume her work when a hand descended on her arm. 'This 'ere's the new girl what's replacing Ruth, an' I want you to show 'er what's to be done.'

It took a moment for the overseer's statement to register. New girl? Replacing Ruth? Emma turned and looked up. Heavens, but it was the girl who had been nice to her that first day at school, the one with the frizzy black hair and big dark eyes that looked even bigger right now because they were wide with surprise.

'Hello,' she said, sitting, at Moll's direction, in the seat next to Emma. 'Remember me?'

'Yes. You're … Jessie … Jessie …?'

'Dobbins. An' you're Emma, Emma Cadman.'

'You two know each other, then,' Moll said.

Jessie nodded over her shoulder. 'In a manner of speakin'.'

'Well, I'll leave you both to get on with it. The work, I mean. I don't mind you chin-waggin', just so long as the work gets done.'

Emma's and Jessie's chins wagged all day long. Locked away for so long in the role of listener and observer, Emma could hardly credit her own talkativeness. But here at last was someone who actually seemed to value her opinions, who treated her as an equal in spite of the fact that Jessie was a year her senior. And the girl was funny into the bargain, with her story of the way she had 'pestered' her way out of the machine room and into the packing department.

'If the truth were known,' she said, ''twas a mite more than pesterin'. Moaned and groaned, I did, all the time. Kept tellin' Mr Booth the noise made me feel proper funny, like I was goin' to vomit. Got so good at it, the pretendin' I mean, that yesterday mornin' I did it – brought me breakfast up all over 'is boots.'

'How clever,' Emma said, passing the wrapped cakes of soap to Jessie, who was boxing them.

'No more clever than you were, clobberin' old Opey.'

Emma paused in her task. 'Oh, but I didn't do it on purpose. I –'

'I know.' Jessie nudged her playfully. 'You were at the end of your rope. Heard all about it from me sister, Gert, an' Ralph an' Luke, me brothers. Comin' home every day, they was, tellin' me about the torment you had to put up with. An' I felt real bad, 'cause if I'd still been in school I'd have put a stop to it. Don't hold with that kind of nonsense.'

Emma smiled. 'You don't have to feel bad, because if you had been there to stop it, then I probably would not be here.' She began stacking the flat oblong boxes into dozens.

'You mean you like it at Brummerley's?' Jessie blinked in astonishment.

'Not exactly. Though it's a thousand times better than school, and ten thousand times better than slaving for my Aunt Kate. She's a positive dragon.' Emma flexed her aching back. 'And I *am* earning my keep and putting a little aside for our futures. Mama says one of these years we may be able to buy our own place.'

'Tell me about your Ma. What's she like?'

For the rest of the morning, their conversation revolved around their respective families.

Jessie's was a large one. Besides her mother and father (a man she described as a 'mean old cuss') and the sister and two brothers she'd mentioned earlier, there were two more boys – Walter, four years old, and a baby, Josh. In order to accommodate so many people, the Dobbinses' house must surely be twice as big as the Sheenes', Emma remarked. For some reason, Jessie thought this a great joke. At least, she laughed as if she did. But Emma detected a darkness in the girl's face – an undercurrent of bitterness to the laughter – that made her blurt, 'I'm sorry,' though she wasn't exactly sure why she should be apologizing. She was glad she had, however, for Jessie immediately brightened and went on to tell about her hideaway, an old boat house on the banks of an abandoned leg of the canal. Someday – if Emma would like – Jessie would take her there.

That 'someday' came far sooner than Emma dreamed it would. Just three weeks later, on a Saturday afternoon.

'It's not Buckingham Palace,' Jessie said, leading Emma by the elbow through the dim interior to the makeshift table and bench in the one corner where the roof was still intact. 'But it's got a carpet' – she indicated the dried grass strewn about the floor – 'and light. See me candle on the table, here? And I can keep plenty warm 'cause I talked Isaac Rubenstein, the rag-and-bone man that does our street, out of a couple of old coats. Here, let's take 'em outside with us.' She rummaged around beneath the bench and came up with the garments. 'You take this one.' She shoved something into Emma's arms that looked and smelled like a dead animal. Horrors, did Jessie expect her to put it on?

'We can sit on 'em,' Jessie said.

'That's a splendid idea.' Emma held the coat away from herself as she followed Jessie outside. Gingerly, they picked their way across the slimy, moss-covered boards of the old landing stage and onto the bank.

A few yards into the tall grass, they stopped. Jessie crouched and tested the ground with the flat of her hands. 'It's just a bit damp.' She spread out the coat and gestured for Emma to do the same. Then they both sat.

'Been comin' here for two years now.' Jessie crooked her knees and clasped her hands under her thighs. 'An' never seen a single soul. Never told a single soul about it neither, not even me sister. You're the only other person in the whole world what knows about it.'

'I am?' Emma's heart swelled at the thought of being privy to Jessie's secret.

It was nice here. Peaceful, with nothing to disturb the quiet except the occasional piping of a bird and the soothing slap of water against the green rotting supports of the landing stage. Only two miles from town. Yet what an utterly different world it was. She arched her neck, drawing the marshy air into her lungs and watching the clouds drift like a bridal veil across the crisp lapis blue of the sky.

'So what do you think?' Jessie prodded her.

'I think,' Emma said, turning and grinning at Jessie, 'that I have just lost a shilling.'

Mama would not hear of it. 'Keep your money,' she said. 'I'm just happy that you've made a friend. Besides, it's not long until Christmas, and you will need every copper you can scrape together.'

Mama was right, of course. Christmas was a time for goodwill, wasn't it? And goodwill even extended to those one had no affection for. Which meant buying gifts for Aunt Kate and Leticia, and spending more than she would have liked because of her desire to show that at least *she* was not miserly.

Once Emma had her duty shopping out of the way, she turned her attention to the selection of presents for her mother and Jessie. For Mama, she settled on a jaunty little hat in the same green as Mama's good coat, and she chose an assortment of colourful hair ribbons for Jessie. Afterward came the joy of anticipating the pleasure her gifts would bring, a joy that not even the thin rattle of her money box could diminish.

But Christmas had come and gone before she had the opportunity to see Jessie's pleasure.

FOURTEEN

Emma paused beneath the sign and consulted the scrap of paper on which Moll Bowers had written Jessie's address: 55 Railway Street. This was the street, alright. Its terraces of soot-draped, red brick dwellings with their dark slate roofs and front steps extending the width of two doorways stretched in sombre monotony up the curve of the hill.

Here was number one. Emma nodded to the two pinch-faced women who stood in her path, gossiping in the frosty January air. They moved aside, staring after her in a kind of grey, empty fashion as she set off, head tucked into her chest, eyes focused on the ice-slicked cobbles.

After several minutes of brisk walking, she reached her destination. The first thing that caught her eye, when the door swung open in response to her knock, was a faint cloud of steam rising from the yellow pool between the spindly legs of a boy who crouched on a floor that appeared to Emma to be part earth, part bricks, and part rotting boards.

Tearing her disgusted gaze away, Emma refocused on the pallid, angular face of the woman. Mrs Dobbins, it had to be, for the eyes, though lifeless, were Jessie's, the hair the same sooty frizz, but with a startling streak of jaundiced white extending back from a broad furrowed brow to her scrap of a bun.

Arms akimbo, she regarded Emma suspiciously. 'Yes, what is it?'

'I ... I wondered if –'

'Give over, Walter.' Jerking her hip at the child, who was now clawing at her skirts, she caught him in the chest. And he let out a wail, then stamped his feet in a purple rage.

'You stop that right now.' Mrs Dobbins swatted him on the seat of his soggy chopped-off trousers, ducked behind the door, and then reappeared holding a tattered coat into which she bundled the indignant child. 'Out you go. Find your brothers,' she said, grabbing him by the earlobe and shoving him past Emma. 'Proper little weasel is that one.' She wiped her wet hand on her skirt. 'One of these days I swear I'll ...' The sentence ended with the slam of her fist in her open palm. 'Now,' she said, smoothing an oily-looking strand of hair behind her ear, 'what was you sayin'?'

'Jessie. I wondered if I might see Jessie? Moll Bowers told me about the accident. I'm Emma Cadman.'

'Come to see my Jessie, 'ave you?' Her face softened. 'Well, isn't that nice. Emma, you say.' Arms folded over her coarse apron, she pulled at her chin thoughtfully.

'Yes. We're friends, Jessie and me.'

'Now I've got you placed.' Mrs Dobbins's forefinger stabbed the air. 'You're the one what works with Jessie – the one what gave Mr Opey what for.' Eyes alive now, she smiled, her teeth protruding slightly over her lower lip in the same way that Jessie's did. 'Come in. Come in. Jessie'll be right pleased to see you.'

'Gert,' she yelled, preceding Emma into the house, 'clean off that chair so Jessie's friend 'ere can sit down without gettin' 'erself all mucked up.'

It was a moment before Emma was able to adjust her eyes to the shadowy interior and see the skinny girl, who appeared to be about her own age, acknowledging her with a nod and a grin.

'The chair,' Mrs Dobbins shouted.

Gert leaped into action, sending up a cloud of dust as she flapped her skirt over what seemed to be the only chair, an unpadded wooden one, with a couple of slats missing from its back.

'Go sit yourself down there, an' I'll see if Jessie's awake. About this time of an afternoon, she has 'erself a rest.' Pausing at the foot of the steep staircase, she added, 'Shouldn't be more than a jiffy. Gert! Don't just stand there gawkin'. Didn't I tell you we needed spuds from the shed?'

Gert scowled. 'Aw, Ma, do I 'ave to? Can't I – ?'

'No, you can't. Just do as you're told for once.'

Gert skulked off, slamming the back door after herself. And from somewhere overhead came a baby's screams.

'Dammit,' Jessie's mother muttered, 'now she's woke little Josh.'

Emma jumped up. 'Maybe I should come back some other time when –'

'Lord love us, no. Sit yourself down. Jessie'd be right peeved if you was to leave. Like as not she's awake now, anyway, what with Josh carryin' on.'

As Mrs Dobbins began her weary ascent of the stairs, Emma sank back in her seat, relieved that she hadn't had to leave. Without Jessie to talk to, it'd been a long, lonely fortnight. She had wanted to come sooner, the very Monday Moll had told her about Jessie's accident. But with Christmas and Boxing Day and New Year, all the preparations and festivities, it had been impossible. It had been touch-and-go, too, whether or not Mama would allow the visit to a section of the town she considered 'decidedly seedy.' Finally, though, after Emma promised to be home well in advance of Saturday teatime, her mother had relented.

Mama was right, it *was* a seedy part of town. Railway Street seemed a regular *Pilgrim's Progress*, with a person having to watch her every step for fear of having slops thrown over her (one woman had barely missed her), and those ragged little urchins collecting horse manure and dog dirt in their buckets and chasing after the tanner's putrid cart. She shuddered and drew in a distasteful breath.

The smell still lingering in her nostrils was enough to turn her stomach. She felt in her skirt pocket for the bag of humbugs. It'd been an extravagant purchase. But when she brought it to her nose and took a deep minty sniff, she was glad she'd been unable to resist the temptation of the sweet-shop window.

Her gaze drifted about the room. Lord, it was no wonder Jessie had laughed when Emma said the Dobbinses must have a large place. The downstairs was no larger than the Sheenes' washhouse.

There were two small windows, most of whose panes were broken and stuffed with dirty rags. Dampness oozed between the bricks and boards of the floor. And the crumbling stone fireplace with stubs of tallow candles on its warped mantel, and with no sign of an oven, housed a feeble fire over which hung a blackened pot. Hers *was* the only chair. Straw pallets lined the flaking whitewashed walls. Around the table, seemingly constructed of a door laid across a half-barrel, was an odd mixture of stools in different shapes and heights.

A corner of the room obviously served as a scullery, for there was a sink (but no pump), a couple of shelves containing three mismatched pans, and a single unpainted cupboard with a bent nail for a handle beneath the shelves.

Poor Jessie, having to live this way. Emma felt a stab of guilt for having so often thought herself badly done to. She would never complain again, never, she silently vowed. She would be thankful every single day of her –

The slam of the door startled her out of her thankfulness. Popping the sweets back in her pocket (not that she meant to be selfish but she had already mentally divided them between herself and Jessie), she glanced up.

It was Gert. 'Where's Ma?' she asked, dropping a sack to the floor and flexing her bony arms.

Before Emma had a chance to respond, a disembodied voice came sharply over the groan of the staircase. 'I'm 'ere. An' if I have to tell you one more time about that bleedin' door, I'll take the strap to you.'

Gert rolled her eyes in mock terror, then said contritely, 'Sorry, Ma,' as Mrs Dobbins appeared, balancing on her hip a baby who, when he caught sight of Emma, hid his face against his mother's shoulder.

'E's a mite bashful is this one.' She bounced Josh on her hip. 'It's like I said. Jessie was sleepin'. Up and about now, though, but wantin' to do 'erself up a bit before she comes down.'

'Ma, what do you want me to do with the spuds?'

Gert's mother sighed audibly. 'Josh, stop your kickin'. You're wearin' me out.'

'Here, sit here.' Emma got to her feet.

'Thanks, luv.' She slipped into the chair. ''E's a bit of a lump. But 'e carries on some'at awful if I tries to put 'im down.'

'Ma-a-a-a! What shall I *do* with the spuds?'

Seeing the telltale flush creeping up Mrs Dobbins's neck and a vein begin to throb at her temple, Emma decided it was time to step in.

'Why don't I help you, Gert? Your Mama probably wants you to set the potatoes down over there.' Pointing to the scullery corner and catching Mrs Dobbins's grateful eye, Emma grabbed the sack from a surprised Gert and began dragging it across the floor.

Just as she was shoving it against the wall, she heard a familiar voice say, 'Now what's goin' on here? You come visitin' an' they put you to work. I don't believe me eyes.'

Stifling a giggle, Emma straightened. 'No, Jessie.' She whirled about. 'It wasn't like that at all, it was … Oh, Jessie!' For a horrified instant, her hand flew to her mouth. '*What* have you done to yourself?'

FIFTEEN

'A proper picture, ain't I?' Jessie struck a pose – chest out, chin up, one hand on her hip and the other gracefully extended, as if to an invisible dance partner.

Her face was exactly that – a picture. But an ugly, painful

one. Skin stretched taut as canvas over the framework of cheekbones. Eyes like twin ink blots underlined in grey, moist with unshed tears. Mouth a tremulous pink smudge. Daubs of faded yellow, purple, and black across one cheek.

'Oh, Jessie, what happened?' Emma whispered.

Jessie's shoulders suddenly slumped. Her arms fell listlessly to her sides. She shrugged. 'Well ...'

'Sprained 'er ankle, she did,' Gert chimed in breathlessly. 'Mucked up 'er face somethin' chronic and doctor says it'll be another week before she can go back to work. Oh, an' she gashed 'er head, too.'

'Thanks, Gert.' Jessie threw her a look of amused irritation. Motioning Emma to follow, she limped across to the table and signalled Emma to sit opposite. 'My tongue's all right, you know. I mean, I can still use it. I didn't sprain it or muck it up or gash it. Though the way *you're* carryin' on, you'd think I didn't even have one.'

Gert pouted. 'I was only ...'

'You was only pokin' your nose in,' Mrs Dobbins said, her tone acid, 'like you always is, and' – pausing to shift Josh from the crook of one arm to the other, she began to unbutton her bodice – 'I've 'ad enough of your shenanigans for one day.' Freeing a breast that was starkly white against her mud-brown blouse, she thrust the dark nipple into Josh's eager mouth.

Still numbed by the sight of Jessie's face, Emma found herself watching Mrs Dobbins with only mild curiosity. One hand tousling Josh's head, the woman instructed Gert to round up her brothers and go scout the railway tracks for coal scraps.

'Aw, Ma,' Gert said, giving a grunt of disgust. 'We were there yesterday and there wasn't none.'

'Sometimes the coal gets spilled when they're stokin' the engine,' Jessie interjected for Emma's benefit.

'Don't you *aw Ma* me.' Josh's hand flew up in the air at his mother's shrill words. Still latched onto her breast, he began to scream as she carried on yelling, 'You get out there right now and don't come back till you've a sackful.'

114

'Lord.' Jessie sighed. 'Peace and quiet. It's as rare as a sovereign around 'ere.' She had to raise her voice over her mother's shouts, Josh's screams from upstairs, and the protesting chorus outside. 'Just listen to them. They've got to argue. And that Walter, 'e's the worst of the lot. But Gert'll soon ...' She cocked her head. ''Ear that screechin'? That's her. *Now* they'll shut up.'

And they did. An abrupt silence fell, broken after a moment or two by the sound of footsteps, like a miniature army on the march.

'They've gone now,' Mrs Dobbins hollered, startling the girls. 'So you two 'ave yourselves a nice little visit while I keep Josh out of mischief.'

'Phew!' Jessie passed her sleeve across her brow. 'Thank God for that.' Elbows on the table, she cupped her chin in her hands, then snatched them away. 'Ouch, dammit. I keep forgettin'.'

Emma winced in sympathy. 'It must hurt dreadfully.'

'Oh, it's not that bad. Not 'alf as bad as it was. An' nowhere near as bad as being cooped up 'ere with them lot all day long.' She rolled her eyes heavenward. 'Not Ma, mind you. Me and Ma get along fine. Never thought I'd say it, but I'm fair itchin' to get back to work.'

'I can see how you would be. Everyone said to tell you they miss you.'

'They did?' Jessie's eyes widened.

'Yes. I missed you, too. Dreadfully. And' – Emma fished the package out of her pocket and slid it across the table – 'I was so disappointed you weren't there for me to give you your Christmas present.'

'Christmas present? For me?' Jessie stared openmouthed. 'Oh, Emma, you shouldn't've. I didn't get ... I mean, I couldn't ...'

'Well, aren't you going to open it?'

'Huh? Oh, yes.' In her eagerness, she ripped the tissue paper to shreds, scattering it hither and thither. 'Oh, Emma ... ribbons. And all me favourite colours.' She held them

115

against her breast. 'I think I'm ...' Her voice cracked. Across the table, Emma's hand sought Jessie's.

'You like them, then?'

As if she didn't trust herself to speak, Jessie nodded for a long moment. Her grip tightened to the point where Emma's fingers began to tingle. Suddenly, she released Emma's hand and said, 'So let's hear it, all of it. How you are, what you've been doin' and what's been goin' on while I've been servin' me time 'ere.'

'Jessie!' Emma slammed her palms on the table. 'You haven't told me a thing yet. I mean, Gert said you fell. What actually happened?'

Jessie gave a nonchalant shrug. 'Just tripped over me feet is all. One minute I was at the top of the stairs and the next ...' Letting the sentence trail off, she began picking at a flake of wood, gritting her teeth in apparent concentration. 'Downright clumsy, that's me.' She looked up, though her eyes seemed to be avoiding Emma's. 'Ma says it's me age. When you're growin', as she says I am, though I 'ope to the Lord I've done all the growin' I'm goin' to do, well, you ...' her voice tapered off. Now she regarded Emma squarely. 'Oh, what the hell. You may as well know the truth. It was me Pa. Came 'ome that night real late. Everyone else was in bed, but I was still up. 'E'd had a bellyful of ale an' I was 'andy. And' – she gestured to her face and the leg she'd propped up on a stool – 'this is what you get around here when you're 'andy.'

'Merciful Heaven! You mean your father hit you.'

'Sssshhh.' Jessie put her finger against her mouth for a second. 'Don't want Ma to know. She has enough to worry about, what with 'im spendin' all 'is wages at the Nag's Head.'

'But that's terrible,' Emma whispered. 'Isn't there something you can do about it?'

'What's to do about it? Short of bumpin' 'im off. An' I'm not cut out for that sort of thing.'

'Couldn't you leave, go and ...?'

'Naw. I'm stuck 'ere. Couldn't leave Ma and the children. Mine's the only wage they can count on.' She shifted her leg into a more comfortable position. 'You don't know 'ow lucky you are, Emma, not havin' a Pa. Let's not talk about it anymore. Would you do something for me?'

'Anything.'

'If I get me comb, would you fix this thatch of mine? You know, do somethin' fancy with it, maybe plait it and work some of these ribbons through?'

In an ecstasy of sucking – Emma had finally remembered the humbugs – Jessie sat with both feet propped up while Emma stood behind her, drawing a comb through the tangled fluff. 'I'm not hurting you, am I?' said Emma, working her tongue over her gums seeking chewy bits of the sweet's soft centre.

'Lord, no. Feels wonderful. Haven't 'ad me hair combed since I was little. I remember how Ma used to do it before the others came along. Now she's too worn out.'

'An' whar've we got 'ere?'

The male voice from behind so startled Emma that she dropped the comb. And under her hand, lightly resting on Jessie's shoulder, she felt the sharp tensing of muscles. Slowly turning her head, she squinted up.

The man seemed to be staring at Jessie's back. As he repositioned a grimy tweed cap on his bald crown, Emma's gaze travelled over a vast expanse of grey smock that covered his huge frame, down the legs to the boots planted a couple of feet from her, and finally back to the face.

She felt herself impaled by hard little eyes regarding her from under a bristling black shelf of brows. Something in the way he looked and the manner in which his tongue flicked over the slack mouth struck her nervously. 'You have company,' she said in a low voice, nudging Jessie in the back.

'Company, is it?' He gave a humourless laugh. Swaying slightly, he sniffed and, with his sleeve, wiped his nose, which had the appearance of a large, overripe plum.

'Your friend 'ere thinks I'm company. Now what do ya think of that, Jessie, me girl?'

'Jessie's back remained rigid.

'Answer me, girl. I said ...'

117

Jessie swivelled about, eyes sparking, and scrambled to her feet, holding onto Emma for support.

'I 'eard you. An' I don't think nothin'.' Jessie spat the words and then out of the corner of her mouth, whispered, 'You'd best go. He's me Pa. An' 'e can be right mean, when 'e's ...'

'What's that you're mumblin', girl?'

There was an ominous quality to the soft thud-thud as he pounded his fist into his open palm. And Emma felt the hairs rise at the back of her neck.

A sidelong glance showed Jessie's expression changing from defiance to fear. 'I wasn't ... I mean, Emma has to be home by four, an' I was just ...'

'She's right. Absolutely. I really must go.' Emma grabbed her gloves and bonnet from the table. And though her skin crept and her heart was pounding in her throat, she managed a polite 'So nice to have met you, Mr Dobbins,' as she made for the door.

Beth was uneasily pacing the flags. Another half hour and it would be time to set the table. Quarter to four, and Emma still was not home. Maybe she shouldn't have allowed the child to go trooping off across town. But Emma had had such a pleading look, and the Dobbins girl, Jessie, did mean a lot to her. Not that she was the kind of friend Beth would have chosen for her daughter – a rather coarse type, from the look of her – but a friend nonetheless.

Beth sat down and resumed her knitting. A shame Emma and Leticia couldn't have become close. But they were worlds apart – Leticia with her grand ambitions and her parade of beaux (though why the girl had so many was baffling) and Emma still so much the child, despite the adult responsibilities she'd acquired.

Setting her knitting in the basket at her feet, Beth rose and poked the fire. She had heaped half a scuttle of coal on it the minute the Sheenes had left to visit Eustace's ailing brother, who would never know how grateful she was. Grateful! Lord, what a dreadful thought to have when, from all accounts, the poor consumptive man was at death's door.

Oh, but it was a splendid luxury to be alone and warm, and to be spared the guilt that came with Kate's constant references to the cost of fuel.

She resettled herself in the chair and resumed her knitting. Today, it didn't seem such a terrible life. And the festive season had been quite pleasant, starting with the Christmas Eve service and a rather nice choral recital. No goose, granted, for Christmas dinner, but a good-sized capon with chestnut stuffing, and afterward a plum pudding. Oh, and the bonnet. Imagine, Emma buying her a bonnet, and so elegant a one at that.

Hadn't Boxing Day been an experience? She chuckled softly. The workers all assembling at the Brummerley home and, in alphabetical order, marching through the servants' quarters to receive their piece of bacon, one apple, and a few hazelnuts from Mrs. And later the treat of listening to the works' brass band play a selection of carols. Treat! A more off-key rendition she'd never heard, with trombones, clarinets, and trumpets positively screeching at each other. Oh, what she wouldn't give to hear Lavinia Parsons at the harpsichord. What glorious musical evenings they used to have with …

The front door slammed. 'Mama, I'm home. I just have to get out of my coat and bonnet!'

'Gracious,' Beth said as Emma entered the kitchen, 'I was beginning to think you were lost.'

'Sorry, the time ran away with me. Is there any tea? I'm as dry as a bone. Cold, too.' Emma chafed her arms and shivered.

'As a matter of fact, there is. I made it a few minutes ago.' Beth gestured to the table. 'Help yourself.' When she completed the last few stitches of the row she was working on, she asked, 'So how was Jessie?'

Emma finished stirring her tea and then took a quick sip before responding. 'In a bad way. You will not believe how she came to have the accident.'

'Really?'

'Her father hit her, gave her a sprained ankle, and her face is black.'

'Merciful Heavens.' Beth dropped her knitting in her lap. 'But what on –?'

Crossing to the chair opposite, Emma sat down. 'He was drunk.' She held out her hands to the fire. 'I met him, Mama, and he's a vile man. Jessie loathes him. She says I'm lucky not to have a Papa.'

'What a dreadful thing to say.' Beth spoke more sharply than she'd intended, for she could feel an unreasoning panic rising. Anxious to change the subject, she said, 'Dear, would you do me a favour and run upstairs. I need another ball of wool. It's in the top drawer of the chest.'

With the sound of Emma's feet on the stairs, Beth relaxed against the back of the chair. Foolish to let herself get agitated. Lord, it wasn't as if the child was interrogating her. Over a year now, and in all that time they'd had only one conversation about George. Why didn't Beth have any pictures of him? Emma had asked. 'Because I have my own picture of your father, here in my heart,' had been her response. And of course, they'd discussed the accident during that final month at Milchester: how Papa had tripped, how ill Emma had been, how her not remembering was practically to be expected …

'Mama.'

Beth jumped. 'Gracious, you scared me half out of my skin.'

With a look of irritation, Emma flopped into her chair. 'I searched and searched, but I couldn't find any wool.'

'You couldn't? How odd.'

'Did Papa drink like Mr Dobbins, Mama? Is that why he fell downstairs?'

'Your father was a fine man, Emma. That's all you need concern yourself with.' She fumbled with her knitting and made an ineffectual stab with the needle. 'And your friend Jessie is right. You *are* lucky; lucky to have a home, a warm bed, a job – and a mother to love you as I do.'

'You're right, Mama,' Emma said matter-of-factly. 'This is

a mansion compared to the Dobbinses' place.' She leaned forward, elbows resting in her lap. 'Do you really think we'll have a place of our own someday?'

Thank God for a different topic. Beth felt all the tension go out of her. 'Oh, I certainly hope so. If Providence smiles on us.'

'Oh, it will. I know it will, Mama.'

SIXTEEN

But Providence frowned that year.

For thousands, 1879 spelled disaster. Its summer of plummeting temperatures and continuous rain was the worst on record. Farmers faced ruin as crops blackened in the fields and sheep died by the millions. Landlords bemoaned their dwindling rents. Mothers mourned the loss of children.

In the towns, industry foundered. Towering stacks that had for so long spewed the black effluvium of prosperity, and served as obscene monuments to the march of progress, breathed their last.

Prices fell cataclysmically. Unemployment reached new heights. And only the most fortunate or most experienced held onto their jobs.

In the taproom of the Bull & Bear shortly before one o'clock on the third Saturday in September, there was the usual pandemonium.

Despair wore the mask of revelry. The din was horrendous, the mood frenetic. Over the chaffing and yelling and the unending buzz of conversation, laced with belches and hiccoughs, shrieks and guffaws, came the clash of pewter and the bacchanalian strains of a fiddle setting scores of clogs to tip-tapping on the worn flagstones.

Seated before an ancient upright piano, at one end of the

narrow low-ceilinged room with its wormy timbers, was a lanky man, his fingers poised like bleached twigs over the yellowing keys. And when he hammered out the first rollicking chords, the quartet of sodden-faced youths assembled about him roared into song, beating time on the scarred mahogany of the piano top. Foaming tankards in hand, they swung into chorus after euphoric chorus, swaying in time to the music and leering at the voluptuous white pillows of the serving woman's breasts, jouncing over her low-cut bodice as she scurried by.

Nimble feet kicking up the sawdust, a gang of lads, flushed with mischief, played tag around the two massive oak tables centred in the room and reserved by unwritten rule for the older patrons. Some sat silent, rheumy-eyed, swigging their ale. Others, with hardly a tooth between them, chewed impotently on the trotters and tripe their tuppences had bought them.

The Berry brothers, an emaciated pair with rosy cheeks that belied their wheezing and constant need to hawk into the brass spittoon on the floor behind them, puffed on their pipes and reminisced about better days.

Mad Dan Pilkington, who had lost a wife and three little ones to the pox back in the forties, muttered to himself, his eyes slithering about. One minute his mouth twisted into the evilest of grins, and the next, turned down at its corners and quivered like a babe's denied its mother's breast. Suddenly, he staggered to his feet and, with a bang of his gnarled fist on the table, called for a toast to 'Her Majesty' and 'Old Dizzy.' Normally, Dan's words would have fallen on deaf ears. But today, there were cries of 'Shut up, you fool,' 'Sit down, you great daft lump,' and 'What the hell 'as she and that bleedin' ol' Jew done for the likes of us, 'cept send us on our way to the poor'ouse?'

Added to outbursts such as this, and the general clamour of the place, was its stench – a fetid potpourri of flatulence and fermentation: stale tobacco smoke suspended in a perpetual haze over the wavering lights of a rusted chande-lier; vomit and sweat; rain-soaked shawls hung to dry before the fire's embers; and dog urine, as a mangy vagabond sniffed among the Eden of table legs, then marked his territory in a steamy stream.

This, then, was the scene that greeted Emma and her mother as they entered the taproom.

Emma stood rooted until Mama urged her forward. Once within the churning crush of people, she felt the inevitable panic rise in her. She had been coming here every Saturday since her thirteenth birthday, and should have been used to it by now. But there was always the overwhelming desire to flee. The hazy, terrifying memory kindled by the closeness of rank bodies. The dread, as she was jostled from every direction. The constriction of her lungs in the malodorous air.

Now, in an effort to compose herself, for her own sake as well as Mama's, whose face was at this moment as white as soap flakes, Emma rearranged her shawl more neatly about her shoulders. She took several long, slow breaths. Her stomach had gathered into such a knot that she was afraid she would lose the bread and cheese she'd hurriedly downed at the twelve o'clock whistle. Hunching over, she clasped herself about her middle, wincing as a band of pain grabbed the back of her neck, then travelled down both arms. Unconsciously, she ran her fingers through her dank hair, then over her face, as if to erase the shadows and lines wrought by sixy-six hours of labour that had begun on the previous Monday morning and ended an hour earlier. And for a time, she became so absorbed in her own discomfort that the tumult around her ceased to exist.

It must have been the commotion behind her, and the cries of 'He's here … Tim Coppins is here,' that returned her to the reality of her feet throbbing against her clogs.

She turned and saw him entering the taproom. A slight, bespectacled man, he struggled under the weight of the square tin box he had clutched to his chest. The crowd cleaved at its centre and became suddenly so silent that Emma could hear the fizz of the foam in the tankard of the man next to her.

Mama grabbed her arm. 'Pray, child,' she whispered, 'pray for all you are worth. For our futures lie in the hands of that man.'

Emma prayed. And her prayers were once again answered. By quarter past one, Tim Coppins, wage clerk for Brummerley's Soapworks, had announced to one hundred unlucky souls – Beth and Emma Cadman among them – that they no longer had jobs.

No more fat. No more soda. No more – what had Mr Theo called it that first day, saponification? – when the horrid boiling mass congealed into soap. No more packing and wrapping and glueing and fetching and carrying and answering everyone's beck and call. And no more Bull & Bear.

Emma was tempted to dance on the cobbles, shining steel-grey in the downpour. But one look at the desperation in Mama's face as they trudged along was enough to stem the temptation and to bring tears of remorse to her eyes. At that moment, Mama turned and looked at her. 'I know, child,' she said, 'we were just beginning to see the light, weren't we? Sometimes, I really wonder if it's all worth it. The struggling, I mean.' Her voice caught in her throat. 'I grow so weary of it.'

'But Mama,' Emma put her arm around her mother's waist, 'don't you remember what you've always said?'

Mama gave a disenchanted little laugh. 'I've said an awful lot of things, dear.'

'I mean about the door.'

'The door?'

'Yes. You remember? When one door closes, another always opens.'

'I may well have said that, dear. But now ...' She shrugged. 'I'm just not sure. All we can do is wait and see. And steel ourselves. For one thing is certain. Your Aunt Kate is not going to be pleased.'

Kate Sheene was appalled by the news.

It wasn't enough that she had lost half a dozen customers

in as many months, and that nowadays it took twice as much coal to keep the washhouse hot enough to dry the clothes because there had not been a decent drying day in Lord knew how long. Now, she had to contend with two nonworkers under her roof.

Granted, Eustace was in no danger of losing his job. And Leticia, with a year's apprenticeship behind her and her wages determined by the number of hats she sold, was doing tolerably well, for it seemed to be of scant concern to the gentry that the price of one frilled and feathered monstrosity could feed a family for a month.

Granted, too, Beth made it clear she did not expect charity. 'You will get your six shillings a week, the same as always,' she calmly said.

It was this very calmness and the apparent lack of concern in her sister's expression that infuriated Kate. Oh she would, would she? But for how long? And once the money ran out, then what? Any fool knew there was not a job to be had in all of Glinton.

As if reading Kate's mind, Beth said, 'Don't worry, Kate, something is bound to turn up.'

Well, it had better, Kate thought. And soon.

SEVENTEEN

Dreams die hard. But on a March evening in 1881, Beth's finally succumbed.

All her hopes down the cesspool, she thought, sitting at her bedroom window and watching the dwindling daylight.

Over three years of mindless monotony, of kowtowing to Kate and playing the stoic in the foolish belief that the end justified the means, the end being a sunlit future far from Glinton. Her fingers closed around the coin in the open cash box on her lap. One crown left after paying their keep. Five miserable shillings to show for their efforts. And next week she would have to dip into their nest egg.

And Emma, what kind of a life did she have to look forward to? Fifteen next week ... on the threshold of womanhood; no, past the threshold. It was six months since they'd had their little talk, the morning Emma had made a certain near-hysterical announcement.

Her daughter fifteen. Beth choked on the thought. Lord, where had the time gone? Thirty-five ... she was thirty-five. With an unsteady hand, she explored the planes of her face. Middle-aged, and here were the crow's-feet to prove it. Middle-aged, and as frightened as a lost child.

'Mama! What is it?' Emma stood, paralysed, with her back against the door. Something awful must have happened, disaster of the worst kind. Her mother never cried. Yet here she was, sobbing as if her heart was broken.

Mama got up and held out her arms. The poignancy of the gesture spurred Emma into action and she stumbled across the few feet that separated them into Mama's embrace.

'What is it? What's happened?'

'Nothing's happened. That's the problem.'

'Nothing?' Emma wriggled free and stepped back. 'Then why are you so upset?'

Blotting her tears with her sleeve, Mama gave a helpless shrug. She sat on the edge of the bed and patted the spot beside her. 'I must look a sight,' she said, running her fingers over her swollen eyes.

'No, you don't. Now – are you going to tell me?'

'What's to tell?' Mama plucked at the fabric of her skirt, then smoothed and resmoothed it over her knees.

'I am not a child. It's perfectly obvious you are hiding something from me,' Emma said, leaning forward and fixing her mother with a stern look.

Now came the smile that was supposed to fool Emma. 'The day. It's been a dreadful day. It rained before I could get the wash in and –'

'Mother, dear ...'

'Mother? Since when have you called me Mother?' She

fussed with her hair and then with a loose button on her cuff, twirling the thread around her forefinger. 'Oh, very well. But it's not nearly as bad as I might've made it sound. After all, we still have the nest egg and there's sufficient there to last us at least two years.'

Now it was time for Emma to mask her agitation with the same little smoothing motions Mama'd used. It wasn't difficult to guess the problem: they had exhausted their savings. She cringed mentally. Depressing news, though not the disaster she'd envisioned when she first caught sight of Mama's face and heard her passionate sobs. And not nearly as shattering as it could have been if she hadn't bumped into Jessie that afternoon. Of course, it was only a rumour, and Jessie had no idea how long it would be. But why not take the optimistic approach and give Mama the lift she so clearly needed. 'Chances are,' she said cheerfully, 'there will be no necessity for you to dip into the nest egg.'

Mama folded her arms and tilted her head inquiringly. 'No necessity? How …'

'I bumped into Jessie Dobbins today, and she was telling me it's almost a certainty that Brummerley's will be rehiring, and within days.'

'Within days?' Mama's eyes widened.

'Yes. So at the very worst, you might have to do a *little* dipping.'

'Oh, my dear, what would I do without you?'

'I dare say you'd manage,' Emma said dryly.

Mama rose and stretched. 'Not today I wouldn't. Here I've been playing the silly ninny, when mothers are supposed to be so strong. While you, my dear daughter' – she lifted her shoulders and made an open-palmed gesture – 'are exhibiting all the maturity of a grown woman.'

'But I am a grown woman, don't you agree, Rex?'

The dog trembled, his bloodshot eyes regarding her dolefully from beneath the halo of soapsuds.

Emma giggled. 'Oh, you poor darling. Don't look so down in the mouth. It'll soon be over.' She picked up the jug and began to rinse him off. 'Besides, think of how nifty you are going to look.' Seeing the telltale expression that warned he was on the verge of shaking himself and splattering the whole kitchen, she quickly grabbed the towel and threw it over him. A deep breath to fortify herself, and she hauled him out of the tin tub and onto the rug. Once he was reasonably dry, she let him go. And he went into an ecstasy of rolling, while Emma disposed of the evidence.

Nowadays, bathing Rex was one of the high spots of her life. It didn't happen often, for it could only be accomplished when the Sheenes were out, as they were this evening: Uncle Eustace at his trade union meeting, Aunt Kate visiting an ailing friend, and Leticia – Lord knew where she was. But Emma had overheard her say that she wouldn't be home until after ten. As for Mama, she was a co-conspirator. And if it hadn't been for the fact that she'd retired early and was no doubt already asleep, she would have been deriving as much amusement from the dog's antics as Emma.

'So ...' She snapped her fingers; Rex strutted over to her and flopped at her feet. 'Do you or do you not agree that I am a grown woman?' She gave an inward chuckle. This was going to be a one-sided conversation. One thump of his tail and he was away, already snoring like an old man.

Curling her legs under herself, she stared into the fire. A sudden sense of moroseness settled over her. What was so wonderful about being a woman, anyway? It meant that you bled once a month and suffered the accompanying aches and pains and the feeling of wanting to weep for no reason at all; you coped with the discomfort of the 'Sunday Dusters' (Mama's name for the bulky cotton pads) strapped between your legs. And you could bear children, though what the connection was, Mama had not explained.

Emma drew in a pensive breath. So many mysteries to unravel.

'No, Emma, God doesn't plant a seed in the mother's stomach. It's a mite more complicated than that.' Jessie, this time, and the first episode of a serial which was to have continued with their Saturday afternoons by the canal.

Except, of course, the afternoons had petered out a year and a half earlier along with the job at Brummerley's, and Jessie had left home to go into service as a kitchen maid.

Just as well. It wasn't healthy to dwell on things of that nature, which was no doubt why she experienced a vague uneasiness whenever she allowed such untoward thoughts to occupy her. Healthy or not, though, it was a challenge keeping the thoughts at bay when you burned with curiosity – curiosity which, according to Mama's 'You will find out when you marry,' must wait to be satisfied.

Marriage, the be-all and end-all. Every girl's dream. No, not every girl's. There must be those, like her, who found the idea somehow abhorrent. Not at Brummerley's, though. There it had always seemed to be the major topic of conversation: this person's beau and that person's beau; who was walking out with whom, whether or not it was getting serious, and when the question might be popped. Surely there was more to life.

Obviously not from Leticia's viewpoint. She had a regular procession of beaux; it was akin to the changing of the guard, with a different fellow every time you blinked an eye. And her taste? Emma shuddered in spite of the heat from the fire, as her mind returned to an August evening the year before when she'd been on her way home from a laundry delivery.

Her route had taken her by the vacant Gibbons house. A place of sombre mystery as solid as the granite of its construction, it was the only detached house in the area; the only one, too, with a patch of garden and an ancient, gnarled apple tree overhanging the front path.

For two years, so the story went, the house had been in the hands of family solicitors. But all attempts to sell or rent it (and at a bargain price) had met no success, for it had been the scene of a violent crime – a triple murder and suicide, with Tobias Gibbons shooting his wife and two children, then turning the pistol on himself. And there were those who swore it was haunted.

Not Emma, though. As far as she was concerned (and in

keeping with her mother's philosophy), it was 'absolute bosh.'

In fact, she thought, pausing before the rusty gate, it was rather a charming house, despite its boarded-up windows and unkempt grounds. And look at the apples, so rosy and inviting.

Well – Emma bit into a golden Cox's Pippin – their loss was *her* gain; if it hadn't been for everyone's unwarranted fears, the tree would long since have been stripped bare, she thought moments later, as she filled her apron pockets with fruit. She was about to continue on her way, when a sound rather like the mewing of a kitten arrested her. Wiping the juice from the corner of her mouth and stopping in mid-chew, she cocked her head. Silence. At the same instant that she sank her teeth into the crisp fruit, she heard the eerie cackle. She dropped the apple and stood transfixed, the hairs at the back of her neck rising. There it came again. She could feel her eyes straining out of their sockets.

'Aw, come on. I didn't come here to play no games.'

Emma blinked in surprise. There was nothing ghostly about that. It was a human voice, a decidedly masculine voice, coming from beyond the front door, which – and she hadn't noticed before – was slightly ajar.

Laughter, now, feminine laughter – high and piercing. And then, 'Percival, don't be a naughty boy.'

Frowning, for something in the female voice nagged at her, Emma stole along the path. An odd grunting, similar to the noise Rex made when he was hot on the trail of some quarry, brought her to a breathless halt on the top step.

'No, Percival … you mustn't. A girl has to think of her reputa-'

Lord … Emma clapped a hand to her mouth. She would know that voice anywhere.

What on earth was …? Peeping around the door jamb, she froze.

The scene paraded across her mind in heart-stopping little jerks. Leticia – and it *was* she, there wasn't a doubt – on her back amid a pile of sacking. A man straddling her, one hand pinning her arms over her head, the other fumbling beneath her skirts. 'No, no!' Leticia thrashed about, worked one of her hands free, and pounded at his chest. But to no avail. With a laugh that had the ring of victory to it, he pinned her again and lunged his face to hers.

Something exploded in Emma, slashing through her trance. The brute, attacking her cousin! She threw her weight against the door and, fists at the ready, charged across the room.

She had no memory of what had happened between the time the man scrambled away under the storm of her blows and when Leticia's face swam into focus, livid as a snake's. 'Leave 'im be, you daft little twit,' she shrieked, seizing Emma by the shoulders and shaking her until she was limp. 'Now, get outta here, snoop. And if you ever tell a living soul, it'll be more than your life's worth.'

And that hadn't been the end of it, either. The next day Leticia had issued a further warning: 'One word in Ma or Pa's ear, or in anyone else's, about what you saw, an' I'll make sure that you and your mother are out on the street just' – her fingers snapped under Emma's nose – 'like that.'

Recognizing the tenuousness of her own and Mama's position, Emma had guarded the secret as closely as she had guarded her total confusion and her simmering fury at the injustice of it: she had jeopardized her own safety only to receive a tongue-lashing, and a threatening one at that.

Leticia's behaviour was no less baffling to Emma now than it had been back then. She unfurled her legs and propped them on the brass fender. But then, who could figure out Leticia? Look at the way her attitude had changed after – Lord – Emma sniggered into her hands. Rex lifted his head and then rolled over onto his back. She trailed the toe of her slipper over his belly. 'Remember that Saturday, Rex? Of course you do. You enjoyed it as much as I did.'

She grinned. Mama might not credit her with quite as much maturity if she could see her now, gloating over the memory of that September night.

Aunt Kate had been out, visiting a friend. Emma and her

mother, occupying chairs each side of the fireplace, with Rex stretched between them on the rug, were chattering to each other and to Uncle Eustace, who sat at the kitchen table, tinkering with a watch.

When Leticia came breezing in and said, 'Where's Ma?' Uncle Eustace answered absently, 'She's off visitin' Hilda Baxter.'

'Hilda Baxter. How could she do that? My hair!' She clapped her hands to her head. 'Ma was supposed to curl it for me. I'd purely die if I had to go to the dance lookin' like this.'

Ma was supposed to curl it for me. The words sounded a little bell in Emma's head. Glancing up from her book, she said, 'Leticia, I'd be happy to do your hair for you.'

'You?' Leticia eyed her disbelievingly. 'But you ...'

'Oh, I've done Mama's scores of times, haven't I, Mama?' Mama didn't respond. She was counting stitches.

Toying with a lank-looking strand of her hair, Leticia studied her aunt's bowed head for a moment. 'Well, if you really think ...'

Emma leaped up. 'Why don't you sit at the table while I heat the curling iron?'

A few minutes later, she stood, with tongs poised, at her cousin's back. 'By the time I'm finished with you, Leticia, you are going to look positively ravishing.'

'I'd better' came the mumbled response.

'Oh, you will, Leticia, you will.'

Rex was the first to notice. He struggled to his feet, nose twitching. Uncle Eustace peered over the top of his spectacles. 'Smells as if something's singein',' he said. Mama, who had apparently been dozing, jerked awake. Her eyes snapped wide at the same instant her mouth dropped open.

'Oh my.' Emma slowly shook her head, 'I'm dreadfully sorry, Leticia dear, I'm afraid I must have overheated the tongs.'

Lord, what a fuss Leticia made. And Uncle Eustace made matters a thousand times worse with his suggestion that all she had to do was cut off 'them frizzled ends' and she'd look as pretty as Emma had when she and Aunt Beth first arrived.

Unable to resist the temptation, Emma had added in a voice dripping with sympathy, 'Your Papa's right. And think of it this way, you will only look like a Charity Girl for a few months, just as I did.'

Oh, what splendid sweetness there was to revenge, Emma had thought, until Leticia's terrible wail pulled her up sharply. Every action had its consequences. The scales had been balanced, all right. But at what cost?

'Struth, but how nervous she'd been, anticipating that at any moment she and Mama would be told to pack their bags.

But things had taken a surprising and happy turn. That childish act of revenge had brought her her cousin's apparent respect. Oh, Leticia hadn't said a word. She hadn't needed to, though; it was there in her eyes, a kind of wary admiration.

A good lesson to remember: You were only a victim as long as you chose that role.

But what a shame one had to be nasty in order to earn respect. What a shame, too, that she and Leticia couldn't have become friends. Though there was something to be said for mutual toleration.

The sound of a piece of coal falling onto the hearth brought her out of her disjointed musings. Rising, she reached for the shovel, scooped up the glowing cinder, and returned it to the fire. She stretched and yawned and then stood with her back to the heat.

My, but she had waxed as eloquent tonight as she had earlier with Mama. What a shame it couldn't have been the truth about the rehiring – the 'within days' part, at least. Enough. She slapped herself on the leg and Rex was instantly on his feet, tail wagging. No sense in looking back. She and Mama had come this far, hadn't they?

There were bound to be brighter times ahead.

EIGHTEEN

Emma was right.

As time passed in its inexorable fashion and spring gave way to summer, Glinton once again donned her smutty mantle and joyfully retuned her ears to the reassuring symphony of Brummerley's going at full bore.

By July, everyone had been called back. Though work was no panacea for Emma, it meant that, after a hiatus of almost two years, she could resume her friendship with Jessie. And naturally, Emma was happy to be a wage-earner again; happier still for the companionship of the girls who, now that she was fifteen, drew her into their coterie, treating her as one of them.

Physically, she was. For her childish skinniness had given way to womanly curves. Others saw in her doe eyes, wide mouth, and slender pointed face a pixieish beauty. Though she thought of herself as ordinary, she was thankful to have inherited her mother's firm, full bosom, tiny waist, and rounded hips, and disappointed that, at just five feet, she was still half a head shorter than Mama. Lack of sunlight had rid Emma of the bane of her younger years, her freckles. And maturity had muted the blatant red of her hair – upswept now in a corona of plaits – to a lush apricot shade. In appearance, Emma was a woman.

But inwardly, she was a child.

During those first few weeks, listening to the girls' gossip, with its innuendoes about men and women and love and Mr Theo (who had married the year before and no longer seemed to pose a threat), though she went through the motions – giggling behind her hand with the rest of them, exchanging knowing look for knowing look – Emma continued to be as mystified as ever and painfully aware of her own naïveté.

134

It was a chance remark of Jessie's one Saturday afternoon, the first week in August, that finally rolled away the stone.

They were lying alongside each other in the grass by the boat house, drying off after their weekly swim, when Jessie said, 'I saw Ruth Frampton last week. Oh, an' that little Ernie's a lovely lad.'

Emma rolled over onto her stomach and propped herself on her elbows. 'Ernie? Who on earth is Ernie?'

''Er son. Two an' a half 'e is an' a right sturdy little fella.'

'Her son?' Frowning, Emma sat up and raked a hand through her damp hair. 'Gosh, I had not a notion she was married. In fact, I thought she had probably died. I mean, she was so ill, wasn't she, when she left and you ...'

'She ain't wed. And ill?' Jessie chortled and turned to look at Emma. 'She wasn't ill, unless you call bein' in the family way ill.'

'Being in the family way? Isn't that the same as ...?'

'Expectin' a baby.' Now Jessie sat up.

'But you just said she wasn't married. How could she possibly ...?'

'Lordy, you don't 'ave to be wed to have a baby. All you need is to have the curse, to start with ... and ...'

Emma blinked. 'The curse?'

'You know, the monthly bleedin'. Like you told me you started with a few months back. I mean, *you* could have a baby ... *I* could have a baby – if we was loose, that is, and we ...'

Emma's mind wandered. Loose? There was that puzzling word she'd heard bandied about so often. Moll had said Ruth Frampton was loose. A baby? So that was the reason she'd been so enormous; there had been a baby growing in her stomach. But the way Mama had explained – she drew a strand of her hair across her lower lip – you could only have a baby if you had a husband. And yet? 'Jessie,' she said out loud, interrupting whatever it was her friend was saying, 'what, exactly, does being loose mean and what does it have to do with babies and ...?'

'You don't know?' Jessie's dark eyes widened. 'Lordy, I thought you bein' fifteen an' all, that ...' She puckered her mouth thoughtfully. 'Well, let's see now, 'ow to tell you?' She toyed with the tip of her nose and then folded her arms. 'Well, first off' - she scooted around and Emma did likewise, so they were facing each other - 'let's find out what you *do* know. Men is different from women, right?'

Emma nodded.

'And you know what makes 'em different?'

'Of course. Men have ...' With the vivid picture that flashed across her mind, Emma's voice trailed off. Bowing her head, she examined the faded print of her calico skirt. She knew about the anatomy of men. She chafed her arms and shivered. But what she didn't know - and this was the disturbing part - was *how* she knew. Jane's brothers, she must have seen Jane's brothers and forgotten about ...

Jessie's voice cut into her confused thoughts, 'Men have things. And to make a baby, they poke their thing into a woman, down 'ere.' She indicated the spot between her thighs.

Emma drew in a sharp breath and plucked at the skin in the hollow of her throat, while Jessie continued: 'Sounds fearful, don't it? But they say it ain't, 'cept at first, when a woman's tight. An' speakin' of tight,' she giggled, 'brings us to your other question.'

'My other question,' Emma said blankly, staring off, still stunned by Jessie's revelation.

'About what it means to be loose.' Jessie tapped her on the knee. 'Are you listenin'?'

Emma willed her eyes away from the brackish waters of the canal and said, 'Yes, of course I am.'

'Well, it's like this.' Jessie stretched and cupped her hands behind her head. 'Men can't help their lustin', see, especially them like Mr Theo' - she smirked - 'who've enough lust in 'em for ten men. It's the way the Lord made 'em. An' it's a wife's duty to submit to a man. Leastways, that's the way any *normal* Christian woman looks at it, 'cause she knows it's what the Lord intended for 'er. Then' - she brought her arms down and plucked a stalk of grass, waving it to emphasize her point - 'you've got them women who ain't normal, ain't

Christian neither. Them what likes bein' poked, what throws theirselves at men. And on top of that kind, you've your honest-to-goodness whore who'll sell 'er favours for a shillin'.'

'Sell?' Emma brought her palms to her burning cheeks. 'Are you saying women actually take money for …'

Jessie's head wagged. 'That I am, and …' She stopped and looked at Emma searchingly. 'Am I tellin' you too much all at once? You look a bit white around the gills.'

'No,' Emma said. She had come this far. She may as well hear it all. 'Carry on, Jessie. I am all ears.'

By the time the afternoon was over, Emma felt as if a storm had swept through her mind.

To think of the pitfalls womanhood held. To think of men pursuing a woman's virtue with all the ardour of a dog panting after a rabbit. It was perfectly horrid. And it only served to reinforce her suspicion that the majority of men must surely be brutes. Look at Jessie's father; imagine Mrs Dobbins having to submit to that disgusting lout. And Theodore Brummerley. And Leticia's attacker. Attacker? Lord, but now it all made sense. He hadn't been an attacker at all, and that was why Leticia'd been so furious.

To think she'd envied her cousin her pretty ribbons and scents and trinkets, presents from admirers, she'd called them, marks of their esteem – Trevor's and Ben's and Abe's and a dozen others whose names escaped Emma. Presents from admirers? Marks of their esteem. Why, Leticia was little better than a … No. She would not say it, that word whose meaning she had just learned. Leticia *was* her cousin. They shared the same blood. And would Leticia come to a bad end, as Ruth Frampton had? If she did, it would certainly be no more than she deserved, for a meaner-dispositioned girl did not exist. And didn't the Good Book say, 'As ye soweth, so shall ye reap'?

It was almost a year to the day later when Emma discovered that Leticia *had* reaped what she had sown.

The first hint had come with Aunt Kate's and Leticia's raised voices from beyond the closed parlour door when Emma arrived home from work on that sultry evening in late July. Not once, in all their years with the Sheenes, had Emma heard her aunt utter a cross word to her daughter. Yet here she was screaming gibberish at the top of her lungs.

'What on earth is going on, Mama?' Emma asked, when she went upstairs.

'I've no idea.' Mama frowned at the fresh tirade from below. 'It must be something quite dreadful, though. And I'm sure we shall find out soon enough.'

A fortnight elapsed before they did. Leticia had spent most of her time at home in her room, making only the occasional pale-faced, red-eyed appearance, while Kate and Eustace, on an almost daily basis, had been conferring behind closed doors with a Mr and Mrs Cooper.

It was dinnertime on that September day. Uncle Eustace had stayed late at work and Leticia was in her bedroom, having answered her mother's pleas to come downstairs with an ear-splitting 'I'm not hungry' and a slam of her door.

Tension hung like a thundercloud in the silent kitchen as Aunt Kate passed the Yorkshire pudding and gravy. Emma grimaced behind her hand, knowing she would be expected to fill up on the leaden pudding, before the beef was served.

Kate took one bite, laid down her knife and fork, and touched her napkin to her lips. Without looking up, she said, 'Reckon you're bound to find out soon enough, so I may as well tell you now. Leticia's landed 'erself in ... trouble.'

'Trouble?' Mama's eyes widened. 'Oh, dear, do you mean ...?'

'Aye.' Aunt Kate's head came up and she brushed a silvered loop of hair back from her forehead. Then her fingers found a crease in the linen tablecloth and worried at it. 'There's to be a weddin' next month. A small one. No fuss and palaver. And of course, she'll be expectin' you' – she nodded in Emma's direction – 'to be 'er bridesmaid.'

'I see.' Emma's bland response betrayed nothing of her thoughts. So Leticia's easy ways had caught up with her. Jolly decent of Aunt Kate to issue her edict. No 'Would you like?'

or 'She would appreciate it if you'd consider.' Taken for granted, as always.

'The young fella's name is Cecil.' Aunt Kate took a quick gulp of water. 'Cecil Cooper. Leticia's known him for quite a time.'

Quite a time. Emma almost laughed out loud. If he was the one she thought he was, that stout fellow with the turn in his eye, he had only been on the scene for a few weeks.

'Oh, and there's one other thing.' Aunt Kate dabbed at her mouth with the back of her hand and then cleared her throat, 'I shall need your help gettin' the room ready.'

Mama arched her eyebrows 'The room?'

'Aye. The young couple'll be livin' here, in Leticia's room. It'll need a fresh coat of whitewash and the curtains and linens and whatnot'll need washing, the furniture rearrangin', too, so as to make room for ...'

'I understand,' Mama said with a weak smile. 'And how soon are we to begin this refurbishing?'

'Oh, right away. I thought we could get started the day after tomorrow.'

The interior of the washhouse was hot as a foundry. At three o'clock, the fire laid that morning and continuously stoked roared like a funeral pyre. Air that was already rife with the odours of soap and soda and starch, and a sodden assortment of bed linens and curtain draped over four wooden maidens, was made even more suffocating by great billows of steam rising from the copper boiler.

With the thump of Mama's sadiron on the ironing table, the swish of the clothes dolly that Aunt Kate was fiercely rotating in one of the three washtubs, and the squeak of the mangle (badly in need of oiling) as Emma fed sheets through the rollers, conversation was impossible. Besides, it was Aunt Kate's philosophy that breath wasted in talking could be better used in working.

What a slave driver her aunt was, Emma thought, turning the handle and gritting her teeth against the dull ache in her lower back. And where was Leticia while she and Mama worked their fingers to the elbow? Where else but languishing in her room? Lord … She paused and closed her eyes. Talk about making her bed and lying in it. The girl certainly …

'Gawd-a-mighty!' The shrill of Kate's voice severed the thought.

Emma came upright and swivelled about.

Hands on her hips, face smouldering, Aunt Kate loomed over Mama and said, 'Downright carelessness, that's what it is. It'll have to be boiled again, if it isn't ruined already. Here, give it to me.' As she made a grab for the pillowcase, her elbow caught the iron. Its scorching tip must have grazed Mama, for she let out an agonized little cry, snatched her hand away, and then cradled her arm to her body.

Righting the iron, Aunt Kate muttered under her breath as Emma wiped her wet hands on her apron and crossed the flags. 'Are you all right, Mama?' she asked, with an anxious dip of her head.

There was no response. Mama was obviously intent on holding back her tears. And when Emma caught sight of the angry red welt above the wristbone, she understood why. She winced in empathy and, unsure what else to do, gently patted her mother's shoulder as Aunt Kate said, 'Well – you didn't answer. *Are* you all right?'

Mama drew in a shaky breath and swallowed hard.

'Or does this mean,' Aunt Kate said, thrusting her thumbs in the waistband of her apron, 'you'll not be able to work for the rest of the day?'

Mama's tongue moistened her lips, and she stared at her sister for a long time. Finally, she spoke through clenched teeth: 'As a matter of fact, you are absolutely right. I shall not be able to work. Nor would I … even if you had not' – she waved her injured arm before her sister's nose – 'done this.'

Aunt Kate backed up slightly, her expression one of puzzled unease.

'For I swear,' Mama carried on, her voice sounding stronger, more confident by the second, 'you are such an ill-tempered biddy, you would try the patience of a saint. And a saint I am not. I am a woman trying to do her best. But the best' – her words were speeding up and a faint wash of pink crept up her neck and into her face – 'is not good enough for you, sister dear. Oh no ...' She paused, her bosom rising and falling rapidly while Aunt Kate, looking stunned now, took a couple of faltering steps backward and steadied herself on the brickwork of the boiler.

'... nothing is good enough for you, Kate, is it?'

'Well, I ...'

'I have made allowances for you, sister. Allowances enough to fill the Crystal Palace. But no more. If you need help, I suggest you get it from that lazy daughter of yours, for we' – she turned and smiled at Emma – 'my daughter and myself plan to take the rest of our afternoon-off *off*.'

The tension at the table was a palpable thing, like some indigestible lump of fat wedged in Emma's throat. Aunt Kate had called them down for tea as if nothing had happened. 'Mama is indisposed,' Emma had said. And so far, that had been the extent of their mealtime conversation, hers, her aunt's, and Leticia's, with Uncle Eustace not expected home until later.

Leticia – doubtless because she was, as they said, 'eating for two' – attacked her food with more than her usual vigour, washing it down with disgustingly noisy slurps of water, her eyes over the rim of her glass gleaming like wet stones.

She knows, Emma thought, staring at the slice of bread on her plate, her appetite lost in the uneasy silence.

Finally, Aunt Kate spoke. 'If you are not going to eat, Emma, then leave the table and –'

Emma was on her feet and pushing in her chair before her aunt had time to finish. 'I'm sorry, I'm just not hungry. I think I shall ... I had better go and ... I'll do the dishes later,' she called over her shoulder as she fled for the stairs.

A dejected-looking Mama – pasty-faced, eyelids puffy – sat propped against her pillows, her hand immersed in the basin of cold water Emma had filled earlier. (Smearing a burn with butter had never seemed to help in the past, and one of the girls at Brummerley's had suggested the cold-water remedy as far more effective.)

'How is it feeling, Mama?' Emma sank down at the foot of the bed.

'Better. At least the throbbing has abated. Oh, dear, dear, dear.' She lifted her shoulders wearily. 'I really did a splendid job of practising what I preach, didn't I?'

'What do you mean?'

'My grand speech about curbing tempers and keeping the peace.' A tear rolled down her cheek. 'Your mother, Emma, is a fool. A silly, silly fool.'

'You are not,' Emma said defensively.

'Oh, but I am.' She slumped back and sighed. 'Of course, I shall have to apologize. There is nothing else for it. Go down on bended knee, if necessary. But not now.' She winced. 'I could not possibly face her tonight, nor do I wish to so much as think about her at this moment. So will you read to me, dear … something pleasant and soothing.'

'Of course.' Emma rose. 'What shall it be? The Bible or poetry?'

'Oh, I don't know. Why don't you choose?'

'Very well.' Emma reached for the Bible on the nightstand. When she picked up the weighty black-leather volume, she saw the envelope hidden beneath it. 'Oh, did you get a letter from Mrs McDonough?'

'Gracious, yes. It came in this morning's post. And it completely slipped my mind. Let's see what she has to say.'

The letter in her free hand, Mama leaned towards the light from the window. 'Let's see now. Seraphine had a lovely birthday party. Albert chipped his front tooth.' Her eyes moved rapidly down the page. 'What else … good Lord!'

'What is it?' Emma said quickly.

'Wait a minute … I am not quite finished,' said Mama. 'Oh my!' She waved the piece of paper excitedly. 'I do not believe my eyes. It is nothing short of manna from Heaven.'

'Mother!' Almost exploding with curiosity, Emma clenched her fists against her breasts. 'What?'

142

'Here.' With an impish grin, Mama dangled the letter before Emma. 'Why don't you read it for yourself?'

NINETEEN

Emma snatched the letter.

'Don't bother with the first few paragraphs,' Mama said. 'Begin where it says, "It seems Lucy's sister Martha."'

'It seems Lucy's sister Martha is emigrating to America with her husband and family and vacating a position as laundress to the Earl of Chearden's family. Chearden, incidentally, according to Benjamin, is some fifty miles west of where you are and quite close to the sea. Well, dear, on hearing this news, I did the most dreadfully presumptuous thing. Because the job must be filled by mid-September, I wrote on your behalf to a Mrs Dawfield, head housekeeper at Chearden Hall, telling her of your circumstances. And Benjamin added a postscript telling of your experience these past years, helping your sister in her business. And he concluded by vouching for your good character. To assure you of the job (I do hope I did the right thing), I said that if she was willing to hire you sight unseen, I would personally guarantee to reimburse your wages if things did not work out.'

Emma stopped reading and looked up. 'A job,' she whispered wonderingly. 'Mrs McDonough is saying you might have a –'

'Yes. Yes. And not just any job. She says later that it comes with a partially furnished house; rent-free, too.' Mama squirmed in obvious excitement, almost tipping over the basin of water.

Emma cringed. 'Your wrist. Be careful,' she said. 'Oh, it's nothing.' As if to prove it, Mama withdrew her hand and set the basin on the nightstand. Her eyes shone and, despite the grey shadows below them and the dusting of silver in her hair, she looked almost girlish. 'Flora also goes on to say the laundress is allowed to take in extra washing. You realize what that means, don't you?'

Emma shrugged uncertainly.

'It means we would have our own business. Our own business, Emma. Just think of it.'

Emma constantly thought about Chearden Hall and the rent-free house and the business over the next few days, which on the one hand turned out to be tolerable ones because Mama apologized profusely and they both did everything in their power to please Aunt Kate, but on the other were excruciating. For the wait seemed interminable.

Finally, it was over. That day – September 7, 1882 – would always stand out in Emma's memory.

As she stood over Mama, who was seated in the chair by the bedroom window, her heartbeat quickened. How queer it was, she thought, watching her mother tear open the envelope and tensely scan its contents in a reenactment of that day five years earlier. Odd, how their lives seemed to be governed by letters. Odd, too, the way Mama was looking at her, now, her face impassive. Not a hint of emotion. Except for, yes, a minute upward quirk at the corners of her neat little mouth, and a slight crinkling about the eyes.

'Oh, dear,' Mama said, swinging her head from side to side, 'whatever are we going to do, now ...?'

Emma's spirits plummeted. Oh, Lord, it had all come to nought. She closed her eyes against the threatening tears, but flashed them open again when Mama said, 'How in creation are we going to furnish half a house with only three trunks to our name?'

'Mother!' She bared her teeth and raised a threatening fist. 'You tease!'

'Listen, listen.' Mama waved her into silence:

Dear Mrs Cadman,
On the recommends of your friend, Mrs McDonough, I

am right pleased to offer you the job what was once Martha Lumsden's, laundress to the Chearden family at a yearly wage of fourteen pound, ten. The job comes with house and coal. If you will kindly report to me on Monday, September eighteenth, in kitchen of Chearden Hall, I shall be waiting. Ask anyone in the village and they shall tell you the way. The train runs every hour to Marespond and it needs a mile walk to the village from there. Send a telegram to me that you accepts.

Beaming, Mama set the letter aside and sprang to her feet. She seized Emma by the shoulders and shook her. 'Do you realize what this means – our sentence is over. Eleven days and we shall be in Chearden. We are going to be free, Emma. Free!' she yelled at the top of her lungs, twirling Emma around on the spot until they were both shrieking with hysterical laughter.

Through it all, though, Emma caught the sound of rapid footsteps on the stairs and brought her mother to a stop, pressing a warning finger to her lips. As they stood frozen, staring into each other's eyes in mock terror, Aunt Kate hammered on the door and said, 'Gawdamighty, what's all the commotion?'

'Commotion,' Mama murmured. 'Did my sister say commotion?' She fluttered her lashes like a coquette and smiled a devious little smile. 'Oh, but we must always give your dear aunt what she wants, mustn't we?' She signalled Emma close and whispered in her ear.

'Are you two goin' to answer me?' Aunt Kate's voice climbed the scale.

'Shall we?' Mama tittered and brought her forefinger up like a baton. 'One ... two ... three,' they counted in unison, trying to stifle their giggles. And then, gripping each other by the shoulders, they uttered an ear-rending 'Hurrah!'

PART THREE

1884-1886

TWENTY

Who would have dreamed that something as ordinary as a line hung with washing could bring such pride, Emma laughingly thought one April morning in 1884 as she pegged out the last shirt and, like a dance master inspecting a corps de ballet, moved along the row of fluttering garments, straightening a ruffle here, smoothing a lace-edged cuff there.

But then – she stood back, thumbs jammed under her apron bib – by no stretch of the imagination could these twenty-three shirts whose finest Indian cotton she had coaxed to dazzling blue-whiteness be considered 'ordinary,' for they were, after all, the property of Lionel Gerard Sedgewick, the nineteenth Earl of Chearden: widower, father of four daughters, and owner of thousands of acres that rolled to the horizon like a bolt of multicoloured fabric, tied with the meandering turquoise ribbon of the river.

Emma had yet to set eyes upon the Earl. But because dirty linen told a great deal about its owner – size, eating habits, proclivities – she already had a mental picture of him. She knew, too, the man was eccentric; anyone who wore three shirts a day and five on Sundays had to be. Eccentric or not, though, the Earl *was* their benefactor. And were it not for him, they would be unable to call Beech Cottage home.

Home ... a comforting word, Emma thought, feeling a surge of pleasure when she turned and surveyed the house.

Named for the stand of beech trees marking the northern perimeter of its half acre of grounds, it was a sprawling U-shaped structure, crowned by a dilapidated slate roof. One side contained the washhouse, the other the henhouse, and the centre the living quarters.

Two hundred years had mellowed the original red of its foot-thick sandstone walls to a dusky pink. Ivy spread over the building's face like giant fingers probing the black-framed windows and under the eaves.

Atop the crumbling chimney stack was a weather vane in the shape of a rooster, its iron plumage one moment silhouetted against the aqua sky and the next instant veiled in drifting smoke. Every so often, the bird pirouetted lazily; its rusty cries mingled with the chirp of sparrows and the bickering of a couple of magpies who strutted like dandies in evening dress before the three worn steps leading to the hefty metal-studded door.

'Stop it, the two of you,' Emma called, squatting beside the flower bed bordering the lawn to touch the proud yellow trumpets of the daffodils. It was too glorious a morning for squabbles, with the day already balmy and the smell of summer, even now, in the air.

She smiled and lifted her chin, letting the breeze massage her face, breathing in the fragrance of apple and hawthorn blossoms, of fresh greenery and newly turned earth.

If spring was like this, then what would summer be like? Splendid, surely. For this year she would have a companion with whom to share her leisure time. Two companions, if one included Hope's son, Oliver. And of course, one must, for mother and child were inseparable.

Sitting cross-legged on the grass, Emma turned her mind to her friend, Hope Windom, a better friend than Jane or Jessie had ever been. Not that the two girls hadn't had their places: Jane as a playmate, Jessie as a confidante, a solver of life's mysteries, and, over the years since their departure from Glinton, a sporadic bearer of news – gossip actually – titbits about the Brummerley girls and that positive *plum* about the Sheenes.

Emma (Mama, too) still had difficulty believing it of mild Uncle Eustace. But from all accounts he had become so fed up with a layabout son-in-law who had not worked since before his marriage, and so distracted by twin granddaughters who had seemingly inherited their mother's and grandmother's vixenish temperaments, that one day twelve months ago, he had up and left with only the clothes on his back. It wasn't more than two months later that Cecil (Leticia's husband) followed suit, but *he* took up with a trollop just three streets away.

With a twig, Emma poked at a clod of earth. She nodded wryly. Leticia deserved all of it; Aunt Kate, too. Still, you couldn't help but feel a bit sorry for them and glad for kindhearted Uncle Eustace – assuming he'd found a measure of happiness.

People's lives certainly *did* take different courses. Imagine, Jane married. Jessie, too, and a mother already, with interests vastly different from Emma's own. It was inevitable that their link, grown threadbare with time, would break.

Emma picked at the dirt under her fingernails. Odd, but no sense of loss or sadness came with the realization. Then, at eighteen, one learned to be accepting. And one looked for something deeper, too, in friendships.

How long had it been now, since she and Hope had met? She clasped her hands and whirled one thumb around the other. Three months? No, two. There had still been a late snow on the ground, which had caused her to lose her footing that mortifying day. Lord – she cupped her cheeks in her palms – the memory of it still made her blush.

The day had begun pleasantly enough with the half-mile walk along the winding, oak-flanked road to Chearden Hall to collect the week's laundry from Mrs Dawfield, including the paper-wrapped parcel with an inordinate amount of twine around it – the 'Sunday Dusters.' Their Ladyships' unmentionables, always segregated from the rest of the washing.

Perhaps … Emma loosened the ties of her sunbonnet and squinted up at the sky … if the 'Sunday Dusters' had not been segregated, those two louts might not have latched onto the parcel. She stretched out her legs and smoothed her holland apron over her knees. The gall of them, waylaying her as they had, tossing the parcel back and forth, back and forth, until it burst and its contents – she covered her mouth with a fist – lay strewn about, obscenely crimson against the snow. She smoothed her hair back and closed her eyes. But then, of course, if the youths had not been bent on mischief that morning, Hope would never have come to her rescue.

She fidgeted inwardly, picturing herself in blind, tearful panic, scrambling around on all fours – sport for those two yokels who gaped and guffawed. She pictured, too, the tall, willowy young woman, elegant hat perched atop her honey-coloured hair, suddenly appearing as if out of nowhere. Lord, but hadn't she put them in their places? Whatever she'd said in a low but authoritative tone, something touching their Mama and the next time she came into the woman's shop, had sent the pair scuttling off like cockerels without tail feathers.

'How do you do,' the woman had said, helping Emma to her feet and then shaking her by the hand. 'My name is Hope Windom. I own the milliner's shop in the village.' She smiled compassionately. 'Rather fortunate that I was delivering a hat to Miss Grisele.'

Rather fortunate? Grinning, Emma rolled onto her stomach and rested her chin on her folded arms. It had been destiny, no doubt about it, the Lord moving in mysterious ways, His wonders to perform. And there was one of His wonders a few inches from her nose – a beetle with an irridescent green body. She plucked a blade of grass to tickle the insect's back when the clang of the gate from behind cut short her nature study. Flipping over, she leaped to her feet, her pulse quickening at the sight of the stranger striding towards her.

He was an elderly man, tall and barrel-chested, with old-fashioned Dundreary side whiskers, silver like the monk's fringe of hair encircling his bald pate. He must have tethered his horse beyond the privet hedge, for she could see its chestnut head.

'So you're the one Dawfield's been telling me about,' he yelled as he reached her.

At the riding crop being wagged a scant distance from her nose, she took a couple of frightened steps backward, her heart hammering in her throat. Lord, but he looked cross, his blue eyes snapping and his jowls, purple against the white ruffle at his neck, aquiver.

'Though dashed if I can believe it, for you're such a little chit of a thing.'

Unsure how to respond, Emma took a defensive stance, feet planted squarely, chin up, as he began to pace and swat flies with the crop's leather loop. Judging from his broadcloth frock coat with its silk-faced lapels, well-cut riding breeches, and handsome knee-high boots, he was a man of some means.

'Nonetheless ...' He paused before her, leaning in and studying her as though she were some unusual insect specimen. 'If Dawfield says it, then by Jove it must be true. Well, is it?'

Emma frowned in bewilderment.

'Shirts, girl?'

She found her tongue. 'Shirts?'

'Dash it all ...' He gestured impatiently in the direction of the washing line. '*My* shirts.'

His shirts. Heavens. She moistened her lips with her tongue. Then he must be the Earl of Chearden!

'Do you or do you not' – his face was so close now, she could see hairs sprouting from his nostrils, hear the faint whistle of breath through the wide space in his front teeth – 'wash my shirts?'

'Yes, I have. I mean, I ...'

Straightening, he flashed a smile. 'Well, my dear, you are doing a damnably fine job – capital, in fact. And a job well done deserves a reward, wouldn't you say?'

Emma's relief was so strong, it rendered her speechless.

''Course you would. Now, what shall it be?' He stared beyond her, forehead knotted. Then with a hoot of laughter he said, 'By George, I've got it. You shall have a title. You'd like that, wouldn't you, girl?'

A title? How preposterous. Emma suppressed a giggle. 'It would be very nice, Your Lordship.'

'Very well, little miss whatever-your-name. Good God!' He lowered his head and peered at her from beneath his shaggy brows. 'Best keep that hair of yours hidden under your bonnet, or I'll warrant my hounds'll take you for a fox.' Bending double, he brayed like an ass. When he finally came upright, crimson-faced, and caught Emma's indignant eye, he said sheepishly, 'A quip, my dear ... just a quip.'

A fox, indeed. Hiding her annoyance behind an anaemic smile, Emma tucked a few flyaway strands of her hair into her sunbonnet.

All at once, the Earl, who had been contemplating his shiny boot toes, snapped to attention and turned aside. Clearing his throat, he raised the crop to his lips and uttered the first of a series of ear-splitting '*Tada-da-dada's*.' At the startling imitation 'bugle' call, his horse reared, flattened its ears, and, in concert with its master, began a horrendous whinnying.

If the strange duet had lasted a moment longer, Emma would have exploded in hysterical laughter. As it was, by the time the Earl lowered his 'bugle' and the horse ceased its racket, she had tears streaming down her cheeks.

''Struth, girl,' the Earl said with a mixture of sternness and concern, 'no need to cry.' He thrust a handkerchief at her. 'Here, dry your eyes, now.'

Once she was finished, he pocketed the handkerchief and said, 'Very well now. Kneel.'

Emma gaped. His Lordship was not merely addlepated; he was madder than the proverbial March hare.

'Down!'

She hesitated. What in Hades did he think she was, one of his hounds? The *whap* of his crop through the air, and her defiance evaporated. She dropped to her knees and cringed, head bowed, feeling like Mary Queen of Scots anticipating the executioner's axe.

After several nerve-racking seconds had elapsed, something touched her, on her head first, and then each shoulder. And the Earl's voice boomed, 'For services above and beyond the call of duty, I dub thee Keeper of the Earl's Shirts.'

Keeper of the ... Lord, what a caution. Laughter spurted in her like a geyser.

'Rise, Madame Keeper.'

Emma obeyed and busily applied herself to dusting off her skirts while she fought for composure.

'The ceremony is not complete yet.'

Slowly, she looked up. How much more could she take?

'For thy excellent works,' he said, his expression one of childish glee, 'thou shalt henceforth receive' – he puffed out his chest importantly –' an extra two shillings a month, which I shall promptly attend to.'

With that, he clicked his heels, gave a smart salute, and marched off. And moments later, Emma watched, thunderstruck, as he mounted his horse and galloped away, yelling at the top of his lungs, 'Tally-ho-oo-o!'

Emma's heart sang as she whisked the iron over the shirt. Two shillings a month, a veritable fortune. Think what she could do with it: save for a pair of plimsolls for the summer, or a Mackintosh for the winter rains; ribbons, perhaps – tartan would be pretty; the bonnet with the white roses and peacock band in Hope's shop. Or something more practical? A volume of verses or …

With each sweep of the iron, her thoughts vacillated until her head pounded. She looked at the clock. Half past twelve. The washing was dry, ten of the twenty-three shirts already pressed. It'd be hours before Mama was home from Market Day at Wilkes Green.

Her decision made, she went upstairs to her bedroom and, fully clothed, slipped under the eiderdown.

The next thing she knew she was being awakened from a sound sleep by a hammering at the front door. She made her drowsy way to Mama's room, where she peeped around the curtains, nervously aware of her mother's warnings about gypsies and tinkers.

Lord save her, it *was* a gypsy! And a giant of a one, his blue-black curls catching the sunlight as he removed his cap and mopped his brow.

Stepping away from the window, she fingered her lower lip. Of course, she'd never actually seen a gypsy, only caught a glimpse of their caravans the summer before. Again she inched back the curtain. Where was he, now - sneaking around and already about his thievery in the henhouse or the toolshed? No, not yet at least. For there went the door knocker again; he must be hidden from view by the roof's overhang.

Wringing her hands, she stepped away from the window and stood indecisively. Naturally, nothing could persuade her to open the door to him. But there *was* the letterbox …

Like a spectre, she skimmed downstairs. He hammered on the door again just before she reached it. Gritting her teeth, she knelt and carefully inched up the brass flap.

Heavens, but he was big. Positively the biggest man she had ever seen. Massive shoulders. Sunburned arms, roped with veins, below shirtsleeves rolled above the elbows. Face, lean and clean-shaven with the look of polished oak of the light golden variety. Square jaw and clefted chin. Bosh. He had turned away, before she had a chance to see if his eyes were as wickedly black as Romany eyes were said to be, eyes that could see into a person's soul, tell the future.

Oddly excited, she rose and slumped against the jamb. He was a cheerful man, it seemed from his whistle. Forthright, too, judging from the direct quality to his receding footfalls. And he sounded as if he knew exactly where he was bound. She chuckled softly. Silly. Of course, he knew where he was bound; the Turners', a half mile down the road, would likely be his next stop. And Mrs Turner would cross his palm with silver, lest he bring down a curse on old Molly and turn her milk sour.

She pressed her hands to her breasts and closed her eyes. What a day this had been: two visitors within the space of a few hours, one as strange as the other.

And as if that weren't enough, there was tomorrow - her day off - to look forward to, with St Helen's Twentieth Annual Sunday School Treat scheduled to begin at noon on the manicured lawns of Chearden Hall.

She gave a decisive sigh and headed for the kitchen. All the more reason to return to the task at hand and relegate thoughts of addlepated earls and mysterious gypsies to the farthest reaches of her mind.

TWENTY-ONE

In her bedroom late the next morning, Emma stood naked before the wardrobe mirror, brushing her hair.

She had never before looked at herself in this lingering, appraising way. It felt sinful, somehow. And yet, was it so awful to think one's breasts well-shaped and firm?

Imagine babies sucking for milk like little Josh Dobbins. The vision of that greedy clamping mouth sent a shudder through her, and she swung about to continue her self-inspection face on.

The fact that she was short no longer bothered her. But was she too thin? Head tilted, she ran her palms over the ridges of her ribs. Perhaps. Though her hips had quite a curve to them and her waist, without benefit of stays, was certainly no eighteen inches. Her stomach was flat, though, and satiny under her fingertips, until she touched ... Her breath caught in her throat and she snatched her hand away at the guilty realization she had been fondling the curly triangle of her pubic hair and experiencing something warm and pleasurable while doing so.

She saw the dark luminance in her own eyes, felt the heat in her cheeks. Now she *should* be ashamed. She plied the brush to her hair with punishingly heavy strokes. Such behaviour, and for a Sunday school teacher scandalous.

Like the outgrown crepe de chine she'd have been forced to wear to the Treat this afternoon – that is, had Mama not been extravagant, bought the sewing machine, and made the violet-sprigged cotton frock that lay behind her now on the bed. There would be no scandal associated with that high-necked, lace-ruffled confection, only envy and admiration.

157

Emma was right. As the Earl cleared his throat for his speech and she slipped into her seat between Alice and Dulcie Higham, her fellow teachers, she felt herself surrounded by approval. It fairly buzzed all about her. And why not? With the new frock, white kid shoes, white stockings and gloves, and her saucy, wide-brimmed straw boater banded in lilac grosgrain, she outshone everyone, including Their Ladyships Cecely, Grisele, Eliza, and Charlotte, who sat flapping their fretful fans and listening with bored expressions to their father's oration about life and duty.

Glancing around at her forty-odd charges, Emma could see duty was the last thing on their minds. Then, who could blame them, with thoughts of swings and merry-go-rounds and hobbyhorses bound to be dancing around in their heads? Not to mention the cricket match and the races, with whips and penknives and gutta-percha tops as prizes for the winners. Their stomachs, too, were probably calling to them with the promise of tea in the tent set up before the conservatory.

Emma's own stomach growled in response to her vision of sticky buns and cold roast beef, and the delicious non-alchoholic ginger beer Mrs Dawfield and staff made each year.

Emma's gaze drifted from the fidgeting, shuffling children to the yellow-and-black pennants, bearing the Chearden coat-of-arms, that were strung across the platform. They ruffled in the breeze and their motion caused her mind to wander.

Being a Sunday school teacher had its drawbacks. No rides. No races. Just an awesome burden of responsibilities.

'It will be your task, ladies,' Reverend Marsh-Hughes had said after church the previous Sunday, 'to ensure everything runs smoothly next Saturday. And please, do keep a sharp lookout. We will brook no fighting, no baiting of the girls by the boys; or for that matter, vice versa. And no *incidents*.' He had flushed over the word 'incidents,' and a look close to pain had creased his earnest face. Later, Emma discovered why.

At the Summer Fete the year before, a frog of the small,

green, slippery variety had turned up in Mrs Marsh-Hughes's dish of strawberries. The sight of the creature clambering out of the clotted cream had seemingly sent her into such a swoon that it had taken a full five minutes to revive her. And her appetite – until then said to be extra-ordinary, for she was a woman of monumental proportions – had never been the same since.

From the admonishing look Dulcie sent her, Emma realized she must have laughed out loud. She realized, too, that the Earl was finally done, for a great cheer went up and, like horses held back at the starting gate, the children bounded off in all directions.

The afternoon progressed with astonishing smoothness. There were only a couple of minor mishaps. The first, when Tommy Beddall shoved Ben Groves into the lily pond and Ben surfaced spouting goldfish. The second, when the Earl split his breeches during a demonstration of his prowess on the hobbyhorse.

By three o'clock, having bribed the Higham sisters (with the promise of a share of her meal) into taking over her responsibilities, Emma was free to wander the grounds at her leisure.

Sauntering through the rose arbour, where the avid-faced Mesdames Crowley, Fitch, and Marples were huddled like witches around a caldron, Emma overheard the startling news that Mrs Marsh-Hughes was 'in that certain condition.'

Masking her astonishment behind an acknowledging dip of her head, she went on her way. Lord, to think of the sparrow-thin Reverend lusting after Mrs M H; to think of him burying himself in that colossal form. Oh dear, here came the unseemly thoughts again. With an effort of will she quashed them, pausing by the sundial to fish her programme from her handbag.

She ran her forefinger down the list. The donkey race. Now that purported to be an exciting event, with something untoward invariably happening. Gracious! She looked up. It seemed something untoward must already be happening.

A woman, crimson-faced and clearly frustrated, came

charging past Emma dragging two children, who squealed like pigs, by the scruff of their necks. Then in quick succession three more women appeared, with youngsters in tow, their voices rising ever higher over the indignant cries of their children.

'Proper disgusting,' Emma heard the first one say.

'Should have had the beast gelded, if you asks me. Shut your mouth, Willy ...' The second woman shook the protesting boy, doubtless her son, 'or I swear I'll give you a good hidin' right 'ere.'

The third woman scurried by without a glance in Emma's direction. But the fourth, apparently noticing her puzzled look, said, 'If you was headin' for the race, you'd best forget it. Cancelled it is. Besides' – she pursed her lips – 'such goings on is no fit sight for a young woman.'

'Hmmm,' Emma murmured, running a speculative finger along her jaw and casting a quick glance over her shoulder as she set off in the direction of the stables.

Great Heavens, what was the beast doing? Emma watched dumbstruck as the white donkey with the odd-looking hairless red tail – or whatever it was – jutting rigidly from beneath its belly tried to clamber onto the back of a smaller brown donkey. The other animals, who had been bucking and braying and milling about, causing great clouds of dust to rise in the air when she had first positioned herself behind the holly hedge, had quietened down now.

A groom suddenly appeared. 'What the 'ell,' he shouted to someone beyond Emma's view, 'let's leave them two be. If old Jasper there 'as a mind to fornicate, then I says let 'im.' A muffled response came and the groom took off across the paddock.

Emma's gaze returned to the manoeuverings of the donkeys. The white animal slipped off the back of the brown one, tossed its head, and snorted. Unconsciously, Emma sidled along to the spot where the hedge ended and the paddock fence began. From this vantage, nothing of the animals' odd behaviour would escape her.

The white donkey reared up again, the tail throbbing, quivering, and – Lord – now it was disappearing *inside* the other beast. They seemed to be locked together in some wild, primitive dance. Great god, *now* she understood. The animals were mating, and here she was *gaping*. Battling the temptation to continue watching, she whipped off her hat and closed her eyes, fanning herself against a hot tide of shame. A picture of Leticia and her man friend flashed into Emma's head, and then another of Reverend and Mrs M-H. She fought off the images. My, but her mind was becoming a regular cesspit ...

'Are you lost, lass?'

Not to mention that it was playing tricks on her. Now, she was hearing voices.

'Miss, are you all right?'

A moment of blank panic, another of searing mortification, and Emma whirled around. She felt the blood drain from her face. The hat slipped from her grasp. It was the gypsy, standing not a yard from her, hands on his hips, a puzzled tilt to his head, and obvious amusement in his flint-grey eyes.

'I said, are –'

She did not wait for him to complete the sentence. Head down, she stumbled by him, striking out blindly, running like a hunted deer and not stopping until she reached the tea tent.

Panting, she collapsed against the canvas. Oh, the pure shame of it, to be caught like that, and by a man! A minute or two of deep breathing and she remembered to smooth her hair behind her ears and check her plaited coronet for loose pins. She was in the process of jamming one in place, when the realization burst upon her: her hat – the new straw boater that had cost her months of savings – she had lost it to that beastly gypsy.

TWENTY-TWO

The next morning, Emma slept soundly through the strident competition of St Helen's bells, those of the Methodist Chapel, and the yips and howls of Chearden's canine population.

When at last she awakened in the warm hollow of her featherbed, it was to a dreary day. Through the open window, beyond the tops of the beech trees, she saw a sky striated with bands of black and grey and faint white.

Swinging wearily out onto the cold wooden boards, she raked back her tangled hair and focused blurry eyes on the slip of paper on the bedside table.

'Since you had such a restless night, thought it best to let you sleep. Fire lit. Meat in oven. See you about noon, depending on Rev. M-H's sermon. Mama.'

So Mama had gone to church without her. Odd. Restless night? She tugged absently at her earlobe. A fleeting recollection came to her of having surfaced once during the night – or was it twice? – drenched in sweat, and with her heart pounding in her throat. It must have been the dream again. If only she had left it behind in Glinton. Why, oh why did it continue to dog her?

Shivering against the unanswered question and the damp air, she drew her nightgown about herself and closed the window. Despite her early night and the fact that the morning must surely be half over, she felt exhausted. And in her stomach a storm was brewing. No wonder; tea the afternoon before had been her last meal, and throughout it – because of her experience with the gypsy and the loss of her prized hat – she'd felt herself on the edge of nausea, unable to eat one bite.

A quick wash, and she would go downstairs and make herself breakfast.

Seated at the kitchen table some time later, she tapped a spoon around the top of the brown egg resting in the hen-shaped egg cup. The lid came off neatly and she dipped a finger of toast, burned black over the fire the way she liked it, into the golden yolk.

What a pleasant room the kitchen had become, with Mama's homey touches. How peaceful it was with the kettle humming on the hob, the sizzle of the joint in the oven, and the muted heartbeat of Mama's ornate Temple clock, which looked incongruous on the mantel's great rough-hewn slab. Not half so odd, though, as Mama's elegant crystal candlesticks with prisms suspended from their fluted tops.

Not for long, this quiet, Emma thought wryly, remembering her mother's words: 'I swear, I cannot endure a day longer the sight of this bilious green parlour sofa. After church tomorrow, Sabbath or not, I shall ferret out that piece of striped damask from my trunk. Olive and rose, as I recall, and perfect for arm covers and antimacassars.'

Mama and her schemes; she'd been full of them last night when she'd come upstairs with the cup of hot milk and sat at the foot of the bed. Though with the dull throb in her head, Emma had found it hard to absorb the chatter.

Emma rose and gave a luxurious stretch. What to do with the rest of the morning? Finish the wax flower arrangement for Hope's birthday in June? Take a walk and perhaps pick a bouquet of cowslips for Mama? The pussy willows were out, too. She *should* do something nice for Mama, after all those hours she'd devoted to making the frock.

Dishwashing first, though. Then her bed, and the slop pail and night commode to be emptied. Oh, and she mustn't forget the meat.

It was doing nicely, she saw, when she opened the oven alongside the fire. Imagine, this leg of lamb had left New Zealand months ago, crossed an ocean, and come through the tropics in a ship fitted with storerooms which, according to Mr Baxter, the butcher, were *refrigerated* so the meat was kept frozen and arrived perfectly fresh.

'Changing times ... these are changing times,' he'd said. So they were, Emma thought, catching a glimpse of the gilded hands of the clock approaching half past ten.

She took the stairs two at a time. As she passed her mother's room, the untidiness of it arrested her. The bed was unmade. Dressing gown, nightdress, and a blouse were draped across the back of the bentwood chair. And the trunk at the foot of the bed was open, some of its contents strewn about the floor.

Emma scratched her head. Unlike Mama not to leave things just so. She must have overslept and departed in a tearing hurry.

Ah-hah. Emma snapped her fingers. The perfect opportunity to do that good turn – tidy the room and find the damask and shawl for Mama; she'd surely be delighted.

She had the room shipshape in no time. She looked around with a nod of satisfaction. Now for the trunk.

On her knees, she began to sift through it. On top was a stiff linen tablecloth with a musty odour and the yellowish cast of age, and beneath it, tied in neat bundles, were dozens of fabric squares of every colour and texture imaginable – obviously, the makings of a patchwork counterpane.

It was astonishing what Mama had managed to cram into the trunk: yarn, knitting needles, twist, crochet hooks, feathers, beads, bobbins of wood, bone and ivory, boxes filled with buttons of all shapes and sizes. Further investigation revealed an ancient sampler with *S*'s that looked like *F*'s and a morbid verse about the inevitability of death, cross-stitched in faded red.

Emma grimaced. Fancy hanging that on your parlour wall, or over your bed. Refolding it, she hastily thrust it to the bottom and continued to dig around. Her fingers came in contact with something hard and smooth. A book? No, more like a book cover, she saw. Inside were a couple of loose tintypes: one of a boy in a woodsy setting, standing at the knee of a dour-faced woman; the other, of the head and shoulders of a man.

Sitting back on her heels, she studied the face. There was a vague familiarity about the light-coloured hair falling over

164

the forehead, the pale-seeming eyes, the half smile. Absently, she turned it over and read the inscription on the small white square glued to the back.

'To Beth, Christmas 1874. Eternally yours, George.'

Mam was Beth. George …? Of course: George Cadman, her father. The tintype face down in her lap, she stared beyond the window. A photograph of Papa. Odd, how she'd never been able to conjure an image of him, not that she'd tried more than once or twice in all these years. Odd, too, that Mama had forgotten the photograph; she surely must have, to have once said the only pictures she had of Papa were in her heart.

Emma now felt the quickening of her own heart. Was that the creak of a loose board on the landing? She cocked her head. No, it must have been the weather vane on the chimney pot, moving in the breeze.

Her gaze returned to her lap. She turned the tintype over, gave it a final uneasy look, and jammed it deep into the trunk.

The damask … she had been searching for the damask. And what else? The shawl, old with a silk fringe.

It was nowhere to be found. But the damask was; and several yards, judging from the weight. She hefted the bolt to the floor and unrolled it, surprised to find concealed within the folds another piece of fabric – pale green silk, from the look of it.

A petticoat, she saw when she shook it out and held it up. A child-size petticoat, and a pretty one; all frills and ribbons and lace and … Suddenly, she dropped the garment and recoiled.

A chill entered her heart and something buzzed in her head. She wiped her brow and pressed her fingertips to her temples, her gaze at once held and repelled by the shimmering silk. The buzzing took form, music, words: 'One-two-three, one-two-three. Dance, my sweet darlin' … dance. Beautiful.'

'*No!*' she cried, struggling against the hand at her throat – her own hand, cold and sweaty. Her own voice, snapping the thread of the dream. And now her mind racing, frantic, clicking like a sewing machine, 'Get-rid-of-it, get-rid-of-it, get-rid-of-it ...'

TWENTY-THREE

'I'm sure Mama thinks me quite mad, and I don't wonder.' Emma stood with her back to the fire and projected her voice towards the curtain dividing Hope's living quarters from the shop, which at nine o'clock was about to open.

She sat at the table by the window and took a mouthful of tea. Replacing her cup in its saucer, she let her gaze drift over the cheerful clutter – spools of ribbons and laces and braids; bolts of velvet and tulle; baskets filled with tea roses of pink and white silk; ostrich and pheasant feathers; head forms; hat forms in felt and straw and hatboxes piled one on top of the other.

'Oh, I doubt that.' As Hope entered and slipped into the chair opposite, Emma experienced a rush of admiration for her friend; wise beyond her twenty-two years; so independent, running her shop single-handed. And brave – Emma glanced at the mantel and the faded Sepia-toned photograph of a man in military uniform – bringing up Oliver alone, without a husband to lean on.

Hope angled her head and narrowed her green eyes. 'My, but Oliver's sleeping late. He's usually tearing about long before this. Now' – she pushed aside a tray of bobbins and leaned on her elbows, regarding Emma softly, penetratingly – 'back to your problem. Look, we have all done things such as you described.'

Emma made a disbelieving sound. 'Come now, people don't ... at least normal, sane people don't ...'

'Maybe not.' Hope's long, clever fingers formed a pyramid beneath her chin. 'But what I mean is, we cannot always be

166

utterly rational.' She laughed a deep, throaty laugh. 'Think of how dull life would be if –'

'Yes, but I told you.' Emma gripped the edge of the table. 'I don't remember much of anything between the time I found the petticoat and Mama discovered me burning it.'

Hope massaged the peak of her proud-looking nose. 'I suppose what you did *was* a little odd ... Oh Lord, I just thought of something.' She covered her mouth with her hands and stared at Emma round-eyed.

'What?'

'The séance at Millie Gant's.'

'What about it?'

'Perhaps some mischievous spirit was called forth and it is trying to take you over.'

Emma passed a hand over her face to hide a threatening smirk. 'But *nothing* was called forth that night, you surely remember. And I seriously doubt that ...'

'It happens, Emma. Really and truly. If you had seen that trance medium in Manchester, the one I told you about, then you would be –'

The shop's bell jangled. Hope turned her palms up and shrugged. 'A customer, let's hope. If Oliver awakens, would you mind looking after him?'

'Not at all.' Emma waved her on her way. 'You go and make your sale.'

Listening to a melancholy rain spattering the glass, she sat back and stared beyond the window at the troubled morning sky. Mischievous spirits? Takeovers? What an outlandish notion. She chafed her arms and shivered. Outlandish or not, there would be no more dabbling in spiritualism for her.

Nor in other speculation; for at this point, discovering what had triggered her insane behaviour that Sunday four days earlier was less important than dealing with the consequences. And they were discomfiting, all right; Mama had hardly spoken all week and her demeanour was one of nervous watchfulness. Understandable, really, when you stopped to consider; she had no doubt concluded she had a lunatic for a daughter. Burning a petticoat! Imagine what her reaction would be if she were to learn of the donkey incident, as well.

Emma ground her teeth together. That beastly fellow ... thanks to him, some gypsy harlot was probably sporting a straw boater by now.

Made restless by her thoughts, Emma rose and cast about for some task to occupy herself. But the abrasive, high-pitched voice emanating from the shop caught her attention. 'Struth, there was no mistaking its owner – Priscilla Seton, doted-upon daughter of one of Chearden's wealthiest families.

Obviously, she was in her usual cantankerous fettle, complaining bitterly about the bonnet Hope must have been showing her. 'I did *not* tell you to use bronze. In fact, it was not chiffon I wanted, at all. I distinctly remember saying tulle.'

'Tulle and cabbage roses,' Hope echoed minutes later as her customer departed with a slam of the shop door, and she swept through the curtain.

Her normally serene face, framed by a bonnet of mustard velvet trimmed with bronze chiffon and ostrich feathers, was flushed and tight-looking. 'Her Highness' – she smiled a clearly counterfeit smile and yanked off the bonnet – 'did not like it.'

'I gathered as much. But it's charming, Hope, utterly charming.'

'I made it exactly as she instructed. And you heard.' Hope's mouth started to quiver. 'I must admit, though, it was hardly flattering. In fact,' she spluttered behind her hands and then clapped them to her breast, 'on her it was an absolute abomination!'

Laughter certainly was the best medicine, Emma thought, on her way home. And Hope's parting words were right, of course. 'Simply apologize to your Mama and tell her you have not a notion what came over you.'

When she entered the kitchen, Emma was all set to follow Hope's advice. But her mother's expression of barely suppressed excitement clearly indicated she was to be spared the necessity of an apology.

A letter from Flora had arrived in that morning's post. And it could not have come at a better time; for Beth had spent several sleepless nights fretting over Emma's odd behaviour.

Bad enough, after the months-long tranquil hiatus, to hear those familiar eerie cries during the early hours of Sunday morning, all the while knowing she'd deluded herself into believing Emma's nightmares were a thing of the past. Even more horrifying to see the vacuous look on Emma's face as she'd tossed the petticoat onto the fire and jabbed at it with the poker as if it were something evil. And in a way it was, because it had been a gift from George. And Beth was oddly glad to see its destruction. She should never have packed it away in the first place, hadn't even realized she had until the sight of the damask on her bedroom floor had caused the pieces of the puzzle to lock in place. But it had been done in innocence, without forethought, like the scores of unconscious acts a grief-numbed widow performs.

When the postman had knocked on the washhouse door and handed her the letter from Flora, the irony of the situation struck her: because of the untruths she'd told Flora, she could never again turn to her friend for counsel about Emma. She would have to look to herself for solutions.

It had been a sobering realization, as sobering as the morning's scudding black clouds. But Flora's news about her cousin Dulcie's son had changed all that.

A newly graduated theological student, Thomas Mondley had recently been assigned his first posting: Wilkes Green, just twenty miles from Chearden. Thinking Thomas and Emma were sure to hit it off, Flora had enclosed the young man's address with the suggestion Beth contact him.

Wouldn't it be wonderful if something were to come of it, Beth thought, losing no time in inviting the fellow for tea the first Thursday afternoon (Emma's half-day off) he was available.

And what better person for Emma, under the circumstan

ces, than a man of the cloth. Someone sure to be compassion-ate and understanding.

Such were the ideas running through Beth's mind when she glanced up and saw Emma on the threshold. Motioning her to sit, she said, 'I've some rather interesting news, dear.'

Emma's face registered momentary surprise and then relief as she joined her mother at the table. 'What is it?'

'Another letter from Mrs McDonough. I shan't bore you with every last detail. But ...' After explaining about Mr Mondley, Beth finished with, 'I've a mind to invite him for tea the first Thursday he has available. What do you think?'

Smiling now that the uncomfortable barrier between them seemed to be down, Emma raised her eyes from her lap. The chap was bound to be an insufferable bore. But from the expectant glow in Mama's eyes, she was obviously counting on an enthusiastic response. What else was there, then, but to give it?

'Sounds like a splendid idea,' she said.

TWENTY-FOUR

Emma's head would have been full of Thomas Mondley if Mama had had her way. She prefaced each of his Thursday teatime visits (which had begun the third week in June) thus: 'There would certainly be no harm in showing him a little encouragement.'

But what was there to encourage, Emma thought one Monday afternoon in early August. Not that Thomas had turned out to be the bore she'd feared. In fact, he was a surprisingly decent sort - pleasant-looking, too, with his fresh, ruddy complexion, rebellious halo of faded yellow hair, and nose Mama termed 'aristocratic' because of its prominent bridge. His eyes were a little odd, though: heavy-lidded and the palest of blues. And he had the demeanour of one who had spent a lifetime ducking through too small doorways. But he was kind, considerate, and they shared a common love of poetry and good music; the recitals at Marespond Town Hall were a treat. And one had to give the man his due – he did have a sense of humour, even if it *was* a trifle acid.

But consider Thomas in a romantic light? Hardly. As a friend, yes. For he was a comfortable kind of person, always maintained a safe distance when they went walking, never tried to touch her. None of those looks that men – some men at least, the lustful ones like Theodore Brummerley – reserved for women. The type of look that slithered over your skin and made you shudder.

'Brotherly' was the word for Thomas, Emma concluded, as she bent over the copper boiler and scrubbed at an obstinate stain on one of the Earl's shirts. Staid, too. And a bit tiresome, the way he was always telling her how good she was, when often she felt anything *but* good.

Massaging her aching back muscles, she unfurled and then trudged across the uneven flags to the rinsing tub, where she stood glaring at the great mound of washing it contained. Anyway, who had time for romantic notions when facing the reality of soggy laundry that would not magically wring itself out, dance from one tub to another, then glide through the mangle's rollers.

She hoisted the laden basket onto her hip. Besides, were she to act the coquette, Thomas would be downright shocked.

'Why, Thomas, darling,' she said to the air, batting her lashes and making an exaggerated gesture with her free hand, 'I had no idea you felt that way.' She tossed her head and then tucked her chin primly. 'My bonnet? I'm afraid Mama thinks it a touch frivolous. But I do *so* adore frivolous things ... frivolous men, too.' Just as laughter exploded in the back of her throat, there was a rap at the washhouse door, which gave her such a start that she dropped the basket. Miraculously, it stayed upright. She hardly had a chance to exhale in relief before another knock came, more insistent than the first. Lord, whoever it was would think her demented. For a moment, she teetered between panic and irritation. Irritation won. So she set down the basket, marched to the door, and flung it wide.

'Struth, no. That man again, the big dark lout who had her hat. Her hand crept through her hair; what a fright she must look. If his expression was any indication – white teeth clamped over a full lower lip and grey eyes as round as an owl's – he was as taken aback as she.

'Well, well.' He ran a thoughtful forefinger up and down the cleft of his chin. 'If it isn't little miss …' He paused and fixed her with a slow, full gaze. Her heart quickened. The skin at the back of her neck tingled and fear flared in her, hot irrational fear that made her close the door partway and shield herself with it. 'What do you want, and who are you?' She spoke sharply, her eyes focused on a crack in the cobbles.

At his 'McKenzie's the name, ma'am, Ewan McKenzie, sometime gamekeeper, sometime Jock-of-all-trades,' she glanced up in surprise. So much for the gypsy theory. The chap was as Scottish as they come, and with the lilting burr to prove it.

He doffed his angled cap, untied the scarlet kerchief at his throat, and mopped his glistening brow. 'Reckon you must be Miss Cadman.' He pocketed the kerchief. 'For you canna be the missus, a wee thing like you.'

A wee thing like you, indeed. This called for some clever comment to cut him down to size. Hmmm. It would take more than just a comment; he surely must be six and a half feet tall.

'I'm right sorry if I disturbed you. I knocked at the front door over yonder an' waited a bit. But there wasna an answer. Then I saw the smoke comin' from the chimney, here.' He jerked his head in the direction of the washhouse roof. 'I've come from the big house.'

Curiosity caused Emma to relax. 'Pardon?' She frowned up at him.

'Och, I mean the Hall. Mrs Dawfield sent me to take care o' the loose tiles on your roof. An' this, here' – he bent over

172

and picked up a brown leather valise – 'is my bag of tricks, you might say. It's right handy for keepin' my tools in.' Dropping the valise, he jammed his hands in his trousers pockets. 'I was by a few weeks back, but there was nobody home. Is your mother here today, lass?'

'Yes, she's ...'

'Run and get her then, will you? For the sooner you do, the sooner I can be finished with my work.'

Though Emma would have dearly loved to quiz the fellow about her missing hat and to tell him she was no child to be ordered about, she found herself unable to muster the courage.

Brushing by him, she started across the yard to the house. She had only gone a yard or two when he called, 'Hold on there, miss.'

'Yes?' She stopped and turned, squinting in the sunlight.

'You didna tell me what you're called.'

'Emma.'

'Emm-e-rrr,' he said resonantly, rolling the *R*'s off his tongue and giving her name an altogether different sound. ''Tis right pretty.'

At her mother's direction, Emma showed Mr McKenzie where the ladder and the roof tiles were before going back to her work. It was a good half hour before Mama had completed her weekly housecleaning and appeared outside. By this time, Emma was hanging out the wash and every so often casting surreptitious glances to the rooftop, where Mr McKenzie hammered and sang at the top of his lungs in an impassioned, melodious voice. Though unable to distinguish the words, Emma had picked up the tune, and she hummed along as she pegged.

Mama yelled something to him and she shouted, 'I'm right happy to meet you, Mrs Cadman. It'll no take too much longer. I've just a few more to do.'

Emma couldn't catch her mother's response. But she heard his 'Thank you kindly, ma'am. I never say no to a wee cuppa.'

Emma smiled. He'd pronounced *never* as if it rhymed with *river*. Oh, and the way he'd said her name earlier, giving it such a soft, musical quality.

How strong he was, too, carrying the ladder as effortlessly as if it had been the stepstool on which she balanced.

How had he come to be in Chearden? And what about his family? A man like that was bound to have a wife, children, too. He was not young (she'd glimpsed a trace of silver in his side whiskers); nor was he old. In his thirties, perhaps. Pausing in her pegging, she tilted her head as she speculated.

Gracious – she jammed the peg over the shirt tail – what had come over her? Here she was burning with curiosity over the fellow, the same fellow who'd lacked the common courtesy to return her property or at least give some explanation as to its whereabouts. She clambered down and smoothed her skirts. Lord, though, come to think of it, she'd just as soon he avoid the subject of *that* day altogether. The mere thought of it made her collar feel too tight.

And at teatime, the sight of Mr McKenzie sinking his even white teeth into the sixth meat paste sandwich and reaching for a third beef pie made her gape. For a man who had expected only a cup of tea (according to his comments when he first entered the kitchen), he did astonishing justice to Mama's spread.

Emma was so absorbed in sidelong looks at him that she hardly touched the food on her plate. What a noble nose he had. *Noble* was the only word she could think of to describe a nose that, unlike Thomas Mondley's, had no aristocratic bump to its bridge, but was straight and in perfect proportion to the planes of the face. And how defencelessly his hair curled over his collar. My, but he was dark as a pirate. She could see him now leaping from the deck of some galleon – a scarlet bandana covering his curls, a gold hoop in his ear, cutlass at the ready –

'Dear, would you pass the cream to Mr McKenzie?'

Emma blinked herself out of her daydream. 'Pardon?'

'The cream.'

Emma slid the jug across the cloth and Mr McKenzie

poured half its contents over his stewed plums, while Mama prompted him: 'You were saying …?'

'Aye, I was.' He paused long enough to take a couple of quick mouthfuls of the fruit. 'You see, the Earl's a chum of the Laird I worked for up north. And it's how I came to hear about the job down here.'

'And where exactly is up north?' Mama took the cozy off the pot and replenished his tea while he gave his attention to the fast-diminishing plums and cream.

'Och, just a wee hamlet in the Highlands.' There was a long pause this time, while he scraped the dish and then mopped his mouth with his napkin. 'I heard about the job, see' – he rested his big square hands on the arms of his chair 'an' I woke up one mornin' shortly after and thought to myself, "Ewan, me lad, you're thirty-five years old. You were born in this here room … lived your whole life in this house …"' He picked up his cup and took a quick swallow of tea. '"An' if you dinna make a move, you'll surely die here." And, to cut a long story short, it wasna more than a month later that I was on the train headin' south.'

Mama licked her finger and dabbed at the crumbs on her plate. 'Did I understand you to say earlier that you are not really partial to gamekeeping?'

'Aye.' He massaged the back of his neck. 'Gamekeepin' is somethin' I just fell into, you might say, my father bein' a keeper an' his father before 'im.'

'It seems rather odd, if you don't mind my saying so, that you – a gamekeeper – should be repairing our roof.'

'Reckon it does, at that.' He leaned back and wiped a smear of blackcurrant jam from the corner of his mouth with his napkin. 'Right now, till old Jess Livermore retires at the end of the month and I take over, the gamekeepin' doesna keep me occupied full time. And since I canna abide bein' idle an' I love to work with my hands …' He stared off for a moment. 'In fact, someday I'd like to have my own cabinetmakin' business …' He refocused on Mama. 'Anyway, I offered to do the repairs at the Hall and the tenants' places. And from what I've seen this afternoon, there's plenty to be done. For one

175

thing, your washhouse bricks are in sore need of repointin';
for another, two of your windows are cracked, and goodness
knows what else.'

'You are right, Mr McKenzie.' Mama gave a wistful smile.
'There is only so much a woman can do.'

'Aye, but you've a grand place here.' He glanced about and
nodded to himself. 'And' – he patted his stomach – 'you
surely do set a fine table.'

'Can I offer you another slice of Emma's Madeira cake, or
a scone?' Mama asked.

'Och, no. I couldna eat another bite. I havena tasted such
cookin' since my dear mother, rest 'er soul, passed on.'

'Oh, I'm sure your wife …'

'Wife? I've no wife. Never met a woman yet who'd have
me.' He winked at Emma. And her mouth quivered in
response.

'An' how is it that a bonnie wee thing like you isna
married?' He cocked his head and tugged thoughtfully on his
side whiskers.

Emma's tongue was suddenly in such a ravel that she could
only look to her mother to respond.

'She's entirely too choosy.'

Emma glowered, and then felt a small stab of victory at his
'Reckon there's no a thing wrong with bein' choosy.'

If the comment surprised Mama, she did not show it. She
pressed him to have another cup of tea. But he declined,
fishing a watch from inside his jacket and exclaiming over the
time. 'If you two charmin' ladies'll excuse me, I'll be on my
way,' he said, rising and towering over them. 'It'll like as not
be a fortnight or more 'fore I'm back, what with the
multitude of leaky roofs hereabouts, an' the pheasant shoot
His Lordship's plannin' for next week.'

Mama began to push away from the table. But he said,
'Dinna get up, now. I can see myself out. I'll just get my cap
from the hook over yonder an' be on my way.'

Mama did get up, though, which was just as well. For if she
hadn't been there to warn Mr McKenzie to duck beneath the
lintel, he would have raised a bump the size of a goose egg.

'What a charming man,' she said as she closed the door after him.

Emma eased back the curtain and watched him stroll toward the gate. 'Yes, he's pleasant enough, I suppose.'

That night, as they washed the supper dishes at a little past ten, Mama swung the topic of conversation back to Thomas. 'Though you may not currently see a future in the relationship – and if you ask me you should, because any girl would give her eye teeth for someone of his ilk – you really should think about getting together a respectable bottom drawer.'

Emma stifled a yawn. 'I know.'

'I started mine when I was twelve,' Mama went on. 'And by the time I was married, I had a half a dozen sets of everything – pillowslips, sheets, bolster cases, towels, petticoats, night-gowns, tablecloths …'

'Yes, Mama,' Emma said wearily. 'You've told me before. And I *will* go to into the village tomorrow, first thing, and pick up the twist so I can start on the pillowslips. Now, do you mind awfully if I go on up to bed? I'm exhausted.'

It was a white lie, but forgivable, surely, since her head was whirring with thoughts demanding solitude, images she was helpless to stem: of laughing grey eyes and glossy black curls and the newfound music in her name.

And when she knelt on the chair beneath the open window, watching the stars stitch their pattern on the navy velvet of the sky, she found herself whispering 'Emm-er-r-rr,' as the wind soughed like a love song through the beech trees.

TWENTY-FIVE

Emma yawned and scratched her head beneath her bonnet brim, as she mulled over the confusing array of spools in the cluttered depths of Williams's Drapers. Choosing the right

177

colour twist was as much of a chore as getting out of bed had been that morning.

She folded her arms and tapped her lower lip. Who gave a jot for needlework, anyway, especially when you had a beast of a headache? And why couldn't Mama have forgotten the subject? She'd fairly pounced on Emma at breakfast, saying, 'I finished the pillowslips last night, and they are ready for you to begin embroidering.'

Not wanting to hurt her mother's feelings, Emma had felt impelled to feign interest. She sighed. No self-respecting woman should be without a bountiful bottom drawer, in Mama's words. But really, embroidering every single item was a dreadful bore.

Besides, after last night, it was doubtful the term *self-respecting* could be applied to her.

The thought of the dream, and the disturbing images it evoked, sent a hot rush of shame through her. She pressed her palms to her burning cheeks.

Unlike the recurrent dream that still beset her from time to time, this one was not frightening; if anything, it was pleasurable – but unsettling, too.

The smiling man – naked, bronzed – pressing down on her. Strong yet gentle hands journeying slowly over her, bringing a delicious lassitude. And when she finally awakened to what she'd thought was the murmuring of the wind, she discovered it was her own low moans. There had been that vague sense of wanting, too – the feeling that had plagued her on and off for weeks now. Wanting, yet not knowing what it was she wanted: an elusive yearning weaving through the edge of her consciousness and leaving her breathless.

Whatever had possessed her? She fanned herself. And Mrs Williams, at that moment emerging from the stockroom, took it as a signal. She bustled down the aisle and said, 'Was there somethin' you needed, dearie?'

Managing a weak smile, Emma said, 'No, thank you. I am just trying to make up my mind.'

'Well, be sure and shout out if ...' With the jangle of the

bell over the shop door, her offer trailed off. She patted Emma on the shoulder and brushed by, calling, 'I'll be right with you.'

Grateful for the diversion, Emma forced her mind back to the twist. She had about decided on the red when the buzz of conversation from beyond the stacked bolts of fabric caught her attention. There was something familiar in the harsh timbre of one of the female voices. She backed up a couple of steps and tipped her head.

'Why, Mignon ... you are just the person I wanted to see.'

Emma gave an inward sigh; the voice belonged to Priscilla's dear Mama, Charity Seton.

'I have some rather glad tidings,' the voice went on in a tone of gushing confidentiality, 'tidings sure to interest your daughter Augusta.'

Emma narrowed her eyes. That meant Augusta Maddox, Priscilla's friend.

'Really, Charity, do tell.' Mrs Maddox's voice sounded like an out-of-tune fiddle.

'Emma shrank into herself. Nothing for it now, but to stay put and pray Mrs Williams would not reveal her presence.

'There's to be a dance at the Parish Hall to celebrate its inauguration, a fortnight Saturday.'

'Oh, how divine!'

'And not just a common or garden affair, mind you. But a grand one, with all the local dignitaries there, people like ourselves *and* his lordship. At least, he's to be invited. And I haven't a doubt he'll accept.'

'Oh my. Augusta will be pleased. And you say it's to be by invitation only.'

'Unfortunately, no; anyone may attend. But it was agreed, at my insistence (and I suppose one should be thankful for small mercies), that there will be positively no admittance to imbibers or to those girls who have, shall we say, forfeited their good character.'

'And quite right, too, Charity, that *their* kind should be excluded. Heaven knows there's an abundance of the type about these days. Two this year. Imagine that! And many more on the road to perdition. Oh, and while on the subject' – Mignon Maddox coughed delicately – 'I was speaking with Grace Penwick the other day and she has a cousin in Lower Crombey, where that Windom woman is *supposedly* from.'

Emma edged closer, holding her curious breath.

'I say "supposedly" because Grace said her cousin had never heard of the woman. If you ask me, there's something decidedly fishy there. Widowed, indeed. I shouldn't be a bit surprised if...' Mignon Maddox's voice sank into a low murmur whose content was impossible to discern.

Gritting her teeth, Emma carefully shifted position as Mrs Seton said, 'I suppose it's all one can expect, with new people moving in these past years and not *our* sort at all. I mean, take that girl with the red hair ...'

Emma frowned and smoothed her chignon.

'That Cadman girl,' Priscilla's mother plunged on. 'Flighty isn't the word. If I were the Reverend, I simply wouldn't allow her in church, looking like a Jezebel with that wild mop of hers loose, and not the decency to pin it up.'

'Oh, I agree wholeheartedly.'

Rigid now, Emma pressed her fists to her mouth.

'But,' Mrs Seton sighed audibly, 'after all, what can one expect from a washerwoman's daughter?'

'Did you ladies find what you was lookin' for?'

It was as well Mrs Williams chose that moment to cut in. Otherwise, Emma's fury might have driven her to apply her shoulder to the bolts of fabric and send them crashing forward onto the two women.

By the time the shop bell announced their departure, Emma had composed herself enough to make her selection. Spools and money in hand, she marched up to the counter.

Startled, Mrs Williams glanced up from her account books. 'Lord love us, I forgot you was here, dearie,' she said. 'Finally made up your mind, have you?'

Emma tilted her chin and bared her teeth sweetly. 'Yes, finally, as you say. And now if you'd be so kind, I should like to look at your dress lengths.'

Mrs Williams came from behind the counter. 'Was you

lookin' for something' serviceable, luv? We've some nice calico or holland and some grand ...'

'Actually, no,' Emma said. 'I rather fancy something pretty. Silk perhaps, or tulle; maybe some torchon lace. Something suitable for a dance.'

'How dare they!' Emma stopped pacing long enough to stamp her foot. Three-year-old Oliver, who was playing with his tin soldiers on the floor beside Hope's chair, looked up, round-eyed and surprised.

Hope shook her head reflectively. 'The poor things. Think of how empty their lives must be with nothing better to do than –'

'Who?' Emma plucked an ostrich feather from the vase on the table and toyed with its gossamer fronds. 'You surely don't mean –'

'Oh, but I do. One should pity them, as one would pity anyone so ...'

'Spiteful,' Emma rushed in, 'and malicious. Old biddies, the two of them.'

'Look here,' Hope said, motioning Emma to the chair opposite, 'there is absolutely nothing to be gained by getting yourself in a tizzy.'

'Are you saying their horrid insinuations are not of consequence to you?'

'Of course they are.' As Hope swept a wing of dark blonde hair off her forehead, her gaze drifted to the mantel. 'But since there is absolutely nothing I can do about it, short of gagging the pair' – her slender fingers closed around the amber beads at her throat – 'and since I never *did* live in Lower Crombey ...'

Emma stopped wafting the ostrich feather. 'You *didn't?*'

'Oh, it's a long story' – Hope refocused on Emma – 'and one which I shall tell you someday.'

How mysterious, Emma thought, resisting the impulse to quiz Hope, who at that moment was saying with a kind of ironic humour in her voice, 'People are never what they seem.'

Emma gave an uncertain shrug and drew the feather across her chin in a meditative gesture. 'Oh, I don't know.'

'Take my word for it.' Hope straightened the lace on her cuff and looked up. 'Which leads me back to my original point: those who gossip are unhappy creatures. And the very best defence against their nasty barbs is no defence. In a word – ignore them.'

'You're right, of course. And I know my urge to retaliate says nothing for my maturity. But' – Emma pinched her bottom lip between her teeth and sat forward – 'what I have in mind is really not retaliation, but more along the lines of … a little innocent sport.'

By half past seven on that third Saturday night in August, the Parish Hall was bursting with the crowd: reverberating with the ceaseless babble of chattering and giggling and cries of greeting and the swish of skirts and the flurry of fans and the scuff of slippers and the tip-tap of heels on the springy new floorboards.

King Arthur's Court could not have looked more festive. From the high-arched ceiling blazed the Sedgewick's gold-and-black ancestral banners. Streamers festooned the dark panelled walls, and crepe-paper rosettes adorned the over-hang of the cloth on the long food-laden table against the one wall, where the ladies of St Helen's Aid Society rustled about importantly. At the head of the capacious room, on a raised platform banked with potted palms and ferns and other exotic greenery, the musicians tuned their instruments.

Herbert Vitch, his fluff of silver hair standing up comically from his bald pate and his plump radish cheeks already shining with perspiration, hunkered over the piano. Centre stage, fiddlers Peckton and Wilde set their bows to whanging and sawing in a discordant prelude, while Tiny Cheadle, cocooned in red-and-white houndstooth check, strummed on a banjo and grinned his wolfish grin.

On upholstered pews at the opposite end of the room, flanking double doors that constantly squeaked wide with a ribbon of arrivals, were perched the matrons – preening and pecking over grains of gossip like sparrows in a barnyard – while their menfolk, pontificating over the march of collectivism and the end of Gladstone's rumoured Home Rule Bill, goggled at the well-turned ankles and milky shoulders and soft peeping bosoms, and dreamed dreams that had not a thing to do with the state of the British Empire.

For Emma, seated next to Hope, the scene was as intoxicating as the knowledge that she had never looked better; that her gown of moss-green watered silk, with its long close-fitting sleeves and demurely scooped neckline inset with ruffles of ecru lace, was the perfect foil for her creamy complexion and the burnished mass of her hair.

What a gem Mama had been; so determined that no one (least of all the Misses Seton and Maddox) would outshine her daughter and her daughter's friend. She had sewn fiendishly that past fortnight, not just on Emma's gown, but on Hope's – an elegant creation of white muslin, with pleated panels and red velvet streamers and bows at waist and shoulders.

What a shame Mama would not be there. 'My dancing days were over years ago,' she'd said, 'and the only waltzing I intend to do is up those stairs to my bed. But I shall expect a full report of the night's activities, with *no* details spared, when you come home.'

The evening was hardly under way, and already there was so much to tell. How the Earl, majestic in burgundy velvet, had singled her out when he was en route to his seat before the platform, and had actually remembered her after their one face-to-face meeting on that spring morning.

'By Jove,' he'd said, scrutinizing her through a monocle as though she were one of the butterflies in his collection, 'if it isn't my little Keeper, grown from filly into mare and looking uncommonly delectable.'

Simultaneously flattered and dismayed by his remark, Emma had blushed behind her fan, then promptly dropped it when the Earl slapped the shoulder of a young man who happened to be standing before her chair, and barked, 'You, sir, are a dashed lucky chap. But you shall not have her all to yourself. Oh, no, my lad. I shall put in my claim this instant. The first polka is mine.'

A tweak of Emma's hot cheek, and off he'd strutted, leaving Emma, Hope, and the young man stunned, until the humour of it struck and they broke into laughter, uproarious and infectious.

And what about their grand entrance? Not that she'd planned it; Hope had been the one to unwittingly plant the seed. And a devilish seed it had turned out to be.

'Over there,' Hope'd whispered out of the corner of her mouth as she and Emma made their way through the double doors at a little past seven and paused on the threshold to absorb their surroundings. 'Mesdames Maddox, Seton, and company.'

Turning, Emma had seen a distinguished clutch of Chearden's elite. Mrs Seton, as formidable as a bobby in dark blue and an abundance of large silver buttons, her elegantly coiffed head rearing above the rest. Dr and Mrs Brownley. Diminutive wispy-haired Miss Cowup and her twin brother, Isambard. Dr Loslett. Reverend Marsh-Hughes and Mrs, as big as a marquee now. Furtive-faced Mignon Maddox and Augusta, cast from the same stocky, thick-shouldered mould. And Priscilla Seton in her countless frills of cheese-yellow organza, looking like a colossal chicken.

'Come on.' Emma seized Hope's elbow and propelled her along. 'We are going to be nice, polite young things,' she hissed through her teeth. With her blithe 'Good evening, ladies, gentlemen,' the austere assemblage's conversation dwindled into silence as deep as a well.

Her first impulse was to flee. But Mrs Seton's expression of frosty contempt and the affronted twitching of Mignon Maddox's wafer of a nose bolstered her courage. 'Good evening, Reverend, Doctors … and Mr Cowup, how delightful to see *you*. You all know my dear friend Mrs Windom. Oh, and Priscilla.' Emma flapped her fan. 'My, what an *interesting* gown.'

There had been a scattering of responses from the group;

none, however, from Mesdames Seton and Maddox, nor Priscilla, whose jaw seemed to have fallen into a permanently openmouthed state.

If the seed had not at that moment germinated and burst into impish life, Emma might have let matters stand. But the temptation was too potent. 'I pray,' she said with a demure flutter of her lashes, 'that when the music begins, you charming gentlemen will not leave dear Mrs Windom and myself to wilt.'

'Struth – Emma came back to the present – what if they were, in fact, left to wilt? She clutched Hope's arm and murmured behind her fan, 'Wouldn't it be ghastly if no one asked us?'

Emma's concerns proved entirely unfounded, for as soon as Mr Vitch announced 'The Blue Danube,' she and Hope were inundated with partners – eager lads with warm moist hands, ponderous old men who waltzed like rusting wheels, Doctors Brownley and Loslett, Reverend Marsh-Hughes, Isambard Cowup. But – no great surprise – not Messrs Seton and Maddox.

The most memorable dance for Emma was her polka with the Earl. What a reckless, dizzying, seesawing journey it was; like being in a carriage drawn by runaway horses. Flashes of jouncing curls and hot glowing eyes, of gaping mouths and beards and whiskers, and stiff starched collars and startled brows. The thrum of their feet and the squeals of mock horror and the rumble of baritone laughter as they sliced through the throng; and the Earl's final triumphant hoot, midway into the dance, when he brought her to a slithering, heart thumping halt and croaked, 'Deucedly sorry, my dear, I'm feeling a trifle done in.'

As Emma sank into a chair, Hope leaned sideways and said, 'I fear your friend Elgin Rutter is headed this way.' Approaching was a strapping lad with a perpetually flushed complexion and protruding eyes; eyes that all evening long had been fastened on Emma with sufficient intensity to make her skin crawl. So far she'd managed to avoid him and she intended to continue doing so.

She and Hope made a quick getaway, elbowing their way through the crowd to the refreshment table. Hope stopped to chat to someone she recognized, while Emma pressed on, her eyes intent on the blackberry cordial.

Moments later, she stood before the open window draining her glass. How wonderful the breeze felt. She leaned against the casement, lifting her hair away from her neck. What a beautiful ...

'Why, Emma Cadman, as I live and breathe!' The voice, instantly recognizable as that of Priscilla Seton, felt like a shard of ice down Emma's back. Reluctantly, she swung about.

'Well, don't you look *divine*.' Fixing Emma with a look of sweet malevolence, she ran a slow finger around the rim of the quart-size cordial jug she held. 'I was just saying to Mama,' she went on, edging closer, 'how nice it is that those who cannot afford quality fabric' – she paused in contemplation of Emma's gown – 'can buy so cheaply at Williams's Drapers, and what amazingly quaint little gowns can result.'

Emma smiled innocently. 'How kind of you to compliment me.' She tossed her head, conscious as her hair settled about her shoulders of the vitriolic gleam in Priscilla's eyes. 'You must be the one-hundredth person to admire my gown.'

Observing Priscilla's face dapple scarlet and thinking delightedly, Parry that one if you can, Emma turned away to catch the breeze again.

It was her undoing. Without warning, Priscilla slammed into her and, as the contents of the jug emptied into the bosom of Emma's gown, shrieked, 'Oh, my, how dreadfully clumsy of me. I was just on my way to pour Mama another glass of cordial ... and look what happened.'

Standing transfixed, Emma felt the liquid run between her breasts and heard the buzz of conversation trickle off into whispers – whispers that gradually grew and merged violently together.

A hand all at once descended on her arm. 'Oh, Emma dear, what on earth happened?' Hope's worried face loomed

186

before her as someone else – a man, the voice familiar – spoke: 'A wee accident is all. But nothin' that canna be fixed.'

Mouth dry, arms crossed over her soggy breasts, and still in a state of semi-stupefaction, Emma cowered in a corner of the Parish Hall kitchen, watching as Ewan McKenzie bolted the door and swung about.

'Dinna worry about your friend. I told her I'd see you safely home.' He removed his tweed jacket, tossed it over the back of a nearby chair, and then began to unbutton his shirt.

Everything reeled and grew warm, and Emma closed her eyes, but not before her mind had registered bronzed skin and rippling muscles and a dark *T* of hair crossing his chest and bisecting his midriff.

'All right, now. Off with the frock.'

Her blood congealed in her veins. And at the terrifying sibilance of the 'Dance ... dance ... dance,' echoing in her head, she cried, 'No ... no, please don't make me.'

'*Make* you? What in Hades are you talkin' about?'

She snapped open her eyes and stared at him dazedly. 'I'm sorry.' She stopped, unsure why she was apologizing and grateful for the tweed jacket now covering his disturbing nakedness.

The caution in his expression matched that in his tone. 'Here's the shirt, on the chair beside you. The idea is, you put on the shirt when you've taken off that soppin' frock, while *I* turn my back.'

As she feverishly struggled out of her gown and camisole, reached for the shirt, and donned it, her gaze stayed riveted on him. The shirt cuffs hung by her knees. Lord, she would look like the village idiot decked out in this gigantic garment.

'Are you decent, then?'

'No.' She frantically rolled up one sleeve and then the other, until each was at wrist level. Thank Heavens she had worn her waist petticoat. Oh, but Lord ... what about the outline of her legs, visible through the muslin if the light caught her a certain way?

'Are you done?'

187

Gathering the voluminous folds of the shirt about herself, she whispered, 'Yes.'

He turned around. Arms folded across his chest and head angled slightly, he regarded her with unabashed directness. 'Well' – a half smile played across his chiselled mouth – 'I reckon it's time I got you home, then.'

For Emma, the journey was a harrowing one spent trying to maintain a safe distance between herself and Ewan McKenzie – a challenge, considering the speed with which he drove the phaeton and the slickness of the leather seat.

When they pulled up before Beech Cottage, she waited in quivering tension, the damp bundle of her gown clutched to her middle. And when he handed her down and walked her to the gate, she stood, head bowed, knowing she should thank him but too overwhelmed to speak.

''Tis a right shame your evenin' was spoiled,' he said.

Still mute, she fumbled for the catch, found it, and slipped through the gate. Only then, with the staunch iron bars between them, was she able to mumble, 'Thank you … and I'll make sure you get your shirt back.'

As she ran down the path, he called after her, 'An' I'll see you get your bonnie straw hat back – the one you dropped by the stables.'

Her heart beat wildly as she carefully closed the front door and slipped the bolt in place. The Rayo lamp burned on the hall table; a candle and matches lay alongside it. Emma's eyes moved from her state of dishabille to the dark stairwell.

'Please, Mama, don't be waiting up for me,' she whispered to herself as she lit the candle, extinguished the lamp, and tiptoed along the hall. She was poised on the bottom tread when she heard a muffled 'Emma, is that you?'

'Yes,' she yelled, then flew upstairs, calling, 'Now don't you get out of bed, Mama. I will be right in.'

TWENTY-SIX

Emma's gratitude toward Ewan McKenzie was shortlived, nullified by the hurricane of emotions that tossed her through the long sleepless night: guilt - for the half-truths she'd fed Mama (oh, she'd told her about the 'accident' and showed her the ruined gown, but said nothing about Mr McKenzie's rescuing her); chagrin - if she'd listened to Hope in the first place, doused the childish desire for reparation with the cool waters of maturity, then none of it would have happened; shame - that she'd allowed herself to be compromised into disrobing like some trollop; dizzying confusion, too, over her inability to expunge the image of those grey eyes and that sardonic smile.

By Monday morning he still gave her no peace. She dumped his shirt in the rinsing water and angrily sloshed it about. Damn the man; it wasn't enough that he had to insinuate himself into her thoughts; he was to become a regular visitor starting next month - one afternoon a week for as long as the weather held, according to Mama. Well, thought Emma, narrowing her eyes and puckering her mouth, she would make sure she was elsewhere. And he certainly would not get his shirt back until he had returned her hat.

It required two months. She returned home one hazy October afternoon to find a large square box on the kitchen table. 'Mr McKenzie left it for you,' Mama said with a look of puzzlement. 'Your hat is what he ...'

'I forgot to tell you,' Emma said quickly, casually, as she lifted the lid and saw her boater - unscathed - lying on a bed of tissue paper, 'I lost it at the Treat last spring.'

'But how did he know?'

Emma fidgeted. What to say? *I was watching the mating of a pair of donkeys when ...*

'Of course,' Mama chirped. 'He must have inquired at Hope's shop and she recognized it as yours. Just the kind of clever thing a man like Mr McKenzie would do.'

Oh, it is, is it? thought Emma with ironic humour. 'Will he be here next week?' She replaced the lid and made a show of dusting crumbs off the tablecloth.

'Yes.' Mama gave a regretful nod. 'But then he'll be finished until spring, he said. So we shall soon have lost both our visitors, if Thomas becomes as bogged down in his parish responsibilities as he seems to think he will.'

'Did he say what day?'

'Who?'

'Mr McKenzie. Did he say what day he would be by?' Emma made each word precise.

'No. Why do you ask?'

Why indeed? What did *she* care? She shrugged. 'No reason.' It had taken him months to return her hat; he could wait for his shirt.

But she changed her mind the following week.

She and Thomas were in the parlour sipping tea on that Thursday afternoon, when she caught a glimpse of Ewan McKenzie crossing the cobbles. She heard him knock on the back door and Mama invite him in.

While Thomas droned on about his parishioners and Emma sat opposite him, her face a mask of polite interest, her ears were tuned to her mother's and Ewan McKenzie's laughter. Finally, she could bear no more. She interrupted Thomas on the pretext of adding hot water to the teapot, and made for the kitchen.

The incongruity of the sight – Ewan McKenzie sprawled in the wing-backed chair by the fire, her mother seated on the footstool right beside him – took Emma aback. Then she noticed the needle and thread in Mama's hand and the basket at her feet. Of course, she was sewing a button on his cuff.

Emma crossed to the hob and bent over the kettle.

'I tell you,' Mama said, 'this man's stories are a match for Mr Dickens's.'

'Really?' Emma said with a note of dry disbelief.

'Och, go on with your bother. 'Tis you, Mrs Cadman, who are the clever one ... wi' that needle o' yours.'

'Now you remember what I told you,' Mama said. 'If you've anything else in need of repair, you certainly do not have to wait until next spring to drop it by.'

'Aye, I do have one or two things that'd no doubt benefit from a bit of stitchin'. Not that I've much in the way of clothes, mind you. And even less lately, for I seem to be missin' my favourite shirt. I canna for the life of me think what could have ...'

With the sudden clatter of the teapot lid, his words tapered off and Emma glided by them with a bland little smile and said, 'Do excuse me.'

She said the same thing to Thomas, after she'd set down the teapot on the tray. This time she made for her room.

With the door ajar so she would not miss the sounds of Ewan McKenzie's departure, she knelt before the wardrobe and opened the drawer in its base. The shirt was as pristine as the day she had studiously ironed and folded it. The garment tucked beneath her shawl, she tiptoed onto the landing.

After a couple of minutes, she heard her mother's voice. 'Goodbye, Mr McKenzie, and remember what I told you.'

Peeping over the bannister, she watched Mama close the door and return to the kitchen. In a trice, Emma was downstairs and outside.

Ewan McKenzie was about to unlatch the gate, when she caught up with him. 'Here.' Avoiding his eyes, she thrust the shirt at him.

He chuckled. 'Well, I never ... my shirt. And to think I'd forgotten.'

Forgotten? Her hands balled into fists at her sides and she brought her chin up. Why, the insufferable tease was making sport of her.

'Och, I'm sorry, lass.' The smile evaporated. 'I was just havin' a bit of fun. 'Tis a habit of mine.'

'So I've noticed ... and one you'd do well to overcome.' The caustic words slipped out under their own power. And Emma felt her eyes widen as his narrowed.

His brows rose slightly and slowly, deliberately he repositioned the cap on his stormy black curls as he passed through the gate and let it swing closed. He came about, leaned on the post and said in as acid a tone as she had used, 'Just as you, my snippy little miss, would do well to mind your manners.'

Emma inhaled sharply. He was right, of course, she thought, as she watched him turn and stride off. She had acted like a fractious child.

'Is everything all right, Emma?'

Thomas. She wheeled about. 'Everything's perfectly fine.'

Thomas plucked at his Adam's apple. 'You and McKenzie were certainly deep in conversation.'

'*Good grief*, Thomas.' Oh, look at the poor chap, so crestfallen. And just listen to her, she was becoming a regular harridan.

It was this disturbing insight, coupled with a vague emptiness that beset Emma as autumn waxed into winter, that led her to join the Society for Aid to the Poor, a Methodist group headed by Hope Windom.

Though taken aback that Emma would affiliate herself with a non-Anglican organization, Mama was delighted, and even went so far as to start the New Year by hiring a girl from the village to help out one afternoon a week.

As the months went by, Emma began more and more to look forward to these afternoons. Though there was nothing ennobling about the work, there was something miraculous in the sight of a lusty newborn who might not have survived but for the weekly donations of food delivered to its mother.

Thoughts of such an infant occupied Emma's head one May afternoon as she took the shortcut home through the copse on the hillside above Chearden Hall. What an ugly, wizened scrap little Isaac Farraday was. And yet, her throat tightened as she recalled how utterly beautiful he had looked, nestled in the crook of his mother's arm.

And the way it had felt, holding the tender bundle. The strange tingling in her breasts; the hot, pleasant spiral surging up in her. Was that the way all women felt, holding a newborn?

She paused and leaned against the trunk of a silver birch. Imagine, Jane McDonough was expecting her first child; Jessie, her second! Fulfilled? She plodded on. By what – children? responsibilities? She pushed aside an overhanging bough, which snapped back in place behind her, sending a startled woodpecker winging up through the diffused sunlight in a flurry of black and white and scarlet.

Oh, to have such freedom. To soar to the top of the world. That little effigy of a newt inches from her foot, what did it have to worry about? A fish had no responsibilities either, except to swim endlessly. The thought stopped her in her tracks and she looked down at her grubby hands, felt her sticky face. Leaning sidelong, she plucked a frond from a fern and trailed it across her throat. Gracious, it'd been years, their first summer in Chearden. Her heart jolted – why not? She was almost there, anyway. And no one ever went to the Well.

Strange it should be called that, when it wasn't a well at all, but a spring tumbling down the hillside and ending in a pool, smooth as a square of freshly pressed silk below the boulders on which she stood.

Odd, too – if the account in *A History of Chearden* was correct – that people years ago should have thought its waters capable of healing their ailments. And all through a rumour that two lads had been cured of fits. Amazing, as well, that the clay dam was still intact after more than two centuries.

Maybe the waters did have powers. As she stripped down to her chemise and drawers, she surveyed the riffling surface. There was certainly the power to tempt in its clear blue-green depths.

She waded in, sucking in a shocked breath at the unexpected coldness. And then she arched her body and dove. As soon as her head cleared the surface, she began to stroke through the water, effortlessly. After a time, she stopped and flipped onto her back and, inert, absorbed the beauty of the place. The sun hung like a chandelier in the domed ceiling of the sky. A breeze feathered the branches of an overarching sycamore, and an insect hovered nearby, flashing turquoise and silver. There were only the moorhens and coots and mallards and a pair of kingfishers for company and a great sleek water rat who inhabited the tall bullrushes that crowded the bank like busbied hussars.

How fortunate that Jessie had taught her to swim. And how different these crystal waters were from Glinton's brackish canal. A noise in the underbrush beyond the bank brought her out of her meditation. She let her legs sink until she was in a vertical position and began to tread water. Some animal, a badger perhaps or a deer. Certainly nothing to be afraid of. Though for an instant, she had had the sensation of being watched. She shivered, conscious suddenly of the chill creeping into her limbs. Her inability to control the chattering of her teeth and a glance at her blue-white hands was enough to convince her. It was time to head for shore.

Emma stole across the cobbles, her fist around the wad of wet underwear in her apron pocket. At this hour of the day (it must be close to four), Mama would be seeing to the tea. She felt her hair. Still quite wet, but fifteen minutes before the fire would take care of it.

Inside the washhouse, she headed for the basket on the bench beneath the open window. Once the incriminating underwear and her damp apron were safely stowed among the dirty laundry, she turned away and began to pull the pins from her hair.

'Afternoon, lass.'

She froze. The swim had diluted her sanity. She could have sworn ...

'You shouldna be standin' in front of the window wi' that wet hair o' yours. You'll catch –'

She spun about. Mr McKenzie. He must have been working outside, below the window, for he was now leaning in, his brown arms resting on the sill, his eyes regarding her in a dark, peculiar fashion. She gave a violent shudder and

194

scraped her tangled curls back, willing them to stay tucked behind her ears.

'What did I tell you, now? You're already shiverin'.'

Blinking confusedly, because a gauze curtain seemed to have descended between herself and Ewan McKenzie, she touched her temples with her index fingers. 'I don't like being stared at. Please just go away.' She tilted her head and frowned. Did she say it ... or shriek it?

The latter, she realized, after the slam of the window brought back reality, and with it the sting of Ewan's parting words: 'Emma, lass, you've the disposition of a weasel.'

TWENTY-SEVEN

With Ewan McKenzie's return, the restlessness beset Emma again. As the weeks passed, she found no relief from those nebulous yearnings that alternately left her cold and hollow and filled her with a suffocating hot tension.

It was the marriage of the schoolteacher, Amelia Peckforton, in the spring of 1885 that saved Emma from herself. Miss Peckforton's decision to continue teaching half days only prompted the Education Committee's search for a second part-time teacher. Eventually, they narrowed the field to one possibility: Emma.

Reverend Marsh-Hughes approached her after Sunday school the third Sunday in May. And that afternoon she broke the news to her mother over tea.

'That's wonderful,' Mama said. 'And when do they wish you to start?'

'June first. Monday.'

'Gracious, that certainly doesn't give you much time to prepare!'

Emma unwrapped her napkin and dabbed her lips. 'Then you think I should accept?'

'Of course. It's the opportunity of a lifetime. Why on earth would you have any qualms?'

'For one thing, I don't know if I am up to it.'

'Of course you are, dear. You're intelligent, well-read. You love children.'

'And for another' – Emma added more milk to her tea – 'Hope asked me just the other day if I'd be interested in assisting in her shop. She's really hard put these days to keep up. But whichever road I elect to take – teacher or shop assistant – it would mean leaving you in the lurch. And I could not possibly do that.'

'I have always been passionately fond of hats,' Mama suddenly said, tucking a silvered strand of hair behind her ear and smiling an odd secretive-looking smile.

'Yes, I know. But do you mind awfully if we return to the subject of my future?'

Mama's burnt-cinnamon brows rose slightly. 'We have not left the subject, dear.' She rested her folded hands on the tablecloth. 'Assume for one moment that you accept the teaching position and …'

'But, Mama, I cannot possibly desert you!'

'As I was saying,' Mama replied, offering Emma the plate of sandwiches, 'you accept the teaching position. And I retire from laundering.' Despite herself, Mama looked as pleased as a cat let loose in Thompson's Diary.

'Retire? But how on earth –?'

'You said Hope needed an assistant, and I imagine she is willing to pay a decent wage.'

'Yes; quite generous, in fact.'

'So what is to prevent me from becoming Hope's assistant – that is, if she's agreeable?'

'Agreeable? I should think she'd be delighted. This way we would both …' Emma caught herself. Her gaze moved beyond the window to the sheared oblong of the lawn, surrounded by flower beds bright with the blues and scarlets and yellows of delphinium and phlox and alyssum – their tranquil heaven. If they were no longer in the Earl's employ, they could stand to lose it all.

'Emma.'

She started. 'Hmmm?'

'I know what you're thinking. It's written all over your face.' A fly flew onto the cloth and Mama shooed it away. 'You are wondering how we can possibly remain here.'

Emma lifted her shoulders. 'Yes, I am.'

Mama regarded her archly. 'It's actually quite straightforward.'

'It is?'

'Yes. We simply buy Beech Cottage.'

Ownership. What a delightful ring the word had to it, Beth thought as she dropped the peeled potato in the basin of water and set the paring knife on the step beside her. She undid the top buttons of her blouse. What a glorious morning it was, hotter than usual for the first week of July, but with a soft wind breathing relief and chasing tendrils of clouds across the flawless sky.

Smiling, she crooked her knees and clasped her arms about them. It'd been a similar morning back in May when she'd marched up to Chearden Hall – her temerity surprised her even now – and requested of a flabbergasted Mrs Dawfield a meeting with the Earl.

What a landmark day it had turned out to be, though not without its moments, especially when Beth had entered His Lordship's study and almost played skittle to a monster. And if the Earl had not risen from behind the cluttered Chippendale desk, wacked its tooled leather top with a riding crop, and bellowed, 'Down, Marcus Brutus,' the huge Irish wolfhound might have drowned her in slobbering enthusiasm.

'So you're Mrs Cadman,' the Earl said when the hound had at last unfurled his great length on the exquisite Aubusson carpet. 'And how is my little Keeper?'

'Emma? Very well, Your Lordship. In fact, she is one of the reasons I've come.'

'Sit, dear lady.' He unceremoniously dumped the contents

of the nearest chair on the floor and returned to his own seat. 'Not satisfied with her two shillings a month, eh?' he said.

'Gracious, yes. More than satisfied. But she has been offered an opportunity ... actually, we both have. And if I may have a few minutes to explain ...'

'By all means. I am at your disposal, dear lady.'

'Struth, but she'd certainly taken him at his word, she remembered with a touch of embarrassment. Before she realized it, she had launched into a meandering saga about their lives. Not that it had done harm; the Earl called her a 'deucedly plucky woman.' And when she'd finally put forth her desire to purchase Beech Cottage, explaining that she had sufficient cash for a respectable deposit, and had calculated future income versus expenditures, and taken stock of her disposable assets, his lordship regarded her with blatant admiration.

'Gadzooks,' he'd said, 'you certainly have an amazing capacity for figures.'

Lifting her shoulders uncertainly and thinking, *in for a penny, in for a pound*, Beth responded with, 'There is one more thing, sir. The repairs. Mr McKenzie was in the midst of them when he left on some business of your lordship's. And I should like, if at all possible, to have them completed as a part of the transaction.' She reached into her handbag. 'I have here, an itemization of ...'

The Earl motioned her into silence. 'That will not be necessary, dear lady. A simple clause in the instrument to the effect that the sale price is based on –'

Beth gripped the carved edge of the desk. 'You mean you are *willing*?'

'Willing to sell. And happily, I might add. 'Twill be one less tenancy to fret about. Leave the pertinent information with me, and I shall have my solicitors draw up the papers. Now we have that out of the way' – he withdrew his legs from the desk top and sat forward, his gnarled hands planted among the clutter and his look so intent that Beth felt herself grow warm – 'tell me more.'

Still nonplussed by the ease with which she'd accomplished her aim, Beth murmured abstractedly, 'More? What in particular, sir?'

'How you managed to build what you term "a thriving business"?'

She drew her wits about her. 'Well, sir, to my mind there are several ingredients necessary for success in any business venture.'

'Several, eh?' He sucked in his cheeks.

'Yes.' Beth made a deprecating gesture. 'Not that there's anything magical to them, and I'm sure Your Lordship is well aware –'

'Maybe so, maybe not. Spit 'em out and let me be the judge.'

She took a decisive breath. 'Very well. First, there's judicious price comparison; you'd be amazed how costs vary from merchant to merchant. Then there's organization of time, records, employees – whether one has two or two hundred. And wages. I feel it's important to pay rather more than the going rate, if one wants to attract people who are a cut above the rest.'

'Hmmm.' The Earl fingered his pug nose. 'Organization, you say, recordkeeping.' He tugged at his jowls, his little eyes shifting rapidly from side to side and finally refocusing on Beth. 'And you think these ideas of yours could be successfully applied in any venture?'

'I see no reason why not, sir.'

'In that case, how would you like to test them, madam? Help me out with this deuced mess.' He scooped up a sheaf of papers and brandished them. 'It's all a lot of gibberish to me – I've been in quite a spot since my financial manager died. But for someone of your ilk ...'

Beth felt her eyes widen. 'Am I to understand, Your Lordship, that you wish *me* to assist you with your accounts?'

He let the papers flutter to the desk top. 'By Jove, yes.'

'But, sir, I have had no formal schooling in ... I mean, I ...'

'Formal schooling' – he swung an emphatic elbow – 'be damned. You've an obvious talent, madam. A head on those shoulders, and not one (no insult intended) filled with female frippery. And I, as I pointed out before, am in one deuce of a bind. So ... what do you say?'

'But, sir, if you recollect, I already have a new position awaiting me.'

'And you cannot see your way clear to doing both – one day a week here, say, with a generous remuneration?'

Generous remuneration. What an understatement that had been. Her pay this past month, for one day a week at Chearden Hall, was more than she received for four afternoons at Hope's shop. But then, he wasn't your common or garden employer – or person, for that matter; witness Emma's 'knighting' and His Lordship's butterfly hunts through the kitchen garden.

Beth stretched and shaded her eyes. The sun was almost at its zenith. Noon, and hardly a thing done. A little more than an hour in which to compress half a day's chores *and* walk to the village. Not to worry. She bent and scooped up the basin and knife. For a woman as 'deucedly clever' as she was reputed to be, it would be no challenge at all.

About the time Beth locked the door and set out for the village, her daughter was entering what had once been the almshouse, but was now, thanks to progress, Chearden's first bookshop.

'I am afraid it has not yet come in, dear,' said Miss Pruitt, the elderly proprietor.

Emma drew a puzzled hand across her brow. 'I beg your pardon?'

'The Tennyson volume.' The diminutive woman came from behind the counter. 'Your young man ordered it a week ago Saturday. I *did* tell Mr Mondley ...'

Her young man, indeed. Oh, the assumptions people made. 'Do you have any books on America, Miss Pruitt?'

The tiny liver-spotted hands fluttered. 'America? Gracious, you are not thinking of ...'

'For a geography lesson,' Emma said pointedly.

'A geography lesson, of course.' She tucked a wisp of hair into her snowball of a bun, as her humid-looking eyes

200

roamed the timbered ceiling. 'I am not sure. If you are not averse to waiting, I can check among the stock.' She sighed. 'Hundreds of volumes and not the time to set them out. I'm afraid it might take me ...'

'That's perfectly all right, Miss Pruitt. I can browse while I wait.'

She was leafing through one of Mrs Gaugin's famous knitting books when Miss Pruitt called, 'Nothing on America, I'm sorry to report.'

'Don't worry,' Emma answered absently, 'I shall find something else.'

'What about Canada?'

'Yes, I sup –' She clapped the open book to her chest and pivoted on her heels. Good Lord, Mama had said he was away, attending to the Earl's business, but here was Ewan McKenzie, lounging against the bookcase a few feet from her.

He tipped an imaginary cap. 'Afternoon, Emma.'

Too flustered by the recollection of their last encounter in the washhouse, she merely stared. How incongruous he looked in a bookshop; too rugged and vital, somehow. He'd grown much darker, his teeth flashing white against ...

'Are you there, lass?'

A couple of fingers snapped before her nose and she felt the rush of blood to her cheeks as she stammered, 'Oh, yes ... Good afternoon, Mr McKenzie.'

'Well, what about it?' He raked back his curls and Emma felt a queer kind of breathlessness.

'I'm sorry, I did not catch ...' Her voice trailed off, and in an attempt to conceal her confusion, she turned and busied herself replacing the knitting book and rearranging its neighbours.

'Canada. Would you be interested in some books on Canada? I've a keen interest in that part of the world, on account of my sister Meggie and 'er husband Will settling there these ten years past.'

'Goodness, you have family there,' Emma blurted, forgetting her self-consciousness and swivelling to face him.

'That I do. An' a right fine family they are. I'm uncle, you know, to four strappin' boys. An' I'm told' – he smiled proudly – 'they've a look of me.'

'And where is it they settled?'

'Saskatchewan. Prairie country.' He rested his back against the bookshelf, folded his arms, and nodded fervently. 'Mile upon mile of rich fertile land. An' rivers teemin' with fish. Fish as any man who's a mind can catch. An' opportunities. Out there, a fella can …'

Miss Pruitt chose that moment to come tip-tapping down the aisle. 'And did you find what you were looking for, Mr McKenzie?' she shouted up at him.

'No.' Bracing himself with his hands on bent knees, he leaned over until his face was level with hers. 'I didna. But I found *someone*' – he jerked his head in Emma's direction – 'a sight better.'

In the few seconds before comprehension dawned, Miss Pruitt's eyes flicked blankly back and forth. And then she gave a delighted cluck of mock disapproval and said, 'You naughty man. Now isn't he a *naughty* man, Miss Cadman?'

Emma shrugged as Mr McKenzie came upright and said, 'Worse than naughty, madam, for I'm about to kidnap this wee lass.'

With that, he spirited her out of the shop and handed her up into the waiting phaeton with a commanding grip on her elbow. 'No need for you to walk,' he said, as he settled next to her, his thigh brushing against hers and thoroughly unnerving her.

The rutted road saved her. As he swerved to avoid a pot-hole and sought to maintain an even course, she managed to slide along the seat away from him. Soon, with a safe distance separating them and the horse moving at a reassuringly steady gait, she let herself relax.

'So how do you like your teachin'?' he said, his eyes focused on the winding road ahead.

'Oh, I love it. This morning, though, we had a visit from the Medical Officer of Health. There I was, all set to give a spelling test, when in he walked unannounced. And what a dreadful old fuddy-duddy he was. By the time he'd completed his examinations of the children, they were ...' She caught herself.

'Like a pack o' red Indians, no doubt,' he laughingly completed the sentence for her and lapsed into silence, urging the horse on with an occasional flick of the reins.

Lulled by the motion and the rush of warm, loam-scented air on her face, Emma let her thoughts float free. Oh, the excitement in his face, in his voice, when he'd spoken of his sister and Saskatchewan. Odd how caught up she'd felt. Not that she had any yen for that far-off wilderness. Never mind the rivers and the prairies and the opportunities. What about the wolves and the naked savages with their tomahawks and ...? She shuddered violently and came back to the grateful reality of the sun-and-shade-chequered lane ahead.

'Are you cold, lass?' Mr McKenzie flashed her a glance.

'No, not at all.'

'So you think you can use my lending library?'

She slanted a quick look at him – they were on *her* territory now, teaching territory – and she felt secure there. 'Indeed, yes. It sounds a fascinating place and one my pupils could certainly benefit from hearing about.'

'Aye, it does that. Some day I shall see it for myself.'

'You are planning a visit then, Mr McKenzie,' Emma asked as he brought the phaeton to a halt before the front gate of Beech Cottage.

'Ewan. My name's Ewan, remember?'

She nodded.

'It'll not be a visit.' He toyed with the reins and stared off.

Recollecting the disturbing sensation of his hand clasping hers when he'd helped her into the seat at the start of the journey, Emma was out of the phaeton in a flash. If he thought it unusual, he gave no sign when he emerged from his thoughtful silence. 'When I do go,' he said, clambering down on the passenger side, 'it'll be for good.'

Emma felt her heart skip a beat. 'For good,' she murmured.

'Aye. But that's a long way off.'

Her breath slipped from between her teeth.

'Could be months, years even, until I have the money for my passage.' His voice petered out and he stared down at her, something swirling across his eyes, darkening them to the grey of a winter morning.

Emma felt a peculiar weakness in her knees, and an all-too-familiar buzzing in her head. Unconsciously, she reached to the horse's flanks for support, and the animal's loud snort broke the spell.

Suddenly, Ewan was all brusqueness. 'Tell your mother I'll be by Saturday to carry on wi' the repairs, an' I'll drop off the books then.' He vaulted into the driver's seat, hardly giving Emma time to utter a bewildered 'Thank you,' before he had the vehicle moving off at a swift clip.

Moments later, as Emma watched the phaeton's dusty wake, the oddest thought struck her: this time, for some inexplicable reason, Ewan McKenzie was running away from *her*.

TWENTY-EIGHT

When Emma returned from the village the following Saturday, after lunching with Hope, the promised books were stacked on the kitchen table. 'Ewan said you were expecting them,' Mama said.

'I didn't see any sign of him.' Emma riffled through the pages of one of the volumes.

'Oh, he stopped by earlier. But he lacked a crucial nut or bolt or some such nonsense and had to go back to the Hall. He'll be returning later, of course.'

But not in time for me to thank him, Emma thought, knowing Thomas was due in forty-five minutes, and true to form, he arrived on the dot of two. The second chime of the skeleton clock on the parlour mantel was just dwindling to a faint echo when Emma caught the muted sound of a departing hansom cab.

She rose from the clutter of books and papers on the sofa and padded across the dense flower-and-foliage-patterned carpet. Thomas was as predictable as the weather was unpredictable, she thought, casting a glance at a sky that had earlier resembled the silk-embroidered blue peacock on the fire screen, but now offered low, threatening clouds. In fact, he was so predictable, she could safely wager ten guineas as to the course the conversation would take when she answered the door:

'And how are you today, Emma?'

'Fine, thank you, Thomas.'

'And your dear Mama?'

'Very well. And you, Thomas?'

'Absolutely topping.'

Emma was right on target until he responded to her 'And you, Thomas?' with a lift of his rounded shoulders and a rueful '*Comme ci, comme ça.*'

He followed her into the parlour. Hurriedly, she scooped up an atlas and dictionary from the leather wing-back chair to which he inevitably gravitated. 'Please sit down.'

'No, thank you, Emma. I am altogether too fidgety.' As if to prove the statement, he positioned himself before the fireplace and rocked on his heels. Then he clasped his hands at waist level and whirled one thumb around the other. 'I'm afraid I shan't be able to stay more than an hour. I've a thousand and one things to attend to, and very little time.'

'Gracious, is something wrong?' Emma perched on the edge of the sofa.

He came to a standstill. 'Well, no, not really.' He hooked a finger inside his starched cleric's collar and twisted his head uncomfortably. 'I mean, it's ... it's actually rather topping news.'

'What is?'

'My posting, Emma. The Bishop's letter arrived last week. I'm to have my own parish.'

205

Emma clapped. 'Why, that *is* topping news. It's exactly what you've worked toward.'

'It is, isn't it?' His hand paused in its journey through the sun-bleached tousle of his hair. 'Trouble is, I'm being sent to Tarletan.' From under their heavy lids, his pale turquoise eyes fixed her sorrowfully. 'Fifty miles away.' Now he slumped in the wing-back chair. 'It'll mean I shan't be able to visit you, at least not regularly. With luck, perhaps once every three months. And I shall hate not seeing you.'

'But, Thomas,' Emma said softly, 'we can correspond, as we did last winter.'

'Yes, but writing is altogether different from …' Pausing, he crossed one leg over the other and jiggled his foot. 'You are such a brick, Emma. And you've been so much of an inspiration to me. Your fine mind, your gentle spirit, your selfless devotion to the needs of the less fortunate.'

Uncomfortable with his accolade, Emma cut in: 'Really, Thomas, you make me out to be a veritable paragon. And I can assure you, I am not. Now do tell me more about your posting.'

'Very well.' He had just finished clearing his throat in preparation for his discourse, when Mama came bustling in, her slim face flushed, her eyes bright as a sparrow's. 'No, please don't get up,' she said as he half rose. She cleared a spot for herself beside Emma and sat down. 'Gooseberry pie, Thomas.'

He inclined his head. 'Beg pardon.'

Mama smiled. 'I – rather *we*, because it was actually a joint effort – baked a gooseberry pie for you this morning.'

'Thomas was just telling me he won't be able to stay for tea.'

Mama's face fell. 'Nonsense, of course he'll stay, won't you? There is absolutely no …'

Emma nudged her mother into silence. 'Mama, Thomas has some rather exciting news.'

'Fifty miles.' Mama, in the kitchen now, shook her head in

disbelief. 'Why couldn't they post him to some town close by? And everything was going so splendidly. You and he ...'

'I told you.' Emma popped one sugar lump in her tea and a second in her mouth. 'We are going to correspond. Besides, it's not as if Thomas is a lover.'

Mama's mouth cinched disapprovingly. 'Really, Emma!'

'Sorry.' Emma stirred her tea and watched several vagrant tea leaves swirling on the surface of the strong brew. 'But you've always persisted in reading things into our friendship – and I stress the word *friendship* – that do not exist.'

Mama curled her lip and looked so downcast that Emma felt impelled to add, 'At least for now, and as for the future ...' She turned her hands palms up. 'We shall just have to wait and see.'

Obviously appeased, Mama said, 'Oh, I suppose so. But it certainly wouldn't hurt to help things along. And speaking of help, here comes Ewan across the yard.' She whipped off her apron, tossed it over the back of the rocking chair and made for the door, smoothing her hair. 'I'd best see if he needs anything.'

When the door closed upon her mother, Emma carefully unlatched the window. As she opened it a crack, she heard Ewan say, 'I'm finished. There's no a thing left to be done.'

'Everything we discussed?'

'Aye ... an' one or two we didna.'

'You're a regular whirlwind. You'll stay and have tea with us, of course.'

'Och, no, I canna. His Lordship's hosting a dinner at the Hall this evenin' for the Hunt Club, an' he's set on me bein' there.'

'I see. Well, I do want to thank you for all your help. I don't know what we would have done without ...'

'Mrs Cadman – Beth – I've been thinkin' that mebbe, when an' if I have the time, I could stop by once in a while an' visit. Then I'd be sure the two of you wouldna be wantin' for anything.'

A sudden breeze flapped the curtain and tipped over the vase of sweetpeas centred on the table. Emma managed to grab it, but not before a pool of water had gathered on the cloth. By the time she had it mopped up, the conversation outside was obviously over, for she heard her mother calling, 'Goodbye then, and thank you.'

Emma had just closed the window when Mama came fluttering in. 'I imagine that,' she said with a laugh, 'Ewan thinks you and I work too hard. He is of the opinion we could do with a spot of jollification.'

'Jollification?' Emma wrinkled her nose.

'A little leisure. Hikes, picnics, and such. I don't know how you feel, dear, but I think it's a splendid idea.'

A little leisure time. Chuckling, Beth plunged her hand to the bottom of the tin tub in search of the elusive bar of soap. Surely the understatement of the century. Why, the man's appetite for jollification was positively insatiable.

As was Emma's. One had only to look at the smile habitually teasing the corners of her mouth, and the spring to her step, to be convinced of it. Well, why not? Things had not been easy for her, and one of these years she was bound to succumb to Thomas Mondley's attentions. Thereafter life would be a serious - perhaps even dull - proposition.

A far cry from this past month or so. Now the evening rides in the phaeton and the weekend picnics brought delight. The hikes were tolerable. But the fetes and festivals? Noise ... crowds ... Beth worked up a lather and soaped her upper body. Like that dreadful Midsummer Festival at Wilkes Green. What a ruckus! Armies of people swarming about the gaudy booths; itinerant fiddlers and organ grinders infesting the side streets; fortune tellers jangling with garish baubles. Sideshows where one could - if one had a mind to, as she had not - toss balls at skittles or shoot toy pistols or dunk some unlucky urchin in a barrelful of water.

Then the Saturday following, the trip to Upper Craxton to see the Morris Dancers. And during their fortnight off (hers and Emma's), the Hiring Fair. Not to mention the Leighton Bridge Steeplechase.

Scrambling to her feet, she began to soap her hips and

thighs. And tomorrow more of the same. Brimsgate – favourite haunt of day excursioners. Lowering herself into the water, she unfurled as best she could in the confines of the tub and then, groaning inwardly, rolled her neck across the rim of the tub. Imagine the crowds this weekend in August. By Jove – she slapped the surface of the water with her hand – that's *all* she'd do this time, view the scene in her imagination and simply stay at home.

Pleased with her decision, she laughed softly. Let those two – Ewan with his astonishing energy, Emma with her youth – have the sands of Brimsgate, black with mothers and fathers and nurses and screaming children. She would take her solitude, an entire Saturday to herself, and relish every minute of it.

TWENTY-NINE

According to her mother, Emma had been two the last time she'd visited the seaside. Imagine waiting seventeen years, she thought, as she stood on tiptoe and watched the locomotive come panting into the station at a little before seven on that August Bank Holiday morning.

When the vehicle ground to a halt and Ewan's hand cupped her elbow, a renewed sweep of nervousness overcame her. Today there would be no Mama to provide a reassuring buffer; for ten long hours she would be alone with Ewan McKenzie. How would he act? The gentleman – entertaining, kind, attentive, as he'd been during their excursions these past weeks? The tease? Or the enigma? Just so long as there were none of those strangely disconcerting looks and she was able to maintain the physical distance between them that was so essential to her comfort. Otherwise, the panic forever smouldering at the edge of her consciousness would ignite.

She need not have worried, for the train was already so crowded, there were not two adjacent seats to be had. So she spent the two-hour journey separated from Ewan by half a carriage length, and sandwiched between a hefty matron who worried incessantly and loudly over what she considered to be the train's excessive speed, and a boy of about six who, every few minutes, grabbed his mother's arm and whined, 'Are we there yet, Ma?'

And once they reached their destination, she forgot her misgivings, as well as the discomforts of the journey.

Outside the station house were parked several horse-drawn omnibuses, plastered with gaudy bill stickers advertising everything from Pears Soap to life assurance. After checking with the drivers, Ewan steered her to the vehicle that he said would take them to the pier. Indicating the upper deck, he shouted over the din, 'Let's go up top, then you'll have a grand view.' Thanking the Lord she'd had sense enough to opt for a simple blue holland skirt (without benefit of bustle), Emma negotiated the narrow iron staircase and made her way to one of the vacant forward-facing garden seats.

Oh, how right Ewan was, she thought some time later, as the omnibus turned onto the promenade. From this vantage, she would miss nothing. Clutching her boater against the brisk, salt-scented wind, she took in the scene with wondering eyes.

To her left, the white-frothed swells of turquoise water glittered in the sun and waves swirled into shore, depositing long trails of brown seaweed. The sands, filled with surging crowds, sprouted brilliant mushrooms of umbrellas. Children paddled and dug and built castles. Dogs yapped after seabirds that gathered in the air currents, rising and sinking in them.

Oh, and everywhere such activity. So many sightseers, shop-gazers. And the noise! Young men and girls calling to each other. People chattering and laughing and singing. The sound of applause from the beach, where a Punch and Judy show was in progress. Just beyond it, a German band *oom-*

pahing from a bandstand. She drew an enthralled breath and turned to glance over her shoulder as the vehicle trundled by a row of imposing-looking homes. 'Lodging houses,' Ewan said, following her gaze. 'An' that great monstrosity there, with all the handsom cabs in front' – he pointed ahead to a three-storied granite building that was a hodgepodge of turrets and battlements and small pointed windows – 'must be a hotel.' Emma gaped as they passed, awed by the amount of luggage, trunks and baskets and bundles, even a flat tin bath, heaped atop one of the cabs.

Ewan gave her a slight nudge with his elbow. 'What do you think of Brimsgate?'

She answered with a roll of her eyes.

Ewan grinned. ''Tis a lively spot, all right.' He hefted the holdall from between his feet onto his lap. 'Are you gettin' hungry, lass?'

She pressed her hands to her midriff. 'I am not sure if it's hunger or excitement.'

'Well, I'm feelin' a bit peckish myself. So as soon as we reach the end o' the line – an' it looks as if we're about there – we'll find a quiet spot an' have the lunch your mother packed for us.'

Since finding a quiet spot turned out to be an impossible task, they ate seated on a green-painted bench next to the pier entrance, where a group of bootblack minstrels cavorted, clad in garish tailcoats, striped trousers, and enormous spotted bow ties, their faces gleaming under straw hats. They cracked jokes, plucked at banjos, squeezed concertinas, and played rousing tunes that made one want to dance, then sang ballads of such poignancy they brought tears to the eye.

Emma was so caught up in the performance that when Ewan tapped her on the arm, she dropped her sandwich. 'Sorry, lass,' he said, 'but we'd best get movin' if we're to fit everything in.'

It took an hour for them to wander the length of the pier, dazzled by its shops and sideshows. On the way back, Ewan paused before a weighing machine. He fumbled in his trousers pocket and held up a copper. 'All right, now,' he said, indicating the metal platform, 'up you get, an' we'll see if you need fattening up.'

Emma clambered aboard. Fattening up? Lord, she was full to bursting after the potted shrimp he'd insisted on buying to replace her lost sandwich.

He popped the coin in the slot and then clapped the heel of his hand to his forehead. 'Seven stone, seven pounds. Och, 'tis a wonder the wind doesna blow you away.'

It was as if the wind had blown away Emma's shyness. She giggled and said as she stepped down, 'Now it's your turn.'

Flashing a smile, he fished out another copper. She gaped as the pointer spun around and came to rest at fourteen stone, six pounds. 'My,' she said, emboldened by the milling throng, 'you surely must weigh as much as His Lordship's prize bull.'

'Bull, is it?' He alighted, nodding slowly. And then, suddenly, he narrowed his eyes, lowered his head, and with a great roar made as if to charge her.

In a trice, she hitched her skirt to her calves and was off, racing over the wooden boards, weaving, dodging, insulated from the cacophony around her by the single-mindedness of her flight.

Reaching a staircase leading down to a beach less congested than the rest, she skidded to a stop. A brief pause to ensure Ewan was in close enough pursuit to guess her purpose, and she descended, but slowly, cautiously, for the treads were narrow, the incline sharp. Just as her feet touched terra firma, he seized her by the shoulders from behind, causing her heart to flap like the wings of the gulls overhead. Then he spun her around and released her. 'Well, aren't you the wily little fox!' he gasped.

'And fast, too.' She undid the top button of her blouse and fanned herself with her hand.

'Aye.' Ewan shrugged off his jacket and slung it between the handles of the holdall. 'Fast as a whippet. You've panned me out.' He drew his shirtsleeves across his glistening brow. 'Och, what I wouldna give for a dip. But since I havena

212

brought my bathing suit an' the sign there says ladies only, reckon I'm out of luck.'

'Goodness, what are those strange contraptions?' Emma pointed to the water's edge.

'Bathin' machines. Come on, we'll have ourselves a closer look. But we'd best not linger too long, or I'll be in trouble.'

They certainly did not resemble machines, thought Emma as they approached. They were more like miniature houses on wheels, with a canopy projecting out and down over the waves on the seaward side, completely screening an observer's view of the bathers. And there must have been several, for one could hear their squeals, whether of terror or delight being hard to tell quite clearly.

Emma shaded her eyes against the sun's glare. Imagine, having to dress to bathe. Mama had dug out an ancient bathing dress from her trunk a couple of nights before. And what a horrid, cumbersome garment it was, constructed of thick serge that surely would muffle her from head to foot. Heathenish. So much better to *un*dress. To feel the water caress your bare skin. Gracious, she had almost spoken her thoughts out loud, given herself away, and to Ewan of all people.

She slanted a sidelong look at his profile. Obviously lost in thought, he seemed a statue cast in bronze, but for the breeze teasing his black curls and ruffling his shirt. She had the sudden desire to touch him, yet the impulse shocked her. To distract herself, she flopped in the sand, removed her hat and boots, then reached beneath her skirt and dispensed with the cotton stockings that clung stickily to her legs. Ewan was too preoccupied to notice until she brushed by him, already breaking into a run and yelling, 'I am going to paddle. Will you please bring my boots and hat.'

The hard ridges made by the tide dug into her bare feet as she raced close to the water's edge. How exhilarating it was, the tang of salt and seaweed filling her lungs and the rushing air whipping her hair about her face. She kept on running, scrambling over rocky outcrops and then back onto smooth, firm sand, until at last she staggered to a halt. She had reached a secluded cove, and there was as yet no sign of Ewan. Sucking in a ragged breath, she collapsed onto the sand and lay spread-eagled, watching the cotton fluffs of cloud chase each other across the aqua sky. When her breathing had returned to an even rhythm, she clambered to her feet and, skirts hitched to her thighs, charged into the sea.

She was some distance out before the water lapped above her knees, and she might have proceeded deeper, perhaps succumbed to the temptation to immerse herself, if Ewan hadn't at that moment shouted from the shore. When she turned around she saw him gesturing wildly, clearly signalling her back.

But why? What in creation could be the problem? With an annoyed little cluck, she raised a reluctant hand in acknowledgement and then dawdled in. When she reached the shallows, she stopped to pick up a starfish. 'Oh, look.' Fascinated with her find, she waved the creature in his direction as she continued her search.

'I'm no interested in what you found.'

Frowning, for she was not certain she had heard him correctly, she continued wading in while he urged her on with an irritable 'Come on, come on.'

Lord, but look at his face, dark as a storm. 'What in Hades do you think you were doin'?' His forefinger wagged before her nose and she shrank back. 'You don't just go chargin' out into the sea like that. 'Tis *dangerous*, do you hear me?' He grabbed her by the shoulders and shook her.

'Let go of me,' she screamed, trying to wriggle free of his grip. But he held firm and a slow paralysis began to creep through her body.

'Look at me, Emma.' His hands slid down her arms and she felt their heat through the thin cotton of her blouse.

But she could not look at him. She closed her eyes in order to hide the threatening tears.

'The sea's a wild beast, lass. And you need to respect it.'

She wanted to respond in some way, but the lump in her throat prevented it.

'Do you hear me, lass?' Feeling herself released, she opened her eyes as a warm, slightly rough finger tipped her chin, forcing her to meet his gaze. Her heart leaped, for his look was gentle, searching, and his voice as he said, 'Well, do you?' soft as a stream.

No longer able to hold the tears at bay, she could only nod mutely and dab at the warm little rivulets on her cheeks with the back of her fists.

'Och, my poor wee thing.' Now Ewan blotted her face with a handkerchief. 'I'm sorry ... I didna mean to shout.'

Emma sniffed loudly and clamped her teeth over her trembling lower lip. He dabbed at the hollow of her throat and she remained quiet, unmoving, staring up at him.

And then a tremor racked his body. Something turbulent rippled across his features and he seemed to snap loose. There was no time for the panic to take hold of Emma; it rose and died in the same instant his arms encircled her and she felt herself swept up and pulled against him, so close she smelled the musky smell of him, felt his heart pound through his shirt, felt the heat and the hardness of him. His lips searched the curve of her ear and his warm, ragged breath kindled a fire in her, a moist throbbing fire between her thighs ... a fire that made her move in some primitive, remembered rhythm under his foraging hand that left the small of her back, inched under her blouse and camisole, and stroked its way to her breasts, cupping each and then teasing the nipples softly, gently until ... Oh, God, please. Some new want begged to be satisfied. She held her breath until everything began to spin. And she was tumbling down ... down ... down ...

... to Earth, jarringly. The sun, the taunting cries of sea gulls, the tangy-smelling wind assaulted her senses. In a torpor, she passed a confused hand over her face and squinted up at Ewan.

Avoiding her eyes, he cleared his throat several times. 'I'm sorry.' He nodded at her boots and boater, lying in the sand alongside the holdall. 'You've some dressin' to do, lass. An' sharp-like, for we've a three o'clock train to catch.'

Lulled by the swaying motion and the subdued silence of their fellow passengers, who all looked as exhausted as she felt, Emma watched the dizzying view beyond the carriage window. She was still in a daze and so, it seemed, was Ewan; he had hardly spoken since they left the beach. Now, though his head was buried in the newspaper he'd bought at Brimsgate Station, something told her he wasn't reading it.

Thank Heaven for these people, she thought. Protection against ... against herself and Ewan McKenzie. She shivered with both lust and shame. In fervent denial, she pressed her burning cheek against the glass. Might it not have been a trick of her imagination a corrupt fantasy? Why then did thoughts of the journey with Ewan from the station to Beech Cottage evoke such feelings of agitation and fear?

Why, too, she asked herself later, as she and Ewan alighted from the train, did the sight of Thomas Mondley fill her with such relief that she careened across the platform and threw her arms about him?

'Sorry.' She giggled nervously, and acknowledged Ewan's dismissing nod as he strode by them with a hesitant lift of her hand. 'What on earth brings you out, Thomas?' She forced her eyes back to his pale face, 'I thought you said –'

'Hmmm. McKenzie's in a tearing hurry. The excursion must have been too much for him.'

'Yes. You were saying?'

'A fortunate schedule change and a switch of days off, Emma, provided an opportunity I leaped at, thinking to surprise you.'

'You certainly did that.'

And you startled me, thought Thomas, still reeling inwardly from the implications of her enthusiastic greeting; she cared for him – his angel, Emma, cared for him, and with more than sisterly affection. Now he dared to hope.

Tucking her little hand in the crook of his elbow and smiling a beatific smile, he urged her towards the station house.

THIRTY

During the following weeks, Ewan McKenzie's and her own behaviour on that August day gave Emma no respite. She was in a constant state of flux: guilt and shame played tug-of-war within her; one moment, unreasoning rage would overtake her; the next, abject fear of something unknown and dangerous.

Thomas Mondley's letters did not help either; there was a subtle shift in their tone, nothing she could pinpoint but nevertheless adding to her confusion.

And the man in her nightmare returned to haunt her on a disturbingly regular basis. Though still faceless, he had lately taken form, had drawn close enough for her to see his red blond hair, feel his cold-fish fingers creeping over her flesh.

Relief – at least on the score of Ewan McKenzie – came in a form she least expected, with Mama's announcement of his promotion and consequent absence of some weeks. He had been made overseer of the Earl's holdings, which included properties in Cornwall, the Lake District, and the Yorkshire Dales, as well as the Channel Islands.

'I gather the job carries with it exceedingly hefty responsibilities,' Mama said that September afternoon as she gave the cake batter a final vigorous beating before spooning it into the pans. 'The first of which is this trip all over creation to make sure things are proceeding smoothly.'

'He has left, then?'

'Oh my, yes.' Mama slid the blue and white pottery bowl across the kitchen table's bleached surface. 'You can scrape it out, now. Two days ago and not due back until Christmas.'

'Hmmm.' Clasping her hands at the nape of her neck, Emma leaned back and contemplated the ceiling. Thank Heavens. She narrowed her eyes and pinched her lower lip between her teeth. Out of sight, out of mind.

'My, that's a determined expression if ever I saw one,' Mama said with a teasing note in her voice.

Because I *am* determined, Emma thought, to erase that man from my mental slate. Ever since he came on the scene, things have become altogether too unsettling. I shall have to be steadfast in my resolve, though, for it will be no easy task. But I *will* succeed. I must.

The only way to meet the challenge, she decided later, was to keep busy, exhaustingly so.

Her busyness began in October, with early preparations for the children's annual party and rehearsals for the Christmas Pageant. She decided to make each of her Christmas gifts, too, and spent hour upon hour hand-painting the Havilland milk pitcher for Mama, embroidering the Stevengraph for Hope, and knitting matching scarves and mittens for Thomas and little Oliver Windom.

Then there were the social activities to occupy her. Simultaneous with the first snowfall of winter, halfway through December, came the wedding of the year – that of Elgin Rutter and Priscilla Seton, a lavish affair to which everyone (Emma and Beth included) was invited.

The Marsh-Hugheses hosted a party and the entire congregation crowded into the Rectory to partake of Madeira cake and non-alcoholic ginger beer, while the mummers performed their age-old drama passed down through the generations.

Baking was a time-consuming proposition; the festive season would not be festive without sausage rolls, mincemeat pies, plum puddings, and marzipan and icing spread on the rich fruitcakes made in October, then wrapped in gauze and liberally doused with brandy during the ensuing months.

A flurry of housecleaning preceded the decorating with sprigs of holly and boughs of spruce, red and green and white paper chains, lanterns, and the laurel Kissing Ring, with its centre of rosy apples and bunch of mistletoe, hung from the ceiling in the hall.

Indeed, the days, the weeks seemed to race by. And suddenly, unbelievably, it was late Christmas Eve.

Seated in church, Emma listened raptly to the story of the Nativity, as if she were hearing it for the first time. And moments after, Mama nudged her and everyone rose and sang, 'Christians Awake, Salute the Happy Morn,' while the bells pulsated their message of peace and joy through the clear purple sky.

The bells had resumed their pealing when Emma awoke on Christmas morning. But they had ceased at noon, when she paced her bedroom. For the tenth time, she paused before the wardrobe mirror to fuss with the collar of her cream voile dress and cinch the mauve sash about her waist.

Lord, should she put up her hair? She checked the ivory combs each side of the centre parting and then fluffed the luxuriant waves.

The sudden sound of the doorknocker ended the debate.

From her room, where she was finishing her toilette, Mama called, 'Will you get it, dear?'

Damn, why couldn't *she*? After all, *she* had asked him; tracked him down through the Earl a month ago, sent the invitation, received an affirmative answer by return post.

The second tattoo on the door and her mother's 'Did you hear me?' came simultaneously.

On the landing now, Emma cleared her throat and shouted, 'It's unlocked. Come on in.'

She watched in breathless silence as he entered, set down an armful of packages, and divested himself of wet over-boots, cap, and topcoat. As he turned to hang his garments on the hall stand, she quietly descended the stairs. Pausing partway down with a kind of studied dignity, she said, 'Merry Christmas, Ewan.' Slowly, he looked up. And she felt something intensely powerful flash between them. Only when he came to the foot of the stairs and extended his hand was she able to move, hesitant step-by-step down to him, her eyes locked in his. She was on the last tread when he took her hand and murmured, 'Merry Christmas, lass. You look ...'

He got no further, for Mama chose that moment to slam her bedroom door and come hurtling down. He dropped Emma's hand and stood away from her.

'Ewan, dear.' Mama threw her arms about him and then released him with a giddy titter. 'How splendid to have you back.'

'Och, 'tis wonderful to be here, Beth.' He smiled a lingering smile at Emma over the top of Mama's gleaming braided crown. 'You have no idea how good.'

It might have been the glass of sherry that loosened her tongue; now there was no stopping her. But God, she was lovely, Ewan thought, the way her tawny eyes shone and her dainty white hands moved in emphasis as she launched into an account of the Christmas Pageant two weeks before.

'So there I was, proud teacher, feeling somewhat smug at the sight of my twenty-odd cherubic charges delighting the audience with their rendition of "Silent Night." Then on stage came Joseph and Mary and the Three Wise Men ...' She speared a slice of goose and popped it in her mouth, and Ewan, suddenly remembering the food on his plate, followed suit. 'I should have known better, of course, than to cast Alfie Plover as Joseph.'

'Go on, go on,' Beth said. 'Don't keep Ewan in suspense.'

Emma chewed and swallowed quickly. 'Well, as I said, they came on stage and, all at once, there was the most horrendous tearing sound.' Dabbing her lips with her napkin, she let the silence build in the manner of a skilled storyteller. 'I thought I would die. For there were Mary's knobby little knees exposed to the World. Joseph had stepped on her gown. And it was no accident, I can assure you ... I had only to look at Alfie's face to be convinced.'

Ewan released his tension in a chuckle and Emma leaned across, signalling him to silence. 'You have not heard the worst of it.' She smothered a grin behind her hand. 'Mary,' she tittered, 'Mary ... that dear little goldenhaired Betsy Watts, who looks like an angel, proceeded to set about Joseph with' – she covered her eyes with both palms and her mouth began to quiver – 'with the swaddled infant.'

Now Ewan let out all his tension in a great guffaw. And a round of laughter ensued that led to his stories about the

Earl's antics during the past months and kept up until after the plum pudding, when Beth held her sides in mock agony and said, 'Oh, my Lord, off to the parlour with you while I get my wind back. You, too, Emma. I'll see to the dishes.'

'Och, no you willna, not by yourself. I'll give you a hand.'

'So will I.' Emma was already on her feet and collecting the plates.

'Then we'll like as not be trippin' over each other. Why don't you take the packages I left on the hall stand into the parlour?'

Emma shrugged. 'Very well.'

'An' no peepin',' Ewan called after her as he took off his jacket and began rolling up his shirtsleeves in preparation for the dishwashing.

In less than forty-five minutes the cleanup was complete. As Beth put away the dinner service in the dresser cupboard and struggled to rise from her kneeling position, she fanned her flushed face with the back of her hand. 'Gracious, one little glass of sherry and I'm hot as a foundry. And I swear every bone in my body is aching. Must be old age catching up with me.'

Feeling a rush of affection for her, Ewan said, 'Rubbish.' He extended his arm, which she latched onto, and helped her. 'You're just a young thing ... an' a bonnie young thing at that.'

She made a deprecating gesture and batted her bright brown eyes. 'I'll warrant you say that to all the ladies.'

'Only the comely wenches and –'

'The good cooks,' Beth laughingly cut in. She was at the table now, gathering up the silver napkin rings. 'By the way, I *did* tell you Hope Windom and Oliver are coming later, did I not?'

Ewan stood with his back to the fire, rocking on his heels. 'Aye, you mentioned it in your letter.'

'It's a shame Thomas cannot be here. He's with his mother, which is only right, of course. Oh, but he did send Emma *the* most exquisite gift – the necklace she's wearing. You must have noticed it.'

Ewan rocked to an abrupt standstill and cracked his knuckles. 'I canna say I did.'

'A family heirloom, I believe, and worth a small fortune. Emma was just beside herself.'

I'll bet she was, Ewan thought, burrowing his hands in his trousers pockets. For wasn't it what women wanted, fancy doodads, and the fancier the better?

Fancy doodads, man. Not some paltry wee homemade ... 'Struth, imagine her face when she opened it, compared it to ...

'I am almost ready, Ewan. Why don't you join Emma while I make the tea? Then we shall have our little gift exchange.'

Relishing the silence, Beth stood on the threshold of the parlour. My, but it'd been a challenge convincing Emma, Hope, and particularly Oliver that she had no desire to go to the party at Chearden Hall. Never mind the carol-singing and the magician who could turn almost anything into a guinea pig and the Christmas tree with its one hundred candles and the lavish spread slated to be served at six o'clock. Solitude was what she needed.

Eyeing the disarray, she sagged against the doorjamb. The carpet was strewn with wrappings and the remnants of the scarlet and gold crepe-paper Christmas crackers they'd pulled; they had gone off like pistol shots and given up a veritable trove of trinkets. There were teacups and plates everywhere. The half-completed jigsaw puzzle Hope and Ewan had been working on occupied a tray laid across two footstools, and the cloth on the round table before the window was scattered with crumbs (not that Oliver hadn't been the perfect little gentleman, but children would be children.) The Queen Anne sideboard was heaped with boxes.

Astonishing the havoc four adults and one child could wreak! Beth drew in a fortifying breath and went to work. But she had barely finished tidying up when she heard Emma's key in the lock. So much for her plans, Beth thought, sinking into the armchair before the parlour fire and

222

propping her aching legs on a footstool. 'What brings you back so early?' she called out.

Emma fluffed up her hair with her fingers as she sat opposite. 'Oh, Oliver was a bit cranky and Hope and I both realized we were worn out. So we decided to call it a night right after the conjurer's show.'

Beth yawned. 'Seems as if everyone's worn out today. Too much of a good thing, I suppose. I must say I was surprised how early Ewan departed. I was under the impression he planned on spending the entire day *and* going on to the party at the Hall. But –'

'If you ask me, it was just as well he left when he did; he was as cranky as Oliver turned out to be.'

'Cranky? He didn't seem –'

'You didn't see what I did, Mama. He came in here after you and he did the dinner dishes, asked – or I should say *snapped* – what I'd done with his packages (and I'd done nothing except set them on the sideboard with the others) and then he shuffled through them, grabbed one and hid it under his jacket, whipped out to the hall and returned, minus the package.'

'Hmmm. That's strange. Obviously he'd made a mistake. Perhaps brought something intended for someone else. But the rabbitskin lap robe he gave us is absolutely beautiful. You knew he sewed the skins together himself, didn't you?'

Emma yawned and nodded.

Beth inhaled the scent of the spruce boughs on the mantel. Odd how dizzy it made her feel. 'It will be splendid for our train trip to Milchester.'

'*Our* train trip?'

'You said you'd come with me, dear.'

Frustrated, Emma closed her eyes and pressed back against the chair. 'No, I did not.' She heard the testiness in her own voice, knew it was as irrational as her vague fears about going back to Milchester were, but didn't care. Ever since Mama's decision to visit the McDonoughs in the New Year, she'd been a regular nag on the subject. 'I said I *might*. Remember?'

After several seconds, the lack of response caused her to lift her lids and peer under them. Frowning, she blinked wide. Lord, what a ghastly shade Mama's face was – a sort of waxen grey. And why on earth was she making those frantic little fanning gestures. 'What is it, Mama?'

'So hot … so infernally hot, I think I shall die,' was her mother's dazed response.

But her mother would live, Emma was assured the next morning. Observing Mama's alternating fever and bone-shaking chills and the bouts of arid coughing that left her gasping for breath, Emma had set out for Chearden and Dr Loslett's house at first light.

'Influenza,' the doctor said after a quick examination. 'Of course, it is not a thing to be taken lightly. But with a constitution as strong as yours, dear lady, and a daughter of Emma's ilk to take care of you, the prognosis for a speedy recovery is excellent.'

Emma could have wept with relief. Instead, she squared her shoulders and threw herself, with obsessive energy, into the task of nursing her mother back to wellness. For the time being, her pupils would have to do without their teacher. Life and health took priority.

Not until Dr Loslett pronounced his patient over the worst did Emma allow herself to think of Ewan McKenzie. Five days, and they had not heard a word from him. Barely had the thought entered her head than Dr Loslett said, 'We've an epidemic on our hands. No doubt about it. I've just come from the McKenzie place, and I've a dozen more calls to make.'

'McKenzie,' Emma said, catching Mama's eye. 'Do you mean Ewan McKenzie?'

'Yes. You know the fellow?' Dr Loslett dropped the tongue-depressor back in his leather bag.

Mama struggled to sit up. 'We certainly do. He's a good friend. Gracious, is anyone taking care of him?'

'Not that I'm aware of. And he is pretty badly hit. Gave him a sedative just before I left that should keep him down for at least a few hours.' He twirled the waxed tips of his moustache. 'Those big fellows have the mistaken idea they are invincible, think they can just carry on. I'll warrant it'll be a good fortnight, though, before your friend Mckenzie is feeling up to snuff.'

'That poor man,' Mama said as soon as Emma returned from seeing the doctor out, 'alone and ailing, and not a soul to look after him.' She fell silent, her shadowed eyes flitting about. Then she sighed and shook her head sadly. 'Men, you know, are as helpless as newborn rabbits, when they are poorly.'

Hard to imagine Ewan McKenzie helpless, Emma thought, rocking impatiently on her toes and heels while she waited for her mother to continue.

Mama toyed with one of the two thick plaits that hung over her bosom. 'Do you know where Ewan's cottage is?'

'Of course.' She rocked to a standstill. 'He pointed it out when he took us for a drive that evening last summer. It's the converted toll house, the red brick one with the half-timbers.'

Mama held up her hand in a staying gesture. 'I wasn't sure if – well, never mind.' She picked up the ormolu clock from the bedside table and regarded it shortsightedly. 'Good ... a little after one. Early enough that you can be there and back long before dark.'

THIRTY-ONE

'Hello.' Emma stepped quietly into the gloom of the interior, pausing to let her eyes adjust, and then closed the door after herself.

A narrow staircase led from the large square room, which seemed to encompass the entire ground floor, to the second story.

She went to the foot of the stairs, a basket clutched to her breast. After drawing in a gulp of air, she called, 'Ewan ... it's Emma.' She cocked her head. Except for the receding echo of her voice, there was silence. Grateful for her reprieve – albeit a temporary one, for sooner or later he was bound to awaken or she would rouse him – she exhaled stertorously.

Lowering the basket, she bounced it distractedly against her thighs. Her mission was to minister to the man; given her experience with the Society, it should not be an overwhelmingly difficult task.

Why, then, this dry mouth? She ran the tip of her tongue across her lower lip. And why her quickened heartbeat and the tremor in her fingertips, these ridiculous feelings of ...? In concert with her mind, her eyes flickered about, searching for definition. But out of the maelstrom of intangible emotions, nothing crystallized except a vague sense of foreboding.

Like an animal ridding itself of raindrops, she shook herself violently. Lord, she chastised her pupils for daydreaming and *she* – oh, grownups *called* it soul-searching – was the biggest offender of all.

She drew in another protracted breath. The obvious answer was to stop all her nonsense and simply get on with the job she'd been charged with.

And it was no easy one, she saw as she wandered across the dim room to the trestle table under the window, taking note of the grittiness of the floorboards under her boot soles, and of the pervasive odour of dust and mildew, and of the clutter on the tabletop as she cleared a space for the basket. Divesting herself of bonnet, gloves, and coat, she laid them on one of the two benches flanking the table.

The problem was where to begin. With her fists, she kneaded the small of her back, while her eyes took in the disorder.

The fire was in its death throes. Among the tabletop clutter, where the mice had left their calling cards, was a slab of partially devoured, moulding cheese sandwiched between two doorsteps of green-pocked bread. A jug that contained milk congealing into sour clots stood next to a bowl of rotten apples, which smelled as potent as a brewery.

A precarious pyramid of pans and crockery graced the drain board next to the sink. At least there was a tap, so there would be no necessity for hauling water from an outside pump or well.

Thumbs jammed in the bib of her pinafore, she hitched her shoulders. First things first. The fire to heat the water, the water to wash the pots. No pots, no soup. Oh, and the light; nothing could be accomplished without the proper light.

It was a good hour before she was done. Work had had its usual cathartic effect. And as she surveyed the room, suffused now in amber from the twin lamps each end of the mantel, and with pans returned to their hooks on the wall beside the stone fireplace, crockery arranged on the dresser shelves, surfaces cleared of debris, tabletop scrubbed to the colour of bleached bones, floorboards swept clean, and the fire resurrected, her mood was one of satisfaction.

She sank onto the bench. Yes, she really had done a capital job. And despite the temptation, she had heeded Mama's warning. 'Whatever you do,' she'd said, 'don't move anything Ewan might consider important. Tools, fishing gear, that sort of paraphernalia. Men detest it when women try to organize their things.'

Smoothing her hair up from the nape of her neck, Emma pinned it in place. There had been no fishing gear. But there were guns – three in the rack on the opposite wall alongside the crammed bookshelves. No danger of her disturbing those, though. She had no desire to go up in a puff of smoke.

But tools – the wood-carving implements in particular – now that was a different story. Those odd-shaped chisels, the miniature mallet, and the knife with the stag handle, at the far end of the table. And the unusual woods with their varied grains, the jars of paint of every conceivable hue. *They* had been tempting.

It was the ship, though, housed in a tissue-paper-lined box, that enticed her most. She slid along the bench and regarded the delicate craft afresh. Its hull of dark, lustrous mahogany must have measured a scant four inches from stem to stern. Furled sails like silk, rigging fine as a cobweb, and on deck a lilliputian captain with an authoritarian stance, and above him, fluttering in the gentle wind of her breath, a minuscule Union Jack.

What an enigma Ewan McKenzie was! Already so many sides to the man and here another. To think those big hands of his were capable of such intricate artistry.

And - she noticed the envelope lying beside a mound of wood shavings - he wrote with unfailing regularity to his sister in Canada. Quite a feat when you considered that most men (except Thomas, of course) were dreadful correspondents.

Emma leaned on her elbows and peered at the postmark on the letter. Saskatchewan, that odd-sounding place Ewan was always talking about.

She chafed her arms. Imagine, crossing endless seas and vast open prairies, fighting for survival. Against the elements. Against wild beasts. And (she gave a shudder) Red Indians. What pluck. She inhaled her admiration and the aroma of soup returned her to earth with a jolt.

Straddling the bench, she looked uncertainly at the dim stairwell. Now it was time to show *her* pluck. Her patient - helpless, as Mama would have said, as a newborn rabbit - was waiting.

Well, what on earth was there to be nervous about?

In the wavering lamplight, all Emma could see of Ewan as she skirted the bed, tiptoeing to the chest of drawers beside it, was the top of his glossy black head.

He lay on his side facing away from her. Judging from the outline of his body beneath the covers, his knees were drawn up to his chest. He had burrowed down so deeply, no doubt against the ague, she could not detect his breathing.

She could hear her own, though; rapid and harsh over the whisper of her feet on the worn strip of carpet. And she could feel the hot steam rising from the soup as she set the tray atop the chest. She bent over to adjust the lamp's wick, straightening when a bright, even flame resulted.

A rustle of movement came from behind, followed by the creaking of the bedsprings and a faint moan. Her heart stopped fractionally, then took off at a trot when something caught her on the hip. She pivoted on her heels and came to a mesmeric stop.

It appeared that his outflung arm had struck her when he rolled to a supine position and tossed the covers back, so that they were now draped just below his navel. His fingertips grazed her pinafore skirt, compelling her to stand as still as an effigy.

Staring down at his nakedness, at the lustre of the skin even where the sun had not bronzed it, and the marvellous symmetry of powerful shoulders to narrow waist, at the crisp, dusky hair covering the chest and feathering down to the abdomen, Emma felt a confusing contraction of breasts and lungs, a prickling sensation at the nape of her neck and a warmth that began as a sweet ache between her thighs, then stole languorously through her body.

She had to steel herself against the overwhelming desire to touch the tender hollow between muscle and collarbone, the column of his neck, his jaw, blue-black with new beard. To smooth away the lines of suffering and the plum-coloured shadows below the eyes, which now were rolling back in their sockets, blinking wide, beginning to focus questioningly upon her.

The cracked lips parted. 'Emma, is that you?'

The sound of her name broke the spell. Turning away from him, she said briskly, 'It most certainly is. Dr Loslett was by earlier, checking on Mama, and he told us you were ill.'

'Your mother's been poorly?'

Emma folded and refolded the linen napkin. 'Yes. Like you, she has influenza. Has had it for almost a week.'

'What day is it?'

'Thursday.'

'What date?'

'The thirty-first.'

'Of what?'

'December.' Good Lord, Emma thought, New Year's Eve. With all the upset, it had completely slipped her mind.

'An' your mother, is she still taken bad?'

Emma continued toying with the napkin. 'Oh, she's well on the road to recovery now. And when she heard you were stricken, she insisted I bring over this chicken soup.'

'Soup, you say?' The question was muffled.

'Yes.'

His voice more distinct now: 'Och, I dinna ken if I could eat ...'

'Of course you can. And you will,' Emma said with false conviction. 'I did not waste my afternoon to have you be stubborn.' Forestalling the moment she'd have to face him and praying the sounds she heard were a signal that he was covering himself, she fumbled with the spoon. Finally, she mustered the courage to round on him.

Thanks be to God, he was now clad in a nightshirt, and the covers were tucked across his chest. He had run a comb through his hair, too, for it no longer clung damply to his brow. He had the look, thought Emma, of a small boy caught in some mischief. Suppressing the urge to laugh, she reached for the tray and set it in his lap. 'Now eat.' She used her schoolmarm voice and stood over him with shoulders squared and arms folded. 'And don't dare stop until that bowl is empty.'

'Yes miss.' His solemn nod belied the twitching at the corners of his mouth.

Her shredded nerve endings knitted together as she watched him. He glanced up and caught her eye, asking, 'You made it, did you?'

'Yes.' Unconsciously, she settled at the foot of the bed.

He tipped the bowl, spooned the last of the soup into his mouth, and then dabbed at his lips with the napkin. ''Twas good, real good. You're a fine cook, Emma my girl.' He lifted the tray from his lap and handed it to her. 'Thomas Mondley is a lucky fellow.'

'Thomas Mondley?' Emma rose and set the tray on the

chest. 'What on earth does *he* have to do with my chicken soup?'

'Well, I thought that you and he were ...'

'We are *friends*,' she said over her shoulder.

''Twas a mighty fancy gift your *friend* gave you for Christmas. Worth a small fortune, accordin' to your mother.'

'My mother?' Emma whirled about. 'What were you and Mama doing, discussing me behind my back?'

'She was just tellin' me how delighted you were with –'

'Well, of course I was.' His expression, something cynical about the angle of eyebrow and set of his mouth, irritated. 'What woman wouldn't be? My fa – someone once said ...' She massaged the centre of her forehead with two fingers as though to coax out the memory, but it eluded her. 'Women and beautiful jewels were made for each other,' she said, feeling immediately inane and even more irritated when she saw a smile flit across his face.

'You dinna need to get your feathers all ruffled,' he said. 'Your mother was only –'

'Mama may think what she pleases. 'But I' – she slapped her thigh in emphasis – 'will plan my own life.'

'Will you now?' He ran a thoughtful finger over the new growth of his beard. 'An' while you're at it, do you think you could mebbe see your way to gettin' me a cuppa tea. I'm right parched.'

'Of course. And be sure to keep yourself well-covered while I do.'

When she returned several minutes later and handed Ewan his tea, he said, ''Tis a miracle you were able to find anythin' in that mess down there. I've not exactly been up to doin' much o' anythin'.' He stopped and gestured impatiently towards the foot of the bed. 'Will you sit down? You're makin' me nervous, hoverin' over me ...'

'Hovering?' Emma sat, her lips pursed in indignation. 'I was waiting to see if you were in need of anything else.'

He stared at her over the rim of his cup. Uncomfortable with his inspection of her, she blurted, 'If you're worried about the mess, as you called it, you may spare yourself. I tidied up earlier and everything is in its place. Except, of course, for the wood-carving tools ... I didn't lay a finger on those. I know how infuriating it is for a man to have his things put away where he cannot find them.'

Ewan set the cup on the bedside table and smiled a lopsided smile, 'You're a wise woman, Emma Cadman.'

Woman. Not lass, or wee thing, but woman. Her heart performed a foolish little somersault. 'And I think it's terribly clever of you to –' The contact of his foot against her hip as he flexed his legs caused her to falter. 'For you to have made that ship, why, it's absolutely –'

'Amazin'. Wouldna credit a great ox like me with bein' able to craft such a wee work? 'Tis a quaint little thing, though, isna it? Now someone like young Oliver would have a grand old time sailin' it in the rain barrel.'

'Gracious, it's far too fine a thing for ...'

'Fine, you say? Well, I'll be.' Ewan stroked his jawline reflectively. 'I take it you like the wee thing, then?'

'Like it?' With a cavalier motion, she smoothed her skirts. 'I *love* it.'

Ewan gave a soft chuckle and his chest seemed to swell under his nightshirt. 'Reckon she is a fine wee craft, if I say so myself. One of my better ones.' Clasping his hands behind his head, he stared beyond her shoulder.

'You have made others, then?' Caught up in the conversation now, Emma wriggled closer to him, one foot dangling to the floor, the other crooked beneath her.

'That I have.' His arms descended to his lap. 'Dozens. When I start carvin', it's as though ...' The words froze between his white teeth, and a strange thing happened to his face. A slow flush washed the edges of his pallor and his eyes, velvet dark, seemed to swallow her up, turning her insides soft and liquid hot. Her heart flapped against her rib cage and the bones of her spine meshed rigidly together, making her powerless to move.

One hand moved across the back of her neck and over her scalp, tangling in her hair, tugging the pins loose; the other encircled her waist and pulled her close, so close against his warm muscular body that her breasts hurt.

Now her hair fanned out about her shoulders, and he was nuzzling into it and caressing her back with slow strokes that grew progressively longer until his fingers found the dip between her buttocks. And there they lingered while she, responding to a gathering rush of sensations, began to undulate in unconscious rhythm.

Through a haze, she thought she heard him whisper, 'God, you're lovely.' She felt him reach beneath her skirts, fingertips like ardent feathers brushing her inner thigh. Lightning raced in her veins; she wanted to rip aside the barriers of drawers and petticoat that separated her from his touch, to feel his burrowing fingers ...

Touch me, touch me, *please.*

Sure, an' Papa'll stroke his darlin' ... stroke her till she's a juicy little sweetmeat. But first she must kiss poor Johnny. Come on now. Be nice to the little fella, for isn't he lyin' here all limp and lonesome and waitin' for the princess to wake him up? Kiss him. Kiss him.

'No. No! *Don't!*' Her own outcry, the sudden grip on her shoulders, and the sensation of being pushed back made her heart sound as if it were beating on the walls of the room. In hollow puzzlement, she looked down at herself seated on the edge of the bed and then up at Ewan.

His tongue moistened his parched lips. 'Emma, love,' he murmured shudderingly, ''tis getting late. I think you'd best to be goin' now, for I'm panned out.'

When he heard the door slam, Ewan slumped back on the pillow and drew the back of his hand across his brow.

God, the fever was on him still; it throbbed in him, clenched like a searing fist in his groin. Oh, it would have been so easy to take her. Like a ripe fruit, she'd been waiting in innocent wantonness to be plucked – until that final moment. Her cry had saved him. Saved *her*.

Just as well. Admit it, lad, there's no place for a woman in your plans, least of all a wee slip of a thing like her; she'd hold you back, just like Ma held Pa back.

Beth's voice echoing in his head. 'Emma thinks the world of you, I know. Admires and respects you. You are like a father she never had, or at least scarcely had.'

If Beth only knew how, this afternoon, he had seen the woman in Emma; passion swirling across those great golden eyes like mists off a loch; that he had travelled the satin path to Emma's warm, moist womanhood, lingered in delight over curves and textures.

Oh, that first glimpse of her – the firm, sweet roundness of her girl-woman's body that day at the Well.

God – he reached over his head and gripped the rails of the bedhead – how long had it been since he'd had a woman? A *woman*? He'd never had a woman; only a succession of one and-sixpenny whores, and not even that since he'd left Scotland. Until Emma, he'd not felt the need.

And yet he writhed against it, now, turning to stare into the lamp's wavering flame.

THIRTY-TWO

'Very well, Mrs McDonough,' Emma shouted into the mouthpiece of the wall-mounted oak telephone. 'Yes, it is hard to believe it's 1886. Uh-huh ... yes, Mama's beside herself with excitement. That's right ... Tuesday the twelfth, a week today, about six. Oh, I shall ... Of course. Goodbye, then.' She shook her head and tapped her ear as she replaced the receiver. ''Struth' – she grimaced at Hope – 'they may well be marvellous inventions, but they certainly play havoc with one's ears.'

'Oh, but I would not be without it. You cannot imagine the time and money that instrument has saved me. But enough of that; come and sit by the fire.' Hope gestured to the chair alongside her own. 'With Oliver at Mrs Barnstable's – I swear he's fallen in love with little Violet and I shall have to pry him

234

loose when the party ends – we have a golden opportunity for uninterrupted conversation.' She edged forward and tapped Emma on the knee. 'Now *do* solve this mystery for me.'

'What mystery?'

'Well, all along you were adamant about not going to Milchester. And now, here you are, making arrangements for next week. What on earth made you change your mind?'

Emma couldn't stop her eyes from darting about in pursuit of her confused thoughts. Why indeed? Another of those spur-of-the-moment decisions that smacked of irrationality. All she knew was she'd told Mama she would accompany her to the McDonoughs', simply rushed upstairs and spouted it when she returned from Ewan McKenzie's that New Year's Eve afternoon.

Forcing herself to focus on the garnet brooch pinned at the throat of Hope's blouse, she said, 'Mama ... I am doing it for Mama. I realized just how much it meant to her and I thought it would perk her up when she was ill.'

'Decent of you to do it for your mother.'

'It was decent of *you* to close up shop this past fortnight. When did you say you were reopening, this Thursday?'

Hope nodded. 'Decency, by the way, had nothing to do with it. Self-preservation, or preservation of sanity – after our horrendously busy November and December – is more like it. This month will be altogether different, though; slower than a tortoise, I shouldn't doubt. Your Mama' – she paused to rummage among the contents of the satinwood box in her lap – 'couldn't have chosen a better time for her sojourn.'

Silence fell, a deep companionable silence broken only by the sporadic moan of the wind down the chimney and the clock's deep strokes marking off the minutes.

Emma traced the cording on the chair's cushion with her thumb, as she watched her friend thread a needle and take up her beadwork. Eventually, Hope spoke again. 'I hear Mr McKenzie fell victim to our influenza epidemic.'

Emma plucked at the nubs on her tweed skirt. 'Hmmm.'

'I was so pleased to become better acquainted with him, Christmas Day. He's a thoroughly charming fellow.'

235

'Hmmm.'

'Oliver was quite taken with him, too.'

'Hmmm.'

'My dear Emma,' Hope said with a faint chuckle, 'you are fast becoming mistress of the monosyllable.'

'Sorry.'

'Such a pity Thomas couldn't have been there.' Hope set the box, and the beaded card case she'd been sewing, on the table at her elbow. 'But, gadzooks' – her green eyes flared teasingly and she clapped her hands against her breast – 'that necklace! Obviously, the fellow is well and truly smitten. Has he declared himself? Said anything that would lead you to believe …?'

Emma crossed and recrossed her feet. 'Thomas is not one to come directly to the point. He hints.'

'Hints?'

'Yes. As in, "the rewards of the ministerial life"; "the qualities required of a minister's mate"; "the sacrifices involved in …"'

'Oh, my. Rather blatant hints, I should say. What will you do if he asks you?'

'Asks me what?'

Hope laughed a single sharp note. '*Proposes*, you goose.'

Ye gods and little fishes … as if she didn't have enough to contend with, Emma thought, bunching a cushion behind her back and resettling herself. 'I should have to refuse him, of course. I'm terribly fond of him. But … anyway, with the New Year, I've resolved to stop crossing bridges before I come to them. Thomas is also a man of extreme caution, and it may well take him months or even years to reach such a step.'

'Oh, I doubt it.' Hope rubbed her hands together, touched her fingertips to her chin, and regarded Emma thoughtfully. 'Something tells me you are going to have to deal with the question much sooner than you bargained for.'

Hope's instincts were correct. Three days later, the letter arrived:

236

My Dearest Emma,

Aunt Flora rang to tell me of your upcoming visit and invite me to participate in the belated New Year festivities. Unfortunately, I shall not be able to get to Milchester until Saturday (about mid-day) which, of course, is the day of your return to Chearden. However, since I am determined to discuss with you – and in private – a question of the utmost importance to our futures, I thought I would accompany you on the train journey home, spend the night at The Hare and Hounds in Marespond, and be back in Tarletan in time for Sunday morning's sermon.

I shall be counting the minutes until I see you.

Yours in profoundest affection,
Thomas

Lord give me strength. Emma crumpled the letter in her fist and squeezed until her hand went numb. The pleasant reunion, destined now to end in *un*pleasantness. Damn. Why couldn't Thomas be satisfied with their friendship? Why did people always want more from you than you were prepared to give? Why couldn't people give you what *you* wanted?

And what exactly is *that*?

What? I want … Oh God, what *do* I want? To be free of this sense of beleaguerment that seems to be forever hovering over me. Just now, though, I want to get this infernal Milchester visit over – the sooner, the better.

Throughout that Monday night, wind and hail had blended together in a howling maelstrom. But Tuesday dawned clear and calm. And just as Mr Pattison, the driver, finished loading Emma's and her mother's luggage onto the hansom cab, the sun made a cheering appearance.

'Gracious!' Mama squeezed Emma's hand as she settled next to her. 'First, you decide to come with me – granted, not for the entire week, but four days is better than nothing – and then the weather takes a turn for the better. If those aren't omens of a splendid trip, then nothing is.'

Emma gave an inward groan. If only you knew, she

thought. All the way to the station, she fretted, playing the scenario across her mind, writing and rewriting her lines. But Mama's 'Oh, dear, I hope you are not sorry you came' as they boarded the train, brought her up sharply. Bad enough she had to shatter Thomas's dream and dash Mama's hopes; the least she could do now was feign happiness. Drawing Mama into her embrace, she said, 'Of course I'm not sorry. I'm as thrilled as you are.'

'Evenin'.' Roscoe tipped his cap and nodded disbelievingly as he picked up their bags. 'What 'as it been? Nine, ten years?'

'Nine. Amazing, isn't it?' Mama said.

His rheumy eyes narrowed with apparent pleasure as they rested on Emma. 'I'd 'ave known you anywhere, miss, with that red 'air o' yours.' His mouth worked over toothless gums. 'Got rid of them freckles, though, didn'tcha?'

Emma ran a gloved fingertip across her nose and chuckled. 'Yes, I did, Roscoe. Finally.'

''Tis grand to see you both.'

'It's splendid to see you.' Emma touched his arm in a gesture of affection.

'Dare say you'll notice plenty o' changes,' he said, shuffling along between them through the station house. 'We've got the 'lectricity, now, on Craven Road, an' that there contraption what you can talk into.'

'Oh, you mean the telephone.' Mama sent Emma an amused look.

'Aye, that's it. Mr and Mrs are ringin' 'ere an' ringin' there. Proper queer if you ask me, talkin' into a box.'

When he handed them up into the brougham, Roscoe said, 'They're all waitin' on you; Mr and Mrs and the young 'uns. Plannin' a right celebration, they are. You make yourselves comfy, now. Put this rug over yourselves an' I'll 'ave you there in no time.'

Emma's eyes took in the tufted red leather upholstery. Surely it couldn't be the same brougham that'd transported them to the station all those years ago. She removed her glove and ran her palm along the edge of the seat. Gracious, it had to be, for here was the little nick made by Albert's shoe buckle the day Mrs McDonough had taken them shopping. How uncanny. Like turning back the clock.

As the vehicle began to roll gingerly downhill, the jangle of its wheels across the cobbles overlaying the thrum of gusting rain, she and her mother exchanged an excited look and then turned away to their respective windows.

At first, all Emma could discern were the shadowy outlines of buildings, and none she recognized. But presently, the pitch of the carriage and the quality of the road beneath the horses' hooves changed; their progress became smoother, quieter. And there, suddenly illuminated by gas lamps flanking its broad flight of steps, was the town hall, appearing smaller than she remembered it. The brougham picked up speed, and all at once, they were bowling along a wide, well-lit street of shops. 'Struth, but they were still here: Hadley's; the dressmaker's; Pratt's Creamery; Edwin & Sons Tailors, and the tobacconist's.

Now they rounded a bend and the carriage's lamps sent twin tunnels of yellow light ahead of them through the downpour. The stone pillars of the park entrance flashed in and out of view. The high red brick wall, thick with ivy. The stretch of giant poplars. Miss Faverley's, unmistakable with its mock-Tudor facade. Emma reached blindly for her mother's arm. 'We must be almost there. We just passed –'

'Your old school. Yes, I know, dear. Isn't it exciting? Oh, and look … Craven Road. I can hardly believe it, Emma. We are here. Actually here.'

Again, the uncanniness of the scene struck Emma, as she stood at the bedroom window at half past eight the next morning. Almost a decade, and nothing had changed.

Opposite was their old house. Except for the curtains, it was exactly as she remembered it. Her room, above and to the left of the front door. Shivering, she chafed her arms through the sleeves of her flannel nightdress and transferred her gaze to the sycamore by the wrought iron gates. As she stared at the tree's bare knurled limbs, etched in black against the ashen sky, a suffocating sense of unease overcame her. Hastily, she turned her back on the scene and padded across the dusky pink carpet to the bed.

The sounds of carriage wheels, slamming doors, and raised voices had roused her earlier. According to Mrs McDonough, breakfast would be served at nine, and in bed. What luxury, Emma thought, scooting down into the hollow she'd vacated moments before. 'You are on holiday,' Mrs McDonough had said. 'And I am going to see to it you are both pampered.'

What a dear she was, so round and rosy, with those bright little raisin eyes. A prideful display of the family photographs, the day before, had revealed a grownup Jane very much like her mother. 'It really is a shame,' Mrs McDonough had said, 'that you will not get a chance to see Jane and meet her husband, Mason, and little Leonard. But I told her you would ring her.'

And what a challenge that'd been, standing in the drawing room, trying to make sense of Jane's fragmented voice and shouting her responses, with the entire family and Mama milling about her.

Emma plumped the pillows behind her head and focused on the ceiling's ornate cornice. The previous evening had been an exhausting one, with Jane's three brothers all vying for her attention: witty Steven, up from Oxford for the holidays; bookish Abraham, doing his best to impress her with his banking expertise; Albert, already quite the dandy, though not yet fifteen, whispering outrageous endearments to her at every turn; and the youngest child, little Seraphine, a golden-haired cherub with impish eyes, hanging onto her skirts and chattering incessantly.

From all accounts, the rest of the week would be equally hectic. Visitors, excursions, calls on Mama's old friends. And then, Saturday, the day of reckoning. She rolled onto her stomach and pounded the mattress with her fist. Thomas, why couldn't you have just continued to be a brother to me?

Emma asked herself the same question throughout Saturday's luncheon, as Thomas's eyes hung upon hers, along with a lingering half-smile that rendered her so nervous she was unable to eat. 'If you'll excuse me,' she mumbled to nobody in particular, 'I have rather a lot of packing still to do.' And she fled the dining table.

Ten minutes later, Mrs McDonough poked her head around the open bedroom door. 'Everything alright, dear?' she asked, padding across the carpet to the window.

For the umpteenth time, Emma refolded her white silk blouse. 'Yes. I'm just about done.'

'Goodness, I never noticed before how tall your tree has grown.'

'*My* tree?'

'The sycamore across the street. Remember how you used to perch up there when your Mama was out? She would have had a fit if I had told her, but I never did – waiting hour after hour for ...' Her voice trailed off, but resumed as she turned from the window. 'Of course, when Thomas used to come and visit – I think that was before your family moved in, though – he was quite the tree climber, too.' She laughed. 'So at least you know of one thing you two have in common. Can I help you, dear?' She rustled to the bedside.

'No, really.' Emma pushed her hair out of her eyes, puzzling over Mrs McDonough's remarks. She made a hasty sausage of her brown corduroy skirt and stuffed it in her suitcase.

'There is no great rush, dear. It will be quite some time until the hansom arrives, so there's no need to get yourself in a tizzy. Thomas certainly isn't. He and Benjamin are closeted in the study, and I dare say they're partaking of a little after-luncheon brandy.' Her apple cheeks dimpled. 'Which is just the ticket, because' – she eased herself onto the foot of the bed and linked her hands below her bosom – 'it has been so hectic these past days, I have hardly had a chance to exchange two words with you.'

'I know.' Emma reached for the hairbrush on the bedside table.

'I should hate to think we had worn you out. I do wish you

could stay on longer, too. I hoped we could go across the way ...'

'Across the way?' Emma paused in her brushing.

'To the Beechams'. Your old house.' Mrs McDonough cupped her elbow in her palm and rested her chin on her fist. 'You know, aside from the addition of a fitted bathroom and water closet, like ours, and a little wallpapering and painting, it is virtually as you and your Mama left it. But then' – she made a dubious face – 'perhaps you are better off staying away.' Her busy eyes moved about the room and at last resettled on Emma. 'I mean, it's not as if the place holds happy memories, is it, dear?'

Emma sank to the edge of the bed and toyed with the bristles of the hairbrush, her shoulders lifted in uncertainty.

'All this time, and it still makes my blood boil that you should have been ...' Mrs McDonough broke off and shuddered. And then she reached for Emma's hand and patted it distractedly. 'I cannot tell you how glad I was, all those years ago, to hear that you and your Mama had together lanced the abscess, so to speak. I knew it was the only way. Exorcise the ghosts and be done with it.'

'Ghosts?' Emma arched her eyebrows.

'Forgive me, dear, I do tend to get carried away, sometimes.' A tweak of Emma's cheek, and she brought her palms together in a soft clap. 'Look at you. All grown up into a lovely young woman, like my Jane. It's no wonder Thomas's letters have been so full of you. And I'll wager a pound to a penny his conversation now with Benjamin is just as full of you.'

Flora McDonough would have won her bet; for her husband was at that moment saying, 'Deucedly fine woman, Emma Cadman. Admirable the way she turned out.'

Thomas Mondley tossed back the last of the brandy in his snifter, gasping slightly as it burned down his throat, and giving himself up momentarily to the pleasant tingle radiating through his body. Liquor was an unaccustomed indulgence. But then this was no ordinary day. He smiled and fingered the tiny box in his trousers pocket. He hoped she liked it, Grandmama's ruby ring. 'Course, she'd like it ... she had adored the amethyst necklace. Suddenly, he remembered his uncle's comment. 'The way she turned out,' he said, inwardly amused. What had his dear Emma been? A wilful child? A spoiled brat? Possibly, during her Milchester days. Certainly not later, judging from her account and Mrs Cadman's of those dreadful years in the factory town.

'Yes,' Benjamin carried on. 'I mean, that sort of thing can ...'

'What sort of thing, Uncle?' As Thomas perched on the edge of the desk, an image of Emma tossing her glorious red hair and stamping a dainty foot flashed pleasantly before him.

Benjamin creaked back in his chair and hooked fat thumbs under his lapels. 'The business with ...' He stopped and looked piercingly at Thomas. 'She *has* told you about her childhood, the good and bad of it?'

'Why, of course; we have no secrets.' Recollecting Emma's confidences about the hardships of life in Glinton, as well as her friendship with Jessie, Thomas experienced a touch of smugness.

'Just wanted to be sure, is all. 'Course, there are certain things – youthful adventures, shall we say – that we men keep from our ladies' delicate ears. However, there is no better foundation on which to build a union than honesty. And,' he said with a knowing nod, 'I suspect that is where you and Emma are ...'

'I certainly hope so, sir,' Thomas cut in.

'By Jove,' Benjamin tugged on his fleshy lip for an instant, ''tis fortunate you came along, my boy.'

'Fortunate? How so?'

'Well, there are plenty of chaps who'd think twice, aren't there?'

Thomas flopped in the nearest chair. 'I suppose there are those who are fearful of the responsibilities of –'

''Twas a lucky day for Emma when you came into her life.'

Thomas waved a deprecating hand.

''Course, she's grown into a fine young woman, despite that nasty business. Fellow was an out-and-out bounder. But as the Good Book says, be sure your sins shall find you out. And by Jove, they did him. Hate to say it, but the wretch only got what he deserved.'

Nasty business? Out-and-out bounder? Thomas scratched his nose in bewilderment. And then, suddenly, he caught on. The schoolteacher, of course; the one Emma had clobbered and who had been instrumental in her expulsion. And wasn't it the truth? 'I should say so, Uncle.'

'Worse than a bounder. A pervert.'

Thomas tipped his head doubtfully. Granted, the man had been a nasty piece of work all right. But Uncle *was* getting a touch dramatic. 'A pervert, you say?'

'Lord, yes. Chap would have to be, to rob a girl of her innocence ... do such vile things ... *and to his own daughter!*'

THIRTY-THREE

The gregariousness of the family who had piled into the compartment with them – parents and four offspring – had first struck Emma as amusing. But now, as the homeward journey drew to a conclusion, the purple-jowled father's jokes seemed inane, the curls of smoke issuing from his pipe malodorous, and the laughter of his wife and lumpy children, a nerve-wrackingly brittle overlay to the relentless clickety-clack, clickety-clack of the train's wheels.

In an effort to stave off the clamorous assault, she reached inside her bonnet and covered her ears until her arms grew tired. Then she returned her hands to her lap and stole a sidelong glance at Thomas's sphinxlike profile. To all appearances he was as weary of their travelling companions as she. Perhaps more so, for he had been acting the mute since their departure from Milchester. And no wonder; the poor fellow had anticipated privacy for their discussion, and look what had resulted.

Emma dreaded the proposal to come; Thomas had been so good to her. She stretched her kid gloves taut over her knuckles. If in the past he'd shown signs of pomposity or nastiness that she could dredge up now, it might appease her guilt at rejecting him. But the worst she could say about him was that he could be a touch self-righteous. And so minor a character flaw hardly alleviated her unease.

Although she *could* conjure up some irritation at him for his ludicrous choice of setting. What in creation had he been thinking about? Proposals – at least in Penny Dreadfuls – took place in heavenly-scented rose arbours or beneath poetic willows or on moonlit verandahs. Certainly not on a train or in a hansom cab, which, since time was running out, was bound to be the stage on which the scenario would be played out.

An unexpected wave of compassion swept through Emma. Oh, Thomas, dear Thomas, she thought, wait until we reach Beech Cottage, where I can say all that is in my heart about my affection for you and then turn you down with the utmost gentleness.

Whether destiny or coincidence had a hand in it was hard to tell, but the cabbie's ceaseless patter during the ride home from the station precluded any conversation between her and Thomas.

'You *are* going to come in?' Emma managed to insert, sotto voce, as they drew up in front of the cottage soon after dusk.

Still avoiding her eyes – he had not met her gaze once since they'd left Milchester – he gave a curt nod of affirmation.

Ye gods, Emma thought with a tinge of acerbity as she alighted and passed through the gate, Thomas was so enormously nervous that he might never rediscover his tongue. 'I'll go on ahead and unlock the door,' she called over her shoulder.

By the time she'd put a match to the kitchen fire and lit the lamps on the dresser and mantel, the two men were at the

245

front door. Obviously, the cabbie had been asked to wait, for she heard his raspy "Alf an hour, yer say. Righto, guv'nor … me an' the nags'll park out there an' 'ave ourselves a bit of a snooze, an' you come an' give me a rap when you be ready fer movin' on.'

Except for the gusting of the wind against the cottage, there was a long interval of silence between the sound of the door closing and Thomas's footfalls. Unnerved suddenly, Emma gripped the back of the nearest chair and braced herself for his entrance.

Ewan could not concentrate on the letter to his sister, Meggie. He had thought it might distract him. But here it was after six, and he had nothing but the salutation written. He crumpled the paper into a ball, aimed it at the fire, and missed. Raking back his hair, he hunched over the table and stared at the note. Damned blasted thing. Ever since he'd arrived home from the Lakes shortly after midday and found it lying on the mat inside the door, it had bedevilled him. As he reread it, he felt his jaw tighten:

Dear Ewan,

His Lordship tells me you will have concluded your brief trip up North by the 16th – the day Emma returns from Milchester. (Yes, to my delight she did decide to accompany me, after all.) I plan on being back by Wednesday, the 20th, which brings me to the purpose of this letter – to ask an enormous favour. I'm worried about Emma being alone those days and would appreciate it no end if you would check on her (without letting on that I asked you, of course) once or twice during my absence.

By the way (I have to tell someone or I shall burst), Emma and Thomas (he is set to rendezvous with us at the McDonoughs') may well be betrothed by the time you see her; all the signs point to it. So keep your fingers crossed with me.

Fondly,
Beth

His big hand closed around the note, squeezing until there was no feeling left. Then he sent it flying across the room to join the aborted letter. He rose and began pacing, cursing himself for the fool he'd been.

She'd bamboozled him, well and truly. '"Thomas Mondley and I are *friends*,"' he said out loud in a mocking falsetto. Dammit, girl, people dinna marry friends.

'"Mama may say what she wishes,"' he continued his mimicry, '"but *I* will plan my own life."' Aye, an' play bloody hell wi' mine. He made a fist with one hand and punched the palm of the other.

And to think he'd spent all his waking hours these past weeks thinking about her, his sleeping hours dreaming about her, that the more he'd gone over in his mind their afternoon together, the more he believed he'd seen his own feelings – the feelings he'd hotly denied for weeks and finally admitted to – mirrored in her eyes.

He circled the room, pacing and punching. Was that what love did – set your imagination to run amok? Oh, it did much more, didn't it? He paused by the bookshelves and his eyes flicked to the volume entitled *Saskatchewan*. Look at how Meggie had chased off halfway across the globe with Will, knowin' full well what it might do to their frail mother. And the worst had happened; less than six months after their departure, Ma had died. Not that he blamed his sister, she'd done what she had to, out of love and loyalty to a husband who had a dream of starting afresh. Then there was Pa, gone to his rest a scant year later, because without Ma he felt he had nothing left.

Ewan made a disenchanted sound at the back of his throat. Love was a fine thing, all right. By God, it hurt. And it broke hearts, shattered families.

Aye, just as *you'd* do with any woman you chose. Like Emma. Though God knows what made you think she'd take to the pioneering life. You'd tear her away from her family and, without so much as a by-your-leave, take her traipsing off to some Godforsaken wilderness.

He brought his chin up at a stubborn angle, brooding

thus: 'I wouldna ... tear her away, that is. I'd have 'er Ma go with us. An' Emma likes the sound of Canada – I know she does; she's read every book I possess, asked a million questions; an' I've seen her face light up more than once when I've talked about it.'

But it's no use, is it, lad? Ewan slumped in the chair by the fire and buried his head in his hands. What she thinks or doesnao think about Canada is of no consequence because she's going to wed Mondley. And she'll have a secure life, a safe one, better than you could ever hope to give her.

Why had he let himself be bewitched by her? The softness of her, the scent of her hair; those gold-flecked eyes he had so often felt himself drowning in.

What a great dunce he'd been. 'Aye, lad, an' a milksop, too.' The clarity of his inner voice startled him. 'You daft thing,' it went on, 'doubtin' what you know in your heart. Willin' to give up without a fight. Lettin' a wee note put you off ... an' a note that may not have a dram of truth in it.'

Slowly, he lifted his head and, glancing at the mantel clock that registered quarter to seven, ran a hand over the day-old growth of his beard.

'By God,' he said softly, 'I may turn out to be a damn sight bigger fool than I thought, but there's only one way I'll find out.'

Thomas paused on the threshold, his lanky silhouette filling the doorway, his face in the shadow. Emma let go of the chairback and chafed her arms against the room's chilliness. Waiting for some opening comment from him, she took off her hat and toyed with its froth of veiling.

Then, unnerved by the silence, Emma said, 'I wish I could offer you a cup of tea, Thomas, but I'm afraid it's going to take quite a while for the fire to –'

'I have no desire for tea ... no desire for anything.' He moved into the circle of light from the lamp on the dresser. 'Except to ask you a question.'

His voice had an odd flatness to it. Emma glanced at him sharply and then looked away, for something in his hooded eyes and uncommon pallor struck her uneasily. Lord, his was hardly the demeanour of a man – however nervous – about to propose.

'Why, Emma, *why?*' The same queer monotone.

Frowning, she unwound the scarf from around her neck and shrugged off her coat. 'Why what?' she asked as she made for the row of pegs on the wall by the window, where she hung up her garments and lifted down her shawl.

'Why' – the word sounded like a cry of anguish between clenched teeth – 'did you allow yourself to be a party to it?'

Blinking like a nocturnal animal surprised by light, Emma snugged the shawl about herself and returned to the hearth. 'A party to what?' She gave the fire a desultory poke and, realizing numbly how exhausted she was, dropped into the adjacent armchair.

Wheeling away, he groped for the wall behind him. Palms flat against it and arms locked straight, he bowed his head. 'Men are powerless against a female's wiles – cannot control themselves – are slaves to their baser natures. But they can be stopped. A word. A gesture.' He straightened and rounded on her, his eyes disconcerting twin coals now in his chalky face. 'You could have stopped it if you'd wanted.'

Feeling her patience eroding, Emma fought for and gained equanimity before she answered: 'Stopped what? I'm sorry, Thomas, but you are not making an ounce of sense. And won't you *please* come and sit down, so we can at least hold a proper conversation?' She closed her eyes against the drum beginning to beat at her temples. The chignon at the nape of her neck seemed too heavy for her head, so she pulled the pins from her hair and shook it loose about her shoulders.

'So. You want a *proper* conversation, eh?'

At the proximity of his voice and its peculiarly high pitch, Emma flashed open her eyes. She drew in a shocked little slurp of air when his face came into focus just inches from her own and her nostrils flared reproachfully at the odour of brandy on his breath. He was bent over her, long skeletal fingers clamped onto the arms of the chair. And it struck her, as she hunched deeper into her shawl, elbows over her breasts in an unconscious gesture of self-protection, that he must have moved with the stealth of a footpad for her not to have heard his approach.

'Thomas, you are crowding me.' She spoke sharply. With a start, he jerked upright and then backed away a couple of swift steps. Emma exhaled her pent-up unease. This man looming over her in his ministerial black, like some ominous raven, was not the Thomas Mondley she knew.

Who was he, then? And when was he going to start making sense?

'I'll warrant your conversations with *him* were anything but proper.'

Him? Emma scrubbed at her hair. Obviously, he was *not* making sense. Lord, how infernally hot it'd grown and with the fire hardly caught yet. Jutting her bottom lip, she expelled a noisy breath designed to act as a cooling breeze. And then she undid several of the tiny mother-of-pearl buttons on her blouse and loosened the collar. 'Struth, the necklace ... Her fingertips explored the amethyst's facets: she'd have to return it; it wouldn't be right to ...

'Emma, I dreamed of a future with you beside me, planned to ask for your hand this evening. Thought you so good, so pure. An angel. The perfect wife for a man of my position. A shining example. But it was all a charade, wasn't it?'

Emma was still digesting his garbled rhetoric. *Dreamed* of a future? *Thought* you so good? She touched her temples and slowly swung her lowered head. Charade? She looked up. What in God's name was he implying?

'Well, wasn't it?' His fists clenched and unclenched at his sides and a crimson tide rose over his starched collar. 'Answer me.'

Anger burst in Emma like a Roman candle. 'For pity's sake, Thomas, how can I answer you when I haven't a notion what you are going on about? If you stopped talking in riddles' – she plucked at the links of her necklace – 'then perhaps –'

'Very well.' He tossed back a wayward hank of his hair. 'If it is bluntness you desire, then bluntness you shall have.' He came and stood before her, then leaned over and braced himself on the chair arms. 'I can have no truck with a harlot.'

Emma shrank from his icy stare. Over her agitated heartbeat she heard herself say in a voice faint, pathetic, 'A harlot?'

'A Jezebel, Emma. A *whore* – for you were your father's whore. Tell me' – one deathly cold hand tipped her chin, then trailed roughly across her throat, tugging at the necklace – 'did *he* give you trinkets as well?'

She cringed under the shower of his spittle. Oh God, she couldn't breathe. There seemed to be a weight on her now, suffocating, crushing her chest. She looked blankly down at the tousled blond head, felt the sobs reverberating against her ribs, 'Oh Emma, Emma, why … why?'

To stop you. Had to stop you. She made tiny circular motions over her scalp with palsied fingers. Leave me alone, she silently implored. Can't breathe. Get away from me. She could feel herself choking. Her head began to thrash from side to side; her fists, limp and ineffectual, to pummel Thomas Mondley's back.

'Please, get off me, Papa, please … and I'll dance for you.' Her voice was that of a mendicant child, low and pitiful.

Thomas Mondley's head whipped back and his eyes fastened on her in frozen horror.

And when she saw his expression, something in her snapped like a wishbone. She arched her neck and screamed, 'Get off me, get off me … *Get off me!*'

Ewan heard the beginnings of her cries as he unlatched the gate. He moved so fast that she was closing her mouth over the last of her scream as he burst into the kitchen.

In that suspended moment before he lunged, his mind eddied around the scene, registering Mondley's kneeling figure and the wild unfocused eyes, the tear-streaked mask of Emma's face and her guttural small-animal sobs.

'Do as she says,' he roared. He latched onto the back of Mondley's collar, snatched him to his feet, and propelled him away, yelling, 'What in Hell were you tryin' to do to 'er, man? Are you mad?'

Plunged back to the here and now, Mondley squirmed furiously. 'Let go of me. This is none of your affair.'

'Well, I'm makin' it my affair.' Ewan released him, gripped his shoulders, and spun him around so they were face on. 'You hear me?' He jabbed an angry forefinger at Mondley's chest and caught him off balance.

Mondley's arms windmilled wildly and a wooden chair went over. He grabbed the table for purchase. But it was the cloth he clamped onto. As in a magician's trick gone awry, he whisked it off and a miscellany of knickknacks, a silver cruet and toast rack and a cut-glass vase full of desiccated holly sprigs fell to the stone flags in a dissonant shower.

The sounds of splintering wood and clashing metal and shattering glass echoed hollowly within the catacombs of Emma's unreality. And terror stalked her, wresting little whimpers from her.

Horror called her name. Those men in the doorway, fighting … shouting. Have to get away. Now.

Unnoticed, she slipped from the chair to her hands and knees and, like a fieldmouse, crawled inch by inch away from the melee.

In the scullery, she pulled herself to her feet. Quick, he's coming … *Papa's coming*.

She eased open the back door and stepped into the enveloping black maw of the night.

Terror pumped courage through her veins. She stumbled blindly on, up and down slopes, slipping on frozen vegetation, oblivious of the prick of gorse bushes and dead brambles clawing at her, twigs snapping in her face.

A gnarled old tree, garlanded with frost, wrenched the shawl from her shoulders, and in the unremitting light of the moon, it dangled from the branches like a gossamer shroud.

On she pressed, still deeper into Chearden Woods. Here the moon wavered on and off, according to the denseness of firs and pines, making the darkness utter one moment, and the next adding an eerie blue-white.

She was without aim, except to escape, and yet her knowing and relentless feet propelled her along a familiar route until she gained the rock.

The surface of the Well gleamed below her, gleamed and beckoned.

While from behind her, far off but unmistakable, came a sound of someone crashing through the undergrowth. Someone coming nearer.

Like a sack of grain down a chute, she slid into the water.

She felt the breath pulled from her body. Dear Lord, the cold. But she *must* move ... away from the shore. Away from him. She kicked off, flung herself forward, hardly able to move for the weight of her skirts, and struck out.

'Emma. *Emma!*'

Oh God! She threw a desperate glance over her shoulder. Papa was there, on the bank. She flailed arms and legs, felt herself being dragged down. He was waiting for her ... she gagged. No. *No!*

'Emma ...'

No. She wouldn't ... couldn't now. Not ever. She took one final gulp of air.

And then she plunged below the surface.

THIRTY-FOUR

The fire on the hearth cast coppery reflections of itself onto the walls. As Ewan heaped on more coal, he kept glancing up at Emma. Swaddled in blankets, she sat motionless in the rocking chair, staring straight ahead, her eyes like dark caves against the pallor of her face.

Thank God he was a strong enough swimmer to reach her in time. His heart caught in his chest. Thank God, too, he'd changed his mind about walking to Beech Cottage tonight and had saddled up Pegasus instead. Otherwise, he might have been stumbling out there yet, with Emma's lifeless body in his arms.

And praise be for his years of tracking, and for the hunter's skill that had led him to her. Digging into the coal scuttle with the brass shovel, he stopped to adjust the blanket he wore like a toga; his garments and Emma's were draped over a clotheshorse adjacent to the fire and an aura of steam had begun to rise from them with the increasing heat.

When, like a man possessed, he'd ripped the blankets from Emma's and her mother's beds, the niceties had not concerned him; nor had he thought about propriety – and least of all, lust – as he undressed Emma and towelled her until her flesh shone pink, and then sloughed his own sodden garments. He had felt only thankfulness for her safety.

The rage over what had been done to her came later. And it rekindled in him now, as he reached and touched her cheek. Her glassy eyes did not waver; his grew moist.

He sank to the footstool and hunkered over, elbows propped on his knees. Cupping one hand, he made it a vessel for his other pounding fist. Mondley, that rotten excuse for a man ... snivelling about purity and virtue ... acting as though she had suddenly become a piece of tainted meat to be tossed away.

Man of God, bah! His mouth curled in disgust.

And father? That bastard Cadman. No wonder Emma had chosen to blot him from her mind. What had Beth said once when he'd asked about her husband? Something about his dying tragically when Emma was a child. Now he remembered her words: 'The shock of it caused her to become quite ill and be left with a loss of memory, which, according to the doctors, is best left undisturbed.'

Well, it was disturbed now – wasn't it? He rose and gazed down at Emma through a wall of tears. Lord, what had the ugly truth done to her? And how could he help her?

An hour had elapsed and the kitchen had grown as hot and moist as the conservatory at Chearden Hall.

Ewan raked his damp curls and then knelt at Emma's feet. 'Come on, lass,' he said. 'Drink this brandy, an' you'll feel better.'

Regarding him blankly, she allowed him to coax her lips apart with the glass. But the instant the liquid entered her mouth, her face contorted and she jerked her head aside. '*No!*' She struck out wildly, catching the tot and spilling the brandy down the front of the newly dried shirt and trousers Ewan had donned moments before.

''Tis all right,' he said soothingly. ''Tis all right.' He dug in his pocket for a handkerchief, tugged it out, and began mopping at the fast-spreading stain.

'I'm sorry.'

The thready little whimper surprised him and he looked up to find her eyes, bulging wide with horror, riveted on his front. 'I'll clean it up,' she said in a breathless whisper, 'as soon as I' – her glance twitched about – 'find something to …'

Ewan captured her restless hands in his own and caressed them. 'Naught to fret about, Emma, lass. 'Tis no catastrophe.'

She tilted her head and frowned questioningly. 'Ewan? Ewan McKenzie? Is it really …?'

'Aye, it is. And dinna worry about the *why's* and *wherefore's*. I'm here, an' that's all that counts.' Thank God. At last she'd recognized him. Like a wee bairn, she was, her thumbnail hooked under her upper teeth.

'I spilled brandy on Papa once. And he was terribly vexed; so vexed, he …' She bit down on the words and began to shiver uncontrollably.

Good … Ewan passed the back of his hand across her cheek in a slow comforting gesture. Now she was starting to remember. He got to his feet and, keeping a wary eye on her, went to the dresser, where he refilled the glass. He would try again to press the brandy on her; she needed it to cleanse the poisons from the festering wound that was her past.

This time there were no protests from her. She downed the drink with the obedience of a child. Indeed, she felt as light as a child when he picked her up, settled in the chair, and cradled her frail-seeming body against his.

'I loved my Papa, you know,' she said tonelessly. 'He used to bring me presents. I was his Princess and he would give me the world, he said. And I'd wait for him in my sitting tree. Sometimes he'd be gone for weeks at a time and when he came home I was so excited. I'd run to meet him, and he'd pick me up.' Her voice died away and she plucked at Ewan's sleeve.

He smoothed back her hair. 'Go on, love.'

'Imagine, my forgetting how wonderful he was.' She made a sound that was part-laugh, part-sob.

Ewan tilted her chin. 'But he hurt you, did he not, lass?'

'Papa hurt me?' She twisted away. 'Papa loved me. More than Mama, he said. He told me I was beautiful, more beautiful than all the fine ladies we saw that week in London, with their creamy shoulders and bared bosoms and painted faces.' Her voice took on a rushed, airy quality as she carried on. 'Whores, all of them. And I was his little whore. I belonged to him. And when I … oh, God, merciful God …' She looked up at Ewan, the bright spots of colour leached from her cheeks, tears welling behind her lashes. 'What am I saying?' She struggled for freedom, but he held her firm.

'You can tell me, Emma. You *must*, lass. Tell, an' be done with it.'

'Very well,' she said in a small voice. 'I was ten when it first began, though I did not become aware of it until that summer, the following year. Oh, and it was such a lovely, lovely summer …'

Ewan sat in the lamplight beside her bed, his mind in a turmoil.

Two hours had passed since she dozed off in his arms by the kitchen fire. The brandy had worked; after those first hesitant spurts and with his gentle prompting, Emma's story gushed out – a horrifying story of abuse and love and hate and guilt.

Oh, how he'd longed to tell her ... to shout his love for her. Only sheer force of will and the realization that now was not the time for declarations of love, but a time for healing, had prevented it.

When at last he'd carried her upstairs, she surfaced long enough to say, 'Ewan, don't leave me,' and for him to respond with calming assurances that he would not.

But staying was out of the question; he couldn't compromise her like that. Besides, there was too much temptation in her nearness. She was too lovely, too bewitching: her hair a pool of russet silk on the pillow; a powdering of freckles across the bridge of her dainty nose; her eyelids, with their delicate tracery of purple veins and long dark lashes, flickering slightly; and the tip of her tongue moistening parted lips, red as a crushed berry against the ivory of her face.

Unconsciously, his fingers went to the hollow of her throat, traced the ridge of her collarbone. Desire surged in him and he felt himself hardening. Ashamed of his arousal, he snatched his hand away. Emma's eyes flew open: dark, fearful, but unfocused. 'Mama?'

'Tis all right, lass.'

'Rub my back, please, Mama.' She turned away from him onto her side, and the cat, Robbie B., who had been stretched out at the bottom of the bed, curled up in the curve behind her bent knees.

Ewan massaged her back through the covers. As soon as her breathing had achieved an even rhythm, he leaned over and kissed her cheek. And then he carefully got to his feet and, chucking Robbie B. under the chin, whispered, 'I canna stay, laddie, so you see you take good care of 'er, you hear me?'

At three A.M., Ewan lay in bed staring through the darkness, too tense to sleep, unable to still his mind, which tumbled with thoughts of Emma.

257

'I love you, my braw wee darlin',' he murmured. 'Need you, want to take care of you. An' nothing … no one'll ever hurt you again, I swear.' He imagined her as he'd left her, curled on her side, small and defenceless. The picture faded and gave way to others: that first afternoon at the Sunday school treat, when she ran away from him like a frightened doe; the night of the Parish Hall dance; their race along the pier at Brimsgate; her tale-telling Christmas Day – those wonderful eyes aglow with golden laughter. Image upon image flowed by him, until sleep finally claimed him.

He was awake before first light, amazed at how energetic he felt and how famished.

Downstairs, he made himself a hearty breakfast of fried eggs, gammon, and toast, washed it down with a mug of strong tea, and then set about tidying the cottage, which had suffered from his week-long absence. Later, he would have to report on his visit to the Lakes. But there was no discussing business with His Lordship before ten. And it was three hours until then.

His mind began to race with thoughts of Emma and plans for their lives. She should have a ring; nothing expensive for now, for he would need to conserve his money. Whistling a jaunty little tune, he began to dance a Highland fling.

'Mr McKenzie.'

At the sound of his name and the pounding on the door, he jerked to a stop and clapped a hand to his thudding heart. Who in Hades would be …?'

When he opened the door and saw the young man standing on the step and a wagonette parked by the gate, he ran a bewildered hand through his hair.

'My Pa sent me … runs the telegraph office in Marespond.' The youth spoke in a breathless rush. 'Got 'ere soon as I could.' He shoved a buff envelope at Ewan and then, with an apologetic lift of his shoulders, tipped his cap and murmured, 'G'day to you, sir.'

Ewan closed the door. The telegraph office, the lad'd said. Now who on earth would be sending …? A sudden chill came over him. And when he began to rip open the envelope, he saw that his hand was shaking.

'God's truth, my boy. Your accounting could have waited.' The Earl fingered his jowls and motioned Ewan to the seat opposite. 'Bloody mess.' He described a wide oval with his hands and glowered at the littered desk top. 'I'll be glad when Mrs Cadman returns. Now' – he winced – 'what disaster – and it jolly well must be a disaster from the look of you – did you uncover up north that has you dragging me from my bed at this ungodly hour?'

Ewan struggled to speak. But the words snagged in his throat. Half-rising, he proffered the telegram.

Suspicion rippled across the Earl's face as he fished a monocle from his waistcoat pocket and jammed it in position. 'What the devil ...?' His eyes moved rapidly from line to line, until he looked up. 'Good God, McKenzie, I'm sorry. Deucedly sorry. It's one helluva thing to ...' He mopped his forehead with his sleeve. 'You must go, of course. No question about it.' He rose painfully, limped to the Landseer watercolour hanging on the dark panelling and lifted it down to reveal a wall safe. A few swift twirls of the combination lock, and he had it open. He searched among its contents for a minute or two, then hobbled to Ewan's side. 'Three hundred guineas,' he said, dropping a leather pouch in Ewan's lap. 'Call it a loan, my boy.'

Ewan found his voice. 'Och, but I couldna. I didna come to ...'

'You will always have a job, if that's what you're worried about. Now let's see; Southampton, no, Liverpool would be your best bet. Know a chap there with the Cunard Line. Owes me a favour. Sit tight while I find out this week's schedule.'

As the elderly man left the room, the great hound Marcus Brutus ambled in and sat at Ewan's feet. In numb silence, Ewan stroked the dog's shaggy head until the Earl returned and said, 'Everything's arranged; there's a departure at two.' He handed Ewan a slip of paper. 'Information's all here –

where to go, who to see. Necessary documents'll all be taken care of.' He clicked open his gold hunter's watch and then returned it to its fob. 'You won't make the eight o'clock train, that's certain. But you positively must catch the nine o'clock – there's not another Liverpool-bound until noon. Come on, then, look lively.' He flapped an impatient hand and Ewan got to his feet.

'Pull yourself together, old chap.' His Lordship frowned up at him. 'You'll need a stout heart and a clear head. Go on home, pack your things and return post-haste. Then Colcutt can drive you to the station. And while you're packing, think of any loose ends that need tying up. Let me know, and I shall make certain they're seen to.'

At a quarter to nine, the Earl stood at his study window, craning for a last glimpse of the carriage as it careered along the curve of the gravelled driveway. By Jove, McKenzie'd cut it fine. And all because of some visit he'd had to make, and something to do with someone he'd been unable to rouse, and some deuced key he'd put through the letterbox the night before when he'd locked up. Drivel – the ramblings of a man at the end of his tether.

The Earl turned from the window. Colcutt would get him to the station on time, even if it was by the skin of their teeth; fellow was an old hand.

Fingering the letter Ewan had handed him a moment before their emotional farewell, he crossed to the desk and then squinted at the envelope through his monocle. If the poor fellow'd said it once, he'd said it a dozen times: 'Be sure Miss Cadman gets this note.'

'Don't worry, old chap,' he spoke out loud. 'She'll get your precious note just as soon as Colcutt returns.' He shook his head disbelievingly. Lord, what a way to start the day. And this infernal gout was enough to drive a man to …

'Excuse me, sir.' His man Everett poked his head in. 'A telephone call from Miss Eliza's doctor.' The usually impassive mouth hinted at a smile. 'I gather the infant …'

'Infant, you say? Come in, come in. You mean my …?'

'Yes. Your grandchild, sir.'

Quivering with suppressed excitement, the Earl made two fists. 'For God's sake, tell me, man. Is it a …?'

'A boy, sir. A fine healthy boy.'

'Well, I'll be damned.' The Earl's hands came limply to his sides. 'A grandson. Bless my soul.'

'You dropped something, sir … by your foot.'

'Hmmm? Oh, yes. Deuce it, man, I cannot …'

Everett quickly retrieved the envelope and propped it against the inkstand on the desk. 'Will there be anything else, sir?'

'Well, confound it, of course there will.'

'Sir?'

'Packing, Everett. Get our things together. Soon as Colcutt returns, we're off to London.'

THIRTY-FIVE

As soon as Emma awoke in the grey dawn, the past – like a predatory beast smelling blood – scaled the disintegrating wall of her defences and tore into her.

Reeling under the assault, she staggered through to Mama's room in search of the seldom-used bottle of 'Dr Whickenham's Patent Remedy, guaranteed to cure all ailments,' then dragged herself back to bed and gulped down a hefty measure of the dark brown syrup.

But laudanum was no palliative. The brutish scenes were inescapable; they played in acute relief across her mind – scenes of perversions committed and submitted to, her father's face overlaying all, its imprint so clear now: broken veins in the ruddy cheeks; brooding hazel eyes; the twin swords of his waxed moutache and the fall of red-blond hair.

She rocked her head from side to side on the pillow,

horror and grief a tight physical pain around her heart. Tears leaked from her closed eyelids.

Two Papas. One, loving and tender; the other a monster who had deserved his violent end.

Two Papas she had alternately loved and hated.

And why hadn't Mama saved her? Mothers were supposed to protect their children. She must have known, or suspected, at least *sensed* something. Unless she was blind or unwilling to accept the horrendous truth.

Fists clenched at her sides, Emma fought for control, afraid that once she let go, she would lose her substance. Biting down on her lower lip, she struggled to a sitting position and plumped her pillow, but the effort exhausted her and she sank back.

Who had told Thomas Mondley? Mama? No, even if she'd known, she never would have divulged such abominations. Who, then? A picture flashed into her consciousness of her childhood tête-à-têtes with Jane McDonough. Of course. But, no - it couldn't've been Jane; Thomas had had no contact with her. It must have been one of Jane's parents.

Lord - she clutched her middle, tossing back and forth - how shaming to have people know such things about you.

A throbbing band cinched around her skull. 'Mustn't ever tell,' the ghost whisper came; and then again, 'Mustn't ever tell.'

She clapped her hands to her mouth. But she *had* told. Yesterday. It was Ewan McKenzie who had pulled her from ... where had she gone? The image was so fuzzy; water, freezing water. She kneaded her temples with her knuckles. Was it the Well, or -? She groaned in frustration; why wouldn't last night focus properly? It *had* been Ewan, though; of that she was certain. He had rocked her and she exhaled a long soft breath as the implications of the thought registered - he had treated her as someone to be cherished. And how gentle he had been with her until he began to force the brandy on her, just as Papa had done ... She gave a violent shudder. And after that? She cast about agitatedly for the elusive memory. Oh God, had *he* – like Thomas Mondley – been disgusted by it all?

And why wouldn't he be? her inner voice taunted. After all, you *are* a woman of easy virtue, sullied and impure. Remember how you allowed Ewan McKenzie to touch you, and how you actually enjoyed it? Like as not, he considered you loose then, and deems you all the looser now that he's privy to your secret. Anyway, he is nothing to you. Or is he?

Her only response to this self-torture was to squeeze her eyes shut and grind her teeth. And then because the sudden image that came to her, of Thomas Mondley's disgust superimposed on Ewan's face, was a sharp knife twisting in her heart, she sought the small brown bottle again ... and oblivion.

The sound of the door knocker echoing through the silent house jolted her into disoriented wakefulness. Daylight filtered through the curtains and the clock read half past two.

Her heart pumped in her throat and when she made her way downstairs, she had to cling to the bannister for fear of collapsing. Oh, Lord, her head! Each blink of her eyes was the blow of a hammer on an anvil inside her skull.

When she hauled open the door – and it required great effort – she saw that her caller was Hope Windom.

Hope swooshed by her and closed the door. 'A rather mysterious and short-lived telephone call which I shall get to later, and a visit from Reverend Marsh-Hughes saying you hadn't shown up at school this morning, convinced me to check on you straightaway.'

'Ye Gods!' Emma hit her forehead with the heel of her hand. 'School. I forgot completely.'

'Don't fret. Amelia has everything in hand, as she has had for these past few days and will continue to do so for as long as is necessary.' Her eyes swept over Emma. 'My Heavens, you *are* ill. Come along. Back to bed with you, and then you can tell me how in creation – when you were supposed to have a nice little holiday – you got yourself into such a state as this.'

After Hope had resurrected the fire enough to heat the beef broth she'd brought, she took it upstairs and hovered over Emma until every last drop was gone. 'Now,' she said, settling herself sidesaddle on the bed, 'tell me why you look so awful.'

It took an hour for Emma's narration. Realizing the wisdom of not stemming the flow, Hope remained still and silent throughout.

'So there you have it.' Emma dabbed at her swollen eyelids with the corner of the counterpane. 'My lurid past. Laughable, isn't it?' Her mouth curled in a bitter little smile. 'I mean, there I was so concerned about hurting Thomas Mondley, and –'

'Oh, my dear.' Hope enveloped her in a long, close embrace. 'What a dreadful, dreadful nightmare.'

'I daresay he's right.' Emma twirled a tendril of her hair around a finger.

'Who? And right about what?'

'Thomas … about my being a whore.'

'Oh, Emma – don't.' Hope laid her hand over Emma's and squeezed. 'Don't revile yourself.'

'I *must* have brought it upon myself.'

'Don't speak such nonsense. Of course you didn't. You were a child … an innocent child.'

'But an innocent child doesn't *want* to be touched … in that way. And I *did* want it, sometimes, I remember.' She eased from Hope's grip. Something akin to defiance showed in the tilt of her chin when she added, 'Does it shock you and disgust you as much as it does me?'

'No, not at all. No more than it shocks or disgusts me when *I* remember how much I wanted Alex's caresses.'

'But that was entirely different; you were a grown woman … and a married one, submitting to your husband.'

'No, Emma.' Hope spoke quietly. Her *own* dark secret, closely guarded all these years, but if its revelation would help Emma see things differently … 'Remember the day when you came storming into the shop, so incensed about

264

the gossip you'd overheard, and I said people were not always what they seemed?'

Emma nodded uncertainly. 'Yes.'

'Well, I am not what I seem. That woman said I had never lived in Lower Cromby and I told you she was right. When I first moved to Chearden and someone asked me where I hailed from, the name popped in my head. I needed a quick answer, a place to be from – any place rather than my true home, which is a village some fifty miles hence whose name would doubtless mean nothing to you.' She lowered her gaze and plucked at the herringbone stitching on the counterpane's hem with her fingernail. 'I had visited Lower Cromby once. It boasts a charming little inn. In fact' – she refocused on Emma – 'it was in the room above the sign, I remember how it creaked in the wind, that Alex and I became lovers … and it was something I wanted as much as he.'

'Lovers,' Emma said in a husky voice.

'Yes. It was the week before he was due to ship out for the Sudan. We were to be married when he returned.'

'Were to be? You mean you and Alex were …'

'Never married. And Oliver – was born a bastard.' She saw Emma flinch and pressed her point. 'It is not a pretty word, no prettier than the word *whore*. But there is nothing ugly or tainted about my son.'

'He is a beautiful child,' Emma said.

'And am I a whore for having given myself before marriage? Surely I must be.'

'Oh no. Of course you are not.'

'And do you still, then, think of yourself as …'

Emma gave a bewildered shrug. 'I cannot tell you what I think. It's all so confusing. I know I feel degraded and horrified.' She shuddered.

'What about your Mama? Would you like me to telephone her and have her come home now, instead of on Wednesday? Ewan's right, you *do* need –'

'Ewan?' Emma's eyes dilated with surprise.

'The mysterious telephone call I told you of earlier. It was Ewan McKenzie. I haven't a notion where he was calling from, though I assume it must've been the Hall. He said, "Will you go to Emma? She needs a friend." Then the connection was broken. Frankly, I'm puzzled. I mean, how is he involved in all this?'

Emma made a dubious face. 'I wasn't going to mention it, because the whole affair is outlandish enough as it is – but he rescued me. I'm not clear about the details or the sequence of events, but ...'

Again Hope listened, and when Emma paused, she said, 'Gracious, it's a wonder you didn't catch your death. No chills or fever?' She leaned over and checked Emma's brow. 'Hmmm. Warm, but not unduly so.'

'I feel all right, really. A bit groggy, but it's no doubt the Remedy' – she jabbed a thumb in the direction of the bottle – 'that caused it.'

'And the entire ordeal. My, but isn't it a good thing you have a psychic for a friend.'

'A psychic?'

'Yes ... the way Ewan showed up precisely when he was needed. A superb friend, too. I mean, from all accounts the fellow saved your life, ministered to you better than any doctor, and then became your father confessor.' She smoothed her blouse cuff, toying with the porcelain stud and thinking that everyone should have such a friend. A lover could not have been more solicitous, more ... She tilted her head and looked at Emma as though seeing her for the first time. Was it possible that – 'Is there something between you and Ewan McKenzie?' she blurted, perturbed with herself even as the words slipped out.

Emma stared at the ceiling, at the wall beyond Hope's back, out the window, and finally at Hope. 'I think there must be,' she said with a kind of questioning wonderment. 'I mean, we have come to know each other rather well these past months, and there was ... *is* ... something powerful growing between us; I suddenly saw it very clearly as you were talking about everything he'd done for me.'

'I was thinking myself,' Hope interjected, 'that there seemed a lot more than friendship in his gestures. And now'

– she smiled – 'I'm remembering the way you two looked at each other Christmas Day. I should have recognized it, but widows like me become a little rusty on that score.'

'I must love him, Hope, because the thought of my past disgusting *him* – I have no memory of his reaction to my unwitting confession – is more than I can bear. The thought of not seeing him again is ...' She folded her hands prayerfully, rested her chin on them, and closed her eyes. 'Too painful to contemplate.'

'Of course you will see him again,' Hope said cheerfully. 'Didn't the fellow go out of his way to telephone me? I should not be a bit surprised if he comes knocking on your door before the day is out.'

The only person who came knocking, though, was Flossie Congleton, the local Jill-of-all-trades, who appeared at noon the next day, saying Mrs Windom had sent her to tidy up and help in any way she could.

You could help, Emma thought bitterly, by just leaving me be. I want Ewan. Oh, why doesn't he come – why?

But Monday passed, and half of Tuesday, with not a sign of Ewan McKenzie. And then Mrs Congleton brought the news.

'Come by that Mr McKenzie's cottage, I did, an' there were Charlie Fowke boardin' up the windows. Proper took back I was. Thought the fella'd passed on or some'at terrible like that. But 'tweren't it at all. Emigrated 'e has ... to Canada.'

Emma's heart fluttered like a trapped bird. 'To Canada?' She heard her own voice, faraway, reedy. 'Who told Charlie Fowke?'

'Orders come from the Hall ... left by 'is Lordship afore 'e took off for London. Seal the place up, 'e says, accordin' to Charlie. 'Twere a shock to everybody. Then I always said them Scotch'uns was a mite queer ... and speakin' of queer, you're lookin' proper peaked, yourself. Lost all your colour, y'have.'

'I'm tired, Mrs Congleton, dreadfully tired. I should

267

dearly love to get some sleep now. So why don't you run along?'

'Not unless you give me your word you'll go downstairs later an' eat some of that broth I left simmerin' on the hob.'

'I will, I promise. Thanks awfully much.' Emma crossed her fingers under the bedcovers.

Eat ... God, who could eat when one's heart was sliced in two? Ewan gone. Forever. Never to see his dear grey eyes again ... that golden face. Never to feel ...

He must have been planning it all along. He must have known it Sunday night. Perhaps that was what had brought him to Beech Cottage. And maybe ...

Oh, what was the use? Whatever had begun between them was over now. If she had meant anything at all to him, her past had obviously put paid to it.

There was nothing left for her now.

Nothing.

THIRTY-SIX

Beth unlocked the front door at six o'clock on Wednesday evening and lifted her suitcase from the step where the cabbie had set it. How grand it was to be home, despite the splendid visit she'd had. Flora had asked her to stay on a few more days, but Hope was expecting her back at work in the morning and then there was the Earl to think about on Friday. Besides, she was fairly bursting with curiosity about the outcome of Emma's and Thomas's talk.

'I'm home,' she called. Lord, not a solitary light burning. It was dark as a mine shaft. She groped her way along the hall, felt for the matches on the gateleg table, and lit the lamp. Once she'd hung up her hat and coat on the hall-stand, she took the lamp with her into the kitchen.

She made an annoyed little click with her tongue against

her teeth. Nothing but cold ashes to greet her, not so much as a cup of tea.

She made for the foot of the stairs. 'Emma, are you up there?'

Silence ... disquieting silence.

Now irritation took a back seat to unease. As she slowly mounted the stairs, the treads groaned under her feet and her shadow moved eerily on the wall, causing her pulse to quicken.

Her bedroom door was closed, she saw, reaching the landing. Emma's was open. She approached nervously and, on the threshold, raised the lamp so its yellow light illuminated the bed.

Lord save her, there was Emma, sitting up in a queer rigid fashion and staring at her through cavernous eyes.

As Emma regarded her mother, an odd thought struck her: the Resurrection had taken three days, just as her destruction had, beginning with her Sunday evening confession.

And now it was time for Mama to make *her* confession.

Contemplating Emma with a worried frown, Beth set the lamp on the bedside table. 'Whatever is the matter, dear?' She rested her warm hand on Emma's clammy forehead. 'My heavens, but you're pale. You must be sickening for something.'

'Not sickening.' Emma spoke without inflection. 'Sick.'

Her eyes darkening with confusion, Mama settled on the edge of the bed. 'I don't ...'

'Sick that you could have stood by, knowing what you must have known. Stood by and let him do those things.'

'Him? I ...'

'Papa. My dear, adoring Papa.' Emma watched her mother's jaw tighten, the colour ebb from her cheeks.

'Oh, God. Please, Emma. Don't.'

'Thomas Mondley, devoted fiancé-to-be, was the bearer of the glad tidings that I was my father's *whore*.' Emma drew out the word, and her mother winced.

269

'And as such,' Emma pressed on, 'a pariah, and naturally unfit to be his wife. Not that I had any inten –'

'But how –?' Mama broke off and then continued in a whisper as though to herself, 'Flora, it must have been Flora or Benjamin. But why would – ?'

'*You* allow it?' Emma completed the question. 'Why, mother, *why*? Did you hate me because he loved me more than you? He did, you know. A cold, unfeeling woman, he called you.' Ah-hah, she had touched a chord. Pain and horror registered in Mama's pallid face.

Now there was no holding back. No keeping at bay the molten eruption of anger and self-loathing and disgust. 'You should have saved me, Mama!' It was a scream. But Emma was unaware she was screaming until her mother, hands clapped over her ears and her head moving in mute denial, appeared to fold in on herself.

The torrent within Emma slowed, dissolved into a despairing trickle, finally stopped. Dear Lord! Mama! What had she done to Mama?

Their eyes met, held for elastic seconds. Then, simultaneously, they reached for each other, clung together fiercely.

'I didn't know,' Mama keened. 'I swear it. Not until Flora told me. And then it was too late. You're right, I should have known' – she choked on the words – 'should have guessed it.' Gently, she pulled back and regarded Emma through wet, brilliant eyes. 'But I couldn't allow myself to … He was my husband, Emma … *your father*. Can you understand?'

'I don't know, Mama. I only know I'm ruined now. There's nothing for me … and I just want to die.'

Darling, darling child, *will* you ever understand? You said that you did. You listened and nodded while I talked the night away … revealed my fears, my guilts, my failures as a wife. And will either of us ever understand the George Cadmans and Thomas Mondleys of this world? Oh, what a poor judge of character your mother is. Who would have thought it of a man of God? Judge, condemner – when the tenets of his faith are based in love and compassion.

270

Beth's shoulder ached from the pressure of Emma's head, but it was a welcome ache. Just as the warmth of her daughter's body next to hers, beneath the eiderdown, was a welcome warmth.

Will you ever forgive me my sin of blindness? She rested her cheek against Emma's hair, listened to the shallow breathing, and stared through the darkness at the phosphorescent clock dial. Two o'clock, the start of a new day in the first month of a New Year.

'Believe me, Emma,' she whispered, 'time *does* heal.'

THIRTY-SEVEN

A week passed, and the first snowdrops thrust their white bonnets through the quickening earth. Another, and the winter air lost its bite. By the end of January, birds had begun to trill on tender new twigs, the harbinger of an early spring.

Locked within her heartache, Emma was like a cardboard figure on the stage of a toy theatre. Every day, she stepped woodenly from the wings and went through the motions of eating and sleeping and teaching. Blind to Creation's awakening, she wandered lanes and meadows. But Nature held no comfort, no hidden truth, no revelation to ease her anguish.

Once she found herself at the Well. It would be so easy, she thought, to swim out to the centre of the winter-grey depths, as she had that night. This time to sink, skirts floating over her head, sink at last into eternity.

But then Mama, thinking the spectres of the past had been the cause of her daughter's demise, would blame herself. And Mama tried – too hard, too much – to make up for the past.

It wasn't the past so much, anyway. With concentration, she could press back the ugly images of Papa and herself. No, it was the empty present, thoughts of that endless void ahead – her future without Ewan McKenzie – that tormented her.

Still, it was life, empty or otherwise. She would survive. Someday, she might even look back and laugh.

She had not laughed in weeks. Her lips had forgotten how, until one sunlit morning in February, when the miracle occurred.

Alfie Plover, the errant Joseph of the Christmas Pageant, was its catalyst.

'Can anyone tell me where France is?' Emma asked, pointing to the map of the world on the wall.

One boy, who for some minutes had been contemplating his lap, raised his head and hand simultaneously.

'Alfie.' Emma gestured for him to approach, and when he drew near, he tugged on her sleeve and urged her to the open window. 'Over there.' He pointed to the outbuilding in the schoolyard.

'Pardon?' With a bewildered frown, Emma glanced sidelong.

'In the closet, Miss. Been there since break 'e has, on account of 'is bellyache.'

Oh, Lord! Frank … France. Emma suppressed a giggle. And then, suddenly, she exploded in laughter so uproarious she was helpless to stem it. She laughed until her eyes streamed with tears, until her ribs ached abominably. She laughed at herself laughing and at her pupils' astonished expressions. And then she laughed for the sheer joy of it.

As the days passed, she found herself smiling intermittently and crying only when the lonely nights closed in on her.

Her relationship with the children took on a deeper meaning. They were her family, her charges. The trust and admiration she saw in those young faces must be nurtured. And she must live up to their expectations.

A poignant truth struck her one morning when Josephine Dyce, a tiny blade of a girl who wore the marks of her ill-tempered parents' abuse as bravely as she wore her thin frock and too small boots, sidled up to Emma's desk and, regarding her through adoring leaf-shaped eyes, whispered, 'Wish you was my Ma.'

The words tugged at Emma's soul. This child – so vulnerable, so innocent – was a victim. We are *all* victims, she thought. I of my father's perversion and my mother's blindness, and, later, of my own gullibility when I imagined Ewan McKenzie loved me; Oliver, of his parents' passions; Hope, of a battle on those foreign shores that robbed her of a husband; and Mama, of a well-intentioned but aborted desire to see me wed and of the frustration she surely must now feel.

Watching Josephine return to her seat, Emma smiled sadly. How she wished she were a mother to that little one. But she would never be a mother, never have a family of her own. Oh, those foolish fantasies she'd entertained: two red-headed boys, tall and muscular; two dainty girls with gleaming dark curls.

No, she would never experience the joy of motherhood. And Mama, poor Mama, would never be a grandmother.

A similar thought was plaguing Beth that afternoon, as she stood at the sink, peeling and dicing vegetables for a stew. Though *never* was a word she refused to accept. Granted, the current prospects appeared dim. But Emma was a lovely young woman, with so much to offer. Somewhere, sometime …

Beth lopped off the end of a carrot. If only Emma didn't continue to feel so worthless, so tainted. If she could just capture some of her old *joie de vivre*.

Remember, though, it takes time. Lord, it might be years before Emma was able to put the past behind her. The past … Beth shuddered. Look at the havoc wrought already. She dried her hands on her apron with a sorrowful nod.

If these first weeks of 1886 were any indication, they were in for trying times. Look at Ewan, taking off, without so much as a word. But for Mrs Dawfield hearing a chance remark of Colcutt's, no one would have been any the wiser, assuming that he was away on one of his overseeing trips.

Didn't make a jot of sense. What did these days? Just thinking about it made you realize how little friendships meant, at least to *some* people. And how empty these weeks had seemed without his visits.

Emma seemed more put out than anyone. The mere mention of his name, and her eyes took on that guarded look, as they had last night when Beth made a casual comment. Clearly, the wisest course from now on would be to completely avoid the subject of Ewan McKenzie.

She carried the iron pot to the hob. Perhaps some light might've been thrown on the mystery, had the Earl not departed for London the very day Ewan left for Canada. She gave the stew a thorough stirring and straightened. Still, thank Heaven His Lordship *had* gone. The situation being what it was, she'd as soon the dear man stayed away another month.

That busybody Polly Clampett. Not brains enough to let things be. Feeling herself tense, Beth marched to the table, took up cloth and polish, and got to work. Better to vent her irritation on the brass than herself. And speaking of brass – she rubbed fiercely at the tarnish on the letter rack – fancy that woman taking it upon herself to 'tidy up,' as she put it.

'A proper mess were that study, till I give it a good do. Not fit for man nor beast, with all them ledges an' books an' papers stacked up. Never seen so much as a feather duster in years, nor the desk a bit o' beeswax. You'll be right surprised when you see it, Mrs Cadman.'

Surprised? Beth had been horrified. The room looked as pristine as a monk's cell. Staring at the burnished wood and leather of the desk top, devoid of everything but its onyx inkstand, she'd asked with counterfeit sweetness, 'And where are the ledgers and the papers you mentioned?'

Polly Clampett's bosom expanded in obvious pride. 'Oh, I stuffed 'em all in boxes, shoved 'em behind the sofa, out o' sight.' Her gaze swept lovingly over the study. 'Don't it look grand?'

And it did, there was no doubt about it. But what a nightmare. Beth flinched. February fifth tomorrow – her fourth Friday since returning from Milchester – and she had still not been able to bring order out of the chaos created by that overzealous maid. Three of the six cartons sorted and organized – she buried her head in her hands – three remaining.

A month later, Beth was feeling decidedly better. Except on the score of the missing three hundred guineas. She finished totalling the long column of figures, slammed the ledger shut, and removed her spectacles. Massaging the sides of her nose where the eyeglasses had left their imprint, she sank back into the depths of the leather chair designed to accommodate the Earl's broad girth. Enough was enough; no use worrying. Only she and the Earl knew the combination to the safe. Obviously, it was some oversight on His Lordship's part, and it wouldn't be the first time. She would just have to wait out the next fortnight until he returned. Then the mystery was bound to be solved.

Anyway, at least Polly Clampett's 'good deed' had not turned out to be the disaster she'd envisioned. In fact, now that the merchants were paid, the cheques from His Lordship's multitudinous business ventures (there'd been enough stuffed in those cartons to finance a war) safely deposited, correspondence sorted and, in some cases, answered, she was willing to admit she might even have overreacted.

There was still one shoebox to be dealt with. But a cursory inspection the week before had shown her a motley assortment of pencils, pen nibs, blotting paper, and the like. Nothing of importance. She could whistle through that one before she left.

She rose and glided to the window. 'God's in His Heaven, all's right with the World.' The phrase skipped across her mind as she took in the view.

The lawns stretched smooth as the bowling green in Marespond Park. The little ponds with their low stone walls lay like hand-mirrors on their backs gleaming in the sun. And beyond terraced gardens painted spring-flower purple, white, and yellow, a row of perfectly balanced cedar trees pointed to a diamond blue sky.

He listened, there was no doubt about it – He listened and He *heard*. That was the miracle. And one had no need to shout or fear a sudden disconnection, as one did with Mr Bell's invention. Only whisper one's desire – sometimes merely think it – and, as the French would say, *voilà*!

Emma on the mend, at last. Praise the Lord! Why, last night she had eaten two helpings of roly-poly pudding and entertained her mother with stories of the children's antics, which brought the two of them close to hysteria. Not only that, she was developing new interests: resurrecting her rusty piano-playing skills, involving herself with the Chearden Dramatic Society. Not that she still didn't have moments when the moroseness overcame her and she cried for no apparent reason. But all the signs pointed to recovery. Yes, there was much to be thankful for. They had forged a life, she and Emma. A good life, a secure one.

True, there might never be the grandchildren she had dreamed of. But at least she had known the joy of mother-hood and forged a precious mother-daughter bond that grew stronger every day. And imagine, Emma turned twenty tomorrow. Lord, how the years had flown.

Now to the last order of the day. The sooner she dealt with it, the sooner she could be on her way. Back to the sewing machine and Emma's birthday gown.

Resettling herself behind the desk, she dipped into the shoebox. It took only moments for her to pop the various odds and ends into the centre drawer.

Hmmm. What was this? She put on her spectacles. An envelope addressed to – she squinted. How odd, it read 'Emma Cadman.' Now who on earth would be …? Ah, she wagged her head like an ancient sage, she must have let slip again (as she had last year) about Emma's birthday, and His Lordship – what a dear, generous man he was – had made out a cheque. No use telling him he shouldn't have. That man had a mind of his own.

She reached across the desk for her handbag and popped

the envelope in it, just as Verity Dawfield poked her head around the door. 'Are you goin' to stop and have a spot of tea with me, Beth?'

'No, Verity, I think not. I still have Emma's gown to finish and the marzipan and icing to put on her cake. Besides, His Lordship left something for her – you remember how generous he was last year – and I cannot wait to get home and see her face when I give it to her.'

'Sounds as if she's in for a right good do for her twentieth, then.'

Beth smiled. 'It does, doesn't it? Oh, and she does so need it, Verity.'

THIRTY-EIGHT

Emma lay on her bed, staring at the sun-dappled ceiling. The end of another workweek; for her, the end of another year – her twentieth on this earth. She touched her cheeks, her neck, so smooth and girlish. And yet she felt so *old*.

Why did people celebrate birthdays, when each brought death that much closer? When each made one conscious of what had gone before: the disappointments, the unfulfilled ambitions, the heartbreak? Perhaps – she made a wry face as she swung out of bed and stood contemplating her stockinged feet – it should be a celebration of endurance, of one's ability to survive 'the slings and arrows of outrageous fortune.'

Tsk, tsk, there you go with your morbid thoughts. And you were doing so well. She padded to the dressing table, peered into its oval mirror, and wagged an admonishing finger. You promised now; no more feeling sorry for yourself. Smile. Good. Oh, better, much better. Put on your shoes and your apron and set those nimble little fingers of yours to work, unpegging the wash. Remember, the busy bee has no time for sorrow.

It was an insane thing she'd done, clambering up into the crabapple tree, the dear old thing. Gnarled and knotted and scabbed with lichen. Tight little buds, waiting to unfurl, to blossom and fill the air with their heady scent.

Smiling, Emma swung her legs and glanced overhead. Not that she was brave enough to climb to any great height. High enough, though, for a woman of her mature years. And … yes, positively insane. If anyone saw her, they would think her a candidate for the asylum.

Oh, but it was delightful. Like those long-ago hours she'd spent in the sycamore by the gate at Milchester, her 'sitting tree.' What joy it had been waiting, watching for … No, she wouldn't, mustn't think about … Still, she couldn't hide from the memories forever, not the good memories. What was it Hope had said? It was all the happy times she had had that kept her going. And there *had* been happy times, hadn't there? He wasn't always … Remember when you'd hear the tap-tap of his cane, you'd have to stretch because you were so small and soon you'd see the top of his sandy head … *sandy* hair, not brown hair streaked with silver.

'Mama! I didn't expect you home yet.'

'So I see.' Beth pursed her mouth seriocomically and rolled her eyes. 'Madame Teacher at her most dignified.'

Emma laughed. 'You should try it, it is good for the soul.'

'Not *my* soul.'

'What brought you home so early, Mama?'

'I finally finished. Everything's shipshape again. And I found this' – she flapped an envelope at Emma as she fastened the clasp on her handbag – 'from His Lordship. A fine thing if I hadn't finished up today – it would still have been in the shoebox and you would have been out of luck. Here.' She passed the envelope up to Emma.

'For me, from the Earl?' Emma scratched the side of her nose. 'Why on earth would …'

'Your birthday, dear. Remember last year?'

278

'Oh yes, but ... Hmmm, he has a jolly nice hand, so bold and ...' She traced 'Cadman' with her fingernail. 'I would have expected an abominable scrawl.'

'Oh, I dare say it's not His Lordship's hand.' Beth brushed debris off a nearby tree stump and sat on it. 'Likely one of the staff's. Anyway, do stop dilly-dallying about and see what it is. I've a million things to do and ...'

'Very well.' Emma slit open the envelope. Her mother was obviously mistaken about its being a birthday gift, for the envelope contained no crisp banknotes. With a questioning hitch of her shoulders, she smoothed the single sheet of paper in her lap and began to read:

'My Darling Emma.' The shock of the words almost knocked her off the branch.

''Struth, be careful,' her mother yelled.

Emma edged along and sought the security of the trunk. She leaned sideways against it. Ye Gods and little fishes ... that silly old man had well and truly lost his wits. Feeling her eyes return to their rightful place in her skull now, she refocused and read on ...

It breaks my heart to have to leave you like this, for I know how much (after last night) you need me. I tried to rouse you so I could tell you all this, but couldn't, so this letter (given to His Lordship for delivery) was the only thing I could think of.

I love you, lass, with all my being and I hope, I pray – God, how I pray – I'm not wrong about your loving me. I want to take care of you for the rest of our lives, see that nothing, no one ever hurts you again. But I cannot do it yet.

By the time you read this, I shall be en route to Canada. The telegram arrived in the early hours. Meggie, Will, and two of the bairns perished in a blizzard, and I'm all the two youngest have left. I have to go, Emma.

It'll be a long journey and it may be weeks before I'll be able to get a letter through to you. But you'll be with me every minute, in my mind and in my heart. Soon as the thaw comes, I shall parcel up Douglas and Trevor and bring them *back here with me. Then I shall come to you and ask you to be my wife.*

Until then, God keep you safe, my braw, wee darling.

Ewan

Beth's attention had wandered to the brow of the hill beyond the low rock wall where a herd of sheep grazed. Soon lambs would be gambolling over the slopes and the swallows would be back building their nests under the eaves and ...

'Mama!'

The cry brought her snapping back. Oh, Lord. Emma looked as if someone had slapped the colour from her face; her mouth hung partly open and her throat was working as though she wished to speak but couldn't.

From her low perch, Beth struggled to her feet. 'What is it?'

'He ... he' – Emma swallowed and tried again – 'oh, it's wonderful, Mama ... too wonderful for words. He ...' She broke off, held her hand to her mouth, and burst into sobs.

Beth clawed like a supplicant at the hem of Emma's skirts. 'What are you bawling for, then? For pity's sake, tell me.'

'I will.' Emma let out a half-sob, half-laugh, and dabbed at her eyes with her apron. 'Climb up here beside me, Mama, and I'll tell you,' she said, her voice thick from weeping.

'*You*' – Beth pointed – 'want *me*,' she said, jabbing herself in the chest, 'to climb up *there?*'

Emma let out a high exultant laugh. 'Yes. I promise you it'll be worth it.'

Like a bird after a dust bath, Beth shook herself and blinked rapidly. Climb? Great God, she hadn't climbed anything but a stepstool in decades. She was no stick in the mud, but really ... About to speak her mind, she tilted her head and stared up at Emma.

But the winsome child gazing out through the young woman's shining hazel eyes struck a responsive chord in Beth, and she said, 'All right, then. Something tells me the challenge of tree-climbing is *nothing* compared to what you have in store for me. Am I right?'

Emma could not respond; her heart was too full, her head dancing with blissful visions of Ewan and a pair of glossy-headed lads who would need all the love two women – one a mother, the other a grandmother, and sure to be an ecstatic one – could give.

'Well, am I?' Her mother tapped her on the foot.

Emma lifted her face for the sun's soft benediction, inhaled the scented promise of spring in the air, and finally said, with a smile of utter contentment, 'Oh, yes, Mama. Indeed you are right.'

EPILOGUE

FROM *THE CHEARDEN VOICE*

July 5, 1888

On July 18th, Mrs Alexander Windom, Chearden's talented and charming milliner, will close up shop for good and, with her young son, join the pioneering ranks. A sad day indeed for our ladies, but an auspicious one for the Windoms, who, after a protracted (and we trust none-too-perilous) journey, will add their numbers to those of the McKenzie enclave in southeastern Saskatchewan.

(Note for the benefit of those new to the district: two years have elapsed since newlyweds Emma (née Cadman) McKenzie and her husband Ewan, his two nephews, and the bride's mother emigrated to Canada. These brave souls, by the way, appear to be getting on famously. Two new members have been added to their clan – a daughter, Victoria, born the very day of the Jubilee, and a son, Bruce, born this past May.)

Additionally – according to His Lordship, who has recently returned from a visit – the wheat-farming endeavours of this enterprising family are proving highly successful.

Delightful news. Let us hope that as time

goes by we shall be privy to more of the same.

Meanwhile, Godspeed, Mrs Windom, and please do pack your cabin trunk with – and convey to our old friends, the McKenzies – a hefty measure of good wishes for continued success and happiness.

Our Loss; Our Distant Friends' Gain.